Out of the Shadows

The metal gray of the sky made Chaplin's brown coat look drab as we darted out of the shadows and into the safe cover behind rocks or more Joshua trees.

It'll be a long time before everyone forgets what happened back at the first homestead, Chaplin said, chewing on his words.

"My lack of control made us vulnerable to Stamp, so I earned the wariness."

Before the big showdown, I'd killed a few of Stamp's men when they'd encroached upon our territory, threatening us. We'd suspected they wanted our aquifer-enhanced dwellings, and I'd made sure they didn't get them. Then Gabriel had appeared one night, wounded, and Chaplin had invited him into our home. My dog had been under his sway, but Chaplin had overcome it, manipulating Gabriel into confronting Stamp for our sakes. But I, and the rest of the community, hadn't been able to stomach his sacrifice, and we'd gone to the showdown to defend him.

So if you went right back to the beginning, the death and destruction had all been because of me.

Mariah, there's always . . . Chaplin began, then cut himself off.

I wasn't dumb enough to believe that my dog had an unfinished thought. He was luring me into something. Intel Dogs had been genetically bred and trained to be practical and lethal when the time called for it. He was my best weapon and, sometimes, my worst.

"Spit it out," I said. A sand-rabbit leaped out of some brush in front of us, causing a rustle. "You gonna say it, Chaplin?"

I could've sworn my dog smiled at my vinegar. It meant that I was fully back to being human. For now, anyway.

There's always hope for a cure, he said.

Ace Books by Christine Cody

BLOODLANDS
BLOOD RULES

BLOOD RULES

Christine Cody

ACE BOOKS, NEW YORK

THE BERKLEY PUBLISHING GROUP
Published by the Penguin Group
Penguin Group (USA) Inc.
375 Hudson Street, New York, New York 10014, USA

Penguin Group (Canada), 90 Eglinton Avenue East, Suite 700, Toronto, Ontario M4P 2Y3, Canada
(a division of Pearson Penguin Canada Inc.)
Penguin Books Ltd., 80 Strand, London WC2R 0RL, England
Penguin Group Ireland, 25 St. Stephen's Green, Dublin 2, Ireland (a division of Penguin Books Ltd.)
Penguin Group (Australia), 250 Camberwell Road, Camberwell, Victoria 3124, Australia
(a division of Pearson Australia Group Pty. Ltd.)
Penguin Books India Pvt. Ltd., 11 Community Centre, Panchsheel Park, New Delhi—110 017, India
Penguin Group (NZ), 67 Apollo Drive, Rosedale, Auckland 0632, New Zealand
(a division of Pearson New Zealand Ltd.)
Penguin Books (South Africa) (Pty.) Ltd., 24 Sturdee Avenue, Rosebank, Johannesburg 2196,
South Africa

Penguin Books Ltd., Registered Offices: 80 Strand, London WC2R 0RL, England

BLOOD RULES

An Ace Book / published by arrangement with the author

PRINTING HISTORY
Ace mass-market edition / September 2011

Copyright © 2011 by Chris Marie Green.
Excerpt from *In Blood We Trust* copyright © by Chris Marie Green.
Cover art by Larry Rostant.
Cover design by Judith Lagerman.
Interior text design by Tiffany Estreicher.

ISBN: 978-0-441-02076-8

ACE
Ace Books are published by The Berkley Publishing Group,
a division of Penguin Group (USA) Inc.,
375 Hudson Street, New York, New York 10014.
ACE and the "A" design are trademarks of Penguin Group (USA) Inc.

PRINTED IN THE UNITED STATES OF AMERICA

10 9 8 7 6 5 4 3 2 1

To Torrey—a lady and a princess and my beautiful friend.
I love everything about you—especially you!

ACKNOWLEDGMENTS

Again, I bow to my Ace team—everyone from Ginjer to Kat to the art and marketing and sales departments to the wonderful editors who catch my errors and the design team. Thank you to each and every one of you who worked on these books! And to the Knight Agency, I salute you, too. Sheree and Judy, you guys are my inspiration and anchors.

My critique partners aren't the only ones who inspire me—there's also Thomas Friedman, whose ideas about the future helped to shape some of GBVille. And a big acknowledgment to the "poet/prophet" William S. Burroughs: Thank you for the "running ones." I have no doubt whatsoever that we will soon see them all over the place!

In a work of fiction, there are bound to be some licenses taken, and there are many of those in the Bloodlands. Forgive my overreaching and any mistakes, but I also hope you "enjoy" your stay in this new land. I so appreciate that you've taken the time to read these books, and hope that you will continue. . . .

1

It'd been a quiet night in Asylum AA-23 until Patroller Hughes decided to check out the maximum-security block.

As he disabled yet another force field that separated the command center from the labyrinthine hallways, his ear communication implant crackled.

"Blok 10 secr," said another patroller, using the casual Text language of the streets to say he'd secured his block for the night.

"Blok 5 secr," said a third employee.

Hughes had already reported in, so he was on free patrol now. This block wasn't even on his normal beat, but he'd had an itch to scratch ever since last night, when Subject 562 had been brought from an asylum in old D.C. over here to GBVille. Subject 562 was supposed to be a high-level preter, and Patroller Hughes had a way of breaking in each new occupant. The staff had been warned about messing around with it, but Hughes knew how to handle even the most intimidating monsters.

He strolled the dim, steel-enforced maze, where cries echoed from each cell he passed. The invisible shields held the subjects captive, muffling screams, hisses, and whatever annoying sounds they made. Hughes could see every one of the grotesque shapes huddled in corners, staring at him with glowing eyes.

He passed a subject waving its lengthened, slimy fingers near its cell shield, and Hughes whipped out his taser baton, threatening the creature. It hunched, backing up, its spine bristling with spaded projectiles.

Patroller Hughes laughed and went on his way. He'd screwed the subject over but good when it'd first gotten here. With one shot of lazy-donna into its veins, Hughes had done his own little experiments. But the creature hadn't been humanlike enough to interest him for long.

Now he came to the cell he was looking for, where Subject 562 stood in a corner, its back turned, its hands hidden in the folds of its bleak, baggy institution gown. Humanlike. Its long silver hair was sheet-straight, hiding its face, skimming over the pale arms scraped with nearly healed, self-inflicted nail marks.

Patrolman Hughes fixated on the wounds. There'd been a lot of vague talk among the patrollers about 562's blood. He wondered just what was so special about it.

He flipped up the goggle lenses from the mask of his protective suit, allowing a panel-bound laser beam to scan his retinas. As soon as the security device recognized him, lasers zapped down from the cell's ceiling, surrounding Subject 562 like a temporary, purple-barred cage. The impenetrable shield dissipated long enough for Hughes to cross the threshold, then hummed back to an invisible wall behind him right after he entered.

Subject 562 remained motionless.

"Hya, wtr rbbr," the patroller said, trying to get the creature's attention.

But it didn't react to being called a water robber. A lot of preters tended to ignore this particular insult, maybe because they didn't steal water in the human way, by siphoning it from dwelling tanks. No, sir, about half the preters here were unapologetic parasites that took the blood right out of humans, getting their liquids in that manner.

Or maybe Subject 562 wasn't reacting because it only spoke Old American, like most preters who'd tried to hide away from society and its goings-on after the world had changed. Maybe the thing didn't understand Text because it'd been tucked away with other water robbers for years and years, avoiding eradication and missing out on all the trends.

Hughes was always happy to teach preters the new ways.

With his gloved hand, he fetched the lazy-donna blaster out of a compartment in his utility belt. The gun held a dose that could put down thirty humans. It'd be enough for one monster.

He aimed the gun at Subject 562, and when the drug bullet slipped through the lasers and hit the creature, the skinny thing didn't even flinch. It just kept its back to him, its head lowered, its fall of hair covering any response.

A minute later, the subject withered to the ground, and Patroller Hughes used a vital sign scanner to determine whether it'd be safe to proceed.

GO, the scanner said.

He smiled, then used a voice command to turn off the laser cage that surrounded the prone monster. Leaving the rest of his protective suit on, he stripped off one of his gloves, leaving his hand bare so it could feel.

As he approached 562, he thought he heard a cry from the monster across the hall: a wail. Maybe even the start of a howl. He ignored it.

"Im not gonna hrt u," Hughes said to his pupil as he bent forward, catching sight of 562's slit eyes glowing through its hair. Red eyes, like something lurking in a forest of silvered trees.

It still didn't move. No preter would be able to, with the dose Hughes had given it.

He crept his fingers over the thing's shin, where a long scratch gouged pale flesh. The abrasion disappeared over its knee, under its institution gown.

He trailed along the mark, but the creature still didn't move.

As always, Hughes wanted to know just how human these creatures could get, so he kept coasting his fingers up its thigh, feeling sleek muscle and smooth skin as he got closer to the middle of its legs.

Then he heard a low laugh.

Pausing, he peered at the subject's face. Silver hair. Red eyes beneath it. A massive set of dagger-sharp teeth.

Before Hughes could wonder how the creature had over-come the drugs, the thing opened its mouth to a grotesque yaw that obscured its face altogether. It sprang forward, clamping down on Patroller Hughes, smashing his head to a pulp, his skull flying in a shattered mess of protective mask, blood, and bone that splattered all over.

Subject 562 turned back to its corner, licking the blood off its fingers before going motionless once again.

2

Mariah

Even though the moon had been in its waning phase for a few nights now, I was seething, my bones shifting in what felt like a brutal melt, my skin hot as it stretched during the fever of were-change.

The murky midnight sky flashed by, blue swishes in my emerging monster sight, while I sprinted over the New Badlands, trying to get away—

But he was right behind me.

"Mariah!" he yelled, his vampire voice gnarled.

A fractured second later, Gabriel crashed into me, driving me to the dirt near a cave in a hill, my chin and palms skidding on the ground and abrading my skin to rawness.

Backhanded, I swiped at him, but he caught my half-human hand, which was more like a claw. Everything was starting to happen as if I were watching from a near distance, remote.

I panted like the animal I was becoming as we struggled, him flipping me to my back as I arched, growled, snapped at him. His eyes blazed against his pale skin, his fangs sprung.

"Stop it, Mariah!" he said.

"Can't . . ."

My voice was just as warped as his own. Hollow beast voices.

Before I could bite at him again, he grasped my head, looking into my eyes, slipping into my mind. My thoughts went watery, as if I were suddenly a pool and he'd dipped into it.

Peace. He was trying to give me the peace, and I opened myself fully, still panting. My temperature was already cooling in the hope of receiving his calm.

Easing. Serene.

As he infiltrated me, my vision wavered; he was on the top of water and I was under it. I felt the flow of his sway over my skin, smooth and numbing.

Thank-all, I thought as my bones started flexing back to their human shape.

I floated in sensation for a few more moments, almost afraid of it ending. I sucked in the dragon's-breath air, which was still hot during late spring here in the nowheres.

Gabriel kept looking deep into me, and I breathed some more, letting him take the place of my turmoil. Then . . .

Then I saw it in his eyes—the resentment. The stifled hatred for what I'd done to the woman he'd come out here to find nearly two months ago.

Abby.

As soon as her name entered my head, it seemed as if the water that'd been calming me boiled. And I could feel it in him, too—he was thinking about how I'd killed her.

The boiling intensified, the water parting, splashing out in a roar that I felt in my own lungs—

Our peaceful connection shattered, my body straining against itself again with the start of another change, my breath rasping. I could also feel the scrapes on my chin and palms healing with preter speed.

"Get . . . off . . ." I growled.

But Gabriel kept pinning me, putting more effort into giving me the peace. With his stronger sway, my body whipped back toward humanity—the watery hush of it, bones and muscle slipping and sliding. For a second . . . then two . . . then more, I stayed in my good, human shape, whimpering because I ached. Ached so bad.

As he pushed me toward that better place, I hurt some more.

Were-change had been natural when me and the rest of my community had been taken by the full moon. My neighbors had chained me up in our new homestead, and afterward I'd thanked them for keeping me restrained. They hadn't dared let me run free after what'd happened with Abby and the rest.

Natural moon change was so much better than the turning that consumed a were-creature because of emotional upheaval. Anger, passion . . . it all hurt a lot less during those three or so nights a month when the darkness combined with the moon's peak to compel a were-creature to madness and terrible hunger.

Gabriel whispered, "There you go, Mariah . . ."

I grunted. A tiny fever still had hold of me.

"Just a little more," he said. "Come on."

My teeth were still long, and I bared them at the vampire, not because of any innate hatred or a need to war against a different breed of preter, but because my wildness just couldn't stop itself.

Yells and barking arose in the background. More than one person was running, no doubt also keeping to the shadowy, hiding cover of the Joshua trees and standing rocks. I didn't want them to see me like this.

My dog came to a dirt-spraying halt next to me in the sheltering cove.

Mariah? he asked. *Running over open ground . . . why . . . ?*

Even in the hazy near-completion of my change cycle, I thought that Chaplin sounded inarticulate for an Intel Dog. I growled, flashed my teeth at him, too.

Chaplin barked at Gabriel.

What set her off this time?

Gabriel could translate Chaplin's sounds because they were communicating mind-to-mind, vampire to familiar.

Although Gabriel was still pinning me, he wasn't breathing heavily, like a human, because vampires didn't breathe. "I don't know what it was, but the peace isn't working so well anymore. I can't soothe her like I used to."

At the mention of something so personal, I turned my face away. It helped not to look at Gabriel, even though my breaths still came hollow and deep, my sight still a little blue-tinged. I just wished he'd get off me, because it reminded me of the first time he'd given me the peace, with his body flush against mine. We'd done sex, and with him being a vampire and me being a were-creature, something strange had happened.

We'd imprinted on each other in some way. I could calm him and he could calm me. It seemed we weren't so much monsters anymore when we were intimate.

But that had been before I told him the truth about the woman he'd loved—how Abby had been a fellow werewolf who'd attacked me, challenging my place in our secretive were-community. Now Gabriel's hatred of me polluted the peace, and I was flailing without it.

Then again, I'd never been the most stable of werewolves. I'd been bitten, not true-born, and my violent initiation had screwed me up but good. I hadn't had much control over my changes—not until Gabriel's peace.

And without it, now? I was back to being a disaster.

By this time, more of the community had arrived. I closed my eyes and willed myself to go all the way human. My bones and muscles obeyed grudgingly, making me buck beneath Gabriel and moan while my skin undulated with the chaos beneath it.

God-all, Chaplin had been right about my running over open ground nowadays. The group was usually so much more careful while in were-form, but I'd taken off, so upset, that I'd just run as fast as I could without thinking about keeping to cover. . . .

When I opened my eyes, breathing shaky, my sight had adjusted to filter in the regular ominous gray cast of a New Badlands night. I saw Pucci first, his bulky chest and grinding teeth belying his true-born were-elk form.

"What the tar is it now?" he asked.

The only reason I never attacked his ass was that, in human form, he could easily take me. But in monster form, another were-creature's blood was like poison, so I had an aversion to his blood—I sought out much more appealing prey instead of turning on the weaker were-creatures. So we were all one big, happy family, except without the happy part.

Another true-born, Hana, had the decency to pretend I was lucid enough to answer. "Mariah, what upset you?"

I couldn't find my voice as I glanced up at her—the mule deer brown eyes and skin, the African-inspired robes and scarf she wore over her head. Hana's and Pucci's animals used to be herbivores in the years before the world had changed, but with the lack of plant life, regular elk and deer had died off, and only the were-creature versions had lived on because their digestive systems had long ago adapted. Same with every other were-form I knew of—like me, they craved blood, which also gave water out here in the nowheres. When we were in regular form, we didn't have were-powers, so we didn't go after blood then.

Gabriel saved me from everyone's interrogation. "I'm not sure chatting about this is going to improve the situation."

But now that I could think more clearly, I *wanted* to talk. I'd spent so much time keeping my rage bottled in, that airing it out seemed safer than exploding. My neighbors deserved at least that much from me. They'd let me stick round. Actually, no one had the power to kick me out, except maybe Gabriel, and he was giving me the chance to redeem myself.

I finally found my voice, tangled as it was. "I was unpacking, and I found my dad's journal. I couldn't help it—everything came rushing back . . ."

My dad's grief after the attack in Dallas, the death of my mom and brother, the fallout from what those bad guys had sicced on me. They'd used a werewolf, and that was when I'd been bitten. Because of that, my dad had smuggled me to our first home in the New Badlands—the one we'd had to leave a little over two months ago. When he'd been alive, he'd taken care of me as well as he could until Abby had come along and we'd had our showdown. After that, Dad had given up on trying to cure me, taking his life and leaving me alone to deal with it.

Oh, Mariah, Chaplin said, as if he were exhausted because of me, too. Then he turned to Gabriel. *I thought we buried sensitive items for the time being.*

"Did you think I wouldn't stumble on them?" I asked. "I spent a lot of time camouflaging the entrance to the cavern, so I'm familiar with every speck of dirt and sand near it." I held my tongue as my last bone locked in place. Then I breathed a bit easier. "I found those journals, Dad's old pipe, his collectible geek dolls without hardly even trying."

Hana had bent to me, running a hand over my forehead, murmuring a foreign chant that she'd learned as a new-age science nurse before having to go underground. Her voice helped me as I tried to stay in control.

Gabriel still held me down while Chaplin and Pucci hovered, ready to take me on. Smart, because I didn't trust myself, either.

"I shouldn't have come with you all here," I said as Hana pushed back my hair. "After I found this new homestead, I should've kept to my original plan and struck out on my own—"

"Do not say such things," Hana said. "If we do not help each other, what is left of the world will surely fall apart."

Chaplin put a comforting paw on my shoulder. *And God-all knows the world's crumbled enough. I wasn't about to leave you behind.*

It was true that he'd eventually persuaded me to come with the community when we'd moved, but that was back when Gabriel's peace had been working. Before his resentment had grown and polluted our connection.

Although Hana couldn't translate what Chaplin had uttered, she must've sensed that he was consoling me. She added, "Johnson Stamp is still out there, and we need to see that he *never* catches up to any of us."

"Yeah," Pucci said. "If Mariah had broken off with us and Stamp caught up to her, he'd probably have tortured our new location right out of our pet psycho. Might as well have her here where we can keep an eye on what she says and does. Unless, of course, she turns into a werewolf and runs all over the place like she's inviting someone to catch her."

His concern would've been heartwarming if I knew Pucci had any love for me.

Chaplin barked, then muttered and whined. *Let's get inside. We can't afford to get caught by anyone, especially if Stamp made it back to the hubs to announce we're out here.*

He didn't have to add that you never knew when Stamp might be round, either, if he'd survived his confrontation with us.

Stamp—who'd been a Shredder, or government-sanctioned hunter, before the powers that be had deemed preternaturals under control years ago—had almost died while accosting the community. Out of defense, we'd killed all his employees except for him and his female lieutenant, but he'd been so torn up that his wounds might've proven fatal.

As I said, you just never knew with Shredders.

Gabriel translated Chaplin's words. Then Pucci turned to me.

"How many times is it going to take until you really do us in, Mariah?"

Gabriel shoved him away, warily backed off from me, then turned and retreated, keeping to those shadows.

I watched him go, my throat tight.

Hana helped me to a sit, and I made a low sound of unease because of the tweak of my bones and joints. She checked me over, seeming to ignore the rips in my clothing, then peered into my eyes. But since they weren't glowing with the fever, I passed her inspection.

Pucci yanked on her robes, almost dragging her up so that she followed him as he walked away, both of them taking care to seek cover, too.

I watched Pucci's treatment of Hana, who never fought back. I could never figure out how such a strong-minded woman loved such a jerk. She always seemed to hold her own against him, but she never left when he seemed to give her good reason to.

As I stood, my legs wobbled, and I sucked in a breath at the piercing reminders of the shift. Chaplin nudged me into a shaky walk, keeping up with my unsteady pace as we sought the boulders, then other camouflage.

Chaplin, my remaining friend. I knew that he also resented me sometimes, but we'd been through a lot together, including the Dallas attack and my dad's death. Hell, my father had trained Chaplin as an Intel Dog in the lab, way back when Dad had still been a scientist, so we'd both lost a father.

"Then there it is," I said quietly so the rest wouldn't hear, although maybe Gabriel would pick up my words because of his heightened vampire hearing. "I didn't mean to put us in danger."

You had a moment, and it's over, Chaplin said. *We'll need to watch those visz screens to see if anyone comes round, but we're very well hidden, Mariah. You've just got to be more careful.*

"Right. I just had a moment." But there'd be more and more moments as the years wore on, and we both knew it.

The metal gray of the sky made Chaplin's brown coat look drab as we darted out of the shadows and into the safe cover behind rocks or more Joshua trees.

It'll be a long time before everyone forgets what happened back at the first homestead, Chaplin said, chewing on his words.

"My lack of control made us vulnerable to Stamp, so I earned the wariness."

Before the big showdown, I'd killed a few of Stamp's men when they'd encroached upon our territory, threatening us. We'd suspected they wanted our aquifer-enhanced dwellings, and, in my anonymous were-form, I'd made sure they didn't get them. Then Gabriel had appeared one night, wounded, and Chaplin had invited him into our home. My dog had been under his sway, but Chaplin had overcome it, manipulating Gabriel into confronting Stamp for our sakes. But I, and the rest of the community, hadn't been able to stomach his sacrifice, and we'd gone to the showdown to defend him.

So if you went right back to the beginning, the death and destruction had all been because of me.

Mariah, there's always . . . Chaplin began, then cut himself off.

I wasn't dumb enough to believe that my dog had an unfinished thought. He was luring me into something. Intel Dogs had been genetically bred and trained to be practical and lethal when the time called for it. He was my best weapon and, sometimes, my worst.

"Spit it out," I said. A sand-rabbit leaped out of some brush in front of us, causing a rustle.

Everyone ahead of us startled toward the sound, even if they were under the cover of the shadows, but when they saw it was only a little flit of an animal, they moved at a faster clip. Anything could be a Shredder or even another preter who'd deserted the hubs. We didn't need to be discovered by either one.

My heart was blipping in my veins because of the interruption. "You gonna say it, Chaplin?"

I could've sworn my dog smiled at my vinegar. It meant that I was fully back to being human. For now, anyway.

There's always hope for a cure, he said.

And that was all, but that final word had the power to give me pause.

A were-cure—that was what he meant, and he'd been mentioning it in private ever since we'd moved into our new digs. He hadn't ever expanded on his thoughts, but it was as if he'd been watering a seed every time he muttered it. Although it was a ridiculous idea, his comments had made me think. They also made me ache that much more, and not in my joints and muscles, either.

"There's no cure for monsters." I'd discussed this with Gabriel before he even knew what I was, and Chaplin had been in the same damned room. Obviously, this rebuttal bore repeating. "Stories about cures are just legends, and every bad guy who doesn't believe that monsters were eradicated probably uses the rumors to lure what's left of our kind into the open. That way, they can beat the location of any hidden preter communities out of the idiots who take the bait."

What if you're wrong about there being a real cure? Chaplin asked.

And there it was—he was about to grow that seed into something I'd have to confront right here and now, fresh after losing control to the point where I hadn't even thought to hide while I was running outside.

"Dad tried every concoction he could think of on me," I said, "and nothing worked. And if he couldn't figure it out, who could?"

He wasn't the only scientist round, Mariah. Maybe Gabriel was right when he said that there was such a sharp drop in preters in the hubs because a cure was found.

Up ahead, hills rose out of the ground like the curves of a serpent's spine. Pucci and Hana had already run ahead to access a trapdoor to a tunnel that led to our homes, but it looked to me as if Gabriel had slowed down before going inside. The moonlight skimmed over his beaten white shirt and pants. His close-cropped hair looked darker than I knew it actually was, and his face, with that slightly crooked nose, had gone back to its normal stillness—like the façade of an abandoned house, the windows gray and cloudy.

His head was cocked.

Was he listening?

His possible interest lit something in me. Hope.

Actual hope.

If I improved my disposition, would that make him look at me differently? Would he feel whatever he'd started to feel for me back before the truth about Abby had come out?

Sorrow and anger began to simmer deep in my belly, but I tamped it down before it resulted in another change . . . and in more trouble.

More than anyone, I needed some kind of cure, and the only one I could think of right now was for me to end my life. I'd already tried that after Gabriel had found out the truth about me, but he'd stopped me for some reason. Now, I still figured he would've been better off.

I realized that, maybe, Chaplin was really going at this subject right now because Gabriel was near, and my response might be affected by that. It was also becoming more obvious that my dog might've asked me to come to this new homestead not only because he loved me, but because he'd wanted to lead me to accept the idea of a cure, all while making it seem as if I'd agreeably arrived there with minimal assistance.

Too smart for his own good, this dog.

If there is a cure, Chaplin said, *what would you do to find it?*

"If it were true, I'd do anything." The comment was out before I could even think, but I knew with all my heart that it was what I'd been feeling for a long time now.

And if the cure required more than just swallowing the contents of some vial?

"What do you mean?"

I mean, what if it involved conditioning, Mariah? Ultra-shock therapy. Mental tooling—

I recalled how Gabriel had tried to slay me after hearing about Abby's death. How, beneath his words and actions, he hated me even now because I was a killer who couldn't help herself.

I suppose, in life, there's always a moment where you run into the wall of yourself. That was what I was feeling now, the crash of knowing there's nowhere else you can go because you can't turn back.

"As I mentioned," I said, "I'd do whatever it takes."

Up ahead, Gabriel glanced partway over his shoulder until he met my gaze.

His eyes . . . red glows in the night.

I held my breath, then used my energies to think to him, willing his vampire mind to pick up my inner voice.

Believe me, Gabriel. I want to be better.

His only answer was to turn round and slip into the cavern entrance, leaving me behind with an Intel Dog who gave me a sympathetic look, then stranded me, too.

3

Gabriel

Gabriel had no sand-picking idea why he'd even slowed down enough to listen to Chaplin and Mariah talking about a cure.

He'd almost gone looking for one himself after learning about Abby's death, but he'd stayed in the Badlands. Who even knew where to search?

Talk of one was nothing more than typical Badlander blab-bity, anyway, he thought, making his way through the rock-faced tunnels, which got cooler the lower he went.

Nothing more than something to make everyone feel better while their world fell apart here, just as much as it had every-where else.

Chaplin loped past Gabriel, who could scent the were-creatures in the main room: clean sweat on skin, dirt worked into simple clothing. Gabriel could even hear the blood running freely through their veins, a trait that separated them from the urban hub normals, who ate such shitty, processed food that their bodies sounded like cell-clogged traffic jams.

Then he heard Mariah, who'd obviously rushed down the tunnels to catch up with him. He always knew her from the rest of the Badlanders, even from a distance, because her angry vital sounds resembled thunder in her veins—a sensation that rattled him, too, though he'd come such a long way in accepting what he was after Stamp had made him face it.

A vampire. A monster who'd never stop wondering if there was more to him than just hunger.

As Mariah's boot steps echoed against the walls and twined through him, he braced himself, his baser instincts urging him to turn around and grab her so he could bury his face against her skin. It happened all the time when she was around, his fangs prodding his gums, his gaze going a deep red. But now, with how he'd tried to give her the peace, with him being inside her mind . . . ?

Gabriel fisted his hands and fought his urges.

He even won himself back a bit, until she came to within about ten feet of him. Tremors lined his veins as he felt that link he'd forged with her when they'd lain together and she'd shown him that maybe he wasn't all monster, that maybe he still did have it in him to be human.

If he was the very definition of what everyone thought a monster was, it'd be much easier to turn his back on her right now.

Her voice flooded him. "Did you hear me and Chaplin talking out there?"

"Does it matter?" Her earthy scent was crazing him, but he told himself she was toxic.

That helped, and he finally turned around to see her standing in the midst of the solar-battery lights edging the tunnel.

Something like emotion tumbled through Gabriel as her body rhythms pulled at him. She was so young, only twenty-three in human years, yet only a few years old as a newer, uncontrolled were-creature. She looked innocent, like what people would've called a waif, with her red hair sawed to her jaw by a knife, her wide, apologetic green eyes. But, then again, she stood like an outlaw, her slim, tall body stiff, her arms at her sides, her hands hovering near the holsters covering her torn, laced-up trousers. Her baggy white shirt was ripped at the shoulders, too—evidence of the latest change that'd almost consumed her.

Her heartbeat played like confused music, and that was what got him the most. He'd heard the same haunting tune in Abby before she'd left him in the hubs, disappearing one night. He'd gone off in search of her, never knowing what she was. He hadn't even known about Mariah or the rest of the community, either, seeing as were-creatures had their powers only when they underwent the change.

They hid themselves so well.

Obviously sensing his desire to get away from her, Mariah lowered her gaze, and it struck Gabriel hard, because though he despised what she'd done, she practically cried out to be saved.

He almost laughed at that. Mariah, a vicious werewolf in need of rescue.

He made himself talk to her. "Are you so at the end of your rope that you're willing to pin your hopes on rumors of a cure out there?"

"I said as much."

"Then you won't mind my adding that pursuing a false dream is an epically terrible idea."

"At least it'd take me away from the community."

Gabriel allowed himself a chopping laugh. "That's Pucci talking. He'd like nothing more than to get you away from here, but did you hear him when he said that if Stamp caught you, you'd be a liability?"

"I'd never reveal where we're hiding now."

"Not easily." He'd give her that. If anything, Mariah was loyal. She'd lied to him, as well as many others, but she'd done it out of protective instinct for herself *and* her community. She was a first-rate deceiver, yet he doubted that'd be enough to bolster her if Stamp ever got hold of her.

"All I want," she said, her tone strangled, "is to keep us safe, Gabriel. If that means I have to chase some wild dream, I'd consider it."

"Supposed cures aren't any kind of answer." He decided to push his point, then leave. "When I was made a vampire, I was converted by a crusader who turned people because she believed it'd save them from the ills of the new world. Her faith was based on the fact that monsters seemed to have immunity to the mosquito epidemics and everything else that dwindled the earth's numbers, and I was one of her lucky lambs. That was *her* idea of a cure."

Even back when he'd been speaking to Mariah on friendly terms, he'd never told her all this before. He'd recently had chats with others in the community, but they hadn't killed Abby.

Mariah opened her mouth, as if to offer compassion, but he capped off the chatter.

"Of course, my creator left me with nothing more than a near-useless pamphlet that described nothing but the joys of vampirism and not a whole lot else. So, if you do go out there, Mariah, I expect you'll get nothing but that, too, yet without the slim paperwork."

He walked off, but she followed, the scent of her heated skin growing stronger as she caught up. The link between them flared with her nearness.

Overcome for a piercing moment, Gabriel reached out, grasped her shirt.

A slight tearing sound offered the only protest.

Control, he thought. He had about as much of it as she did when they were together. They drove each other's passions up, and that was no good for either of them.

He let go of her, almost as if in violent disgust, and her eyes went shiny with what had to be oncoming tears.

Sadness. He knew it well by now. Being here in the New Badlands had schooled him in most of the emotions he'd lost upon becoming a vampire. He wished he didn't see sorrow so often in Mariah, though she'd done so much to deserve it, especially with Abby.

The name wandered through Gabriel, as if it'd strayed from the center of him long ago. Thing was, it hadn't fully deserted all of him yet.

Would it ever?

He held up his hands, showing Mariah that he wasn't going to touch her again. She looked . . . crushed.

The part of him that was still hopelessly addicted to helping her made him say, "There're solutions other than a cure, you know."

She swallowed, as if gathering herself. "Are you the one lying now, Gabriel?"

Nothing to say to that, so he kept himself shut right up.

She sighed. "What if there *is* a cure? Wouldn't I be irresponsible in ignoring the possibility?"

It felt as if his chest were being pried open, and he knew that he was connecting to her emotions again through the imprint. They shared so much, and even the vague dream of a cure made him yearn just as she did.

Then it hit him: Because of the imprint, would a cure affect him, too?

He brought himself to continue walking away from her. The only vampire cure he'd ever heard of was when the death of a maker resulted in the return of humanity for a vamp.

Mariah gave him space, then followed at a distance. Their imprint connection faded, but beats of her vital signs still possessed him. Sometimes he thought that the echo of her was the only thing that made him feel alive.

Shit, he hated this dependence on someone else's life to feel like he had one of his own.

They arrived in the main area, a cavern with stalactites and stalagmites stabbed with beige and brown artistry. Among them, three visz screens silently flashed pictures from some hidden cameras outside. Otherwise, the area was stark, with a few empty aluminum casks serving as chairs while others, filled with turtlegrape alcohol, lined the right side of the room like a bar. During the rushed move here, Pucci had found the casks near an abandoned semi-truck filled with black-market goods. The bleached bones of smugglers had littered the sand around the seemingly ancient, gutted vehicle.

Pucci often drank the turtlegrape, but at the moment, everyone, including him, was soberly waiting in the room: Hana. Chaplin. Sammy Ramos, a bitten were-creature whose orange hemp clothing matched the hues of his skin whenever he shifted into Gila monster form. Right now, though, he only looked like a stocky middle-aged man with dark hair, pocked skin, and a barely contained frown.

Then there was the true-born oldster, a no-name who could assume a modern-day scorpion figure during his changes, like the huge, previously unknown, meat-eating mutants that'd come out from the holes under the Badlands after the world had gone terrible. He sat on top of a cask, his skinny legs dangling, encased in the earth-toned denim he favored.

"Next time," he said to Gabriel and Mariah, "you two might think about how them tunnels are a conduit for sound."

Mariah stayed near the entrance. "Then we don't have to catch you up on our conversation."

From the way the Badlanders avoided looking directly at Gabriel and Mariah, he knew that they'd also intuited the hard feelings that'd gone along with the exchange.

Pucci dove straight in. "So when're you leaving, Mariah?"

Everyone shot the big man a dirty glance, though no one contradicted him.

Mariah crossed her arms over her chest, taking it as she always did. If she hadn't decided for certain whether she'd be on board with this hare-brained idea about a cure, Gabriel was pretty sure a decision had just been finalized for her. It seemed as if tonight's excitement had been the final blow, and the silence from the community spoke volumes—a group of books slamming shut.

Then Chaplin spoke, woofing.

"No," Mariah answered. "You're not going anywhere. The community needs you as protection."

The dog barked, his tone vehement. He wasn't bothering to block what he was saying from Gabriel this time.

I promised your dad I'd always be there, Chaplin said. *And I want to be.*

Gabriel hooked his thumbs in his belt loops. This was definitely going past the idea stage.

Was she *seriously* thinking of leaving?

Even if he wasn't a vampire, he wasn't sure how he'd be feeling about this turn of events. All the pieces clashed in his mind: Abby. The profound link he'd created with Mariah during the imprinting. The rights and wrongs of her being out there all alone.

Gabriel's remaining sense of right wasn't sitting well with him.

"Chaplin," Mariah said, "have you thought about what would happen if you were uncovered as an Intel Dog? Your kind was set upon, too, right along with preters, and one DNA test from a cop or official would result in your immediate termination. From what I hear, there aren't even many regular pet dogs round anymore, and you'd attract attention, boy. *I* can hide my abilities because I'm a were-creature, and if anything happened to you . . ." She shook her head.

A thought invaded Gabriel: A vampire could hide, if he tried hard enough.

He ignored it, but it seemed as if his mind connection with Chaplin had allowed the dog to hear Gabriel's musings.

Double shit, because Chaplin was shining those huge brown dog eyes at him in a sad plea that Gabriel could read loud and clear, even before the canine thought, *Mariah wouldn't be able to go to the hubs alone to get a sense of what might be possible as a cure, Gabriel, and you know how much she needs this. How we* all *need her to do this.*

He could feel Mariah looking at him, too—could feel that link between them—but when Gabriel turned to meet her gaze, she'd already averted her eyes. Her stubbornness nagged at him, because a woman like her wasn't going to ask anyone to go with her if she undertook this journey.

She'd pile everything upon herself like some martyr seeking redemption. He knew the type all too well, because he'd done it when Stamp had called him out. He'd been willing to suffer for the Badlanders because, at the time, he hadn't known what they were; he hadn't thought them capable of handling the Shredder themselves, and he'd believed he was the only one around who had the power to save them.

Pucci opened his big mouth, and Gabriel could see Mariah bristle.

"You'd need a heat suit," the man said.

"I suppose I would." She said it without fear, as if the more her neighbors showed relief at the idea of her leaving, the quicker she'd go, whether or not she wanted to.

Pucci continued. "Even with heat suits, I'd take care to travel at night, when it's cool and when I could run in were-form to get where I was going as fast as the powers that be allowed me to."

In his corner, Sammy Ramos was fidgeting. "Mariah, are you sure . . . ?"

"Sammy," she said, "let's not pretend you all don't want this."

Then the oldster gave voice to what everyone but Pucci had to be feeling. "I wouldn't wish your situation on anyone, Mariah. I'm sorry it's fallen on you."

"You think that way even after what happened to Zel?" Mariah asked.

Even Gabriel was taken aback by the comment. It was as if she had a yen for self-flagellation.

Did she *want* everyone to push her out?

Zel Hopkins had been one of them, murdered by Stamp and his crew after she'd had enough of his threats and gone after him. A were-owl, she'd done quite a bit of damage to his men with her claws, but she'd been beaten in the end.

The oldster had been in love with her, and now he was silent, holding on to the cask, white-knuckled.

"Mariah," Gabriel said, hoping to keep the calm, "let's discuss this."

She peered around the room, seeming like she was already a thousand miles distant from all of them.

It felt as if Gabriel's gut dropped, and he knew it was because he was linking to Mariah. Devastation, isolation . . .

She was also mortified, dejected by how the community was acting, but she'd definitely decided to go.

She tried to act as if it were no big deal. "Gabriel, there's nothing to discuss."

Chaplin whined, and it didn't mean anything more than that. A deep-down sound of sorrow.

Acceptance settled on the room, and Hana was the first to respect it. She reached under the collar of her robes and undid a necklace.

Gabriel had caught sight of it peeking out of all that hemp once—a golden star with seven points, framed by three circles.

She went to Mariah, who appeared wary at first, until Hana laid the necklace in the other woman's hand.

"For luck," Hana said.

"I can't—"

"It is a traveler's star." Hana smiled. "That is what my mother told me. My great-grandmother passed it down."

Mariah's brows drew together as she stared down at the necklace. It looked like she was fighting tears again. But then she lifted the jewelry, putting it on as if daring someone like Pucci to take it away. It caught a glint of light from a solar lantern as Hana went back to where Pucci was standing with his hands planted on his hips. There'd be no parting gifts from him.

"Thank you, Hana," Mariah said softly. It sounded final.

She's actually going on this wild-goose chase, Gabriel thought, still not able to grasp it.

Sammy gestured toward the exit, which led to other tunnels where everyone's private caverns and the aquifer/storage room were located.

"I've got a comm device in my quarters," he said. "You'd have to be close enough to a hub for good reception, but . . . Well, here it is, just in case."

Though the Badlanders used viszes to survey the area around their homes, they'd turned away from higher technology. They'd removed the chips from under their skins, avoided getting personal computers implanted in their arms, and refused to have any powerful comm items anywhere near them, but Sammy, who used to be a computer specialist, still messed with smaller devices.

Mariah seemed touched by the man's gesture. "Thanks to you, too, Sammy."

"It's nothing fancy," he continued.

"It's . . ." Her smile wobbled. "It's good, all the same."

The oldster made a cranky sound and ran a liver-spotted hand through what remained of his gray, wiry hair. "I could give you one of my zoom bikes."

Going, going . . .

Sammy said, "Unless you can provide her with enough of that homemade fuel you concoct, oldster, she'd have to ditch the vehicle at some point."

"It's okay," Mariah said. "Changing into my other form at night and running is fine. I'll make it. And if I do locate a cure . . ."

She didn't say she'd come back, and no one asked her to.

Gabriel's blood thudded, but he didn't know why he should want to feel sorry for her.

She touched the necklace charm, then lifted a hand in farewell, moving toward the tunnel.

"Wait," Gabriel said.

When she did, everyone else looked at him, too.

"That's it?" he asked the group. "Off she goes without any other—"

"Fanfare?" Pucci asked. "You'd better fucking believe it."

Gabriel's fist itched to land right in the man's righteous face. "Do you all remember what's out there?"

Hana stared straight ahead. "Demons."

Gabriel nodded. Stamp had caught such a creature and tortured it to perdition. They'd all wondered why a demon would be in the New Badlands, if there was some exodus from the hubs for the preters who managed to still secretly exist there.

And not all preters might get along as they, a vampire and were-creatures, had been doing.

The oldster added, "Humans are out there, too. Stamp had the tools to kill us, but the rest of them . . . they have the attitudes. Humans used to be just as bad as Shredders when it came to hunting. We threatened their place at the top of the food chain, and they were doing all they could to hold that chain together."

Sammy laughed darkly. "We weren't the ones to blame for what got them into such a situation."

The wars, the terrorism . . . Zealots had decimated the West Coast with clever ultracharges planted along quake faults, and change in general had caused catastrophic physical alterations throughout the globe. Disease, melting ice caps, more freak earthquakes . . .

The bad guys had taken advantage of every bit of it, seizing control in the name of safety. But everyone should've been more afraid of the people in charge instead.

And that was just where Mariah would be headed: straight to where they lived, en masse.

He could feel the fear in her, and it yanked at their connection, scorching him inside as if she were marking him.

If he'd been able to breathe, he would've felt suffocated. But he wanted to keep *on* feeling her, didn't he? With her gone, he might not feel half as alive or . . .

Human.

Again, the reliance on her needled.

A cure. Would it get rid of this ailment for him?

It was enough to make him say something he probably shouldn't have.

"Tomorrow night would be a better time for us to leave instead of now, when we've already burned part of the darkness," he said.

They all gaped at him. Mariah especially.

Then Chaplin yipped, a little cheer.

Meanwhile, Gabriel kept hearing his words over and over again. . . . *for* us *to leave* . . .

But he'd said it, and he couldn't take it back. He wasn't even sure he wanted to, because he could feel Mariah's pulse hopping in him, animating him beyond anything he'd experienced when he was away from her.

Relief. Happiness. Gratefulness. He fed off it all, and he saw it for what it was—another addiction, stronger than what he'd experienced with the alcohol he'd soothed himself with after his family's deaths.

Stronger than the fear he'd heard in Abby and Mariah, qualities that had attracted him to them in the first place.

As the Badlanders started firing questions at him, Gabriel left the room before anyone could figure out that he needed help just as much as Mariah did.

4

Stamp

Twenty-Three Hours Later

"Did you ever hear about the boy who cried wolf?" asked Goodie Jern from her side of the shack.

Johnson Stamp backed against a scuffed wall, knowing he was in for a talking-to from the other ex-Shredder. All the chairs except for hers seemed to be broken here in this watering hole on the outskirts of the Bloodlands, where he'd tracked her down.

Like every Shredder who'd been indoctrinated young so that they could learn and absorb the passé ways of preters, the woman spoke Old American. Stamp would've even said that the years since retirement had been rough on Goodie Jern—she was in her early thirties and still had a sense of slim femininity, but otherwise looked as used-up as a shriveled whale-skin jug.

But Stamp had post-service issues, too, even though he was about a decade younger than she was.

He adjusted his slight weight, favoring the reconstructed leg he'd crushed during the showdown with the vampire Gabriel and his were-creature friends. Although it'd been repaired, phantom pain had a habit of singing to him every so often. It was more a reminder than a physical sensation, though, and he took a swig of turtlegrape alcohol to chase away the bitter taste in his mouth.

Then he said, "Refresh my memory. They didn't exactly tell me bedtime stories in the orphan camp after my parents exploded."

Goodie Jern, candlelight making the stubble on her head shine, said, "None of us grew up with the sweetheart version of fairy tales, did we?"

"Not unless you count the ones I saw in my nightmares." The monster sympathizers, human bombs in a marketplace, murdering Stamp's mom and dad while he watched from a near distance. He'd been trying to catch up to them while they played tag among the crowd. Through his six-year-old eyes, he could still see them there and then gone in a blast of blood and ripped flesh.

The only other person in the room, Goodie Jern's teenaged, prairie-braided female companion, lit up a smoke from her place behind the bar. She wasn't much younger than Stamp.

"Just make your point," he said to Goodie Jern.

She considered him with a piercing set of dark eyes, much like his, then decided to grant Stamp this boon.

"I think 'The Boy Who Cried Wolf' goes something like this: There was once a kid who went to the nowheres, trying to make a better life for himself than he had in the hubs. But he came back, wounded very badly. After he healed somewhat through reconstruction, he told a few well-selected friends that, out in the nowheres, he'd seen a wolf . . . or a few monsters. Somehow, he rounded up a few of these friends to go back out there with him, weapons in hand, ready to spray some Shredder bullets around. They didn't find anything except a deserted compound that held no evidence of were-creatures, and when his friends went back to society, the boy cried about how monsters were really out there and he just needed a little extra help—"

Stamp didn't have the patience for this. "When the boy went out there to put the final whomp on those wolves and other were-creatures, they had obviously cleaned up after themselves, Goodie. They're smart, these monsters. They know how to hide, and I guarantee they're somewhere else by now."

Goodie Jern chuckled, showing silver where regular teeth should've been.

She hadn't gotten all of the thinly veiled story correct; it'd been his right-hand woman, Montemagni, who'd gathered some of his old Shredder friends while Stamp had quickly healed with the help of laser medicals from the minor chest wound Gabriel had inflicted, as well as the leg he'd crushed when he'd fallen down a mine shaft during the showdown escape. He'd recovered in enough time for them all to go out to the Bloodlands again, and even though they hadn't found the monster community that time, Stamp knew it was still out there.

It'd taken a couple days to track down Goodie Jern for his next hopeful trip. "You'll see I'm right if you just come with me."

"Why should I listen to you when the other ex-Shredders won't listen anymore? Water robbers were wiped out a few years ago, babycakes. That's what the government told us when they cut us loose."

"And you believe them?"

Goodie Jern's flask had been halfway to her chapped lips, and she stopped there, glaring at him. No one questioned the government—especially the ex-Shredders who'd received a tidy sum to shut up about preters and live the rest of their lives quietly. None of them even complained when they heard rumors about how they'd been replaced by newer models—ones that were said to be faster, stronger, more efficient.

She went ahead and took her next drink, and Stamp waited, hearing her companion playing a lone game at the bar, lazily stabbing at the wood with a knife.

Stamp almost smiled at the attempt to intimidate him. He didn't know if Braids was anxious about Goodie liking Stamp more than her, or if the teen just plain didn't want Stamp and his preter stories in here. Either way, she was amateur hour.

When Goodie Jern had finished with her flask, she said, "If there *were* anything out there, the old bosses would know it. Since the government's got new investors and they pulled out of that economic sanction trouble with India, they'll have enough funds to be doing new surveillance sweeps, if they haven't already started."

"The preters would know how to shield from surveillance with camouflage. We discovered steel plating at their homestead, and that might block government eyes."

"So you want to do your civic duty by wiping out the last of the monsters, is that it?"

"I want . . ."

His conviction trailed off. At first, he'd gone out to the New Badlands—or the Bloodlands as he called it now—because he'd truly wanted a new start in life. He'd wanted neighbors who didn't know he'd been raised to kill, and he wanted to help the bunch of former criminals he'd hired as employees to farm water and carve out peaceful existences.

Then his men had started dying, one by one, just because they were a little curious about the neighboring community over the hills. Turned out that community was a bunch of were-creatures who'd adopted a vampire, and Stamp had declared war, because monsters were built to kill, and you had to get them first.

Yes, he knew what he wanted.

Payback.

Stamp pushed away from the wall, putting his weight on his leg and hearing a few gears ease into place. He still wasn't used to the sound of the robotic parts the doctors had used, and he hoped that Goodie Jern hadn't heard them.

Then he made his way to the bar for more turtlegrape. Goodie Jern's companion looked at him with blank eyes and silently gave him what he wanted while her knife rested on the blade-scarred bar just within reach.

Meanwhile, Stamp kept talking. "You won't come with me, then?"

"Not unless you're offering a lifetime of riches."

Her voice held a hint of pity, and it rankled him. Obviously word had gotten around that he'd lost his severance money because he'd invested everything when he'd moved out to the Bloodlands. His one remaining employee, Mags, had filched enough water-currency to pay for his healing, as well as salaries for that first batch of ex-Shredders who'd gone to clean out the scrub compound. All he had left now was the hope that other Shredders would feel the same fire in their bellies to hunt down any and all preters before it was too late for humanity.

But Stamp was finding that the fires had been put out with his old friends. They kept telling him the preters were done for, the government had even said so, and the busted adventure he'd taken his comrades on to the Bloodlands only proved it.

They thought he was loco, and sometimes Stamp even wondered. If it hadn't been for Mags and how she'd gone through the same trials with the monsters, he might've found his own shithole outpost bar like Goodie Jern and stayed there for the rest of his damned life.

"You were good at what you did," Goodie Jern finally said. "That's a fact. One of the youngest Shredders ever, with quite a few kills to his name. But it's time to let it go, babycakes. If the government still deems monsters a hazard, they'll take care of it themselves."

He turned toward her, ready to argue that.

Goodie Jern leaned forward, serious now. "You were lucky to find any ex-Shredders who went with you the first time, do you know that?"

In back of him, he heard the companion stabbing her knife into the bar again. This time, it didn't sound like jealousy.

The rough woman in front of him shook her head. "Shredders stopped being Shredders the moment we accepted our severance. The government has ways of containing everything, even those who think they're looking out for the greater good."

"Are you saying they became cautious of us, like they did with Intel Dogs and local government councils who actually had the balls to think? That's why they disbanded us?"

The stabbing paused, as if the companion had the knife in midair.

"I'm saying," Goodie Jern answered, "that when our time of greatest contribution is up, it's up."

Stamp stared at her. Goodie Jern had boasted a few government connections back in the day, and that made sense for a Shredder of her standing. She'd racked up more kills than most and had been given special assignments that were said to be stored in the black-files.

Maybe he shouldn't have come here.

Or maybe he should just listen to her now.

Yet common sense didn't stop his blood from boiling whenever he tried to move his bum leg, whenever he thought about the vampire and the weres that'd gotten away from him and no doubt lived scot-free in the Bloodlands.

"Word to the wise," Goodie Jern said. "You stop now or you expect some higher authority to interfere. Understand my meaning?"

Stamp didn't understand at all, but he nodded, knowing when to argue and when not to. Then he glanced back at her companion, who was watching him, her dirty hand gripping the knife handle as she held it in front of her.

Without another word, Stamp left the shack and stepped out into the tepid night. Ten yards away, Mags waited in an archaic blue van that'd been painted on the outside with big-breasted women in bikinis. Quaint, in these times of carnerotica.

They'd salvaged the vehicle from a garage back when they'd fled the Bloodlands after his showdown with the preters. The weapons they'd been carrying on them—a chest puncher, a corner shotgun, a deathlock gun, a few knives—were stored in the cab next to his Shredder uniform and heat suits.

He limped to the van, where Mags already had the door open on the passenger side. She'd known he was coming because she'd been listening in on the comm connected to his personal computer, which had been activated the entire time.

Slipping into the front, he closed the door.

The throttled moonlight shone over Mags's dark skin and battered shirt, pants, and boots. She wore a yellow bandanna that held back her curly black hair, and it gave her bladed cheekbones and slanted brown eyes that much more prominence. There had to be Korean blood in her, along with some Afro-American roots.

"No go?" she asked him in her husky voice.

"Drive," he said.

And she did, over the uneven ground, sending the van to bumping. They passed a mob of loto cactus, with their swirled, needled shapes; passed stranded old cars from humans who'd tried to live outside the hubs with no luck. Most who'd come out here had been soft and ill-educated in even the most basic survival methods, such as how to derive fuel from the tymol roots discovered under the desert ground after the world had changed.

Most humans had ultimately stayed in the hubs, locked inside their own homes, strangers to even their neighbors. Too much terrorism, too many bad guys outside the door.

That was survival enough.

Before Stamp and Mags had gone even a few miles, she slowed the van, bringing it to a grumbling idle.

"Might want to check your computer," she said.

"Why?"

She lifted an eyebrow and smiled a little.

He rolled up his shirtsleeve and pulled down the glove that covered him up to the inner forearm, where his personal computer screen was embedded, hooked up to his chip implant. When he accessed his new data, a message from Mags popped up.

It featured grainy satellite images taken from a long, sky-high distance, then focused to a closer view: blips of light blobs against dark. He made out what looked to be hills. Sand. Trees.

Then the film slowed severely down, as if Mags had taken the action frame by frame, and he thought he saw two blobs moving over open ground until they disappeared into the shadows.

In spite of Goodie Jern's warning to back off the hunt for preters, excitement rolled through Stamp.

"Is this what I think it is?" he asked.

"The Bloodlands, about a hundred and six klicks from the first scrub compound. That's footage from last night from one of just a few satellites the government had already started using for abandoned-area surveillance again, and it came to the attention of an analyst when her computer alerted her to the speed of movement in a place that's supposed to be filled with slower creatures."

Goodie Jern had told him that the government was putting in a new watch program. Here was evidence of it. "How do you know it might be the scrubs?"

"I don't. But it looks mighty interesting to see something moving that fast in the open. That's why it came to my attention."

"And how did you get this?"

Mags gave him an *oh please* look. She was a hell of a hacker as well as a gunslinger. In a business world, where they still relied on Old American, Chinese, and Hindi, she'd needed to learn fast-talking in all three languages, plus computer skills and the occasional weapon work as a white-collar criminal

who'd diddled a few corporations without them even knowing
it. She'd retired to the Bloodlands with Stamp's group before
ever getting caught and put to execution on a carnerotica channel
for screwing with the government and its corporate partners.

She said, "I have an old . . . friend . . . who thought I'd be
interested in the footage after I told him about our adventure
out there, and we're close enough to a hub for me to receive it.
If an analyst thought it was worth his or her while, they could've
sent someone out to the location by now."

"Are you saying new Shredders are employed to do that
kind of thing?"

After talking to Goodie Jern, he wondered if he sounded
neurotic.

"I don't know," Mags said. "Maybe the government would
just send out a 'bot to inspect the area." She was talking about
Monitors, who used to venture into situations too insignificant
for human labor before the government had cut back because
of the financial trouble with India.

She kept the van idling, and he knew what she was asking
without having to say it.

What now?

To the Bloodlands?

Or back to the hubs where he'd pretty much been told to
stay by Goodie Jern?

As he kept seeing those shadowy hints of preters in his head,
Stamp's adrenaline surged, icy and urgent. It made his leg keen,
made the memories of Gabriel and his buddies dig into him
like fresh wounds that rose up every day, never healing.

A frown lined Mags's face.

"You have something to say?" he asked.

She gave him a look he didn't comprehend, because there
was something in her eyes . . . a flicker that seemed to run deep
into her for some reason.

Just as he thought she might be looking at him a moment
too long, Mags gunned the engine and turned the van west,
toward the Bloodlands, and Stamp's pulse picked up vengeful
speed, as well.

5

Mariah

We'd left hours ago, shortly after dusk had fallen and Gabriel had awakened.

Right from the start, he'd walked far ahead of me in the gray night, never looking back to see if I was behind him. But that was okay. He'd come with me, and that was enough. Hell, it was more than I'd even dreamed of in the first place. When he'd blurted out that he'd be accompanying me, I'd feared shattering my jaw because of how it'd just about crashed to the floor in my shock. Well, maybe I hadn't had such a dramatic reaction, but in my brain, it'd sure felt like it.

Even as we trekked miles over the dirt, I still had no idea why he'd made this decision. I was almost afraid to ask, in case it'd make him come to his senses and turn right back round. Not that I'd shown it, but I'd been dreading taking this trip alone. Sure, I could've done it, but . . .

Alone was the worst punishment I could think of.

As the witching hour struck in my veins, we crested a hill, seeking the cover of a rock. From there, the moonlight slouched over the ruins of a diner near the old road we were following. The pavement was nothing more than cracks amidst dirt, but

I remembered this path from when Dad and I had come to the New Badlands. Now, I was certain it'd lead me and Gabriel to a so-called civilized place where we could begin ferreting out clues for any kind of cure.

Chaplin had begged to escort us this far—about fourteen miles distant from our homestead—and out of respect for my dog, neither Gabriel nor I had called on our preter abilities in order to move faster. The mutt could run, all right, but not as fast as a vampire or a fully changed werewolf.

My pet growled low in his throat as he surveyed the diner from our spot atop the hill.

"What is it, boy?" I asked.

Something on the air, he said.

I bent to him at the same exact time Gabriel did. But then, as if our dual actions extended some kind of simpatico with me that he didn't want to own, Gabriel stood right back up.

He blocked the moon, more a shadow than a man, and as with the first time I'd seen him, he reminded me of a mythical cowboy: long coat, boots, a carryall slung over his chest. He had a weary bravery about him, and it gave his shoulders a slight hunch, as if, at a moment's notice, he might draw the revolvers or knives I'd seen him load into his bag and coat.

My chest clenched, as if trying to shut him out, but I couldn't. Not with that buzzing imprint connection that kept us linked, whether he wanted it or not.

He began smelling the air, just as Chaplin was doing. I'd read once in my dad's monster book that the thousands of olfactory receptors in a vampire's nose had way more power than a human's, and they could detect scents without inhaling. Half of the information in that book probably wasn't true, but if he couldn't breathe, this explanation made sense.

Then my dog spoke. *Food. Your pick of it, if you want to rest here and stock up.*

I relaxed. I'd been expecting Chaplin to pronounce something troublesome. "You gave me a scare."

He wagged his tail. *There's a feracat, sleeping nearby. I'll bet it's in a burrow under the diner, and it has no idea we're here yet.*

Feracats were bigger, meatier versions of feral cats that'd migrated to the nowheres from the hubs and mutated into something carnivorous, stiletto-toothed, and fast. Just one of them could supply Gabriel with more sustenance than he'd probably need for a few nights. And I could roast a fera with a campfire stoked with the flint I carried along with my heat suit, small weapons, and other survival items in my backpack. I also had revolvers and knives in my holsters, and that would make hunting all the easier.

I don't need to mention that there was another way to hunt, and it would allow me to eat the animal's meat raw, which would satisfy my werewolf side if I changed into that form. Truth was, I'd *have* to call upon a change soon, just to make speedy time during our trek. Walking at a human pace wasted precious hours because we had only twenty-three nights until the next full moon, and, naïve or not, I was hoping I'd come upon a cure before that. Plus, lollygagging in the desert would leave me and Gabriel more vulnerable to discovery if the government was watching. Of course, an analyst might take us for migrating humans, but why take the risk?

We all just stood there on that hill, because we knew what had to occur next. We'd been building up to it, putting it off for miles now.

"You gotta get home, Chaplin," I finally said. "Dawn's just a short time away, and no one in their right mind would be out here during full-day heat."

My dog shuffled as Gabriel waited, almost as if he didn't know whether to walk ahead or linger.

Then he put his hands on his hips, peering down into the valley. "I suppose I'll go on and check out that diner. . . ."

No, Chaplin said. *Please don't leave her behind, Gabriel.*

Both me and Gabriel froze, because we knew that my dog was making a request for the entire journey, not just now.

Don't ever leave me behind.

Awkward.

There were no words that could cover what I was feeling, so I just threw my arms round Chaplin's neck, hugging him for dear life, thanking him for asking this of Gabriel, even if it humiliated me. But, more to the point, I couldn't believe my dog wasn't coming.

He buried his muzzle under my ear, and we stayed like that for as long as we could, the night barely moving round us. My very best friend. The only one who truly believed that I could be more than the killer I'd become.

My dog was the first to back away from the embrace, and he nudged me away from him, as if thinking that a little cruelty would make this easier. Then, with a final glance at Gabriel— one in which I knew Chaplin was silently communicating with his vampire—he turned round and ran full speed down the other side of the hill. He'd probably maintain that pace until he reached home, too, keeping to the shadows, never stopping until he fell to rest in the cavern.

There was nothing I could do but watch him disappear, maybe forever. God-all, if I moved, I'd cry. It might even happen if I breathed. So I merely stared at the dirt, as if the grains could piece themselves together, as I sorely needed to do myself.

Then Gabriel said, "Before Chaplin left just now, he made me vow that I'd stick with you."

When I glanced up, I saw that he hadn't moved from his spot. He hadn't left me behind yet, just as he'd told Chaplin he wouldn't. But I wondered how long his promise would last.

He started down the hill, making his way toward that diner. I followed him, keeping my voice low so as not to disturb the wild things round us that were no doubt hiding in the brush and in holes under the ground.

"I'd let you out of a vow, if you just asked," I said. Gabriel was a vampire of honor. He'd proven it enough times, and I didn't want to hold him to anything he didn't want to do.

He didn't answer.

Sand slushed round my boots, and I slowed at the bottom of the hill near a boulder, where the dirt was firmer. "Why *did* you say you'd come in the first place?"

He kept right on walking. "Because I wasn't about to see you forge into the great beyond by yourself. Unlike humans or even weres like you, I'm meant to live a long time. Having your destruction on my conscience when I could've prevented it wouldn't sit well for a decade, much less hundreds of years."

"I don't doubt your gentlemanly concern," I said, although I knew I didn't deserve it.

He slowed down, his tone more casual, as if he'd admitted far too much and wanted to correct any assumptions I'd made. "Also, I'm just as curious about a cure as you."

Was he talking about how a cure for me might affect him, too, through our link?

All right then. He was here for himself, and I was incidental. It didn't taint this trip, though. I would've welcomed him along even if he'd confessed to bringing me out here at the request of the community to kill me and bury me where I'd be out of sight and mind.

"Don't worry about it," I said. "The reason for your being here doesn't matter so much. Having you along is the main thing."

A grunt was my answer, but that was fine in my book.

Truth to tell, now that we were doing something about my malady, *everything* seemed finer. I guess hope has a way of pumping up a person, and with every step I took, the better I felt. I even started having a fanciful notion or two: When I came back to the Badlands, I was going to help them all, if they wanted it. I was going to be like Gabriel, when he had come to us and volunteered to protect us from Stamp. My neighbors would look at me differently, not with trepidation, but with relief, and maybe even gratefulness.

I'd be their hero. . . .

Dare to dream, right?

It seemed that this trek could stand a little small talk, so I said, "I wonder what life would be like after a cure. There's a chance I'd be able to look in a mirror again without wanting to look away."

"Not to burst your bubble, but a cure's not a guaranteed outcome of this trip. You still might be . . . who you are . . . afterward."

Why couldn't he just say it? Was he still so intent on keeping Abby alive in his heart—or whatever he had—by refusing to talk about what'd happened between me and her? Could he avoid confronting what *she'd* been if he didn't label me, either?

"And what am I exactly?" I asked.

"Forget it."

"If we're going to be traveling together, we need to get this out. Just lay your cards down and tell me what I am."

He shook his head, as if I were a supreme moron for bringing all this up. Just over his shoulder, the diner loomed with its falling burger joint sign and faded, slouched aqua-and-pink siding.

"If you won't supply a word for me," I said, "then I'll do it for you. I'm a killer."

"Mariah—"

"Just like Abby was, because the both of us had to be to survive. And you, Gabriel? You're one of our own, too, whether or not you like to see yourself that way."

That brought him to a complete halt.

"We're monsters," I said, as if I needed to clarify. "Maybe you don't know it yet because you spend so much time thinking you can still be human. You're only about a couple years old—"

"Different folks have different definitions of what a monster is." Now his tone was icy.

"And what's your definition?"

He was so still that I might've mistaken him for a standing dead person. Undead was technically more like it.

"A monster," he said, "is an accident. A thing with appetites that go against the laws of man, but with the consciousness to still regret its hunger. Humans don't realize how we struggle with what we survive on. If they did, they might be able to come to terms with us."

"There're monsters like my neighbors who live just fine with those appetites. They're at peace with what they are."

"And *you're* at peace?"

He had me there. Right after I'd killed Stamp's employees—bad guys, one and all—I'd truly believed I'd been justified. Someone had to stop them. Someone had to step forward and be the force of reckoning if nothing else in the world took care of it. It was only afterward, when the consequences started falling on me and my neighbors, that I pulled back from what I'd done; I'd been a coward by not sticking by what I'd set into motion.

And you know what? It scared me to realize that the consequences of killing were the only things that made me fight my ingrained instincts. Otherwise . . .

God-all, otherwise I might be one of those monsters who lived just fine with themselves. With a cure, I didn't even necessarily want to be human as much as I only wanted my lack of control to be remedied. I liked the power I had as a were-creature, but if I had to go human to protect my neighbors, I'd do it.

I tried to explain all this to Gabriel. "Were-creatures can stop themselves at a half-change point, but that leaves us with the consciousness you mentioned. So we don't have much call for that state of being. When we're in full were-form, though, it's almost like our minds are separate from our bodies. Our hunger leaves morals way behind until we come back to humanity. That's when you realize the damage. But the thing is . . ."

I warned myself against saying it, but omitting the truth would be just as good as lying to him, and I couldn't lie anymore after all he'd been through because of me.

"The thing is," I continued, "bad guys like Stamp's employees . . . and like the men who killed my mom and brother and then turned me into a werewolf . . . Gabriel, sometimes I wonder if there's a reason we were given our powers. Have you ever thought that monsters evolved and then grew in number because we were meant to balance the bad guys out?"

"Are you saying this is nature's plan?"

"Could be."

It seemed to take him half a night to turn to me, and when he did, he was glowering. When a vampire glowers, it ain't pretty, with his gaze a slow, crimson burn, his expression downright mean with a threatening change.

And, help me now, but it sent a monsterish thrill twisting through me.

I talked away, as if that'd smooth me out. "I used to be so afraid of what I can do—it's part of the reason I never went outside unless I had to. Outside was where I could be a wolf and run as wild as everything else out here. But after Stamp came along, and with some time to think about how the world works, it's made me wonder . . . Can I be better than those bad guys? *They* kill because of greed or sometimes no reason at all. I killed out of defense."

"And that makes you superior."

"No. It's just that I love most of my neighbors, although it's hard to say the feeling is returned. So isn't wanting what's best for them—the good guys—the superior part? Wouldn't it have been wrong to *not* protect them? You used to tell us to fight."

"Your fighting went far beyond the methods I was talking about."

"Why? Should I have just used shotguns against them instead? How is that different?"

He kept right on glowering, and it mangled our connection. Instead of just humming, it sizzled, electric under my skin.

"There's even a part of me," I continued, "that wonders if, someday, I was meant to track down those bad guys who tore my family up and visit justice right back on them."

The notion of bringing karma on those men made me full, as if it were a meal I'd already feasted on in my fantasies. I dreamed in karma. You could even say it was what kept me going.

If a vampire could look gobsmacked, Gabriel would qualify. "You're not some kind of reckoning god, Mariah."

"Then who's taking care of what gods should be doing?"

Obviously done with the discussion, he left.

Was he put off by my logic? Or had the final straw been the religion talk? I'd heard once that you shouldn't gab about religion or politics if you wanted to keep on someone's good side. Nowadays that was doubly true.

Back Before, when the world had been so much simpler, there'd been established religions. There'd been scriptures, which had led to the expectation of rewards for being a true believer. But after the calamities, many believers had fallen, telling everyone that there'd been no rapture or repayment for their faith; their patience had been stretched enough because, to them, the calamities had been the predicted Armageddon. All but the most devout had turned to other objects of worship until newly organized religions ran legion with everything from followers of blogs to fans of entertainers to converts of slick-tongued politicians.

Everyone needed something to believe in, and the more immediate the returns, the more attractive the group. As I said, no one likes to be left behind.

I ran to catch up to Gabriel. We weren't moving with preter swiftness, so I wasn't as worried about catching much surveillance attention.

"If *you* haven't accepted what you are," I said, "why're you out here with me in search of a cure? Don't you have to admit what you are before you set out to correct it?"

"You're really testing me."

I probably should've paid heed to that, but, again, I was beyond lying these days.

"In a perfect world," I said, "everyone might come to respect each other, and there'd be no need for monsters to balance anything."

"This isn't a perfect world," he said in that gritty vampire tone.

Then I went way too far. "If it were perfect, Abby would've stayed with you in the first place. She wouldn't have left and you wouldn't have had to come looking for her."

He turned, his gaze flaring, and I stepped back, even though there was a world of space between us. But I'd been wanting to say all of this for a while. I guess I was even seeing how far I could push him before he ditched me. Might as well know his limits now before we got close to the hubs.

"You didn't know her that long," I said. "You didn't know me, either, Gabriel, before we—"

"Don't say 'became intimate.'" The tips of his fangs peeked out from his lips. "What happened with us didn't even approach the definition."

Bam, right in the gut. He'd been my first, so it'd been intimate for me, at least.

Disappointment pulled me down, as if my skin were so heavy that everything was falling with it.

"You want revenge on me then?" I asked softly. "Because this is the best time for it. Who would know if you reckoned with me way out here? Who would even care besides Chaplin?"

Gabriel just red-glared at me. The link between us grew to a sawing screech, cutting into my nerves.

Then he somehow regained control, his eyes cooling to the normal gray of his human façade, just like the color of the unforgiving sky.

It was as if he'd snipped a cord, and I felt switched off.

"Revenge is a fake, temporary concept that doesn't matter in the end," he said. "It wouldn't make *me* feel any better."

"It might."

Before I knew it, he'd zoomed over to me, stopping just short of my face. His eyes were back to burning into mine, and I reared away, pushing my hands against his chest as he hissed.

"If you tempt me," he said through his elongated fangs, "I just might take you up on it. So don't."

But I did, perversely leaning my head to the side so that the ugly moonlight would shine over the thudding vein in my neck. I could hear my pulse beating throughout my body, even between my legs, where my sex was going achy and damp.

His skin was cold, but mine was heating, and the balance of temperature seemed to clash in the small space between us, resulting in a hammering dirge.

He hissed again, obviously hating that I was doing this to him. I hated myself a little, too, but I wanted him in me again, healing me.

When he kept restraining himself, I looked up into his blazing eyes. Fevered, I locked onto his open thoughts, sensing the struggle of a man in an ancient tale trying to push a boulder uphill. And Gabriel had never been taught by his maker how to do anything but keep pushing that weight forward, even though he always ended up backtracking because of the fruitless effort. . . .

Stung by his tragedy, I closed my eyes.

Why was I goading him? I was acting like a true monster—the kind humans thought we were. No wonder they'd wanted to kill us.

My fever seethed over and through me. A change was coming—it was pounding harder and harder—and I shrugged out of my backpack, then my holsters, sprinting toward the diner.

The feracat, I thought, juices flooding my mouth. Time to hunt for it, to divert my growing appetite toward something less destructive.

As my skin and muscles got hot enough so that the growth and thrust of bones came fast, I wiggled out of my shirt. My heightened werewolf senses sprang to the forefront—the piercing bluish sights, the vivid scent of night and dirt—and I skidded to a halt, shucking off the rest of my clothing just before my body shot up and out, so much taller, wider.

My claws sprouted, and I panted in hollow time, my teeth thrusting out of my gums, hair flowing out of my skin. I bit back a howl, then sniffed the air, tracking the feracat near the diner, which was only yards away by now, and finding its tangy scent.

I was an animal who saw through that blue-hazed vision,

latching onto a hole beneath the diner and pouncing to it, then howling again as the massive, black, glow-eyed feracat scream-hissed at me and I lost all humanity with one, fast swipe.

. . .

When I came to, I was lying on my heat suit, which covered a dirty, uneven linoleum floor. My clothing lay on top of me. Round me, upset tables and lopsided aqua-upholstered booths loitered like shocked observers. The murk-weakened moon spied through the broken shades on the windows, creating barred shadows.

I sat up, clutching my shirt to my chest, my pants to my lowers. Sore. Damn, my body was sore.

Across the diner, near some stools, Gabriel sat, reclining against the counter panel, staring straight ahead at a long fluorescent bulb that hung from the ceiling, scratched by wires.

"I already checked this place inside and out," he said in a near whisper, but I suspected his forced calmness wasn't so much about his trying to be quiet as it was about his coming off a blood high. His chin was streaked with red. "No other preters about. No Shredders, either."

I felt so very naked in front of him, and not because I literally was, either. He'd seen me change. And it wasn't just about turning into a were. I'd confronted him with some disgusting words, and it'd happened way before I'd gone wolf. I'd exposed my true thoughts, and they'd been grotesque.

He kept talking, as if that would keep him from looking at me. "I already buried the feracat's remains and cleaned out its cove underneath the diner. Lots of critters have settled in there, but they can come back after we've rested in their home for the day. It'll be cooler down there than in here, and you can wear your heat suit, besides, while we get some sleep."

I cleared my throat, then gestured to the upset booths. "Did I do all this?"

"It was destroyed before we got here."

"Gabriel, I'm . . ." *Just say it.* "I'm so sorry."

He still acted nonchalant. "Don't worry—you left enough of the cat for me. You ripped out its side and worked on that while I had a feast at its neck."

Hearing him talking about our wild feeding so matter-of-factly should've shaken me up, but to tell the truth, it bothered me more that Gabriel had obviously refused to dress me, even after I'd turned back into my human form.

He couldn't stand being close to me.

Was it because my nakedness would make him lose more control? No, probably not. He just couldn't stand to be round *me*.

I slid into my shirt, and he suddenly became real interested in the spot of pink paint-stripped wall on his left.

"I'm not apologizing about the food," I said. "I'm sorry for talking to you like I did. It was wrong. I overstepped."

"You were right, though. There was some clearing that needed to happen between us if we're to travel together."

I'd already put on my pants and was working on my boots. He'd brought in my weapons and backpack, taking good care of me, as usual.

"It's all cleared, as far as I'm concerned," I said. "There'll be no more of it from me. You can be sure of it."

He rested his forearms on his bent knees, slouched, but not in a defeated way. He was shielding his reactions, acting as if my every move didn't matter to him.

I knew it just as well as I knew most things about him after we'd made the imprint through sex. Reading a vampire would've been a hell of a lot tougher without our link.

"I'm done now," I said.

He finally looked at me, the blood on his chin bright against his pale skin. The sight of the red sent the same fear and hate through me as it always did—memories of those bad guys and what they'd done to my family.

I stood, grabbing my heat suit from the floor. It was time to get into that feracat's cove before sunrise hit.

"After we rest," I said, "we should leave shortly after dusk in our preter forms," I said. "With enough speed, we might hit some population in Salts"—what they called old Utah—"pretty soon. Maybe we'll come across a batch of people who can point us in the proper direction if we ask the right questions."

"Sounds good."

"I'll follow your lead, Gabriel. You were out here traveling more recently than me."

He got to his feet, too, graceful as all vampires probably were. "What I need more from you is trustworthiness."

I wished I could promise him that. "And I want the same thing from me. But wanting isn't necessarily enough." I tried to lighten both of us up. "I guess that's why a cure would be dandy, huh?"

For the first time in . . . well, it seemed like ever, Gabriel smiled. It wasn't much—just a tip of one side of his mouth, really—but it sent a fizzing high through me.

It was a smile that made me want to live up to its cautious optimism, and at that moment, I told myself that I *could* do that.

I really could.

6

Gabriel

Gabriel had a passing acquaintance with necropolises because he'd passed a few on his way to the Badlands in his search for Abby. The stench was one of a kind—a musty decay that carried over through years of hopelessness. And, here, in a nameless outpost they'd reached that was obviously about a hundred miles distant from a town of the dead, Gabriel detected the odor, even over the wood smoke that rode the main street.

But the smell wasn't as heavy as the weight he was carrying—the cost of traveling with Mariah. As planned, they'd burrowed under the diner, where he'd battled with himself until darkness had swallowed him at the sun's rise. Thank-all for that slumber, too, because he couldn't have imagined what it might've been like to lie awake next to her, obsessing over the sight of her without clothes, her flesh pale and smooth.

That wouldn't have been the only thing keeping Gabriel awake, though. He'd never seen her enjoy changing into her were-form before, and his vampire body had been pulled to her animal freedom while she'd altered.

Even after she'd changed back, the attraction remained, but

forced rest had saved him, and he'd woken up with the dusk, crawling out from their cove before Mariah had even opened her eyes. She'd soon joined him, and there hadn't been much conversation as she'd willed another change upon herself so they could cover as much ground as possible—hundreds of miles. They'd run most of the night, trying to keep to some hill and tree cover until they'd come upon a small fox pack. Gabriel had taken enough blood from the animals to last for a while, but he couldn't shed the image of Mariah, half panting woman, half towering beast, tearing at her food with those long teeth.

His bewilderment had continued as they'd both scented out this way station, which squatted in the middle of the nowheres with no name, no identity. Mariah had put her clothing back on so they could blend with the humans, but, to Gabriel, there was still a huge difference between her and the stilted flows of human blood he could detect. The place also had a sour twist of unwashed skin that hung below the necropolis and smoke smells, but at least the heat was lessening slightly. The farther they got from the Badlands, the more improved the temperature would be. Relatively, at least.

At the foot of the main street, dust seemed to veil the lone eatery and the spatter of sun-shield tents opposite it. Gabriel also identified a trace of old opium that humans still used for mellowing themselves. When the sudden sound of unholy screech-howls and human yells arose, he cocked his head.

Sounded like a tournament of sorts, Gabriel thought. An entertaining contest where someone . . . or something . . . was getting hurt. He could smell the blood now, too, and he took a piece of old shirt from his bag, fixing it over the lower half of his face. He wouldn't look out of place since humans routinely wore masks in the hubs to fend off disease.

A scraggly man with a straw hat stumbled out of a tent, accompanied by a skeletal wisp of a dog that he must've found in some hole outside a hub since the government had gathered up most canines around the time they'd banned Intel Dogs. They'd cited a canine flu, claiming that they'd wanted to get it under control.

Gabriel wasn't sure why, but it reeked of bullshit, just like most things bad guys did.

As the near-distant yelling stopped, he looked into Mariah's eyes, wanting to communicate with her nonverbally. It was supposed to be a simple vampire ability, according to his introductory pamphlet, which he'd discarded long ago. However, mind-reading hadn't always come easy to him. He was getting better at it, though.

Even so, he'd be keeping the vampire tricks to a minimum when they were around people. He had to be quietlike about what he was, just like Mariah.

I say we greet that man, Gabriel thought to her, tilting his head toward the straw-hat guy who was clearly supervising the whiz his dog was taking by the tents.

Mariah just nodded, almost as if she were surprised he'd cared to enter her mind.

Together, they ambled toward the straw-hat guy, who didn't hear them approach until they were upon him. He gasped, his hand going to his jeans pocket.

Gabriel held up his palms, speaking Text. "No hrm hre, frnd."

Mariah didn't repeat that she also meant no harm to their new friend. She was, after all, loaded up with weapons in those holsters and the backpack she was wearing.

Nonetheless, she had her hands up, too. For the moment.

The dog growled weakly. It'd barely even had the strength to whiz; Gabriel knew as much because he'd connected with the animal and heard the feeble movement of its vital signs. He had an affinity for canines—Chaplin, this dog . . . and werewolves like Abby and Mariah.

The straw-hat man relaxed but kept his hand near his pocket. He wore a long-ass mustache that was waxed to points below his chin. "Wht u wnt?"

What did they want? Probably a sight more than this poor man could give them.

Just as Gabriel was about to begin some subtle questioning to hunt down rumors about a cure, a tinny, small, very elderly voice came from the direction of the tents.

"Which one of you asswipes took my can of beans?" Then, as if that hadn't been good enough, he repeated it in Text.

Mariah was already headed in the voice's direction, and Gabriel nodded to the straw-hat guy in the best thanks he could muster.

She whispered over her shoulder to Gabriel. "Old American's a better bet than one of those Text-hawking ignoramuses."

He knew what she meant. There was someone speaking an upper-level language in this dump, and maybe this person would be halfway educated and tuned in to the bigger world picture.

They circled the tents, seeking the most likely spot where the Old American had come from. Meanwhile, the screeching and yelling they'd heard from the main street got louder as they approached its source.

A shade fight.

Unbelievable. These tent-dwelling cretins had two gargoylesque, hulking black carrion eaters with ropes tied around their necks and stones strapped to their wings. The hideous shades were lunging at each other, snapping their beaks, leaving tracks of blood on the dirt from their wounds while soil-caked men and women leaned forward, cheering them on.

The sight of blood deeply unsettled Gabriel, and he pressed the cloth against his face, walking away.

"Where're my *beans*!" shouted the small, elderly voice again.

Thinking that Mariah might've been affected by the blood, too, Gabriel took her wrist, handling her while navigating the maze of tents until she disengaged from him. His flesh burned where her warm skin had touched his.

"I've got a hold of myself," she said under her breath.

"Never can be sure," he said right back.

She didn't parry, so she must've taken his comment to heart. At any rate, there was no time for a lively discussion because they found a bent little old man standing by a campfire outside the only tepee in the copse of tents.

And *little* was certainly the best way to put it. Even with the high-crowned cowboy hat he was wearing, he couldn't have been more than five feet. He was like a mini general from the handheld screen of a history e-back, with a gray soul patch under his bottom lip and military-style pants with a multitude of pockets. A steel pipe cane kept him standing, as if he were on his last legs. Judging by the lines on his face and the deliberation of his movements, he had to be even more ancient than the oldster back in the Badlands. Maybe even over a century.

Gabriel stayed away from the fire, and Mariah remained at his side as the little old man barked out his bean question in Text again. Then he paused, finally noticing Gabriel and Mariah with a gaze that was more cloudy-white than blue.

"You're looking for beans?" Gabriel asked in greeting.

"Have you seen anyone around with a can of 'em? If you do, they're mine."

"I suppose they are, but we haven't witnessed hide nor hair of any beans." Gabriel put on his friendliest expression and proceeded to give the little old man a false name—a precaution he and Mariah had agreed upon. "I'm Gary and this is Michelle. We're new to this place and we couldn't help noticing that you spoke Old American. We haven't heard that in a while."

"You wouldn't, out here." The little guy kept peering around with his milky gaze, as if his beans were going to roll right up to his feet and all the fuss would be over. "When did you arrive at our illustrious palace?"

Mariah had clearly given the floor to Gabriel. That was another thing they'd planned—one of them would talk at a time. This way, there was a lower chance of them fumbling any cover stories.

"We got here tonight," Gabriel said. "Lost our high-business jobs in the hubs and decided to come west. We needed a place to rest for a spell."

Gabriel didn't know why, but the little old man's lips parted, as if he recalled something secretive and rather delightful. He seemed to forget about his beans, focusing on them instead and running his fuzzed gaze up and down their clothing.

Great. Gabriel had wanted this guy to be sharp enough to give good information, but not *too* sharp. What was he noticing about them?

"You," the little man finally said, and Gabriel had the disconcerting feeling that . . .

No, it couldn't be. This guy couldn't have recognized them.

The old man looked smug for some reason, and Gabriel could sense the confusion in Mariah, as well.

"Son, this is a way-camp," the little guy finally said. "You'll find other people here who also 'recently' lost their high-business jobs, but they don't quite have the balls to cross over into the Badlands. There're more and more lately who come here, then tell themselves they'll stay for only a week or two, just to get used to the higher heat and the strange sounds of the night that you don't hear when you're sleeping in a secured hub home. Then, the next thing they know, they're speaking Text and stealing beans from an old fart."

Mariah's imprint began to thud inside Gabriel. Was she thinking what he was? That, among these humans, there might also be preters in this camp because of an exodus? Was this man one of them?

But his blood flow was clogged, just like an ex-hub human. . . .

As Gabriel tuned in more to the pulses around them, he at least knew that this camp held more ex-hubites than he'd sensed anywhere in the nowheres during his own trip out to the Badlands only a little over two months ago.

"There do seem to be a lot of people with the same idea we had," Gabriel finally said.

"They're getting sick of the bad ways, just like you, I imagine. More citizens than ever are running the streets these days, stimulated out of their minds. I saw it coming, and that's why I skedaddled."

"How long have *you* been here?"

"Pretty, pretty long." The little guy gestured them to come closer, probably so he could see better.

Maybe this was a good thing, because the old man would realize he'd been mistaken in recognizing them. He'd find out that Mariah and Gabriel were strangers, just as everyone was to each other in the world these days.

Mariah went to the little guy first. She didn't have much to fear when it came to the campfire where the man was waiting—not like Gabriel.

In the background, a horrific screech-howl went up from the shade fight, then a raucous cheer.

"Ah, another one bites the dust," the little man said as he leaned heavily on his cane with one hand and reached for Mariah's fingers with the other, as if to shake her hand in an official greeting during which he'd introduce himself.

But it didn't quite turn out that way as the man touched her fingers and closed his eyes. Immediately, he jerked back from her, then let go of her hand. But, as if sorely determined, he grabbed her fingers again.

This time it was Mariah who quickly let go.

Gabriel felt confusion swirling in her, and he couldn't push it out of himself, either, because the little man was smiling, as if he had indeed come across a long-lost pal.

Who *was* this guy, and what'd happened when he'd touched Mariah?

"You've had lots of blood in your life, haven't you?" the man asked her.

Time to go. "We've all seen blood. Michelle, let's turn in."

"No, don't." The little guy held his hand out to Gabriel now, those cloudy eyes making him look like a half-blind sage.

"Michelle?" Gabriel said again.

But Mariah hadn't moved.

The little man said, "Michelle isn't your name. I don't know much more than that, because you do a good job of blocking, so all I understood about you for now was the blood and how it covered you and the people you loved. You're looking for . . . something. Can't quite put my finger on it, though. It'll probably take a minute. . . ."

Crap. Now Gabriel knew exactly what was going on.

They'd run into a rogue psychic.

The government had driven them out, probably fearing that psychics could feel and see things that they didn't want made public.

As if noticing that Gabriel had hit the mental jackpot, the little old man smiled. "I knew you two would be introducing yourselves before I died, and let me tell you, time was getting short. I was starting to think I was wrong and my clairvoyance was on the outs, right along with a lot of other parts of the old body."

"Your clairvoyance must be mistaken."

The little man started talking in earnest. "I can help you . . . for a small price, of course. I'll put you on your path."

"I—"

But the man beat Gabriel to the punch. "If you can't trust someone who's been in this camp ever since the government ran him out of house and home, who you gonna call?"

Mariah looked into Gabriel's eyes. *What should we do?*

No answers there. As for trusting this so-called psychic, he'd only made a fairly vague guess about Mariah's past and their present—after all, who hadn't suffered in this life? Who wasn't searching for something more? The guy hadn't even guessed that Gabriel was a vampire and Mariah was a were-wolf.

Maybe he was a good con man and they could still leave unscathed.

"Come on," the little man said. "Help a fella out. Since my beans were stolen, I could use something substantial to eat. Haven't had much but root juice for the past couple of days, and with all these people coming from the east, the salvaging has been a tough haul lately."

Mariah seemed pained by his confession, and the little man hitched onto her sympathy.

"You really think a put-aside psychic and an old man to boot is gonna have any bad-guy connections? Please."

And that was true enough—people like this man and the oldster were usually sent to pounds in the hubs, where they were considered to be next to useless.

"If you're really a psychic," Gabriel asked, "why don't you know where your beans are?"

"If I had the ability to control the information I received, I'd be water rich." The little man coughed, and it seemed to rack his whole body before he dove right back into talking. "But I *can* use touch"—he motioned toward Mariah's hand—"and focus my thoughts on getting a reading. I'm an excellent conduit for prophecies every once in a while, too, just like when I saw that you'd be coming here. I saw the change of the world right before the mosquito epidemic hit. No one listened to me, but back in my younger years, my talents put some real major evils to justice. . . ."

A wistful smile tugged at his mouth. Then he coughed again.

Gabriel and Mariah locked gazes once more, and he

communicated with her, mind-to-mind, careful not to be obvious about it.

Maybe he's already got our number, he thought.

Should we just talk to him then?

He could feel the rise of desperation in the rush of Mariah's blood, and it mocked his own need.

So he made a decision. *No guts, no cure.*

She smiled, as if she'd been praying he'd think this, and the psychic seemed to feel their commitment, holding back the flap of his tepee and inviting them inside while Gabriel took the long way around the campfire.

He stepped into the tent, tugging down his face mask, and he *really* smelled the opium. But it wasn't in smoke form. The drug wouldn't have any effect on him as a vampire. However, the more humanly inclined Mariah might be susceptible to it if the old man slipped it into a drink or food.

Gabriel turned that over in his mind for a second. Would opium mellow her out? Could it even be a type of cure?

But that was doubtful, because even the feyweed back in the Badlands hadn't done anything to help. Why would opium?

The tepee's flap stayed partway open, lending a smoky angle of light to the area, almost like colorless neon, lazy and foreboding. The psychic brushed by Gabriel, and he could've sworn that the little old man made contact with his coat for a second too long.

I can use touch, the psychic had told them. . . .

Laughing to himself, the man plopped down near what looked to be an entrance to a small bed dug under the ground. He gestured for his guests to hunker down, too.

"I can't read you," he said to Gabriel.

Gabriel minded his breathing, which he needed to keep steady if he was to portray a convincing human. He rested his gaze on an open canteen next to the old man's blankets. It became obvious where the opium smell had originated from. The raw scent of it was mixed with stemorick root juice.

Maybe the little old man took the drug because of the physical pain of aging.

As he motioned for Mariah to extend her hand to him again, then grasped her fingers, Gabriel corrected his assumption about the drugs. Maybe they were a way for the psychic to shut off his own abilities when he didn't want them.

They all seemed to have a way of doing that somehow.

This time, the little man didn't let go of her. "Ah."

Mariah leaned forward. "What?"

"My beans." The old man chuckled. "I just put two and two together to come up with the fact that an ex–small business owner filched 'em. He's got a kid, though, so I just might let the issue drop because you and Mariah, here, can hunt for me instead. I see quite a bit of sand-rabbit in my future."

Gabriel frowned at him. The psychic had gotten Mariah's name. What else had he intuited?

The man laughed again, reminding Gabriel of the oldster's cackling wheeze. But, unlike the oldster's laugh, this ended on a serious sigh.

"I'm telling you two now," he said in that tinny old voice, "you better be careful about what you're looking for."

"Why?" Mariah asked.

"Because you'll find a change for you, all right . . . and everything that comes with it, too."

Mariah's heartbeat joyfully blipped inside Gabriel, and pounding blood rushed every part of his body. The scent of her wove through him, heady as a summer's day back when there used to be a real summer. Happiness was bringing out the best in her, and it sent his hunger to rising before he quelled it.

The psychic said, "You want to go ahead and tell me why you'd need a cure? You look robust enough."

If only the man knew. "It's more of an emotional thing. Did you get any feel for where we should be headed?"

"If I told you 'east,' that'd be a real 'no shit, Sherlock' moment, wouldn't it?"

"It probably would."

At this turn of events, Mariah's desperation lanced through her happiness and traveled on to Gabriel. She was impatient, and she offered her hand to the psychic again.

"Can't you read any more than that?"

Gabriel wanted to snatch her back. What if she offered too much?

But the little guy didn't take her hand. He merely stared at her with those semiwhite eyes. "A long time ago, I would've had a gun to your head by now, Mariah. There would've been silver bullets in it, too."

The meaning of that dawned on Gabriel. *Shit.*

By some miracle, Mariah hadn't gone and lost control yet, though her breathing was coming faster. "You know about . . . me?"

She hadn't given Gabriel away, and, through the imprint, he warmed at that. She didn't want to put him in danger.

"I'm not stupid," the psychic said. "The world has altered, and somehow, some way, it was us humans who became the bad guys. Your kind could've taken over at any time, but you didn't. Now it's too late, for both werewolves . . . and vampires."

The little man glanced at Gabriel, emphasizing that he knew his monsters.

"Don't freak out," he added in that faded old voice, lowering his volume. "I'm not gonna hurt you or turn you in. I've known a few good vamps and even were-creatures in my time. That was before the Shredders came along and didn't differentiate between good and bad. . . ." He shook his head, then shrugged, as if the past was the past and there was no getting around that. "Besides, as I said, I saw you two coming, and I've been prepared. It's been a long, long time since I met one of your sort. Heck, I even forgot that I can't read vampires until I tried with Gabriel." So he'd gotten Gabriel's name from Mariah's touch, too. "And in all that waiting time, a million questions came to me."

"Like . . . what?" Gabriel asked.

"Well, it'd be sweet to know what happens when weres and vampires travel together."

"It's a long story," Gabriel said. "Maybe you can read it off Mariah's skin while I quietly hunt for those sand-rabbits."

The man seemed satisfied by that. "I'm not sure anyone really knows the dynamics between your two kinds, but *you* seem to tolerate each other."

"Has it always been that way?" Gabriel asked. He'd often wondered why he and the were-community hadn't hated each other on sight. It would've been real helpful in identifying their monster status.

"Heck if I know how it used to be," the psychic said. "I ran into way more vampires than were-creatures in my travels. But I'll tell you this—I've heard rumors about places in some hubs where you could find history."

Gabriel was curious about what this man had been, once upon a time, but he wasn't about to cut the psychic off when it sounded as if he might have a lead.

"Places?" Mariah asked, because the word had seemed ominous.

"Asylums." The little man pointed outside. "They started popping up quietly, almost like they were evolving ghost stories. The official word is that asylums are facilities for the humans who came down with lycanthropy and other mental afflictions caused by world change."

After things had gotten intense in the world, people had contracted more head maladies than ever, and lycanthropy was one of them. Supposedly, it was based on a depression that resulted in psychosis. Supposedly.

"You heard me right," the psychic added, "asylums are out there. Maybe there'd be a cure in one of them." He grabbed his canteen, as if thinking about taking a hit of the opium-laced juice. He toasted them with it. "I used to get real bad reception whenever I was on meds. Now I just take a sip or two of my jungle juice every so often, to make the creaks shut up. Know what I mean?"

Then, just like that, he smiled a devilish smile, as if he'd been waiting to sling another curveball their way.

He set the canteen back down, obviously changing his mind about taking a drink. "Here's where I prove just how awesome I really am."

"Really," Gabriel said.

"Yup. There was a name that kept floating into my mind along with the knowledge you guys would come around here someday. She can help you. I can feel it." He put some drama into his presentation of the name. "Taraline."

"What?" Mariah asked.

"Is she a fellow monster," Gabriel asked, "or another psychic?"

"Neither one." His words all but spilled out, maybe because he'd been waiting for them to come around so long and he was eager to show off. "I've intuited a few superficial things about her, like how she used to live in GBVille, which isn't too far away. And she caught a skin disease before she had to leave the hub."

Gabriel lowered his head. Diseased people weren't technically monsters, but most humans treated them like it. He'd even done his share of avoiding them after the mosquito epidemic had left so many scarred. They'd ended up leaving the hubs to find new homes, knowing they weren't wanted.

The psychic said, "The only other piece of information I know is that she's in a necropolis now, and I suspect it's the nearest one. That's probably how I've gotten vibrations from her. I'll be headed there, too, when the time is right. No decent human would leave themselves to die in a camp where their beans can be snatched up like so much trick-or-treat."

Mariah asked, "Where is she in the necropolis?"

"Anyone there who's still left moving should be able to tell you. I know she speaks Old American, too, so you should be able to chatter with her just fine."

A necropolis. Wonderful. "She'd have information about what's in each asylum?"

"I don't know," the psychic said. "But I'm intuiting the name and details for a reason. And if you doubt me, don't waste your time. As I said, I'm king of prophecy. Years ago, my skills helped take down the motherfucker of all vampires. You, Gabriel and Mariah, are small potatoes next to that."

Gabriel took a big chance then, looking into the psychic's mind. And he felt a genuineness, no duplicity at all.

But the man cut him off as he realized what Gabriel was doing. He glanced at Mariah, as if to ask her what kind of asshole vampire didn't ask to go into a person's mind.

Then his expression changed to one of sadness. Empathy.

When Gabriel turned to Mariah, he saw that she'd pressed her hands over her face, and Gabriel wasn't sure if he heard her laugh or sob into them. Maybe it was a bit of both.

She seemed so . . . human. A suffering person who was only searching for the peace no one could give her.

Gabriel laid his hand on her shoulder, and she glanced at him, her gaze profoundly optimistic. When she smiled, it was tremulous but halfway to joyful.

We're on our way, she said via her mind. *A cure really might happen.*

Gabriel didn't want to tell her that they still had next to nothing. Instead, he kept his hand on her shoulder, their imprint allowing him to take on the pain that she'd conquered for the moment.

He just wondered when it'd catch up to bite them again, just as it always did.

7

Stamp

Out in the Bloodlands, Stamp saw the Monitor 'bot before it
saw him.

He and Mags had camped in a nearby cave, then posted
themselves on a rise about a mile from where they thought the
scrubs were living now. They'd compared the stored satellite
footage from Stamp's computer against some geographical
software he carried in him, isolating this particular spot.

Then the 'bot had shown up, confirming their suspicions.

Adjusting his electronic field glasses to filter out the muddled dusk, Stamp zeroed in on the Monitor, which kept changing its hues, so it blended with its surroundings. It looked like
a miniature old stealth airplane, and it hovered near the base
of a bunch of low, strung-together hills, using a laser to sweep
over the rock face of one rise in particular. It was a careful
model, and it was making sure it had a solid target so it wouldn't
waste ammunition.

Next to him, he heard the high-pitched whine of Mags's
field glasses adjusting, too.

"You were right about the 'bot being here," Stamp whispered. Because Monitors had obviously been returned to wide

use only recently, after Stamp had retired from Shredding and left the hubs, he wasn't very familiar with them. But he kept his voice low, anyway, just in case the Monitor had high auditory capabilities.

Mags lowered her glasses. Her slanted eyes were dark in the night. "So what's the plan now?"

"I'd like to blow that hunk of junk to kingdom lost and take care of the scrubs mano a mano." Stamp could almost see himself standing in front of the outlaw community, reveling in their horrified surprise as they slowly recognized him in his Shredder uniform, with its bandolier, gauntlets, and armored bulk. With his chest puncher lashed to his back and lurking over his shoulders like a modified turbo crossbow. They wouldn't ever know he was coming, because he knew how to move with the darkness. Knew how to mask his scent with the government formula he usually kept stored in a compartment on his suit belt—a ritual he'd made Mags undergo, too.

Who the hell needed other Shredders?

Her lips drew into a straight line. Disapproval.

"Hey." Stamp put down his field glasses. "I'm not daft enough to assassinate a piece of government equipment. Maybe we can use the 'bot for our own purposes, though. Let it do the work for us."

"That'll go over really well when it sends footage of you back to a surveillance center. Do you remember what Goodie Jern said about staying away from the scrubs, John?"

Her comment made him dig his fingers into the thigh of his techno-improved leg, where his Shredder suit was leathered and nearly impenetrable over a layer of body armor.

He wanted those scrubs. Walking away and letting a machine corner them seemed dead wrong because *he'd* been the one who'd suffered, not the 'bot.

Mags's expression had altered again. If Stamp didn't know any better, he'd say that she cared about what happened to him.

But that was all it was, he told himself. Concern. And he wasn't used to it, what with growing up on his own. After retirement, he'd wandered the hubs, furthering his education through observation of humanity. Thinking he could help the state of things, he'd brought employees out to the Bloodlands to give them new opportunities, but he'd been their boss, not their friend. Having a single partner was foreign to him, and he wasn't sure he liked it.

She'd raised the field glasses up to her eyes. "Would you look at that. . . ."

When Stamp glanced in the 'bot's direction, he didn't need surveillance equipment to see that it was using lasers to slice open a hole in the hill, where it obviously intended to enter.

Adrenaline pushed Stamp to a stand, and he accessed his own glasses again. He wasn't sure just what he aimed to do—stop the Monitor?—but in the next half second, it didn't matter, anyway.

Something else had noticed the 'bot, too.

Whatever the creature was, it rose behind the Monitor, as if coming from the shadows of the hills . . . a sausage-thick body that stood on two legs, its skin a clutter of beaded pale desert colors. Claws extended. A snout with a black tongue flickering.

But its face . . .

As Stamp's glasses zoomed in, he saw that the damned thing had the exaggerated face and eyes of a man, except with the scales of a Gila monster and a glowing preter gaze. . . .

Before the 'bot could whip around to lock in on the creature, the lizard ripped the machine in half, then tore into the Monitor's casing, reaching inside its body with a claw to gut it. Wires sparked as what remained of the 'bot reared back, attacking bottom-first with spinning blades.

But the Gila creature had already darted back into the shadows, and the Monitor crashed to the ground, bellowing smoke and vomiting more sparks before it sputtered, then died altogether.

It'd happened so fast that it took Stamp's brain a few beats to catch up.

A Gila . . .

Then he thought of those visz screens the Bloodlanders used. Of course. The scrubs had seen the 'bot and sent their Gila-man out through a secret exit to confront the threat.

Stamp ducked back behind the rock, shoving his field glasses into a belt compartment, next to a gun that could peek around corners and offer him a view to a kill.

"Seems as if the presence of my enemy has been confirmed," he said, smiling.

"They'll be watching for whatever they think the Monitor brought with it."

"They'd never see *me* coming, Mags. I'll sneak up on them and—"

Almost violently, she grabbed him by the hair at his nape and brought his face close to hers.

"Do you *hear* yourself?"

Stamp was a trained assassin; his heartbeat didn't quicken. Not until he focused on Montemagni's eyes.

The caring.

He gripped her wrist and forced her hand away. Her chest was rising and falling as she held up her hand in a *Well, screw you then* gesture.

"What's with you, Mags?" he asked. "Good God-all."

She began to go over her weapons, checking a revolver for silver ammunition, avoiding his gaze. "You're going to get yourself killed, that's what's up. And where would I be then? Back in the hubs trying to score riches off white collars again? That isn't my idea of fun anymore."

"I won't get killed."

"Did you ever stop to think that you're not in the same shape you were before the scrubs ambushed you?"

He flexed his leg; faintly he could hear gears moving. "I'm as together as ever, so stop henpecking."

"You're out of practice. You were even off the job for a while when you called out Gabriel, and he beat you."

Slowly, Stamp turned to her. "I had him, Mags. Then the rest of his friends sucker-attacked *us*."

The ambush was the first time he'd ever been bested. It'd be the last time, too.

She gritted her jaw, refusing to back down, so he blew her off, doing his own weapons check, making sure his guns were loaded, his knives in place. He wasn't going to think about Mags getting angry at him for what he'd come out here to do. He wasn't going to think about Mags, period. The last thing he needed was a big sister or a . . .

Or a what?

She recommenced her field survey, sweeping her glasses over the terrain, but in a pissy way that hinted she thought he was being too rash. Then she sighed.

He ignored that. "You just stay by the van and have it ready to speed off, should I need it."

But he wouldn't need it. He was going into the scrub compound alone, even though he'd been training Mags in Shredder techniques. Still, he was just as good as he'd been before he'd hung up his suit and come out of retirement. He hadn't been a success as a peaceful farmer out here in the Bloodlands, yet he'd always been and always would be a hell of an enforcer.

In spite of his confidence, a thought niggled at him. If he wasn't a Shredder, he wasn't sure just what he could be in this new world. That was why failing with the scrubs wasn't an option.

Mags was having none of his bravado. "By my count, there're five weres, one Intel Dog, and one vampire in there, cowboy. Those odds aren't in your favor."

Stamp laughed. He didn't mean to sound cocky, but . . . why not? He'd never told Mags every minute detail about his past— like how he'd taken on a nest of ten vampires years ago and dispatched them all within five minutes. As Goodie Jern had said, he'd been a teenager, but he'd been climbing the ladder of success faster than most established Shredders. He was that good.

"Mags," he said. "Just get to the van, would you?"

As she left for their camouflaged vehicle, she muttered something about pride going before a fall, and he wanted to tell her that pride wasn't what was at stake. It was something bigger than him or her.

Stamp watched her climb over a rock, her body lithe under the bodysuit she was wearing. He frowned, not really knowing why.

Then he cleared his mind, slowed his heartbeat by taking deep breaths, and slid around the first rock until he reached the next one.

And he continued rock after rock, on his way to give those scrubs what they were due.

8

The Oldster

In the main cavern, most of the Badlanders were on the edge of their cask seats, watching the visz screens, but Pucci, who'd hastily put on some clothes, was pacing, the stalactites hanging over his head like knives ready to thrust.

The oldster wanted to punch him.

But as Pucci passed by, the oldster stuck out his leg instead, sending the other man to stumbling before he righted himself and delivered to the oldster a death look.

"Sit down, Pucci. Sammy only did what needed to be done, and you ain't doing us any good by working the floor like a crone who's got bowel problems."

Pucci looked at Hana, probably to see if she would take his side, but she was watching her own visz, where the trespassing robot still lay on the ground, its shell nearly blending into the dirt but for the wires sprawling out of it. Next to her, she had a double-barreled shotgun. All of them had something or another nearby, in case they needed weapons.

But they were also ready to change into their lethal forms. All they needed was a sign from outside.

Hana's failure to defend Pucci seemed to make the man

even whinier. "We're screwed. Mariah probably did something lame-brained out there to tip off other creatures as to where we live. Sammy did us even worse."

Over near a visz that showed a wide view of the east, Sammy stuck up his middle finger. Next to him, Chaplin cast a long-suffering gaze at Pucci; the dog was still tired from escorting Gabriel and Mariah as far as was prudent. He'd been in a bad mood ever since, but now that the robot had shown up, he was even closer to snapping.

No one knew if the machine had gotten to Mariah and Gabriel first, so that put them *all* on further pins and needles.

"Oh, real eloquent, Sammy," Pucci said about the middle finger. "I'd rather hear you explain why you thought it necessary to turn into your Gila form and jump that robot rather than just come in here and hide."

"In case you're deaf, dumb, and blind, that government surveillance 'bot was coming for us."

"You don't know for certain that's what it was doing or if that's what it really was."

"No, you're right, Pucci. It was probably someone's pet droid that nosed its way out of the yard and was sniffing round the neighborhood." Sammy usually kept his tongue in check, but not now. "Before I came out here to the Badlands, the grapevine round my professional tech circles would talk about Monitor 'bots like these. I never thought I'd see the day when they were put into circulation, but I was pretty sure I'd know how to shut one down tonight before it registered anything on its receptors. It was either that or risk having the thing enter our shelter, and that's just what it was doing when I caught it using those lasers on the rock."

Pucci rolled his eyes. "Government issue or not, that Monitor's got you off your rocker if you think it didn't get you in its sights."

"I don't know what it did, hoss, so back off, shut your everbitchy mouth, and watch the viszes for signs of anything that might've accompanied the machine."

Having no response to that, Pucci merely ground his teeth. Hana still ignored him, although the oldster wasn't sure how she managed.

Meanwhile, the oldster kept track of his own visz screen,

which featured a view of the west, where nothing was stirring yet. But he knew the community's time here was over. They'd have to get a move on soon, just to be certain they weren't discovered.

A twinge of weariness made the oldster sink on his cask seat. The good times out here in the Badlands had clearly passed. Back in the day, he and the other were-creatures had enjoyed free run in this area, all of them tired of the hubs and seeking a new home. He'd invited those he cared to invite into his community after he'd lived well enough among the humans in the hubs, his were-ness undiscovered. Then he'd been age-phased out of his graphic designer career. Jobless and older than dirt, he'd wondered what to do with himself. Round that time, he'd become all too aware of the pounds where they sent old human people, and damned if he was going to allow anyone to phase him out for eternity when he still had a lot of living to do, were-creature or not.

But that was then, this was now, and he was sick of feeling hunted, whether it was for being a were or for being an oldster. He was sick of losing people like Zel.

Sick to death.

"We need to evacuate," he said, "maybe even before the sun comes up."

Sammy seemed to notice the oldster's dispiritedness. "And go where? Goddamn it, first we had a Shredder on our heels. Now a government 'bot. Where's it going to end?"

Chaplin let out a series of barks and grunts, but none of them understood his talk. If only Zel were around to trans-late . . .

His chest felt speared by loneliness and loss. "They're gonna come with bigger weapons, Sammy. Last time with Stamp, Gabriel told us to stand up and fight, and we happened to survive the ordeal. But this time it's not just a Shredder and his buddies we're facing."

Sammy didn't say anything. He just kept watching his visz.

Pucci spoke. "I think we should scoot right now."

The oldster was in no mood for Pucci's opinions. The fact that they were the same as his own made the oldster feel just as weak-minded as the big man.

He distanced himself as much as he could from Pucci by

saying, "If you've got an ideal location in mind, by all means, inform us. But Mariah scouted out this area before we settled here, and she said there's not another viable living place within miles." Gabriel had taken a few outside night trips to seek a backup homestead even farther away, but there hadn't been enough time to find a decent one.

Pucci was working his mouth as if he meant to spit at the oldster. It would've been the ultimate insult. But when the big man refrained, the oldster wasn't surprised. Pucci was all talk.

Luckily, he became *no* talk as Hana rose from her station.

"I will pack water, then scant clothing for all of us. We will need an extra set for travel in case a were-change overtakes us and shreds our wardrobe. Without a human appearance, we haven't a prayer of passing ourselves off as people if a second robot should find us out there and have the capability to question us."

A sense of inevitability fell over them as Hana and Pucci left.

Chaplin took Hana's place at her visz while the oldster and Sammy kept vigil, too. But as the minutes ticked by, the oldster told himself that maybe Sammy *had* gotten to the robot before it'd identified their presence, because there didn't seem to be any backup mechanisms outside querying into the robot's fate. Maybe a government analyst had chalked up the machine's malfunction as just that—a natural disaster that didn't require looking into.

But the oldster knew the government better than that. They'd be sending something or someone to check on their spy—a robot that'd probably been dispatched because of Stamp, though Mariah's careless, open-field running could've been a cause, too.

The oldster heard a rustle back in the main tunnel, where the sound carried so clearly. But he didn't pay much mind, figuring Hana and Pucci were making quick work of the packing.

Sammy was getting restless at his own visz.

"You want to pack up a few of your tech doodads?" the oldster asked.

"I wouldn't turn down the opportunity." Sammy gestured toward his screen. "Watch my screen?"

"Hurry up."

As Sammy left, the oldster positioned himself so that he could glance back and forth between the viszes. Chaplin helped him out by watching two at a time also.

Seconds later, the dog sniffed the air, losing focus for an instant. Then he shook his head, going back to the visz screens.

The oldster wished he could ask what that had been about, but what could the dog tell him?

So he kept surveying the screens, scratching at his whiskers, the flinty sound of hair against skin seeming to fill the cavern.

Then he felt it.

A prickle on the back of his neck.

Heartbeat flicking at him, he turned round on his cask, glimpsing the tunnel entrance.

Nothing.

The oldster laughed at himself. Was he afraid that Pucci had come to sneak up on him and whine him to death?

When he turned back toward the viszes, Chaplin was on his feet, stiff-bodied, staring at the tunnel.

Now the oldster wasn't laughing. "What's going on?"

The dog slunk forward an inch, his silence indicating that the oldster should be quiet, too. Slowly, the oldster reached for his shotgun, his pulse banging, powered by adrenaline. His temperature rose, needling his skin on its way to heating.

Chaplin sniffed the cool air again, then seemed confused.

Was it a smell he didn't recognize?

Or maybe there wasn't a scent at all, and that was what was making the dog frown. Maybe he was hearing something but not smelling it.

The oldster moved toward the tunnel, his shotgun raised, his skin beginning to waver as the change threatened. He didn't attempt to control himself—a change might be just what he'd need if something had gotten inside without them knowing. . . .

Bristling, he wanted to call out to his friends, just to see if someone was there, but he didn't.

Chaplin went before him into the tunnel, where the solar lanterns burned in what seemed to be a flickering menace. Other tunnels, which branched off to various nooks, felt like eyes that followed the oldster. There were a few unlit tunnels up ahead, too, leading to areas they didn't use.

Those felt even more dangerous.

He heard Chaplin trying not to breathe, so he attempted to do the same thing, inhaling and exhaling with his lips pursed, hoping he didn't sound as loud as he suspected.

Something smacked the rock wall to his left, and he swung the shotgun round, ready to fire.

Chaplin barked, and it was almost like a dog scream.

Then everything slowed to a baleful crawl: Chaplin, springing forward into the nearest darkened tunnel, his teeth bared as his muscles moved under his sleek brown fur; the oldster's were-change making his skin into an exoskeleton as his muscles and bone shaped a tail and pincers out of his body; his clothes ripping, his shotgun dropping to the ground, the fine hairs on him feeling the vibrations of a predator . . .

All the while, in the bluish tinge of oncoming were-creature vision, something emerged from the shadows of the tunnel where Chaplin was flying.

A robot?

No. As it unfolded from the darkness, it became a human—one who had masked his scent. One who was wearing a dark leather armor suit with gauntlets and FlyShoes strapped to his boots, making him a few feet taller than a regular normal. One with bullets slung across his chest and guns at his sides.

Shredder.

Stamp?

The oldster's were-perception had almost fully distanced itself from his human mind, and he felt himself raise his scorpion pincers, then ready his tail to strike venom at the enemy's neck. At the same time, Chaplin finally reached the Shredder, aiming his teeth at Stamp's dimmed face.

But with a dodge that was worthy of a preter, the human Shredder avoided the dog's bite, sending up an arm to slam Chaplin behind him into the darkness. The dog yelped as Stamp whipped round, raising his revolver to target the canine.

He also had a gun in his other hand.

Dual explosions signaled a bullet blasting toward the oldster, too, and agonizing pain tore into where his shoulder would normally be. Right away, silver anguish rayed out from the wound.

He didn't hear the outcome of Chaplin's bullet, because he'd already hit the ground, his body bending and pulling back into human form because of the silver poisoning in him. Human reality zipped back, bringing quick darkness and flashes of gunpowder as the Shredder fired into the tunnel again.

The oldster didn't hear Chaplin react this time, either, but maybe that was because he was too busy cupping a hand over his injury as blood seeped out. Pain. God-all, he'd never felt such screeching pain as the poison kept spreading from the entry point outward.

How long until the Shredder put a silver bullet in his heart?

He dug into the ground with his fingers, trying to crawl away.

Then . . .

Was there a hissing sound coming from where the Shredder had last been standing?

The oldster looked behind him to find Stamp gone and Sammy in his place, massive in his full Gila monster wereform, his eyes humanlike except for the preter shine in his scaly lizard face. He had long claws and a flickering tongue, and stood on two feet, hunched.

"Sammy," the oldster tried to say, but he could hardly voice anything. "Shredder . . ."

His voice turned to a gasp as Stamp eased out of the shadows again and slid behind Sammy. The only sound the oldster heard was a very faint buzzing, like gears turning.

By the time Sammy heard it, too, the Shredder already had his revolver aimed at Sammy's back.

Bang!

The explosion seemed to last forever as blood splattered over the oldster, coming down on him like a rain shower.

Somewhere in the oldster's mind, he thought, *If I hadn't been talking, Sammy would've heard the Shredder. He was too focused on me. . . .*

He opened his eyes through the blood, seeing Gila-Sammy with a red bloom against his scales, right where his heart was located. As the half–Gila monster fell to his knees, his body contorted, skin waving while the change consumed him, sucking the scales back into his skin, twisting the bones back to where they belonged, shortening them, bringing him back to plain old Sammy.

With a bewildered frown, he slumped the rest of the way to the floor, his cheek smacking the ground, his eyes and mouth shock-open as blood ran red.

Stamp kept his revolver targeted on Sammy, but he leveled his cold, dark gaze on the oldster. Then he smiled, giving his gun a little, cocky twirl as he adjusted his aim toward his new target.

The oldster didn't close his eyes. He stared right back at Stamp.

Kill me, you bastard. Go ahead.

But before the Shredder could fire a silver bullet into his heart, Chaplin flew out of the dark tunnel, knocking Stamp to the other wall, his flailing paws batting the Shredder's weapons away. Sammy's blood seemed to streak over the oldster's eyes, or maybe he just saw the red on Chaplin's fur as the livid dog clawed and bit at the Shredder with frenzied speed.

Intel Dog-Fu, the oldster thought vaguely.

He had no idea what happened from there, because he heard a yell just before someone scooped him up and started running with him.

Someone with hooves.

Pucci?

While the oldster's eyelids grew as heavy as his heart, he only remembered the ground rushing past him as Pucci carried him out of the cavern, galloping over the Badlands dirt.

9

Stamp

By the time Stamp stood and brushed the dust off his suit, the scrubs were gone—the elk-man carrying the scorpion-guy away while a mule-deer woman rescued the Intel Dog.

Gone in a flash.

No matter how good Stamp was, he wasn't as fast as a preter, even if he was wearing FlyShoes that could increase a human's speed if he fired them up. There wasn't cause to fret, though. Stamp knew how to track, and the monsters would be leaving quite a bit for him to go on during their haste to escape. The two rescuers had carryalls with them, but the bags hadn't been bulky enough to contain heat suits, so there was little chance they'd be able to keep running in the daylight. They'd be resting somewhere, and that'd give Stamp ample opportunity to catch up.

His only big disappointment was that he hadn't seen Gabriel or the werewolf he'd witnessed during that showdown over two months ago. . . .

Stamp inspected some tears in the leather of his suit and damned that Intel Dog for getting a jump on him. The glorified pet had played dead when Stamp had blasted bullets at it, and

Stamp hadn't had the time to check the thing's vitals because he'd known that the others would be attracted by the gunfire and would be upon him soon. That was the danger of silver bullets: They weren't quiet, but they pierced a were-creature's hide better than blades.

The canine had obviously dodged the bullets. Facing an Intel Dog was always tough, but this one was rougher and readier since it'd probably learned its tricks from the preters.

Hunt and learn, Stamp thought. He was a little rusty, so he'd take every piece of information and put it to good use for the next encounter.

With his technologically enhanced leg, he used his toe to nudge the naked, humanized body of the man he knew to be Sammy Ramos. A dead were-creature was a good were-creature, no matter how human they looked. Monsters had gotten Stamp's parents killed, no matter how indirect the process, and seeing one here with the life gone out of it went only a fraction of the way toward making Stamp feel better.

One down. Four weres, an Intel Dog, and a vampire to go.

Before he left, he took out a scent-catcher unit from his belt, turned it on, and ran it over the scraps of clothing that had fallen from the old fella when he'd turned into a scorpion-man. Once the smell was locked into memory, Stamp gave the machine a moment to process. Then, keeping his revolver skinned, he jogged on his spring-stepped FlyShoes down the tunnel, hoping Mags had seen a flash of the were-creatures leaving in such a hurry.

But if she hadn't, no big deal. He'd soon find out which direction they'd taken.

He emerged into the outdoors, where sunlight was still hours away. Even so, he knew it was going to be a great day.

Inspecting the upset dirt, he saw the sure trail of hoof tracks, the signs of a group that didn't have much time left until Stamp caught up. And, right next to the disturbed ground, the Monitor 'bot rested, its wire innards busting out of its sleek dirt-hued stealth airplane casing.

Stamp glared down at it. The government had sent a 'bot. Good move. As if a Monitor could ever take the place of a Shredder . . .

A *whoo*-ing sound made him step back, just before a light beam flashed at him.

He raised his firearm, but the 'bot shut back down.

Stamp's heartbeat knocked in his temples. Had the Monitor caught an image of his face? Even now, was there a satellite focused down upon him?

Would the government think he'd destroyed the 'bot?

The roaring of an engine took over Stamp's attention—Mags was here with the van. He put the 'bot out of his mind, thinking that if it'd seen him, then the government could come after him. Or, at least, it could try.

Opening the door so he could talk to Mags, Stamp stayed outside the van, already working off his Shredder gear so he could put on his heat suit. "I didn't see Gabriel, nor that werewolf."

"And the rest?"

"Gila-man? Dead. The remainder of them—the old guy, the dog, and two more—took off. You drive on ahead while I walk, Mags. Their tracks and the scent of the old man are going to lead me right to where they'll need to hide when the sun rises."

"They're going to do everything they can to mask themselves once they come to their senses."

"But I'm not going to be fooled." Never again by these weres.

He stored his weapons in the back of the van, pulling out his heat suit, which would provide for easier travel in the Bloodlands. When he knew where the scrubs were hiding, he could always change back, but he wanted to be prepared for the sun when it came up. He didn't want the unforgiving heat to suck the energy out of him, because he'd need every bit of it when he found the scrubs.

As he peeled off the upper half of his Shredder outfit, he looked up at Mags. She was watching him, but when he caught her, she glanced away.

Oddly embarrassed, Stamp stepped to the side, where the van blocked him, and he continued undressing. When he'd slipped into his heat suit, with its sun-shield hemp material lined by coolant, he stowed his Shredder outfit in the vehicle, then stood by the door, ready to close it.

"You can drive ahead to find us a place for later, about five hours after sunrise. My suit will need to restore itself by then, anyway."

"Understood." She sounded detached, as if she were just as embarrassed at having been caught with the ogling.

Stamp shut the door, and she drove off slowly, the engine purring. The sound remained behind in Stamp, as if something were rumbling in his body that he had no former acquaintance with. It buzzed through him, settling in his belly.

As he walked, he thought about cold blood. Soon, he felt it chilling his veins, a method he'd been taught when he was too young to really understand how much it'd benefit him.

Then he pulled on his heat mask and followed the hoof-prints, a hunter on the loose.

A Shredder through and through.

10

Mariah

Gabriel and I didn't set out to the necropolis until the next sunset. That was because we'd promised to provide the psychic with vittles, so we had to hunt far away from the outpost. After that, we slept in our host's tepee, burrowing under the ground and covering ourselves with sun-shield blankets until dusk came round.

When it did, the camp rustled to life, since everyone burrowed during the days. There were more carrion feeder fights and people wandering aimlessly in and out of their tents. I was already wearing my backpack as the campfire smoke rolled over my view of the moon.

Twenty-one more days until a full one. If I didn't turn my life round before then, I wasn't sure I ever would.

The little old man hobbled out of his tepee with his cane and tall-crowned hat, meeting me at the edge of his fire pit. Gabriel trailed him, keeping his distance from the flames.

The psychic shook my hand one last time. "Maybe I'll be seeing you in that necropolis if you stay there long enough."

Gabriel rested his hand on top of his leather carryall. "Is that a prediction?"

"That's just a fact. I don't have too many more dusks in me. I hope you make the most of yours."

This was his way of saying good-bye, so I bent to him, offering a hug. He patted my back, and when I let him go, he was blushing.

Cute, that blushing.

Gabriel obviously noticed it, too, and he grinned to himself as he shook the psychic's hand. The guy had never told us his name. I even wondered if, like the oldster, he'd abandoned it in the hubs. All oldsters were in the process of fading off, and maybe their names just went first.

As we walked away, the psychic stood near his fire, leaning on his pipe cane, then tipping his hat. A shadow seemed to stretch behind him, even in the night, and, for a second, it looked like death was inching up on him.

I waved back until we rounded the corner of a tent and couldn't see him. My chest felt a little hollow because I wished good things for the psychic, not shadows. But, as I well knew, life didn't always see fit to give us what we desired.

"Do you think he wanted to come with us to the necropolis?" I asked Gabriel.

"I think, when he feels it's time, he'll get there fine on his own. If I were him, I wouldn't want to arrive too soon."

"You ever been to one?"

"No. Just heard about them."

I'd heard, too. Necropolises were part graveyard, part a place where the half-living gathered. Never in my existence did I believe one would be on my itinerary.

We wandered onto the main street, where a glance into the eatery showed a bunch of vacated tables topped by rickety, stacked chairs. Probably no one had any currency to spend on food. This was a hunting and gathering camp for certain, and last night Gabriel and I had found sustenance together again, and damned if we weren't using some teamwork.

I wasn't sure if he realized it as much as I did.

We kept walking—we weren't about to use our preter speed this close to camp—and, about a half mile away from the outpost, the yelling started.

"Shade fight," Gabriel said.

"If you want to go back to try your luck, feel free."

He lifted an eyebrow at me, like he was trying to figure out if we could kid with each other or not. When he barely grinned, I got a glowy halo round my heart. Dorky, I know, but that was what it felt like.

"Not my sport of choice." Then he just as quickly changed expression, leaving me wrinkling my own brow. "You have Sammy's comm on you?"

I'd hooked it on my belt, so I worked it off. It was a palm-sized item, square and black. I rubbed my thumb against the "on" panel and a screen appeared. It was blank. I circled my thumb the opposite way over the panel to turn on the audio function, which Sammy would've tuned to one of his own little simple receptors.

I spoke into the comm. "Hello?"

Static answered, just as blank as the screen.

"No reception," Gabriel said. "We'll just have to try later."

We kept walking, not bothering to take cover as we had before. We were amongst more humans now, and we could be more lenient about being in the open if we moved like they did, without preter speed. At this point, we wouldn't stick out to surveillance like sore thumbs amongst other people who were wandering round.

Soon, the clamor of the outpost melded with the wind and desert silence. After that, the sounds seemed not to exist at all. And, believe you me, the silence got to be overwhelming. It put Gabriel and me back in our places, reminding us that there was nothing for us to talk about. Or maybe too much.

I had to break it. "Gabriel?"

"Yeah."

I felt dumb for sounding as if I'd been checking if he was still there. "I'm curious about what the psychic said about vampires and weres. . . . What's *your* theory about how we're able to coexist?"

"Are you asking me if there was anything concrete about our pasts in that introductory vampire pamphlet I used to have? I barely know about my own capabilities from that little piece of crap. And it's not as if I go to a fang convention every year to share the latest discoveries in Vampireland."

He was in a mood. Maybe he'd remembered that he was supposed to be mad at me.

"Just making conversation," I said.

He made a low sound, like he was chiding himself, then reached into his bag to bring out a scrap of long cloth that he used when a smell was bothering him. He wrapped the hemp over the lower half of his face, and I wondered if he was trying to block *me* out.

"The necropolis," he said, his words muffled. "It's getting stronger."

"Ah." That brightened things a bit. Not that I wanted him to smell foul things, but I was just glad it wasn't me.

And that was where the vampire versus were-creature topic ended. But it didn't keep me from thinking about the history between our kinds and how it'd been lost through the years. It'd be interesting if we could uncover something about it along with a cure in one of those asylums. Maybe I'd even get some peacemaking hints from past lessons.

Would this Taraline lead us to answers?

I walked faster, bypassing Gabriel. He kept pace behind me, our connection like a line that attached the two of us. A leash of sorts. I felt him watching me, and once, I even peeked behind me to find his gaze on my fanny.

He pretended he was considering my backpack instead, but I turned back round with a tiny smile on my face, my chest warmed, the sensation trickling down in a melt that wasn't as violent as usual.

It felt real good until I thought about having to change into were-form, just so we could gain some significant ground that would result in our arriving at the necropolis well before sunrise.

I didn't want to change. I liked walking like this, knowing Gabriel was right here, the sky over us clearer right now. But, like all nice things, this wasn't meant to last, and Gabriel accessed his vampire powers, blasting ahead of me to the nearest brush covering.

Halting, I undressed, shoved my clothes and holsters into my backpack, then kept hold of the bag as I brought the change on myself.

Soon, I caught up to him, even though I barely recalled it in my were-state. I only remember Gabriel grabbing me, pulling me to the ground, and saying, "Rumbler ahead!"

Stamp's men had used rumblers, with their small aircraft bodies and jagged wheels that ate the ground. The word forced me to change back to human form right quick.

By the time the giant vehicle rolled over a hill in the distance, I'd gotten my clothes back on. I rubbed my arms, helping my skin to stop pounding and the hurt to go away. The air felt cooler on my skin, too; it'd kept getting that way as we ventured farther out of the desert. It'd never be as cool as our cavern homestead, though.

The thought stayed with me. Homestead. And then that thought led to Chaplin.

I rubbed my skin harder to chase off the isolation.

The rumbler flashed its blue lights at us, requesting a palaver. The occupants must've caught us on radar at about the same time Gabriel had heard the contraption.

"We're not far off from the necropolis," Gabriel said, tugging down the facecloth. "I'll take charge of the talking, if you don't mind."

He'd done the same with the psychic, so it was fine by me. Gabriel had a strong grasp of Text, and my weakness in the dialect was suspicious, to say the least. I wasn't a businesswoman, didn't work for the government, and wasn't a hub shut-in—every one of them humans who generally still spoke Old American. The only category left for a poorer "person" like me was monster because, after humans had started hunting us in earnest, we'd gone into hiding, avoiding outside trends. Hence, some of us either had never learned Text or just never used it, unless trying to blend in with society. I'd been trying to absorb more of it, though. Gabriel had been teaching the others, and Hana had been tutoring me in return.

I could understand superficial conversations in Text, but anything more than that and I was a goner.

The rumbler tossed dirt at us as it jerked to a halt. As the engine whined down, a single man jumped out. Well, I think it was a man. He wore a veil that covered him from head to waist and long gloves that disappeared under his covering.

The link between me and Gabriel froze with a cautious zap, and I kept my hands hovering near my holstered revolvers. He was wary, too, and I could feel it all through me.

The man slurred out a Text question. "Wh'r u goin?"

"Ncroplis," Gabriel said.

"No. Far enuf." The man had his hand up, as if he could push us back.

Clearly, this guy was some kind of guard, most likely not a preter who'd abandoned the hubs, either. It was just his job to patrol outside the necropolis for some reason—maybe he'd even taken it upon himself. Could be that he wasn't even a patrolman and this was his way of robbing us.

Silly man.

I glanced at Gabriel, but I didn't send any thoughts to him. He'd warned me about using that ability too much round strangers unless we were sure we could get away with it.

Gabriel, who was so adroit at putting on a nice-guy act, hooked his thumbs into his belt loops. When I'd first met him, he'd done pretty well with the *Howdy, pardner* routine, but I'd caught on fairly quick that he was a vampire. Maybe this robber/patrolman/whatever wouldn't notice.

Gabriel explained in Text that we weren't here to cause any trouble, that we just wanted to pay a visit to a resident of the necropolis.

"Who?" the man asked.

"Taraline. Kno her?"

The veiled man seemed to think about it, putting his hands on his hips.

As his veil stirred, I saw the bulge at his side just before he reached for it.

He skinned an old semiautomatic at the same time I drew my revolver, but Gabriel was faster, zooming toward the man and batting the weapon away from him before my finger could even squeeze the trigger.

The man's shot banged into the air, echoing, but Gabriel already had the guy's arm twisted behind his back.

Then he yanked the veil off.

As it freefell to the dirt, I gaped at the scars decorating his face. It looked as if a child had spilled blue and red and white paint on his skin, then dragged a stick through the colors so they swirled in raised layers. One eye was at least an inch below the other, his lips swollen to the point where they seemed as if they might burst open.

The living dead. I wasn't sure if he'd survived the mosquito epidemic or something worse.

"Wht r u?" he asked Gabriel.

Gabriel tightened his grip on the man. "Wht'r *u*?"

The guy whimpered before mumbling, "Srry. Lt me go, k? Wont bthr u agn . . ."

"R u gard?" Gabriel asked.

"No."

"A rbbr?"

"Yah," the man said, truly seeming apologetic.

I suppose I'd be, too, if I had my arm wrenched behind my back by an undercover vampire.

And Gabriel didn't let go as he asked, "U kno Taraline?"

"Yah."

And then the man spewed out some directions that I couldn't even keep up with. Something about rights and lefts and lanes and structures. I trusted that Gabriel had it all down.

Gabriel then whispered something in the man's ear, and I knew it wasn't lighthearted chatter. The terror on the guy's face told me so.

His expression went blank, and I figured that Gabriel had swayed him into forgetting what'd just happened. Why not, while we were out here where no one else could catch him doing it?

Gabriel looked into the man's eyes, as if seeing whether he'd done the job correctly. His maker hadn't taught him jack shit, so he was a self-taught vampire. Besides that, he was a young preter, and he was never sure of just how powerful he was.

Then, obviously content, he pushed the man away. "Go."

The man pointed to his firearm, which was on the ground nearby. Gabriel merely glowered. I don't have to describe a vampire glower again.

As the guy scrambled to his rumbler, Gabriel picked up the semiautomatic, inspecting it. The weapon was old-school, just like all the ones I'd collected and maintained. He kept it, even pointing it at the man as he started up the rumbler and put the pedal to the metal.

The vehicle spurted away, leaving nothing but flying ground. Gabriel cocked his head at the semiautomatic, then shrugged, putting it into his carryall. As he adjusted the cloth over his lower face again, he kept looking down, so I couldn't see his expression. Our link was pretty much nil, too, as if he'd blocked me out.

I was impressed that he hadn't turned super vampy. And kind of impressed that I hadn't changed, either. Then again, the robber man hadn't scared me, maybe because there'd just been one of him and I didn't have much to protect right now— no home to hide, no dog to defend. He'd just been a bad guy that I could've taken all on my own, and there probably wouldn't have been many consequences for killing him. . . .

The thoughts trailed me as I went over to the man's veil, just to look closer at it. Or maybe I just wanted to be nearer to Gabriel.

He kept squinting at the ground, and I swear our link came alive, starting to pulse.

Was it because he was just now allowing himself to get vampire-excited because of the near violence? Or was it because I was standing next to him?

I should've walked away, but I didn't. "Did you use some sway to tell him that, if he gathered up friends to come after us, he'd be nothing but blood and bones afterward?"

"I suggested something similar."

"Judging from how he looked like his buns were on fire, I think whatever you did say was effective."

He didn't laugh at that, so I shut right up, not wanting to assume we were chums now. But then he looked at me, and I saw his gaze burning.

Our link throbbed, getting louder, warmer.

This wasn't about being chums. I was getting to him, and that raised my passions, too.

I whispered, "Gabriel . . . ?" I didn't know what else to say. *Did acting as the hero turn you on?*

As if he'd heard me loud and clear, he sped off in a blur, toward the direction in which the rumbler had disappeared over a hill. Dust clouded in his wake.

I followed, fighting my own change, walking far behind him, knowing he'd thank me for it later.

11

Gabriel

Gabriel had halted at the crumbling wrought-iron-and-adobe necropolis gates, where a moan of wind lethargically circled dust around his boots. Under his cloth face mask, his gums had finally stopped throbbing with the needled threat of his fangs. He was almost back to being as human as possible.

What was it about Mariah that pushed him? She was the opposite of Abby, who'd been so polite on the outside that he'd never remotely suspected she was an animal-were underneath it all. Mariah was at the opposite extreme—volatile. A mass of chaos that scrambled him up, making all the orderliness he'd tried so hard to create in himself fall to pieces. She was everything he'd been running from as a monster, but she always managed to slip into him as if she belonged there.

He heard her long before she caught up, and he inspected the gates as if this were his original intent. He surveyed the stars embedded in the dark iron as well as the deadened bell that hung overhead; it was missing its clapper so it didn't ring out as the wind sent it to creaking on its hinges. Color-bled paper flowers slumped on the ground, stray petals everywhere, as if they'd broken from their fake stems and were on the fly from the necropolis. And he didn't blame them—through his improvised bandanna, he could still smell the odor of disease and death.

Her boot steps halted yards away from him. "You got directions from that guard. Are you ready to follow them?"

Thank-all Mariah wasn't going to torture him with personal talk. "He told me about a place where the live ones gather. Said that Taraline is usually there more than anywhere else."

Then he got a move on, walking past the gates. Mariah was right in back of him. He could feel her on his skin.

Not far ahead, the main avenue branched off into smaller lanes edged by crumbled adobe that offered gaping peeks into the buildings. Graying moonlight invaded them, revealing wooden tables, benches, and broken ceramic pots. Some spaces even looked occupied, with sun-shield blankets wadded into corners.

As Gabriel and Mariah moved through the passages, he witnessed a person standing in the middle of one dwelling, a veil draped over its head so that all you could see were gloves and legs peeking out. He could've sworn that the person watched them pass, even though its head didn't swivel to track them.

If Gabriel had been human, he'd be chilled to the marrow, but all he could sense was Mariah's linked warmth behind him.

They turned down another lane, just as the robber said they should, and Gabriel's senses immediately shifted to the walls. There were skeletons embedded into them—death in motion, with bony fingers reaching out, mouths agape as if in eternal cries. And . . .

Wait. They were actually *moving*.

He stood still, realizing that the wall-bound creatures were only craning their necks, looking him up and down. They weren't attacking.

Instinctively, Gabriel guided Mariah ahead. Like him, she was more curious than afraid, but, even so, she walked with her hands by her firearms, her heartbeat stomping and then echoing inside Gabriel.

As they made their way down that lane, the walls moved even more, the skeletons parting to reveal other forms using the walls as cover; they were veiled people, just like the guard.

They blended in and out of the adobe and bones, snakelike, clearly following Gabriel and Mariah.

He could feel her skin beginning to heat up—the kick-start of her fear. Soon, she'd be boiling, her body altering, and they'd have a lot of explaining to do.

"They won't hurt us," he whispered to her calmly, a mite of sway to his voice. "They're just seeing what we're about."

Though he wasn't sure it was the truth, his voice worked on her, and her pulse leveled off. It also helped when they emerged from the constricting lane into what looked to be a town square.

Yeah, he would've described it just that way, except, instead of a green park with a gazebo and fancy ironwork benches, there were slanted tombstones and small, chipped concrete houses of the dead, with angels and Celtic crosses silhouetted against the choked-moon sky.

One of the houses was bigger than the others—basically a plain domed hut. A dim light emanated from the doorway, and so did a smell that practically made Gabriel do a double take.

Chemicals on dead flesh. And more disease.

Mariah was breathing hard, her pulse gathering speed as the veiled shadows hovered just behind them, back in the lane.

"Is that it?" she asked. "The gathering spot?"

"Seems so."

And they'd have to go inside to see if Taraline was there. Joy.

They wove through the graves, some of them only ragged holes in the ground, and it wasn't because robbers had invaded them, Gabriel thought. The resting places had merely been prepared for occupants ahead of time, waiting for a body to be dumped inside and covered up.

After they passed the holes, they came to the hut. Mariah stepped inside, and Gabriel readied himself to do the same. But would he be blocked from entering?

Normally, he needed to be invited into personal dwellings, but he supposed that this hut belonged to everyone, and he proved that idea correct when he stepped in, unimpeded.

That smell hit him right away, and he saw why: The place was decorated with the preserved remains of humans. Chemically treated limbs, with fingers, hands, and arms sticking out of the walls. Faces framed by adobe with their rotted teeth bared in freakish smiles. They'd been pieced together into semblances of whole bodies and, beneath each one, a fancy silver vial waited, attached to the wall.

Water tributes. These must've been important people who'd been worthy of a sacrifice, and the fact that no one had stolen their water signaled the amount of respect the necropolis residents possessed for these walled-in relics.

Everyone else in the place was staring at Mariah and Gabriel from their seats at the bar and their chairs at tables. A few wore the same veils Gabriel and Mariah had already seen. Others, like the bartender, presented their scars proudly, maybe because they weren't as atrocious as what they'd seen on the robber, who'd probably suffered side effects from black-market mosquito epidemic medicines.

But not everybody here seemed to have the same maladies.

Were any of them monsters? Or, worse yet, were any former Shredders like Stamp who'd retired out of the hubs?

Gabriel kept Mariah close to him while a frail, veiled woman wearing a long black skirt sat at the bar and fingered an earthenware jug with the tip of her glove, taking stock of the new arrivals. Next to her, a man with pustules on his cheeks spoke in a graveled voice.

"Why r u healthies hre?"

Healthies. Gabriel assumed it was a nickname for those who wandered into the necropolis from the outside and didn't quite belong.

He tugged down the cloth from his face, almost grimacing at the smell. "Taraline."

Several people stirred, and the bartender occupied himself by sliding a canteen with a wide, slickened base to a wizened prune of a customer down the bar.

The pustule man barked out a laugh. "Taraline? Fncy nme."

Gabriel toyed with the idea of looking into the pustuled man's eyes. But what if the others in the bar noticed? What would they do to a true monster?

Then the pustule man switched to Old American, as if to mock Taraline's fancy name.

"By gum, when's the last time someone came round asking for Taraline?" He nudged the veiled one next to him. The woman merely sat on the stool, still touching her jug.

Gabriel sensed Mariah glancing at him, and he looked down at her. They didn't have to mind-speak for her to tell him that this man knew something.

Probably the most secure way to get out of here would be for Gabriel to do some mind-looking. He'd gotten much better at it since coming out to the Badlands. Plus, he'd taken care of that robber outside the necropolis well enough with mental vampire tricks.

The temptation was overwhelming, especially when he thought of the cure. If he and Mariah found one, maybe there'd be a day soon when he wouldn't have to act like a vampire. He'd gladly play the monster now just so he wouldn't have to later.

He connected thoughts with Mariah. *So how do we get it out of him?*

She paused, then smiled. *Would a distraction give you enough time for a peek?*

He could feel her yearning for a cure, just as if she were yelling it out loud. It echoed in him, too.

Do what you need to do, he said, moving toward the bar and standing next to the pustule man. It'd be the first time he was putting true faith in her. He only prayed she wouldn't bring the roof down on them.

When he heard the sound of a body slumping to the ground behind him, he had an idea of what her plan was.

He turned back around to see Mariah lying on the floor.

"Dn't wrry," he said to everyone. "Sh'll cum 2 soon."

Some of the veiled people at a nearby table leaned over to get a closer look at Mariah, who was still doing a fine job of being passed out. No one got out of their chairs to help her, though.

The pustule man stared at Gabriel, as if he were thinking Gabriel was as heartless as they came for leaving his woman lying there on the ground.

He locked the man into his sights. *Where's Taraline?*

The man immediately pointed to the veiled person next to him.

As Gabriel disengaged—reading this one had been incredibly easy—he used the sway in his voice to whisper, "You won't recall a second of what just happened. Now go back to your dwelling."

The man blinked, his pupils enlarging back to normal size, just as Mariah "awakened" on the floor, then sat up and glanced around. Without any more drama, she shrugged, as if she had a fit like this every night.

Even the living dead gave her space as she made her way to the bar while the pustule man deserted his position, obeying Gabriel's sway and creating an open space next to Taraline. A rush of something like pride in doing a job well infiltrated Gabriel as he sat on the stool next to the veiled person, reaching into his bag and extracting one of the flasks of aquifer water he'd thought to pack. He'd anticipated that it might come in handy for trade, since he didn't drink the stuff himself. Besides, he could smell the junk they served in that jug of hers, and it looked as if he had some superior product here.

"Wtr?" he asked, offering it to her.

She didn't accept. From under the veil, her voice was deeper than Gabriel could've predicted.

"Wht u wnt?"

The bartender was at the other end of the bar, so Gabriel was free to get to the Old American point with Taraline. That way, Mariah would be able to understand, too.

"We heard you'd be able to communicate some information to us in a nice, expedient manner," he said.

Taraline huffed out a choppy laugh, her veil belling. When it settled back down, he inspected the outline of her face—an elegant forehead, high cheekbones . . . but where there was supposed to be a nose, there was next to nothing.

She picked up Gabriel's water flask, opened it, and put it under her veil to smell it. He heard her sigh, as if she hadn't enjoyed the prospect of quality water for a long time. Then she slid off her stool.

He supposed it was an invitation to follow.

Mariah grinned at Gabriel. Once again, she didn't have to access his mind, because he could already tell that she was thinking, *Can I set up a situation or can I set up a situation?*

He resisted the urge to grin back at her, just as he would've done when he'd first gotten out to the Badlands and hadn't known she was a hard one to trust. Instead, he jerked his head toward the exit, and they stepped out, after Taraline.

She led them past the graves, but not too far beyond as she stopped near a small house of the dead with a broken pair of wings serving as a steeple. She slipped the water flask under her veil, throwing back her head to gulp in the nectar.

Next to Gabriel, Mariah waited, her longing evident in their connection. Her raised temperature pricked at Gabriel's flesh.

When Taraline was done, she gasped. "Pure. We can only collect water here when it rains, and storms come so few and far between that the water tastes old."

He didn't tell her that what she'd just drunk had been pumped from their Badlands aquifer. They didn't need more refugees out there.

"You willing to talk with us?" he asked.

Taraline was clasping the flask for dear life. "Are you from the government? Associated with it?"

"No," both Gabriel and Mariah said at the same time.

"You speak Old American, just like a higher-level would."

Mariah said, "We had proper educations before coming out here. I suspect you did, too, but that's not important."

Gabriel got out a second flask. A further installment on their initial down payment of water. He'd rather use this means of persuasion than voice swaying at first, should someone else happen by here in the open—like those shadows they'd seen in the lane.

He didn't give the water to Taraline just yet. "A friend told us that you might know about the asylums where they keep lycanthropes."

Under her veil, their informant glanced from Mariah to Gabriel, then back again, as if wondering who this "friend" was. He raised the water again, and that seemed to erase the question from her.

"I used to have a homebound administrative job for contract workers, and I have an acquaintance associated with an asylum. Hardware design. Why do you want to find out more about the asylums?"

Mariah opened her mouth to answer, but hesitated. Gabriel felt despair from her, and he wondered if it was because of all the lying she'd done previously and how she didn't want to do it anymore. How she wanted to refrain for *his* sake.

It gnawed at him, and before he knew it, he was saving her

from having to backtrack on her personal promises. "My sister . . . She was taken from her home about a year ago. She'd been depressed, and was acting . . . Well, she thought she was a wolf."

"And she went in for treatment." Taraline seemed to have sympathy for this story. That and the promise of more water obviously loosened her tongue. "Most asylums are back east, but they established some out west to see if different weather and conditions would affect the patients. That was what I gleaned from the vague memos I read, anyway."

The wind bit at the fringes of her veil, and Gabriel wondered just what was under it. Exactly what disease had she contracted?

But those weren't the answers he wanted or needed.

He held the water flask just that much closer to Taraline, as if she would have to earn it with a little more effort than this. "Do they have lycanthropes in the nearest asylum?"

"GBVille? Yes."

It was short for General Benefactors–ville. Years and years ago, it'd even been called Denver until the GB corporation had taken it over. Interesting that "lycanthropes" had been brought out there, because the air was still thinner than most places. Since the same amount of oxygen didn't get to the blood as it did at normal altitudes, did they think that might weaken and stunt the healing process for preters?

Mariah turned to Gabriel, but they didn't communicate mind-to-mind. Her hopeful grin said that maybe they were close. So very close.

Gabriel's belly warmed, and not only because of their link. He was picturing her as a human, free of everything that haunted her.

He pulled himself out of the wishful thinking. "Can you tell us what this asylum looks like?"

"The GBVille location is red stucco. It was one of the only old buildings left in the area and has fortifying brick walls outside. The doctors who established it had a sick sense of humor, thinking it was clever to have the most Gothic surroundings they could in the hub, like their very own scary story."

He could practically feel the focus of her gaze from under the veil as she stared at the flask.

But was she just telling them what she thought they wanted to hear in order to get the drink?

"You do know that asylums don't take appointments from loved ones, right?" she added.

"We can think of ways around that," Gabriel said.

"They have heavy security. I heard about top-level consultants that roam the grounds."

Did she mean Shredders?

If the asylums dealt with something other than patients who had psychological disorders like lycanthropy, the government would need Shredders there, even if the enforcers were supposed to have been dumped by the government, leaving only remnants like Stamp around.

Gabriel itched to ask Taraline more about it, and he actually flirted with the idea of whipping off her veil so he could look into her eyes.

She seemed to be staring straight at him instead of the water now. "What lengths would you go to in order to get inside?"

Mariah didn't even pause. "Great lengths."

Gabriel covered up what he thought to be too much information coming from Mariah. "We were all the best of friends, so you can understand why we'd be emotional about this."

"Yes," Taraline said. "If you're anything like me, you wouldn't hesitate to take matters into your own hands when you come to believe that justice won't otherwise be served. Getting your sister back seems enough to warrant extreme measures."

Mariah clenched her jaw, but Gabriel knew she wanted to agree with Taraline. She'd confessed as much back when they'd started this trek, when she'd told him that she'd go after the bad men who'd killed her family, if she had the opportunity.

The warmth between them went cold, and he barred his arms over his chest, keeping this side of Mariah as far away as possible.

Taraline motioned to her veil. "I wish there were an avenue of justice for every wrong."

"What happened?" Mariah asked softly.

"I caught dymorrdia."

Gabriel took an unintended step back from her, then regretted it. So obvious.

Mariah's heartfelt gaze told Gabriel that she'd been in society when dymorrdia had introduced itself. It'd been around for a while—a social contact disease that had somehow supposedly originated in the monster community. That was what the scientists had said, anyway, and a mere touch from a carrier could spread it if you had the genetic disposition to catch it.

It seemed to infect the most beautiful among the population and, as if envious, infected sociopaths had gone around touching people, just for the fun of knowing how it'd slowly disfigure their faces. It'd even gotten to the point where diseased burglars had used it instead of weapons. Rumors had even circulated that carriers were undercover monsters wreaking havoc.

All in all, it'd infected only a small segment of the population, though it'd seemed like many, many more. Scientists had come up with a cure as fast as possible; the victims had taken the remedy to kill their ability to transmit the disease while the rest of society had gotten inoculated against it, just in case. There wasn't a cure for those who already had it.

Not long afterward, dymorrdia had ceased to become a concern for humanity, except to serve as a reminder of how ugly anyone could get. It was also just another way to blame the monsters for society's downfall.

Taraline's veil rustled in the breeze, and it seemed like so much more than a covering now. It was her own perdition.

"Are you really going to the asylum?" she asked. "Back just before my dymorrdia started to show and I was still working, I got the feeling that, among the cures they might be developing for lycanthropy, they might—"

So this was what she'd been leading up to with all the questions.

"No," he said. "There's no way you can come with us to see if there's a cure for dymorrdia that they've been holding back from the public. Besides, asylums are supposed to be for mental patients . . . not anything else."

Or everything else.

Now he felt as if he were just as bad as any of the humans who hated monsters. As if he were just as prejudiced, only in the most ironic way he could think of.

But he didn't want to take the risk that dymorrdia was only a selective disease and that it'd been vanquished altogether.

And they needed to travel quickly, without a human to slow them down. They also couldn't afford to blow their cover with someone who stood out as much as Taraline.

They had too much at stake for Mariah and the community back in the Badlands. And, he thought, maybe even for himself. He hated that he thought it, but there it was.

Taraline spread her arms under the veil. "You don't understand . . . I may as well be dead out here."

Gabriel gave her the second water flask, then took Mariah by the hand. Seriously time to go.

"I'm sorry," he said to Taraline. "I wish we could help you. If we find something, we'll try our best to come back."

And that was all he could do.

Mariah was like a plow behind him. "Gabriel . . ."

He'd have to talk sense into her later, but as he looked behind to see Taraline standing by a grave, her veil blowing around her as if she were a dark ghost, he felt deader than ever, too.

12

Mariah

I let Gabriel drag me only so far out of the main graveyard and into a darkened lane before I wrested myself away from him.

He made as if to grab me again, then held his hands up, clearly realizing that he was going too far. Round us, those figures in the walls—cryptic and far too curious—slithered nearer. It was like they were attracted to us.

Nosy? Or . . . lonely?

Maybe they felt that last quality in me.

Gabriel glanced at the interlopers, then at the lane in general, as if looking for somewhere private—a place where shadows weren't pressing down on us. With one sniff of the air, he seemed to determine a perfect spot, pointing to a building on the corner that seemed to have all of its decrepit walls intact. The door to it was open.

Even in my human form I could smell the more pleasant aroma of the space. When we went inside, I saw it was an herb house, with ropes of dried tawnyvale hanging from the ceiling and draped over scrawny chairs and tables. The herb had a mild, sweet fragrance that probably did its part to cleanse the diseased odor from some of the homes of the living dead in this necropolis. Probably the people who still cared enough about smelling decent were the ones who used it.

Gabriel closed the door to the shadow creatures outside, and I stood amidst the herbs, which brushed my shoulders.

"I realize," I said, "that Taraline would've proven to be a lot of baggage, but couldn't we have heard her out?"

"If there's a cure for dymorrdia and we find it, then we can always come back here, just like I told her. Listening to her beg wouldn't have gotten us anywhere tonight."

There was a slat in the roof, and it lent a bit of drab sky through the herbs. It was enough to allow me to really take a look at Gabriel.

The good guy, with his laconic, easy way of moving. The gray eyes, which didn't seem to have much in the way of emotion right now.

Even as a vampire, he'd always seemed far more human than I was. But not right now.

"It's almost like you couldn't get away from her fast enough," I said.

He looked flummoxed by that, but I was puzzled, too. After all, wasn't Gabriel the hero who came to everyone's aid? Or was that only when he thought his rescuees were entirely human and somehow deserved a second chance?

What was it with him and his own inner monster . . . ?

The questions butted at my lungs, wanting to get out of me once again, just as they had back in the Badlands when I'd confronted him about Abby.

I couldn't hold it back this time, either. "If I didn't know better, I'd think that you despise even a woman who's lost her human appearance."

He cocked his head, frowning, and through our link, I could feel him scattering, then trying to construct the right emotion within himself. As if a semblance of feeling would help him figure everything out.

"Gabriel?" I asked, wishing I could help him know just who he was.

Who *any* of us were.

He righted his head from its tilt, looking at me straight on. "No need to say more. I take your meaning."

Did he? Because I had a lot more I could've contributed.

But I refrained from telling him that maybe, in death, Abby was the only "human" who'd always remain perfect for him. He'd never seen her change into anything else. He'd never seen in her the monster he'd despised in his own self. I even thought that she was kind of like a Madonna to him—a painted image to worship from a comfortable distance.

That was the saddest part, because I could never be that innocent and untouched ever again. I'd been his whore, and maybe that was all I'd ever be to Gabriel—something he wanted with every fiber of his needful body but something he didn't want, just the same.

Mortification descended on me. A whore. My prim mother would've dug herself a hole and stuck her head in it if she could see me now . . . especially if she realized how much I didn't even care so long as Gabriel wanted me again.

The link between Gabriel and me felt like a tangle of live cords that were getting frayed under heat and wear. But they were intact enough for me to detect in him the closest thing a vampire could feel to sorrow. Heaviness, numbness—his own punishment for falling short of what he truly believed he could still be.

A good man.

But he'd never be that again unless his creator was killed and he went human. The tragedy of that gripped my heart, squeezing what felt to be every last bit of blood out of it.

I moved toward him, the tawnyvale skimming my shoulders and head. "We're going to find all the answers we need. We've just been traveling the toughest part of the road, but it'll get easier. You'll see."

He barely smiled, as if recognizing a cosmic joke. Or maybe he thought it was funny that I was the one selling optimism these days.

But I didn't give up. "We *have* come a long way in a short time." I stood right in front of him now, where our link was expanding, just like lungs taking a stifled breath. "We didn't have much direction when we started out, but now we know where we're headed."

"And here I thought *I* was the speech maker."

He said it with an appreciation of how things used to be

when he'd first come to the Badlands. He'd been our great hope, and then our conscience.

Was *I* sounding like that now?

I almost laughed. Not me. I was still a killer who needed to be stopped. Nothing more, nothing less.

Even so, I grinned at Gabriel, thankful we'd avoided another blowout. Again, he looked like he didn't know how to take my smile.

Trying not to be put out by that, I took off my backpack and glanced round the room, thinking that a bit of tawnyvale wouldn't come amiss if I stowed it in my bag. Gabriel could use it until we got away from the necropolis and the smell abated.

"How long do you think it'll take us to get to GBVille?" I asked. When I thought about what Taraline had told us about the asylum, my excitement pulsed, making me feel ultra-awake. The hub wasn't that far off, and I felt like I could fly there right here and now.

He was back to being the gallant. "Two nights, if we can speed our way along for part of the journey. But maybe we should take a rest before we head out. You've been pushing yourself."

"I'm not tired."

"You don't have to wear yourself out as penance, Mariah."

I looked into those gray eyes of his, not because I wanted to go inside his mind, but because I wanted him to see the truth in my own gaze without having to use any vampire tricks.

His pulse became mine with one fierce jerk as our connection ramped up. It was like my heart was on the outside of me, exposed.

I don't exactly know what got into me then, but I went and did it—I touched the back of his hand, where his skin was pale and cool, the matter underneath harder than any human's. The contact gathered his blood under my fingertips; I could feel the rush of pressure with every passing thud in my chest, in my belly.

I could feel what I did to him.

My temperature pushed upward, as if it meant to spike through the ceiling if I didn't stop it. But when his gaze turned bloodred, I didn't have the will to control myself.

Brain-addled, I reached up to him, wanting to brush my mouth over his. Just once. If he pushed me away, I'd accept it. But I wanted to know what he'd do now that his eyes had gone vampy and our link was yelling at me that he wouldn't say no.

I got closer . . . closer, and when my lips touched his, our connection imploded—an electric burst that left my mouth tingling. It pressed with zinging insistence against my sex, making me ache in such a good way.

The electricity branched out from my lowers, taking hold of the surrounding cells, then all my muscles, up through my skin, breathing heat.

Pounding, stretching . . .

Change was on its way.

Surging with primal need, I grabbed what I could of his short hair as my fingers lengthened with the onset of my change. He groaned against my mouth and, from our link, I knew that he was trying to pull himself back. But everything about me was going with him, sucked into his body, fusing and not letting go.

My sight began to go bluish, and I stopped myself there, on the cusp of absolute change. I have no idea how I mustered the strength. Could be that this connection with Gabriel had bolstered me—that our link had twined through us during these last few nights as an understanding between us had started to grow. The connection seemed to have taken over the peace he used to give me—it'd become something else entirely.

I wasn't sure what, but I liked it.

Nonetheless, my control beat at me. "Gabriel?" I asked against his mouth, my voice warped, but still my own.

The pierce of his fangs scratched my lips, sending my willpower to wavering as I tasted a hint of my blood. He obviously tasted it, too, and our link folded back into itself for a lulling moment, as if collecting itself, reveling in the lust for more.

Then it burst outward, enveloping and then attaching us completely.

He grabbed my hair now, bringing the length of my body to him with his other hand. My pulse thumped against him, and my heat gathered his blood to his groin, making him hard.

I wiggled against the ridge of him, loving the feel, missing it, because the last time I'd experienced such a thing with him, he'd held some affection for me.

He hadn't known what I was yet.

We stumbled backward, bumping against a table strewn with herbs, and he lifted me onto its surface, spreading my legs and forcefully rubbing up against my sex. Our link battled with itself, as if he were trying to keep some order while my chaotic vitals tried to tear us into scraps.

As he rocked against me, I leaned back on the table, arching against him, wrapping my leg round him to get everything I could. His hardness agonized me, sending sharp nips of pleasure up, then out . . .

I moaned, and in my state, the sound emerged like a tiny, building howl.

He buried his face against my neck, and I knew it was because he was lured by the pulse there. Alive. Hungry.

He wanted a bite.

Wickedly, I wondered what would happen if he took my blood and I took his. An exchange. A werewolf and a vampire combined . . .

I dashed away the idea, then reached up to fumble with the catches on my blouse. When it gaped open, the famished sheen of his eyes nearly sent me to really howling.

My nipples went hard as he visually devoured my breasts. Our link turned itself inside out again, flipping my stomach while he cupped me, circling his thumbs over me, our imprint heating through his hands and into my skin. Wherever he moved, a burst of my blood followed, and it made me go wet, needful.

Wanting to give him the same pleasure, I went for the fly of his trousers. I coasted my fingers over the bulge there, and our link surged, swelling the stiff spot between my legs.

As he hissed in feral response, I undid his fly, taking him out, tracing him and knowing that the imprinted blood flow would drive him even further. My hands were hot, pounding, and they'd be sending the same beats into him.

His fangs had fully emerged by now, and when he leaned his head back in utter ecstasy, they were white in my near-animal vision.

Our link huffed like driving steam, almost to the point of scalding my skin. God-all, I was nearer to a change than I'd ever been without giving in to it. But this felt too nice to ruin, with my fingers on him, with his cravings blasting me onward and keeping me strong at the same time. I wanted to be a part of him in every way, so I did the unthinkable—I raised my hand to my chest and drew a lengthened nail down my skin.

He smelled blood the moment it bloomed over me, and with a wild growl, he lifted me to his mouth, latching to the wound. I cradled his head, urging him to drink while our link spun, as if he were trying to pull himself back again but couldn't gain traction.

Spinning and spinning . . .

His thoughts surged through me: *Can't escape . . . animal . . . monster . . . that's all I'll ever be . . .*

The very idea seemed to shake him, and he raised his head, my blood on his chin and mouth. We connected gazes, and I fell right in, although there was no peace for me to cling to inside him.

No temporary cure for me.

All I heard were more of his thoughts: *Gluttony. Stop now . . .*

But I didn't want him to stop. So I offered my neck to him. My pulsing vein.

He paused, our link pounding violently. That must've been what pushed him, because suddenly he was on the table, poised above me, his eyes livid as he pulled me to him.

Needing something to hold on to, I reached up with one hand and grabbed a strand of herbs. With the other, I held the back of his head as he struck fang into my neck, the sting of his entry making me growl and pant.

The herb strand broke, and we fell to the table, where, with every suck, my body contracted, as if it were getting ready to explode.

Another suck, another painful, pleasure-filled draw of sustenance from me to him, his mouth against my neck, my blood gathered round the bite, swirling and heating . . .

A howl palpitated in the center of me, a gale of whispers, then a low moan of growls, stronger, higher, until—

I cried out, digging my nails into his shirt, then tearing through the cloth until I ripped at his skin.

He kept sucking, ramming against me, and I rode every movement, whimpering for more, splinters abrading my own back through my blouse. My were-body was already starting to push out the wood and heal as he thrust me farther, farther down the table, until I started hanging over the side.

I churned against him even as I slid to the ground, but he grabbed me, whisking me back up to him, his fangs dripping with my blood.

Then he smiled, as if taken over by his vampire and—

We both heard a sound at the same time.

The creaking door.

When we looked, there was a black veiled shape standing against the night, and just by the water flasks it was holding, I could tell that it was Taraline.

13

Stamp

One Night Later

Tracking the monsters to this point had been simple.

Stamp crouched amid a batch of tumble trees, whose slender network of branches offered prickly spaces of sight much like the tumbleweed of old, except that these things had mutated and expanded in size. While avoiding the brambles, he watched the scrubs through his field glasses as they trudged over the nightscape, toward what looked to be a human-occupied way station, with its sun-shield tents.

The monsters were a motley group who'd probably blend in well: There was the elk man, a big guy who'd put on some khakis and a nondescript white shirt culled from one of those bags the group had apparently grabbed before evacuating. There was a robed woman whom Stamp knew to be a were–mule deer. Then the old man, who'd have stung Stamp like a scorpion if he'd gotten close, as he'd clearly intended to back at their settlement.

And, of course, the dog who could bite quicker than any of them.

In spite of their pedigrees, the scrubs were definitely the worse for wear. But what if they found shelter in this place?

Stamp put away the field glasses as well as the scent-catcher unit he'd used to follow the group when they'd started covering up their progress a little more carefully. It'd be extremely risky to terminate the monsters in the midst of humans, and Stamp had to admit that he still wasn't in top form, just as he'd been back in the days when he'd taken out nests of vampires.

But he would be as efficient and deadly as he used to be soon enough.

Taking out a penlight, he flashed the beam through the darkness at Mags, who'd been trailing him at a distance. His best bet would be to wait until the scrubs emerged from the other side of the camp;.there, they'd be far enough away from the humans not to raise an alarm. He didn't want anyone to report the presence of a Shredder to the government, if that Monitor 'bot hadn't already done so. The last thing Stamp needed was the degradation of getting caught.

And Shredders didn't get caught.

He waited, watching the scrubs get even closer to the camp, and with each of their steps, he began wondering if they'd choose to stay in that outpost, hiding in plain sight among people.

Damn. That wouldn't do at all. He'd have to think of a way to get them out in the open again, where the hunting would be freer.

Just as his mind settled into the groove of problem solving, he heard a pained croaking sound behind him, by a clump of rocks, and he used the penlight to see what was going on.

The pinpoint beam filtered over a strange frog-bird creature with bulging eyes and scaly skin. Something was coming out of its mouth, as if it were vomiting a miniature version of itself or . . .

Giving birth?

Stamp laughed a little. He'd never seen the likes of this, so he sat there for a bit longer. The Bloodlands, and obviously the fringes of the area, certainly contained a few creatures that defied description—mutants that had adjusted in order to survive, and species that hadn't even emerged until the world altered—but this one took the cake. Maybe this little critter kept its eggs in its belly, and this was how it produced its babies.

As the frog-bird bent over to ease the newborn from its

mouth and to the ground, Stamp couldn't help comparing this creature to the monsters. There were some people who said that preters were just mutations of humans—ultimate survivors who'd end up outliving them all. But if that was what Stamp needed to become in order to carry on through life, he didn't want any part of it.

Monsters.

Mutants.

A split of anger made him claw his hand as the newborn stretched and opened its mouth. Stamp wanted to squish both abominations, showing just who was the survivor.

The mom or whatever it was must've sensed his ill will, because it opened its beak and stuck its tongue out at him, hissing.

Ooo. Scary.

It was only when Stamp saw how the tiny, spittle-covered baby blinked at him in helpless, wide-eyed fear that he relaxed his hand. Then the parent made a whining sound, as if trying to play on Stamp's better instincts. And, indeed, he felt like shit.

Did they know that Shredders didn't kill the innocent? Mutants weren't technically like any monsters he'd ever been assigned to hunt. They didn't suck blood and rob the water from humans and animals.

The two mutants didn't move, clearly knowing that if they did, Stamp might change his mind. Perversely, he wallowed in that fear, wishing the old scrub scorpion-man had given him some of the same when the guy had been flat on the ground in the cavern, after Stamp had been concentrating too much on that damned Intel Dog and shot the ancient man in the shoulder area instead of the heart.

Stamp had wanted to see terror in the old guy's eyes, but his foe hadn't given it over. The old one had even been contrary, as if *daring* Stamp to just kill him.

Fear. Stamp had felt robbed of the rush. What would it be like to catch up to the old guy, aim a revolver at him again, and watch while that fear of reckoning settled into his gaze?

The more Stamp stared at the frog-bird mutants, the more he thought about the power of a good scare. Of having all the control and how that might translate into corralling the scrubs back out into the open.

When he didn't threaten the mutants further, the parent shielded its baby. That conjured anger in Stamp all over again, only because it made him think about how his parents would've thrown their bodies over him, too, if they'd seen the bomb from the monster sympathizers in the marketplace coming. . . .

He shut off the biting emotion that memory brought with it. The adult frog-bird kept covering its child, and Stamp fed off its remaining fear.

One moment.

And another.

Feeling stronger now, he stood, the gears whizzing in his leg as he rose above the height of the tumble tree with the aid of his FlyShoes. When he'd picked up the scrubs' trail, he'd changed from his heat suit and into his Shredder gear. All the same, it protected him from the air, which had grown a little cooler here on the desert's outskirts, but was still warm enough to bring out the sweat on a man's skin unless the suit prevented the scent from leaking.

Fear. It was his best weapon right now.

As Stamp watched the silhouettes of the scrubs moving toward the camp in the distance, he shadowed them, a bringer of terror in the pall of night.

14

The Oldster

"Thank-all," Pucci said as the group approached the outpost. "I never thought I'd be so glad to see humanity."

The oldster silently agreed with Pucci, knowing it was becoming a disturbing habit.

Still, he marched onward with the rest of the group. He was doing his best to keep up with them, but he was dragging, even though Hana had worked some of her nursing skills on him by sucking out the silver remnants from Stamp's bullet when they'd rested in an abandoned old shack. There, they'd debated about what to do now. Where to go.

Should they find somewhere else in the Badlands, where they'd be discovered all over again? Or should they do what Stamp might least expect—hide amongst the humans in society, just as they had years ago before fleeing to the nowheres?

They'd decided on the latter, even going so far as to use Chaplin's superior scenting skills to track Mariah. They'd decided to regroup with Mariah and Gabriel, hoping to God-all that the two were on the path to a cure. As far as the oldster was concerned, finding a remedy might be their only shot at stopping this mad game of cat-and-mouse, because, if they were human, what kind of Shredder or government would want to chase them anymore? Sure, the oldster was a goner, anyway, just by virtue of being ancient and supposedly useless, but his friends still had a chance.

That was what logic dictated, anyway, yet something about finding a cure bothered the oldster.

He liked being a were.

But he wasn't about to get fussy about what seemed to be their best option when there was so much else to consider first, such as night-to-night survival details. Hana and Pucci hadn't been able to grab everything they'd packed before they'd come to the oldster's and Chaplin's rescue at the homestead, but they had brought a couple bundles of human clothing and some canteens of water. Unfortunately, they hadn't secured heat suits during the escape, which meant the group needed to stay out of the sun. However, in were-form, they could hunt at night for sustenance and water gained through their prey's blood. The trick was keeping the *human* parts of themselves satisfied.

That included a proper place to rest for a while, and maybe this outpost would be able to provide one. After some rest, it wouldn't be such a strain for the recently wounded oldster to turn into his were-form again. This camp also seemed to be a blessing in that, if the group could blend in, they might even be that much safer from the scent-tracker Stamp was sure to be using on them. The oldster only wished the Shredder hadn't nullified his own smells, because the were-creatures, plus Chaplin, would've been able to catch Stamp's scent nearby.

But that was probably why Shredders had caused as much destruction as they had in the past—because they knew what they were doing.

Chaplin was sniffing the ground, the air—everywhere, it seemed. His super-duper Intel Dog abilities lent him a better sense of smell than even the weres had in animal form, and he'd been hunting down Mariah's trail when the group wasn't were-speeding over the landscape, carrying the dog with them.

The canine wagged his tail and glanced up at the oldster as they neared the outpost.

"Mariah was here recently?" he asked, guessing as to what the dog's good humor might mean.

Chaplin nodded, obviously happy that his mistress hadn't been overtaken by one of those government robots to this point.

Hana waved a hand in front of her face. "It is a wonder he can still smell her with all this smoke."

The dog muttered, and the oldster thought that he might be agreeing with the woman.

They were about twenty yards from what looked to be a main street, with a lone wooden building across from the tents. Cheers and screeches provided a nerve-scratching balance to the otherwise quiet night.

Hana reached into one of her two travel bags—the second was Sammy's, which she'd put together before knowing he was dead. Then she extracted the one thing that had survived their friend—a little comm device that he was supposed to have tuned to the unit he'd given to Mariah.

Hana accessed it, but the reception didn't cooperate. As she put it away, depression hung over the group.

Sammy.

Then, as if grieving didn't sit well with him, Pucci opened his mouth. "What I'd give to just be back home."

The oldster had been trying not to think about how things used to be. Only a short time ago, his Gila-man neighbor had been alive. Sammy hadn't needed to eat as frequently as the others, so they hadn't hunted a lot together, or even liked to be round each other much while in were-form. But as humans, they'd gotten on like brothers.

Never in the oldster's life had he ever thought he'd outlive the younger ones like Sammy. Or like Zel.

"Don't talk about it, Pucci," the oldster said.

But it was too late, because Sammy's murder was getting under the oldster's skin again: the naked shock on the younger man's face as the silver bullet had flown through his heart. His blood pooling over the ground . . .

Pucci actually sounded reasonable as he said, "I'm sure Sammy wouldn't have wanted us to mope, oldster. He—"

With no warning, Chaplin reared back and nipped at Pucci's leg, taking a bite of material from his khakis. The big man stumbled back, his hands raised as the dog readied himself to pounce again if Pucci didn't shut up.

"Call him off!" he said.

But Hana had already looped her arm round the dog's neck, hauling him back.

"No, boy." It almost seemed as if she didn't blame Chaplin for losing his patience. "You cannot give any indication of aggression here. It will be odd enough for us to have a dog, but if they find out what you really are . . ."

Chaplin had already heeled. That didn't mean he'd stopped glaring at Pucci, though.

All of them were glaring, and the oldster hated to think that Pucci was right—that Sammy wouldn't have wanted them to act like this.

So far, there wasn't anyone from the outpost to greet them, so the oldster took advantage of their privacy while it lasted.

"You know Chaplin could've done much more than nip," he said to Pucci.

"Damned dog."

And here the oldster had just about been ready to cut the whiner some slack. "He's just as sick of your mouth as the rest of us are."

"I can say what I want to say, and no dog's gonna stop me. Right, Hana?"

His partner kept holding on to Chaplin, not saying a word. The oldster wanted to shake her, ask her why she tolerated such behavior. When the oldster had first invited them into the community, Pucci had been decent. Strong. Glad to hunt away from the oldster and then Sammy during their were-trips outside. But then just as surely as Pucci had adapted to the Badlands, he'd flown his true colors, and everyone had wondered just how the hell a good woman like Hana had ended up with him.

"Hana?" Pucci asked with more emphasis.

She sighed, and Chaplin trained his big brown eyes on her.

"For goodness' sake, Antonio," she finally said, coming to a stand. "There is a time for talking and a time for thinking. This would be a thinking moment."

The big man bristled. Hell, the oldster could've testified that Pucci's brown hair was about to stand on end. Maybe his olive-toned skin even went a little ruddier, although he wasn't sure Pucci's ego allowed blushing.

But Hana didn't shy away. No, she gave the man a look that told everyone just who held the power in the relationship. And maybe that was why she stuck with Pucci—because she liked controlling a person no one else could tame.

The oldster was no therapist. However, he was astute enough at picking up unsaid vibes to know that it was time to move on, before Pucci decided to be twice the dick he was.

He pointed toward the tents. "Should we mingle, ask round for a place to stay and for water sources?"

Hana agreed, leading Chaplin and the oldster toward the tents. Pucci trailed behind like the caboose he was.

The smoke grew even thicker because of the campfires. Near one of them, outside a tent, some sort of meeting was in progress. Seven humans surrounding a long-bearded man who was writing in the dirt. Once he was done, his audience leaned in to read whatever he'd written.

Followers, the oldster thought. They weren't using computers out here, so they were simulating the act of following their leader's Texts.

Whatever entertained the masses.

More cheers went up from the opposite side of the camp, but there was an even louder sound nearby—and it was in Old American.

"Where's my sun-shield blanket?" a small, old crotchety voice yelled.

Hana, Chaplin, and the oldster exchanged surprised glances.

They turned a corner, going toward where they thought they'd heard the voice when they were stopped short by the sight of a nightmare waiting just beyond the tents.

A leathered, tall figure wearing FlyShoes, a chest puncher rising from its back like a network of cables and steel . . .

Pucci's voice came from behind the oldster. "Stamp?"

The oldster's body temperature blasted as he jumped backward, behind a tent, where the rest of the Badlanders had darted, too. But he kept himself from changing.

Doing it here would be a death sentence.

Breathe, he told himself. *Don't change. . . .*

Hana and Pucci were holding to each other, as if it were the only way they could ward off their changes, too. Her hand fisted his shirt, and he clung to her like a safety blanket.

Chaplin was sticking his nose round the tent, peeking to see if Stamp was approaching. The Shredder wouldn't just stroll into a populated area, would he? People would freak because the presence of a monster hunter would mean just one thing . . .

Monsters.

When Chaplin looked back at the group, he seemed bewildered. He jerked his snout toward where they'd seen Stamp, as if asking the oldster to check round the tent, too.

When he did, there was nothing out there.

Just the dirt and tumble trees and rocks.

"He's gone," the oldster said.

Pucci asked, "Like he was never really there?"

"Just like that, yeah."

They'd all seen him—it hadn't been a figment of the oldster's imagination. For some reason, he thought that maybe Stamp had wanted it that way—uncertainty. Fright.

"What should we do?" Hana asked. "Run?"

Chaplin was shaking his head, and Pucci seemed to understand.

"In order to run fast enough, we'd have to change here in the camp," the big man whispered. "Everyone would see us . . . or at least the blur we'd leave. We might cause an uproar and someone would alert the higher authorities."

Hana glanced up at him from the cradle of his arms. "What other choice do we have?"

The oldster's smile was a dim one, but it held respect for the Shredder. Not a bad plan to make the prey weak with doubt.

"He's flushing us out into the open, blurs or not. Afterward, Stamp will go right back to tracking us. Or, if we stay here because we know he's out there, he'll only wait, and he'll do that until there's a full moon. Then we'll be forced to leave because there's no way we can control a change or the need to hunt."

No ifs, ands, or buts about it, the oldster thought. Stamp had shown himself because he wanted them to know that they were cornered.

But the oldster wondered if Stamp expected a geriatric to have some game left in him, too.

"He expects us to run," he said, "and we damned well should. We can rustle up some heat suits to carry with us so we don't have to find shelter during the day. Then we get us an empty tent near the very edge of camp where we can undergo a change, then bust out undetected. It's a chance we'll have to take, and Stamp thinks we wouldn't dare risk it. But if we do, we'll at least get a head start on him. Hopefully Mariah and Gabriel will have gotten to the nearest hub by now, and once we arrive at it, too, it'll be harder for Stamp to track our scents with all the other peoples' smells."

The oldster got no arguments from the others as the dawn crept ever closer in the sky, no doubt moving as surely as the Shredder who had tracked them here.

15

Gabriel

One Night Later

This was the second night that Gabriel and Mariah had been on the outskirts of main GBVille, and already he wasn't loving the alteration in their plans.

And that alteration was named Taraline.

Yeah, Taraline. They'd had little choice but to bring her along.

They'd settled in a long cave that'd been created by a gathering of boulders just outside Little Romania, one of the many burgs where offshore vendors and local labor stayed until it was time to go into this main urban hub itself to work their General Benefactor jobs. Other burgs—Singaporetown, New-New Delhi, Saigon41—surrounded GBVille like lower satellites rotating the hub that was set on the higher, leveled tree-bare rise. GBVille was nowhere near the size that old Denver had been; it was far more concentrated, the population whittled down after the mosquito epidemic in particular. It was even the smallest hub in the United States, though a lot of them had shrunk in size and scope during the recent Indian sanctions.

Gabriel glanced at Mariah, who was looking up at the hub, too. At this distance, the gray buildings looked like stabs of sculpture, all celebrating the hope and devotion that the General Benefactors Corporation extended toward its populace. The structures took on the forms of clasped hands, old-time cathedrals, domes that resembled pregnant bellies hinting of fertility and fruitful promise. Below that, shaded boulders and smoke lingered, almost as if they held up all that shiny-murky urbanness.

The place buzzed with vibration, even from this distance. Gabriel could feel it in his very bones. He wondered if Mariah could, as well, though he doubted that a were-creature would feel it out of her most powerful form.

Reluctantly, he glanced to the other side of him, where Taraline took in the sights.

Clamping down on his vampire temper, Gabriel crooked his finger at her, then guided her back into their boulder cave so no one would see her standing there in that veil. Not that this remote location they'd camped out in had a lot of humans coming and going, but you could never be too careful with a companion who practically shouted, *LOOK AT ME! DISEASE!*

He stopped in the solar torch-lit dimness of the cave—Taraline had thought to bring a few of her own supplies when they'd left the necropolis, but he didn't have it in him to be thankful for that.

"You shouldn't be out there for anyone to see," he said.

Even under her veil, he could've sworn Taraline was smiling at him. And it'd be a satisfied smile, too, because after she'd caught Mariah and him in that herb house, she'd become queen of the castle.

"I'm sorry," she said in that deep voice. "I haven't seen GBVille in years. Even from down here, it seems so very different."

Mariah walked up behind him, giving him room. She'd been doing that ever since they'd sped out of the necropolis, and Gabriel wondered if it was because of . . .

Well, what'd gone down in that herb house.

The claw marks Mariah had abraded into his back still burned, though Gabriel knew they'd healed by now. It was the brute inside him that kept the reminder alive—the urges he hadn't been able to ditch when she'd brought out the beast in him.

But now was the time to handle the other difficult woman in his life.

"Taraline," he said, "just to be clear, you're to stay here while we canvass the hub. There's no way you can go with us."

When they'd arrived, they'd decided to get comfortable in a camping area outside the actual hub while they came up with a mode of operation. And just as Taraline had done last night during the planning phase, she butted heads with him now.

"But I can blend."

"Yeah, I saw all that blending back in the necropolis, with the people who moved through those shadows. I'm sure you're just as adept, too, because that's the only way the living dead can exist among others. But you won't blend here. Believe me."

"I see. Even if I'm not contagious, I'm hideous, and that's a worse disease."

Gabriel tamped down the urge to wipe her mind with some voice sway, but just after Taraline had discovered him and Mariah in the herb house, he'd tried some hypnotic words on her and they hadn't worked. Taraline had a real strong mind, and just before he'd even considered speeding toward her to whip off her veil so he could look into her eyes for a stronger moment of persuasion, she'd beaten him to it.

Now, she repeated the same gesture she'd made back at that herb house, calmly lifting up a flap that blended into her veil so expertly that Gabriel hadn't noticed it before.

Below it were two more flaps.

When she raised those, Gabriel saw her eyes. Watery blue eyes, and he peered into them, sensing the same thing he'd known the other night—that she wouldn't ever expose him and Mariah. She would genuinely aid them as much as she could.

Her thoughts were so pure that Gabriel couldn't refute them. He couldn't even bring himself to look into those eyes to see if he could hypnotize her into leaving altogether because, as Mariah kept reminding him, Taraline had gotten them this far. Was it possible she'd be even more helpful?

Had the psychic foreseen *that*?

"Listen," Gabriel whispered. "Just leave the hub for another night. Are you getting me?"

The woman smoothed down her eye flaps as well as the top

flap, almost like a lady demurely adjusting a blouse that had gaped open to show her necessaries.

"I understand," she said softly. Mariah took a step closer, and his imprint-link with her began thudding. This made him even angrier, because the last thing he needed was to feel her so acutely. She only reminded him of the worst when he only wanted the better.

Taraline held up her hands, and Gabriel knew he was about to hear another plea to come with them. Wonderful.

"I wasn't sure before today that I could think of a way to carry through with a plan that's been brewing in my head, but now I think I'm more confident in its execution." She paused, as if presenting something grand to them. "The friend I spoke of? The asylum contact? She was sympathetic to me before I left society, and I think I can find her, if she's still here. She worked from her home, so—"

"Your friend's a shut-in?" Mariah asked.

Of course she'd be interested in another fellow recluse. Mariah and her father had also been the type who'd cut themselves off from society for fear of bad guys everywhere. Hubs were full of shut-away humans who weren't nearly as overstimulated as the people who'd chosen to go outside in the streets. Mariah and her dad had left their hub a while ago, so who knew if they would've ended up like a lot of the rest of the city people—too spastic and distracted to think for themselves if they should ever come out of their homes.

Taraline was nodding as she said, "If I could contact my friend, ask a few questions without her ever knowing why, maybe we could all make our way into the asylum together."

Gabriel ignored her assumptions. "You want to talk to her without her knowing why we're asking about that asylum? Let me guess—are you suggesting that I sway her?"

"If she were on excessive job neuroenhancers, your sway probably wouldn't be of much use. But she had her intake under control."

Gabriel wrapped his mind around what Taraline was suggesting: swaying a human while they were in a hub. He'd wanted to avoid the act even more than he'd done out in the nowheres. Here, there'd be fewer places to hide if he should be caught. Here, there'd be computer reception and arm cameras everywhere, and humans could capture him committing his monster crimes. . . .

"We'll give it some thought, Taraline," he said, mostly to assuage her. "Just stay here while we scout things out. We'll be back before you know it."

"But—"

Gabriel raised a finger, and she stopped right there. Maybe she was remembering his fangs and red eyes. And maybe that was a fine thing.

Leaving Taraline in the cave, he went outside, where he stood on a flat rock that offered a view of GBVille in all its questionable glory.

As the vibrations from the hub dug into him, the scent of meat soup wafted by, souring the air with a tinge of vinegar even from about a half mile out of Little Romania. Hunger didn't affect him or Mariah, as they'd done their best to hunt before entering the more populous areas. Until the full moon, Mariah would do all right eating the human food they could trade for with the remaining pure water they had from the Badlands, but finding sustenance would get a lot tougher for Gabriel from this point on.

Would he have to drink from Mariah in a few days . . . ?

Out of the corner of his gaze, he could see her profile— delicate, with prim, soft lips and a gamine chin edged by that razored hair. Though a nick of desire cut him, he wouldn't bleed from it, in spite of pretending that nothing had happened between them.

It was as if she sensed his perusal, and he could see her glance at him, then back at the hub.

Gabriel leaned away from her. But even with a couple of feet separating them, he was still too close. Their impromptu liaison had only strengthened the link between them, and he could still taste her. Could still feel the fiery life she'd imprinted on him, reminding him of what he was.

"I'm ready to go when you are." She'd made an effort to look like a hub dweller by tucking in her shirt and draping a simple old scarf around her neck, plus she'd stuffed all her weapons into her backpack, making do without the holsters at her sides. She seemed like a random hubite who'd be coming or going. More important, they'd also talked about acting a little loopy, as if they were as overstimulated as the thugs Stamp had brought with him to the Badlands.

"I'm ready," he said. There wasn't much he could do about his own wardrobe, but he'd pass.

"First things first." She accessed the comm unit Sammy had given to her and spoke into it. "Is anyone there?"

When there was no answer, she stowed it away again, frowning.

He said, "The homestead is probably too far for a trinket like that to work now."

"That's what I keep telling myself. Then I start getting nervous, thinking, 'What if they *can't* answer the comm? What if I attracted attention when I was running outside without cover?' "

Her genuine fear pawed at him, as if stripping off his defenses bit by bit.

"Don't torture yourself with ridiculous thoughts, Mariah. You know as well as I do that it's the comm's lack of reception, not some kind of tragedy."

She must've liked the tone of his voice, because she started to look up at him, her heartbeat quickening.

Shit, if she really focused those green eyes on him, he might do something dumb.

He just about jumped off the rock vampire-style, arcing through the air and landing in a gentle crouch on the ground, just so he could get away from her all the quicker. But he got control of himself before he did a fool maneuver like that and instead climbed down like any normal human would.

Sure, he did it a mite too fast, but it beat exposing his preter side.

Mariah followed him, and he could sense tautness in her, as if she were wondering when they'd talk about the herb house.

Never, probably. Because talking about it would've meant that it'd actually happened—that he'd crossed a personal line back into near gluttony. That he'd given in to everything that was base and unnatural.

Or *too* natural.

They took a road upslope, where zoom bikes and solar-batteried box-looking cars wound up to GBVille. Every vehicle sported digital advertisements for General Benefactors, which produced media toys as well as spiritual tools like high-fashion yoga wear and do-it-yourself altar kits. Some windows even flashed personal self-made "collages," which featured provocative images that went by faster than the naked eye could grasp. Subliminal art from invasive artists.

Humans had more disposable income these days. It hadn't been that way since India had beaten down the United States with economic sanctions, so it was only recently that mercenary global investors had banded with the United States to buy most of its assets back. The country itself was behind on a lot of the most advanced technologies available, but it was obviously beginning to catch up again. On an individual level, its confidence also seemed to be growing back to where it used to be during the days of Before.

When Gabriel heard the gasp from a pair of FlyShoes behind them, he instinctively reached for Mariah, guiding her farther to the side of the road so the person could pass. The man's FlyShoes made him a few feet taller, the implements strapped to his legs just under the knee as he lurch-sprinted by.

In response, Gabriel kept his head low. Stamp's men had used FlyShoes.

As he bristled, he kept his senses open to detect any vampires like him, just as he'd been doing ever since leaving the Badlands. He'd found that it didn't do much good with were-creatures and demons, who were far better at masquerading.

His blood felt thinner in his veins, thanks to the altitude, and he could hear Mariah making a bigger effort to breathe, but at least the air was milder than it'd been in the desert. Maybe GBVille wouldn't be so bad after all.

But Gabriel changed his mind as they got closer, to where he felt those vibrations even deeper. They made him remember a time when he was very young and a military jet plane had roared over his home, low and fast. And that was what it felt like now—low-frequency sound waves riffling through him.

"You hear that?" he asked Mariah. "You feel it in your chest?"

"The beats?" Mariah asked.

While Gabriel nodded, he took a pair of earplugs from his bag and stuffed them in, but they didn't benefit him, so he packed them up again. The vibrations weren't just about hearing.

Soon, they found the source.

Clear booths lined the road like a stiff welcoming committee. Inside them, humans stood as if in silent ecstasy, swaying back and forth, their heads thrown back as the low-frequency vibration waves pounded out of speakers. But they weren't listening to music. Just . . . bangs.

Mariah clearly sensed Gabriel's keen vampire discomfort, because she hurried her steps uphill until they came to some platforms where guaranteed, disease-free, government-sponsored prostitutes posed like statues. Several men stood around one altar that held a naked woman who wore nothing but a snake, and they had their hands in their pants.

The woman didn't seem to care much. She just stared over their heads, petting her own snake.

It was quieter here, so Gabriel decided it'd be okay to speak. He'd have to avoid eye contact and thought sharing with Mariah, though. He had no choice, because other outside-dwelling hubites—distractoids, they were called—didn't really look each other in the eye. He needed to imitate that. Also, in a place where Text was the norm, he'd have to make sure he looked pretty clueless about body language.

"We entered through one of the red-light districts," he said, keeping his voice low. He couldn't speak Text with Mariah, who wasn't so fluent. "Not that there'll be a big difference when we step out of it."

"Wow," Mariah said, wide-eyed as they passed the platform of the last prostitute—a drag queen in red sequins and satin who fanned himself with a blaze of old peacock feathers. "Wow."

Maybe she wouldn't have to act much like a loopy distractoid if she was so entranced by the sights. But what did he expect? She was a shut-in from Dallas, one of the last traditional holdouts in the country.

Gabriel's blood welled as he tried to reconcile that innocent side of her with the animal who'd gone at him in the herb house. But he still couldn't put the two of them together.

"Wow, what?" he asked. "The women?"

"The . . . everything." She glanced back toward vibration

row, whispering, "I've never seen those vibe stations before. And certainly not . . . those kind of women. In my part of the country, there was too much fear of purity enforcers for that to be in style."

"You know that Dallas wasn't the same as most other hubs. As for those vibe stations, they discovered somewhere along the way that vibrations can change things like heart-rate patterns and contractions in the muscles. Just one more way to get a rush outside of drugs."

"And I thought neuroenhancers were bad enough. When my dad was working, they tried to get him to take some, just so he'd turn in top-grade performances. That's what they said, anyway."

Gabriel lifted an eyebrow. He and she kept mentioning a "they," but he often wondered just who "they" were. Maybe no one really knew, aside from assigning them the term "bad guys."

Mariah distractedly looked ahead to where the red-light district ended and the corporate buildings rose; she was doing a pretty good job of acting urban, adding a few spastic quirks here and there as she talked to him and avoided that eye contact, too.

"My dad resisted the request," she said. "It's one reason he ended up quitting. He saw where the world was going. Actually, he thought it was already too late, and he was right." She still hadn't slowed down. "When schools started suggesting that kids take enhancers for tests, that's when my dad began talking about leaving. Even if we hadn't been . . . attacked"—she obviously wasn't going to talk about how becoming a werewolf had driven her and her father out of society right now—"I think Dad would've taken us to the nowheres, anyway."

Gabriel thought of the outpost camp where the psychic lived among the exodus of humans. Seemed that there were others who didn't like the direction society had taken, either, and they weren't just preters.

Now the buildings seemed to swallow the sky, hovering over them like watchers. It was almost as if he and Mariah were enclosed indoors in a way. Honestly, the place was just about as oppressive as a lane in a necropolis, but sleeker, with hints of bonfires and ragged shadows from a group of thugs lighting off one building while a whisper fountain that espoused positive thoughts burbled from a granite square across the way.

The profane blending with the sublime, Gabriel thought. Just like every hub he'd visited. But no one around them seemed to give a crap about the nonsensicalness of it all as they Fly-Shoed by or walked in a straight line toward their next destination. Everyone was focused on the distraction that owned them at the moment. Pleasure freakin' Island.

Sterile and empty, even with everything so polished.

The air was even devoid of the earthier smells from the outskirts. The liveliest elements seemed to be sounds, like the echoes that only Gabriel could hear from the red-light district vibe stations and the whiz of motors from vehicles and Fly-Shoes. Even the vital signs from these hubites was stifled because of all that processed food they ate, slowing down their blood flow with blocked arteries.

Then he felt different vibrations through the ground, like a stampede, and he gestured for Mariah to settle under a concrete canopy with him.

It was just in time, too, because while he and Mariah got out of the way, thirty or more wild-eyed people clambered past them.

Gray business suits, withered street clothes, a lot of disease masks over the lower halves of their faces . . . The running ones wore all different kinds of fashion as they barreled by.

"We had those in Dallas," Mariah said, craning her neck to follow them.

"They're everywhere."

Word had it that the running ones had started with a few smart-asses who'd listened to a poet prophet who'd predicted these groups. "Everything is permitted because nothing is true," the man had also said. Gabriel, never a scholar, couldn't recall his name, but he'd remembered these words because he'd started running away, too, just not like these idiots.

To the original runners, the activity had no doubt been a joke, or maybe even an attempt to merge fantasy with reality, just as video games and old-time movies had done. But the initial groups had never disappeared after being introduced into society; they existed in perpetuity, regenerating, even after losing people to exhaustion. They were constantly replenished by one more who'd probably had enough of the vibe stations or carnerotica shows. Then another person would join as they tried to run away from whatever they needed to. Then another . . . another . . .

Everyone had gotten so used to them that all you could do was step out of the way, concentrating on your own distractions.

When this group vanished around a corner, it left a city square full of concrete under the harsh slants of shadow and gray moonlight. To the left of Gabriel and Mariah, a man sneaked up on another guy who was wearing a water necklace—a string of liquid-filled beads that flagrantly symbolized his wealth. No one intervened when the disease-masked hooligan snatched it, but a teenager did take a photo with her arm camera. The culprit left without the necklace, knowing the girl would be sending the picture to the authorities, who depended on citizen nosiness. She'd also get a touch of fame from posting the film to the Nets. The police monitored those, too.

All in all, none of the people Gabriel saw right now were interacting as much as they were merely aiming shit at each other or watching things while standing next to each other. A good example of the latter was the game therapy corners, where people let out their frustrations on virtual scenarios—jolly boxes. In them, you could die, but then you were resurrected for another go. Some distractoids spent days with this government-approved pastime, dying, living, back and forth until there was no line between the two.

Gabriel could smell every one of the distractoids as if they were his next meal.

Nearby, a zoom bike came to a stop, and it brought Gabriel back to the moment. He'd forgotten that even a vampire could get overstimulated in a hub.

He thought he detected a . . . familiar . . . smell. A scent he didn't like, but before he could get a bead on it, he and Mariah walked on, trying to stay to the shadows as they looked for a building that matched the description Taraline had given them. It'd have to be something old, with stucco that had withstood the years. Something just out of the center of the hub—inaccessible enough so the scientists could act in secrecy behind the possibly Shredder-protected brick wall while everyone else went about amusing themselves.

After Gabriel and Mariah walked around some more, they finally came into view of a massive building with red stucco and steeples that rested on the slope of a bland hill.

They traded a glance from their spot below it, near a streamlined structure with GENERAL BENEFACTORS embossed on the gleaming overhang.

"What do you think?" Mariah asked.

There was a catch in her voice, as well as in the connection between them. Gabriel didn't want to break her heart by telling her anything other than this might be the place that could hold a big change for her . . . and their . . . future.

"Looks like it could work for an asylum," he said. "But I sure wish we had that psychic with us now so he could tell us for certain."

He smelled something nearby—the familiar scent—and he put a hand on Mariah's shoulder. She knew better than to ask him what was wrong as he kept still.

That smell . . .

The necropolis?

Then he saw a figure blending with the shadows of the office building where they were standing.

A veil.

Gloves on the hands.

Taraline.

Without calling on his vampire speed, he made fast time over to where she was just now disappearing, as if knowing she had been caught. Mariah kept up with him.

"That'd better not be you," he said to the pillar where Taraline had ducked.

"Don't be angry," she said, her low voice bouncing off the concrete. "I knew you'd be coming here."

"I told you—"

"I told *you* I could blend. And guess what? There are a lot of others like me who know how to do the same. It's just that everyone is too busy to notice us."

"Taraline," Mariah said, half-chiding, half-accepting that this was how the woman wanted it and this was how it'd be.

Taraline's gloved hand appeared from behind the pillar, and

she pointed toward the hill. She was telling them that they'd come to the asylum.

A pump of profound happiness pistoned in the link between him and Mariah, and he traded a glance with his for-better-or-worse partner. She was smiling to beat the band.

Their connection expanded even more until Gabriel stepped away, into the shadows toward Taraline.

Mariah didn't follow, maybe because she knew it was best for them both if he removed himself.

Taraline was already talking. "You need me. Admit it."

Gabriel grunted. He'd give her that much.

Warily, he reached forward, clasping her gloved hand. She sucked in a breath—she didn't have vampire sight so she hadn't seen him coming.

He didn't have to say anything, because their joined hands said it all. They were in this together.

Mariah's voice owned him just as much as her presence always did. "Gabriel . . . ?"

He could feel her trepidation, as if she were thinking that he was going to hurt Taraline for betraying their instructions. Before he could dwell on the irony of Mariah trying to hold *him* back, he released Taraline.

And maybe he was also recalling the dymorrdia.

Anger burned in him because remembering the disease had been too simple.

But Taraline didn't seem to mind. She was already planning their next steps, and Gabriel could hear Mariah's vitals beginning to pump with the same excitement. She stepped into the shadows, and Gabriel's chest clenched.

"I'll contact my friend discreetly," Taraline said. "I'm pretty sure she'll meet me, even just to see what became of me. She was immune to dymorrdia in the first place, and she was never afraid. From her, we might get descriptions of the asylum's inner workings, details. But you'll have to put your work in, too, Gabriel, if I bring her to you."

Swaying. That was what she was talking about.

By now, Mariah's blood was practically singing to him, and he couldn't deny her this.

"When do you think you'll have your friend ready for me?" Gabriel asked.

But there was no answer, because Taraline had already left, melding with the shadows, gone just like that.

After a second, Mariah said, "This is it, then. No going back."

In the darkness, he could see her with his vampire sight, like the outline of a ghost who couldn't see him back. The near voyeurism sent his blood to tingling, and from the way she sucked in a breath, he knew she felt it, too.

When he pulled away, she closed her eyes, as if wishing he would've stayed.

He headed toward the subtle light of night. "Let's just hope the course of our adventure is a little more predictable than Taraline. I don't know if I can take any more surprises."

He would recall those words later, when Mariah's comm came alive with the last voice they'd expected to hear in the hubs.

16

Mariah

Gabriel and I were on the road back to our resting place near Little Romania when we heard the voice crackling over the comm.

"Mariah!"

The oldster?

I almost dropped the comm after I dumped my backpack and brought out the device.

"You there?" the old man asked. "God-all, *answer* me, girl!"

I darted behind a boulder, Gabriel right behind me, avoiding the parade of vehicles going to and from the hub.

"Oldster?" I waited a moment, trading an anxious look with Gabriel. My heartbeat seemed to ping out of my chest and into him.

A garble of static came back at me. Or maybe it was the oldster's relieved and tetchy laugh. Then, "We need to find you, quick. Chaplin's having a hard time tracking you here near the hubs."

Oh, Chaplin.

I swallowed, my throat aching. It stopped me from asking

why they were here instead of out there, but that wasn't as important as giving the oldster the location for our hideaway.

Afterward, he broke off without further comment.

Gabriel and I rushed to our site before the oldster and the rest of them could get there, but we took care to keep blending with the hubites all the way.

"Not to be base," Gabriel said as we rushed down the hill, him a few feet behind me, "but do you think the scent of Taraline's belongings masked our smells so Chaplin couldn't find us?"

"Could be."

In my human form, I wasn't terribly offended by her scent. Taraline had even used the masking effects of the tawnyvale herb to freshen herself up before we'd left the necropolis. But to Gabriel the full-time vampire, she was off-putting, although I didn't know if it was because she'd had dymorrdia or because of what the disease had brought about on her.

We arrived at our boulder cave about a half hour before everyone else did, and, boy, did they ever enter at a gallop. Chaplin just about knocked me backward as he said hello.

While he licked my face, I saw Gabriel exchanging hearty greetings with the group, who were wearing heat suits. They took their masks off one by one, and that was when I noticed that someone was missing.

"Where's Sammy?" I asked.

Chaplin stopped licking me as a fraught second passed, and even in that stitch of time, I knew. It was in the way the oldster stared at the ground, his heat mask in his hands. It was in the way Hana closed her eyes and how Pucci touched her shoulder and how Chaplin tucked his muzzle against my neck.

Pucci was the one who said, "It was Stamp."

"Stamp," I repeated, as if I didn't comprehend, even though I actually did.

Then a hunger shot through me—anger. A thirst for vengeance. A second later, I realized that I wasn't even the one from whom the turbulence was originating.

Gabriel. He was as stiff as death, his jaw clenched, his eyes an echo of red.

"How did it happen?" he asked.

My own body heat began to simmer, but I held it down as

Pucci told us about the government robot, the stealth attack from Stamp, how Chaplin had used my scent to follow my and Gabriel's progress as the group sped across the nowheres to get away from Stamp.

A bad guy. Just another one who needed to suffer for the sins he brought upon others.

"I guess," the oldster said, "that we all need a cure now as much as you, Mariah. Shredders like Stamp have a code about not killing humans, don't they? We figured that, if we became people again, that would surely keep him off our backs."

He wore a frown, and I knew why. The oldster liked who he was already. He had no big desire to be human, if a true-born even had a prayer of it.

"Is Stamp still on your trail?" I asked.

The oldster set down his heat mask to the side of the cave. "Your guess is as good as ours. He masks his scent from us so we don't know where he is."

Hana said, "And we have not seen him since the outpost."

"But," Pucci said, "Stamp must have a mechanized scent recognizer. We think he's an expert tracker, besides. That's why he was on us like sweat on skin. We tried to take care of the problem by . . . finding . . . some heat suits in that outpost, just so we could travel by day and get here all the speedier."

Hana was already unbuttoning her gear. "We have been subsisting on prey blood every night, and left our entire supply of water in place of the suits we took. It would be unconscionable to strand someone without items of value in their stead."

It seemed as if she felt guilty about stealing, but I surmised that, in the bigger picture, my neighbors had needed those suits more than someone in that outpost would have. I had seen how the occupants could burrow during the day to avoid the sun, but they seemed to lack water. Frankly, the burgled people might have gotten the better end of the trade for the time being.

But I had good reason for guilt, too. "The robot that pinpointed the homestead . . . It might've been out there because of me."

Hana had stepped out of her suit, revealing that she wasn't wearing her robes underneath. Gabriel turned away from the sight, but no one else cared much. We were used to each other's bodies in a functional, were-creature manner.

"Or the robot might have been there because of Stamp," she said. "Sammy had told us that robots were only recently being put into use again, and the one that found us might have been part of a first wave of new surveillance. The government seems to really be getting back on its feet to take care of the smaller details."

I sent her an uncertain smile, thanking her for standing up for me, and Pucci took hold of her bare shoulder.

But no one's forgiveness was going to make me forget Sammy. Quiet Sammy, who didn't ever do much to draw attention to himself. Sammy, who went about being useful without a need for recognition. I was a lone wolf in more than one way, and I hadn't hunted with him. I hadn't much hung out and shot the breeze in human form with him, either. But he'd always brought me meat after hunting during the full moon, during the times I was restrained. He'd always made sure I was comfortable in the chains that my neighbors bound me in to keep me under control.

Sammy.

By now, Chaplin had gone straight to Taraline's bag of belongings. All this time, he'd obviously been waiting for a good moment to cock his head at me, pretty much asking whom we'd picked up during our trek.

Time to put Sammy aside. As it was, thoughts of him were going to keep me awake during our day rest, so there'd be time enough for me to spend private hours with my sorrows.

I gave my neighbors the short version of our trip: how Gabriel and I had found the psychic at the outpost—or how he'd sort of found us, more likely. How he'd told us about the asylums and Taraline.

A wave of excitement traveled between all of us. It was a nervous type of trill, mostly made up of a new desperation for that cure.

Then Pucci said, "A psychic. I wish we had discovered him, too. He might've been able to tell us where Stamp is now."

The oldster was taking off the rest of his heat suit. "We can just assume that the Shredder is on our heels."

I supposed that when they were out of were-creature form, they'd tried to pass themselves off as humans who'd been traveling between hubs while wearing those heat suits, and they hadn't taken them off when the atmosphere had ceased to become hostile enough to need such gear. They'd probably switched off the protective functions, though. Plus, I suspected that the suits were maybe even hiding their scents from Stamp's tracker. Maybe. But the clothing would draw attention here in the hub, and that was the last thing we needed.

While Chaplin kept nosing through Taraline's stuff in the corner, I told them about meeting her in the necropolis. I thought it best to omit the part where she caught Gabriel and me in the herb house and highlighted how she was even now in the hub gathering information. All in all, I made it sound like Gabriel and I had thought it best to bring her with us, seeing as the psychic had urged us to seek her out in the first place. I added that she knew we were all monsters because we'd had to speed here to the hub in our basest forms, but Gabriel had seen in her mind that she wouldn't betray us.

The oldster went along with my explanation fine enough. The others looked skeptical, but what else could they do? Taraline was the psychic's chosen one, and we needed her.

Maybe my neighbors were too worn out to ask a lot of questions, but the oldster, at least, was already lying on the ground, half asleep, the heat suit acting as his pillow. Probably he was still weighed down from any remnants of his silver poisoning, which would disappear within a couple of days, I suspected. Maybe he hadn't healed fully during his time in were-form, or maybe he was just plumb spent.

Chaplin had nipped some clothing from Taraline's bag and dragged it over to the oldster. It looked like a black pair of pants and a shirt.

The oldster opened an eye, inspecting the wardrobe, while Chaplin dropped the material and chewed out some sounds.

I think the skinny oldster will fit into these clothes.

I repeated this for the others, then went straight into asking, "Since Stamp has record of his smell, are you aiming to mask it with Taraline's?"

Chaplin nodded. *This Taraline has a distinctive scent. Dymorrdia, right?*

"Right," I said.

When I translated Chaplin's sounds for everyone, there was a stir. Hana, the ex–new age nurse who'd been educated about the disease and the successful attempts to curb it, didn't over-react. Pucci and the oldster sure did, casting knee-jerk, horri-fied glances at Taraline's stuff.

"We won't catch anything," I said. "They never proved that monsters were the ones who originated the disease. I don't see how we could've, anyway, with our immune systems."

"But—" the oldster began.

Chaplin wasn't about to deal with wussy-minded monsters. *Oldster, your clothes got torn off during Stamp's attack, and I believe that the Shredder's been using your smell as a track-ing marker. I doubt he took the opportunity to search the home-stead to find anyone else's clothes and run them through his scenter unit. It would've used up valuable time for him because he would've wanted to be on our trail as quickly as possible.*

Again, I told the others what my dog had said. Then I added, "I'm sure Taraline won't mind sharing clothes. She thinks there's a cure for dymorrdia along with any other cures in the asylums, and if you dressed in her duds, it'd be a small sacrifice for what she thinks she'll get in return."

And I understood Taraline's thought process more than any of them could imagine. After Gabriel had looked into her head to gauge her loyalty, I'd decided to accept the honesty he'd sensed and trust her completely. Hell, maybe I would've even taken her willingness to help us at surface value, because I could almost taste a cure now.

As the oldster gingerly touched Taraline's clothing, I felt Gabriel watching me. When I looked over at him, he was wear-ing an expression that made me go jellylike, but he glanced away real fast.

Still, I held on to the moment. He'd been acting like nothing had gone on between us in that herb house, and I'd let him get away with it, mostly because nookie was the last of our con-cerns right now.

But I was going to call him on it when this was over. You bet I was.

Before the oldster entirely fell asleep, I helped him up and guided him and everyone else farther back into our cave, where it was even cooler and less accessible to anything outside. Chaplin stayed by the entrance, guarding it, attuned to Taraline's scent so that he wouldn't raise an alarm if she returned tonight.

And she did return, shortly after we ate some jerked meat from my backpack and drank my ever-dwindling supply of water. A were-creature doesn't *have* to eat fresh meat or fill up with blood every night, since we can sustain ourselves through human nutrition until the full moon comes round, but it sure does wonders for our systems if we can have a consistent diet that appeals to our primal sides.

Everyone but me was day-resting as Taraline crept into the cave, obviously having already met Chaplin.

She glanced at the snoozing oldster, who was wearing her black shirt and the only pair of pants she seemed to own, his ankles exposed by the ill fit.

"I hope you don't mind," I whispered. "We think he's being tracked, and . . ."

"It's all right," she said.

I could tell the sun had already risen because Gabriel was slumped on the floor, out like a broken lantern. I kept watching him, unable to stop until Taraline lay on the ground, too, hugging her bag to her, the veil like a blanket over her face and upper body.

"I asked my friend to meet me tomorrow at the same place I found you tonight, in view of the asylum at eight P.M.," she said. "We'll find a secure place to talk. She didn't want us to come to her home."

I myself remembered the days of barring other people out of my own Dallas home before the bad guys had attacked my family. "I don't blame her."

"I'm glad Gabriel is going to see to it that Jo doesn't remember the delicate conversation we'll have," Taraline added. "And what I'm going to ask her to do."

The cryptic comment gave me pause. What the heck were we going to ask her friend to do that she'd probably like to forget?

Before I could query about that, Taraline added, "Jo is already very curious about why I'm back in the hub. Gabriel's mind powers will keep us safe from her curiosity."

I didn't know how agreeable he'd be to swaying people in

so public a place, but he was just beginning to feel his oats with his vampire powers, thanks in no small part to my unfortunate influence on him. It seemed as if he was getting more comfortable with himself all the time.

And I'd be glad that he was finally accepting his nature if it didn't make me feel like such crap. I didn't like being the temptation that dragged him into a darker state.

Conversation done, Taraline sighed, her veil puffing, and that soft sound made me feel better about our future. She was going to help us get there.

Then I lay down, too, closing my eyes and finally thinking of Sammy, who was hopefully sleeping somewhere far better than this.

Chaplin had no cause to awaken us during our rest, but that didn't mean Stamp had ceased to become a menace when dusk fell. It'd just be a matter of keeping our eyes and ears open for him as we went to meet Taraline's friend, Jo.

We cleaned ourselves up as best we could, even going so far as to alter our clothing and appearances with hats that we could pull down just above our eyes, plus disease masks Taraline had somehow snatched. I even coached the oldster to walk and move as if he were younger than he was, because if anyone saw that he was advanced in years, they'd scoop him into the nearest pound for certain.

Basically, we *all* needed to be the blendiest citizens ever to reside in GBVille, where the throngs of people—plus the precautions we'd already taken—would hopefully cover any identifying scent markers Stamp might have on us. Meanwhile, Chaplin would stay back in our camp, not only to guard it and get some rest, but because I didn't want an outlawed Intel Dog to be so exposed.

He didn't even argue as Gabriel, the oldster, Hana, Pucci, and I braved the night and mounted the slope. Taraline had left before any of us had even awakened, but we knew just where and when to meet her.

We had at least an hour to get to that General Benefactors building near the asylum, but I realized that our progress through GBVille would be slow, thanks to having to watch for

Stamp as well as running into all the wonderland obstacles of the hub. It'd been a while since Pucci, Hana, and the oldster had been out of the New Badlands, and they'd be just as flabbergasted by what they'd see as I'd been.

And, indeed, as we walked through the red-light district with its vibe stations and prostitute platforms, we moved at a snail's pace while trying to seem as if we weren't interacting with each other. Just like any distracted Text citizen.

Nonetheless, Hana subtly nudged and bumped Pucci through the whore avenue, where he kept gaping at the near-naked lady displays. Much to his credit, he pretended that he really wasn't very interested in them, but even a dunce in a deprivation chamber could tell that wasn't true.

Anyway, it wasn't until we got farther into the hub that we really slowed down.

As a stampede of wide-eyed running ones came at us from round a building corner, the oldster started running, too, as if not knowing how to get out of the way. It made me wonder if there'd been a few running ones who'd joined the group because they didn't know how to avoid the crowd.

We chased the oldster, who'd veered away from the group and off to an unfamiliar concrete square.

"Well, I'll be," he panted under his disease mask as the group rounded another corner. One business-suited man fell to the ground, utterly exhausted. Citizens walked round him, as if he were part of the decorative plan. A cop would probably pull him to the side soon enough so he could continue his sleep, then join another group.

Not wanting to be noticed, we moved ahead, allowing spaces to fall between us. To anyone who might be checking us out, we were wandering aimlessly, but I was betting that the distracted populace wouldn't give a fig about who we were or why we were here.

We passed an alley with bonfires stabbing out of cans. I'd seen the glow of this area last night, and although I'd been curious about how something so dirty could exist amongst the gray-clean buildings of the hub, we hadn't gone close. That was probably a fine thing, though. Now that I could see, the alley seemed to be a meeting place of sorts, with a filthy, muscled, braid-bearded man chanting Text at the equally tough crowd below his perch. He was holding a chicken by its neck, a machete in his other hand.

> *I kill & gut*
> *& maim & rut*
> *dn't fck w/me*
> *cuz ded yul b*

We left the scene behind right quick, and about a block away, where the surroundings were slightly more welcoming, Gabriel seemed to think it was safe to talk. Trusting a vampire's heightened senses seemed a good bet, so we slowed down to hear him while pretending to watch a General Benefactors show screen that featured its logo changing shapes. Pretty.

"Lowlord," Gabriel said from under his disease mask.

"Is that what he was?" The oldster panted. "But just what was a lowlord doing with a chicken?"

"I can't be sure, but lowlords are thugs who answer to even worse bad guys, and they keep any malcontent distractoids in line by controlling their own little groups—usually the people who don't gravitate toward game therapy and the like. Maybe the chicken was a meal for them, and he was using it as a reward for appropriate behavior."

Lowlord ganging—it was another way to disassociate. No wonder bonfires and chickens fit into the hubs, side by side with everything else, even if the buildings were sophisticated and cosmo.

"Man, it's gotten bad for humanity," the oldster said, resting his hands on his thighs, struggling for breath, maybe because of the altitude. "Maybe that chicken was actually some kind of sacrifice."

Hana said, "It is like the Middle Ages, isn't it? No one has any purpose but to get from one day to the next."

"I'd sure like to know just what he was doing to that chicken," the oldster said, seemingly fixated.

Gabriel stared at that GB logo screen. "Your guess about a sacrifice might not be far off base, come to think of it. It's something to excite his followers. Everyone needs something to believe in, right? And even lowlords have to entertain to earn a following."

Something to believe in. It seemed that whether we lived in the hubs or out of them, we were all searching for the same thing. A lot of us didn't even know what to believe about ourselves, so we had to look everywhere else for an answer.

And I'm sure the bad guys depended on that. My dad always used to say that the government especially wanted everyone to keep our eyes off what they were doing—that they hoped no one would ever take their focus from the gossip pages and pseudo scandals to really see what was happening round them.

I guess that was a hundred times truer these days.

"Supposedly," Gabriel said, "some police look the other way with the lowlords. Or other police can be just as bad, working for the lowlords as well as the government. A few cops go vigilante, though, and they have their own followings."

"Zel wouldn't have stood for any of that," the oldster said, straightening up, and even beneath his hat and disease mask, I could see a muscle ticking in his whiskered jaw.

"No," I said softly. "Zel sure wouldn't have."

We were quiet for a moment. Even the lowlord's shouting had faded into the air, seemingly eaten up by the hovering buildings.

I hoped that, somewhere, Zel had welcomed Sammy into the best home they'd ever known. That she was there to mother him and watch out for him while he settled in.

We ventured on, still watchful of Stamp while we moved past screenboards with carnerotica available for all to see. In fact, a small crowd had gathered beneath one of the screens—an execution in what looked to be a country the United States had isolated itself from long ago. Some people were even watching on their arm screens, just to get a closer view, I suppose. Or maybe they were monitoring other channels at the same time.

Rushing past, we came upon one woman who had her arm raised, filming herself as she babbled Text to her screen, documenting her day. I'd seen others doing this last night, and Gabriel had told me that they were in their own "shows." Amazingly, these people were even sponsored, mostly by General Benefactors, and they wore clothes with the corporate logos all over them.

Lots of people seemed to be a brand, a product, an

advertisement of themselves when it didn't seem there was much content to sell. I didn't get hub life.

I don't think any of us did, especially when we saw two teen girls hand-polishing the FlyShoes of a gray-garbed businessman. They were doing the labor the old-fashioned way, without mechanical tools; humans could be more detail-oriented if they were focused enough.

When they finished, the businessman jerked at the two leashes that held the girls, and they walked on. The girls kept their gazes on the ground.

"Water slaves," Gabriel said from behind me.

I looked again, hardly believing what I was seeing. I'd heard stories from my dad, but . . . "They indentured themselves to that man?"

"They thought it was a fair trade for survival."

From farther behind us, the oldster must've overheard, and his voice got gritty. "He treats them like showpieces."

"That's the idea," Gabriel said.

Indenturing had become common practice after the world had changed—survival could be more important than pride. It seemed as if no one had bothered to look back to decades ago and think how people would've reacted to the sight of leashes round someone's neck. Hell, I didn't even put a leash on Chaplin because . . . Well, first, he wouldn't tolerate that nonsense. Second, he was no animal.

We all watched the businessman and his girls stroll away. He was a bad guy. I knew it in my bones because decent people didn't humiliate others just for sport.

The oldster branched off from the rest of us, and I knew what he had in mind. His dander was up, and we couldn't afford it.

"We've got an appointment, oldster," I whispered.

He made a wretched sound but fell back.

Trying to concentrate on the topic at hand, I didn't think about the girls or the lowlords or any of the other garbage that the hubs seemed to breed.

I tried real hard not to think about anything but that asylum and how we were going to get into it.

We made it to the meeting spot far ahead of time, in the shadows of the General Benefactors building where Taraline had found Gabriel and me last night. After we inspected the area with our hand weapons subtly drawn to see if Stamp had set up an ambush, we settled into the darkness.

Soon, Taraline slipped in. I could feel that Gabriel sensed her before she even spoke.

"Is your friend coming?" he asked.

If Taraline was impressed that he knew she was there, she didn't indicate it. "Yes, Jo is a minute behind me."

"Then I'll do what needs to be done," he said. He hadn't complained about needing to sway this person. I'm sure it was because he could taste that cure just as surely as I could.

Gabriel obviously heard our "Jo" outside the shadows, because he began moving out of the darkness and toward the concrete park where she'd probably be waiting. We'd already agreed that I'd go with him while Taraline stayed back with the others, who'd be scanning for Stamp or other interlopers.

But before we left, Gabriel asked Taraline, "Has your friend been taking more neuroenhancers than she used to?"

The answer would matter. If Jo was hopped up, he'd have a hard time grabbing hold of her thoughts.

"Her intake is still minimal." Taraline's deep voice was serene. "Jo has been resisting them. Even back when I was still living in the hub, she talked about leaving behind GBVille and this life, so she's a perfect candidate for giving us information. She's a workaholic, so she hardly needs to be inspired to do a turbo job at work, but she's tired, just like so many others."

So work was Jo's own personal distraction. It wasn't jolly boxes or running the streets.

"Why didn't Jo ever leave here?" I asked.

"Why don't most people leave?" Taraline asked.

Even as monsters, we were all familiar with fear of the unknown. We'd felt it when Stamp had visited the New Badlands, and it'd taken Gabriel's influence for us to stand up to the dangers, even if we should've done so long before.

Without Taraline, Gabriel and I left the shadows, then approached a woman wearing a stiff, blandly colored suit. Her back was to us as she sat on a park bench in a square with stepping-stones and piped-in fountain noises. In back of her, the asylum waited on its hill, a red-stucco contrast to the sterility.

I almost expected Jo to be holding a facial recognition scanner, and when I saw that she was empty-handed, I sighed in relief. It would suck if Stamp had gotten cozy with the government and already reported us, putting those of us he knew in the database as identified monsters. I wasn't sure I even wanted to find out.

Before she heard our stealth approach, I noticed that she was wearing a disease mask, and as she turned round at the sound of us, all I could see were her big brown eyes and slicked-back mahogany hair.

Gabriel locked Jo into his sway before she could even comment on the two strangers who'd sneaked up on her.

"Good to meet you, Jo," he said, not including me in his sway.

"So good to meet you, too," she said.

Yup, locked and loaded—and, afterward, Jo would be left to think that we'd all had a much less intense conversation.

I kept an eye out for anyone nearby who'd notice us, but the park was deserted, maybe because there weren't any carn-erotica screens or jolly box corners to attract folk. The government hadn't even put any cameras round here because it was so dependent on the hubites' filming habits, which saved them loads of money they could use on themselves and their pet projects.

"You know about the asylum?" Gabriel asked.

"I contracted with the government for some of the weapons they use inside."

They used weapons inside? Maybe on the monsters . . . ?

"Thank you, Jo," Gabriel said.

My heart pounded, my chest buzzing as I connected to him.

"This is what I'd like you to do," he said. "We need to know the layout of the property. Can you quietly get blueprints for us through any of your connections at the asylum?"

"Yes."

"And security information, too. That's very important, Jo."

"Security information."

Gabriel glanced to the side, as if he'd sensed something. And then, from an angle of shadow near the concrete steps, I heard Taraline's voice.

She'd blended. "Gabriel, I didn't dare ask her about this

before, but now's the time for us to bring up how we're going to get into that asylum. Years ago, before Jo came to GBVille, she contracted with the military, so she'll be able to construct something for us without us having to go on the Nets. She can also procure materials for what I have in mind, because she'll have access to them because of her work."

I checked Jo out a little more. The military, huh? Ever since the end of the Before years, the military had turned into an all-defensive body rather than an offensive one. They kept our country to itself except for key business arrangements with the investor/allies who also owned us.

"What exactly should I ask Jo?" Gabriel said to Taraline.

"Ask her if a weapon based on a smaller version of an e-bomb would work for our purposes. It could disable power—generators, vehicles, communication, all with an electromagnetic pulse."

Holy crap.

Taraline had *really* thought this through. Her willingness to do anything—even take advantage of a friend's exposed mind—impressed the hell out of me and Gabriel. Long ago, one terrorist group had hatched an e-bomb plan on Chicago, but they'd been caught and slaughtered before they'd succeeded. After that, the government had cracked down on security and performed tons of executions, preventing more attacks until the terrorists' money had dwindled and they had seemingly gone underground.

Maybe they were still there. Or maybe they were distractoids now.

"The bombs were designed to act like lightning strikes," Taraline added. "My boyfriend . . ." She paused. "My *ex* used to be a science online teacher. He would talk about science and how it applied to everything from defense to cooking. That's why I thought of it."

Her ex. It sounded as if he'd left Taraline—or Taraline had left him—after the dymorrdia had come visiting.

"The thing is," Taraline added, "there's a very high chance that our device could affect more than the asylum. Databases and hardware here in the hub might not start up again. It could fry just about everything, but it would level the playing field for us."

I smiled at the practicality of it. I should've thought more about the consequences of knocking out power in a hub, but all that mattered for me, my neighbors, and maybe all of us monsters in the end was a cure. "Our device wouldn't do a thing to *our* primal abilities."

Gabriel laughed at Taraline's chutzpah. I just kept smiling, thanking-all for the night we'd met that psychic in the outpost.

Taraline was as silent as the shadows, but I'd bet in that hiding place of hers, she was smiling, too.

17

Gabriel

Several nights passed as the Badlanders prepared for their sneak attack on the asylum. Now, the night before its launch, when the moon was just a crescent, they'd done everything they could think to do, even going so far as to stock their safe rendezvous point—an abandoned mine shaft that was a couple human-travel days distant from GBVille—with their extra supplies.

Then they had come back here, to the front of their cave, where the Little Romanian scents of that sour meat soup and a cornmeal mush floated past them, not even tweaking their hunger. In addition to everything else, they'd hunted far away from the hub, goading their animal cravings with blood from some stray felines, smaller than those Badlands feracats.

Blood nourished them for what was to come.

"So this could be it," the oldster said from his seat near the boulders, where Chaplin napped against his leg. "Either we find what we're searching for up there or we die trying."

As he looked up at the outline of GBVille, Gabriel thought that the lantern light made the old man look like a rusted antique trussed up in the black clothing he'd borrowed from

Taraline. Next to him, Pucci leaned against a boulder, also watching the hub. Hana reclined near the cave's entrance, her eyes closed, meditating, the mellowest of them all.

The most high-strung Badlander had to be Mariah, who was with Taraline back in the cave. The two women were checking over the pair of what Jo called her own version of old e-bomb technology—"power blasters." She'd constructed modified versions while under Gabriel's sway, and he'd justified using his mind powers because it was for Jo's own good; she didn't need to recall that she'd aided and abetted a bunch of monsters.

Yup, he'd wiped Jo's mind of the past several nights well and decently. His absent vampire creator might've even been proud if she'd cared enough to hang around and see how her little progeny had grown up. But he'd even gone beyond just mind-wiping Jo. He'd sensed a bitterness toward the government in her, and when she'd finished her work, Gabriel had suggested that she might find better happiness in another place. She'd been open to it, and he wondered if, someday, she'd end up in an outpost like the one that housed the psychic.

No matter where she eventually resided, Gabriel wished Jo all the best, because she'd funded and given them the key to their attack. One of the cylindrical power blasters would serve as backup, just in case the first malfunctioned. However, merely a single device, which Jo had called a "model based on a flux compression generator bomb," would be enough to take out every technological advantage that the asylum and the hub around it held, even if the item was detonated outside the asylum's wall. She'd said that they needn't worry about effects from the blaster, as it wasn't supposed to harm people.

Too bad the government hadn't shielded anything in the hub, which meant that they hadn't protected their vital equipment by encasing it in what she called a Faraday cage. Since computers and other hardware required outside power, shielding wasn't practical, and it would put that equipment out of contact with the world outside, where it was needed.

Truthfully, Gabriel hadn't listened much to Jo's technical chatter. He had no interest in engineering—as a human he'd been a craftsman, a career that was simple and straightforward— so he didn't give a rat's ass about the things Jo had been saying about the power blasters acting like a majorly powerful old microwave oven or how they could generate "a concentrated beam of microwave energy." All he'd heard while she was updating him was "blah, blah, and blah" as he'd studied the blueprints he'd drawn from what Jo had been told about the inside of the asylum—a place she'd never actually gone into.

The layman's version of their plan was this: Taraline would set off a power blaster, and then the Badlanders would enter in monster form during the resulting confusion. The chaos of no power—lights, communication, cameras, the whole bit—should give the Badlanders enough time to strong-arm any human who could advise them or even lead them to a cure. If all went well, the group would be able to speed out of the asylum and the city before the humans even discovered what'd hit them. Afterward, they would go into deep hiding for a while.

Not a bad plan, really. Not perfect, either, but then again, what was?

Gabriel just hoped that there'd be no remaining Shredders guarding the wall. The only security plans that Jo had been able to get hold of had been vague about that, referring to "sentinels." She also hadn't been able to tell him if there were definitely monsters being kept in the asylum, only the old standby—lycanthropic, mentally deranged humans.

Next to him, Pucci spoke, sounding wistful. "If there were one thing I'd wish for tonight, it'd be that Jo could've told us for certain whether there really is a cure up there. We just might be running headfirst into nothing."

Just like back in the Badlands, when Gabriel had been trying to get the community to stand up to Stamp, he wasn't about to hear any negativity now. "If there's nothing definitive up there this time, we'll find something at the next asylum in another hub. We'll just have to figure out a different way to get into it, seeing as I'm sure the staffs will be advised in the future about power blasters."

Pucci said, "So we'll be doing this over and over again until we find a cure?"

"*I* will be."

The oldster preached up a responding "Amen," which got Gabriel right in the gut. It wasn't only because of the religious connection, either. It was because he wanted to stop Stamp from chasing down the Badlanders, too, and a cure would remedy that. After all, the Shredder had hesitated to attack Gabriel when it hadn't been clear to him whether Gabriel was a vampire or not. Shredders had their own rules of conduct.

And then there was Mariah, who needed anything they might find tomorrow night most of all. . . .

Something streaked across the drab sky. A shooting star?

If so, it was a good omen.

The link between him and Mariah banged, as if it'd come more awake than ever. It even felt like the trail of a shooting star in itself. Obviously, she'd come out of the cave and, as she stood near Gabriel, he scented her earthiness. He heard the music of her vital signs, which weren't as wild as they'd been in the New Badlands, when she'd been nearly suicidal. Now that she'd focused on a mission and calmed down, she sounded more like Abby had—a song played over the nerves of his body. Notes that were a hungry part of him.

"I'm with Gabriel, too," she said. "No matter how long it takes, I'm not going to give up."

He could smell that Taraline had stayed behind in the shadows.

A sense of togetherness stole over the group, as if they *all* agreed for once. They wouldn't quit if this particular visit to the asylum wasn't successful. But what else could a crowd like this do when their last two homes had been raided? There was no choice but to find somewhere better . . . even if it did kill them, like the oldster had said.

Pucci stood away from the boulders, as if getting ready to turn in for the approaching day. "I'll be dreaming blueprints, that's a guarantee."

Hana spoke with her eyes still shut. "All of us will be. I almost wish we could go to the asylum now, to get this over with."

"We only have about a couple of hours until daylight hits," Gabriel said. They'd need more time than that because, once that power blaster went off, the asylum wouldn't have any far-reaching main lights, and the longer the humans were in the dark, the better. Besides, he kind of wanted to be awake for everything.

Mariah's voice pulled at him. "I can't believe monsters haven't thought of this before—and I'm not just talking about barging into an asylum to see what they're storing in there. I'm talking about facing up to the bad guys in general. Taking away their weapons and means of existence. I mean, just what are they without their technology?"

"Could be," Gabriel said, "that if everyone hears about what we've done, they'll want to do it, too. It's just that no one wants to be the first to try it."

The oldster laughed. "Only idjits like us would dare."

They all joined him in nervous laughter, an outlet. There was a chance that they might not be able to laugh at all come the end of tomorrow night.

But the oldster's mirth died before anyone else's. "How many power blasters do you think it would take to get people like the girls we saw the other night out of their indenture-hood?"

The water slaves. The oldster had been mentioning them off and on. It didn't take a vampire to sense that the sight of them had profoundly unsettled the old man, maybe because he felt shut into such a corner himself lately, with being driven out of the New Badlands. He felt caught and leashed, though he still had the ability to run.

And then there was the fact that Zel would've been just as furious about those slaves. Perhaps the oldster felt doubly offended for her sake.

Pucci's voice was mild when he said, "Maybe someday, oldster. Maybe someday."

Gabriel lifted an eyebrow in surprise, but Hana just smiled, her eyes still closed. It was as if she'd known Pucci had a non-asshole side and she'd just been waiting for him to show it. But, of course, Pucci was just ornery enough to reveal it right before they embarked on what could be a suicide run.

The big guy wasn't done talking. "I know I've harped on this before, but there's just one thing I can't reconcile myself with when it comes to our plan. Jo couldn't tell us for sure that there're Shredders providing outside security, since she created weapons only for the inside employees. But if Shredders *are* out there and they're using weapons that differ from what Jo provided for the others, they might *not* have high-tech gadgets that'll be affected by a power blaster. They might still be able to shoot us up with whatever yippee-yo-ki-yay warfare items they have. Gabriel, you told us about that chest puncher Stamp almost used on you. We saw it ourselves, and it's clearly hand-cranked. It used to be said that Shredders were proficient with blades, too."

"Then we'll fight them as nature intended."

They were all hanging on his every word, and Gabriel realized that he'd missed feeling looked up to. Respect did something to a man, and it didn't always come to a guy because he had a set of fangs.

Could he remember that the next time he was too close to Mariah? The next time blood called to him?

He was already unsure enough when he caught scent of her on a hint of breeze. Among the dirt and musk of her, he recognized the sweet, clean scent of the dry shampoo the group had traded some of Mariah's water for.

Head down, Gabriel contained himself, then talked so he wouldn't have to think about her. "If I hadn't been so set on proving to Stamp that I wasn't a vampire, he would've been an easier fight for me. But I was protecting you all, and I didn't want him to know that you'd been harboring a monster, so I hid my powers. And I almost got him in the end, too." He nodded. "Shredders are trained well and they're vicious, but never forget that they're flawed."

The oldster ruffled Chaplin's fur and the dog rolled over, begging to be petted on his belly. "Stamp hasn't harassed us for a while, so that goes to show that he has his weak spots—in fact, he might've lost us altogether."

"From your mouth to fate's ears," Pucci said. "The last thing we need to be worrying about right now is handling that little boy during our bigger task."

"The little boy packs a punch," the oldster said. "Sammy would testify to that."

Everyone but Gabriel sighed. For them, it was automatic, a human attribute, and the fact that he didn't do it naturally only reminded him that he wasn't nearly as human as the were-creatures. Still, he felt the heaviness of Sammy's memory.

But maybe that was only because Gabriel was borrowing the emotion from Mariah and their connection.

Pucci said, "Sammy could've made that power blaster for us. He could've been just as much a part of our activities if Stamp hadn't wasted him."

Anger roughened his voice, as if, like Pucci's decent side, the emotion had finally decided to show itself tonight.

Hana opened her eyes. "He and Zel will be with us, in some way." She touched the travel necklace that Mariah had given back to her. Its pointed pendant gleamed just under her robes.

Taraline's voice came from behind them. Gabriel had almost forgotten she was there. Maybe he was getting used to the smell.

"The dead are never really gone," she said in that husky tone. "What they've done for us stays behind. All we can do is remember them and thank them the best we can."

Gabriel thought of what he'd seen in the necropolis. Things like the arms, legs, and faces sticking out of the walls. The water that'd been sacrificed to them.

"Those people back in your necropolis," he said. "You were honoring them?"

"Their remains are relics for the necropolitans," she said. "They're reminders of people who gave themselves up for others when a predator animal would breach our gates or when a healthy would come inside to rob valuables from the graves. The relics gave us hope just by being there."

The oldster raised his hand, as if he were holding a glass in a toast. "Then here's to Sammy and Zel, our mental relics."

"Sammy and Zel," the rest of the community said together.

On that note—one that didn't leave much else to say—Pucci paused, then went inside the cave. Hana and the oldster followed, intending to sleep until waking before the next sunset. Even Taraline left Gabriel and Mariah standing alone under the hub above.

Near the cave entrance, Chaplin paced. Mariah went to him, then bent to run her hand over his brown coat. As always, something vised Gabriel's chest as he watched them.

"Don't be nervous, boy," she whispered.

I want to take watch, Mariah, the dog said, also opening his thoughts to Gabriel. *Just for my peace of mind.*

"I wish you'd get some more sleep instead," Mariah said. "You're gonna need it. We all will."

I napped already. You get going, now.

She kissed her dog on the crown of his head, and he sat where Pucci had been standing, looking up at the hub.

When Mariah rose to her full height again, she found Gabriel watching her, and she smiled at him. He got snagged in it, just as he'd been doing more and more lately, as if it were a web that he couldn't find his way out of.

This mission was redemption for her, and it was addictive to him, too. Maybe their quest was even really a cure for her in itself, and having a higher purpose would somehow save them all if they kept going, hub after hub, asylum after asylum.

Trouble was, as Mariah got better, Gabriel seemed to be getting worse, and that shouldn't have been the case if their link truly worked. Shouldn't he be getting some peace from her these days if having hope and purpose tamed her?

"I guess this is where I say good night?" she asked, but she didn't go anywhere.

"We should probably talk while we have the chance."

From the slight flush on her face, he could tell she knew that he was thinking about the night in the herb house and all the apologies that still had to go with it. Her blushing skin whipped him up inside, chewing at him, making him feel those healed claw marks she'd left on his back as if they were as fresh and raw as ever.

"We don't need to do that, Gabriel. Really." She glanced at Chaplin, who was still standing near the entrance, his ears flicking, as if tuning in to every little sound.

"If you're worried about the dog," he said, "I wouldn't. He's listening for Stamp."

The canine made a sound as if he were clearing his throat.

Mariah laughed slightly. "Don't underestimate his ability to multitask. Besides, he already knows about us. He could sense it on me from the second he saw me."

Durn Intel Dogs.

As if the canine were satisfied with the direction of the conversation, Chaplin lifted his chin, then trotted away, bounding up a few boulders to higher ground, where he disappeared behind a rock.

Gabriel rested his hands on his hips, not sure how to go about wading through these sexual-emotional weeds that kept cropping up between him and Mariah. "I regret my loss of propriety."

"It's best to regret it." She swallowed. "I want you to be better, not worse, and round me, you can't help being the latter. I used to be like that, Gabriel, until I decided there was something besides dead ends for me."

The link between them vibrated, as if it were remembering how she'd kissed him, the tingles and thrills she'd planted in him just by doing the simplest things.

As the breeze carried her scent to him once again, something turned over inside Gabriel.

He was a vampire. A hunted creature. A monster. And if he was to be tracked down for it, wasn't it good that his worst side was coming out? Wasn't that the only way he'd survive in a world that seemed to get worse by the year?

The visceral hum of Mariah's vital signs sang through him—he'd been wrong before about how she sounded, because now he could hear that she was still wilder than Abby, that her song was something that made his blood pump and surge. And he wanted to give in to it. To slake every thirst and craving with her.

Unaware of his turmoil—this attraction to confusion and chaos that made no sense—Mariah braved another smile. "If everything goes well tomorrow night, we won't have to deal with talks like these anymore. I'll improve, and you with me."

Her optimism spun into him, too, but, as she walked into the cave, her hope went with her, fading and fading with every step she took away from him.

18

Stamp

Stamp and Mags stood on top of a building that housed GBVille police headquarters. They were looking down to the plaza below, where the cops watched a lowlord's crew using massive hammers to pound the pavement. Since the thugs were only having fun, the authorities weren't interfering.

"No wonder I left this scene," Stamp said while holding the scent tracker in his hand. He was trying to get a reading from up here. The device had been just about useless for nights now, as if the old were-scorpion man had erased his smell from existence. The only thing that made Stamp think the scrubs were somewhere close was an occasional blip on the screen.

Maybe they'd found a way to block Stamp out most of the way, but that wouldn't stop him from finding them.

Mags had one long leg propped on the building's ledge as she surveyed the lowlord's crew hopping up and down, drugged out of their minds. Like Stamp, she'd dressed in the insipid pants and shirt that hubites favored. When the two of them got back down below, they'd blend as well as they could by affecting the hyperkinetic faces of the distractoids. The only ways they might stand out was in how their eyes were reddened, their breath more labored, from the atmosphere since they hadn't fully acclimated yet.

"Even a short time in the nowheres makes me realize that the hubs are bullshit, John," she said. "Just look at them. Makes me happy that I never swallowed a drug in my life."

Stamp didn't have to tell Mags that the dumber the populace, the easier they were to control. In Shredder training, he'd read old sci-fi literature and seen movies to study the notion.

At first, he'd just told himself that humans could be misguided, that most of them could snap out of it if given the chance. He was human, too, and he wanted to believe there was something worthy about his race, even if they had the propensity to willingly lose all reason and become things like monster sympathizers.

But the more Stamp watched the thugs with the hammers, hooting and hollering and flying in the face of the humanity Stamp had sworn to defend as a Shredder, the more he thought that no one but ex-hubites like Mags and him seemed to get it.

A blip flickered on his scent tracker screen. Then it blipped again, only to disappear before he could get a good read on a location.

Somewhere on the west edge of GBVille . . .

Stamp picked up his bag, which contained small weapons, and walked toward a ladder that would take him and Mags back to the ground. In his eagerness to get going, he reached for her, brushing her wrist.

She startled away from him, and he held up his hand, feeling a weird tingle on his fingertips.

Mags gave him a look that meant she was either angry or kind of pleased. He wasn't certain which it was, but he wasn't about to analyze it.

Just as he was willing his heart rate to a deliberate Shredder-paced crawl, Mags rolled her eyes at him and started down the ladder.

"Let's find our scrubs," she said.

Somehow, he thought she was mocking him.

But it wasn't a Shredder's priority to determine why that'd be, and he went down the ladder, too, on the trail once again.

19

Mariah

As I and my neighbors huddled beneath the outer brick wall of the asylum, I kept glancing up at the dark sky, where the new moon hid. In eleven nights, a full one might rule me again if tonight was a bust.

Gabriel hunched a few yards away, where I could barely detect him with my human sight. Subdued brightness from beyond the walls, where the asylum bled light from its windows, was my main source of illumination.

It showed me how Gabriel remained a few feet from the rest of us, probably because we were all as naked as newborns. Our bareness was necessary because we'd be changing real soon, if everything went according to plan.

As silent and still as always, he watched the top of the wall. He was listening, anticipating sentinels. Shredders.

The rest of us—Chaplin, the oldster, Hana, Pucci—were waiting for *the* signal, which would come in the detonation of a power blaster. Taraline was much farther down the length of the asylum's wall, as near to the hub as possible, and she'd told us what to look for when she unleashed the device.

That we'd definitely know when it hit.

So we counted the seconds, listening for any noises in the building beyond this tall wall . . . or from behind us where anyone might've seen our group edge up the hill or had found our clothing behind a mass of rocks.

The noises never came. Hell, my heartbeats were way louder than anything else. My breathing seemed to dominate, too, because it was so heavy and sharp.

Pucci released a near-frantic whisper. "What if Taraline detonated both blasters already and they just aren't working?"

"Pipe down," the oldster said.

"I'm just—"

Hana said, "You are only nervous, Antonio."

He chuffed. "That's because we're gonna die, and when that happens to a man, he tends to get—"

The oldster must've clapped a hand over Pucci's mouth because he didn't finish.

I turned back to the wall again, then sucked in my laden breath when I found that Gabriel had slid up right next to me. I hadn't heard him or felt him. Then again, I'd all but shut out my perception of our link, focusing instead on my adrenaline.

He put his fingers under my chin, directing me to look into the almost feral shine of his eyes so he wouldn't have to speak out loud. *There's something up there, all right. I can't scent it, but I can hear a hint of it. Something as careful as a Shredder.*

Then he seemed to recall that I wasn't wearing a stitch of clothing, and his gaze flared to a spark of red. He backed away, quiet and smooth.

My pulse flooded me, sending prickling heat over my skin, making me sweaty, my flesh waving with the threat of my change. My heart twisted round in me, thudding with a chipping cadence.

Thank-all Chaplin was on the other side of me, nudging me, as if relating that Gabriel had opened his thoughts to him, too, and we needed to be frosty when it came to Shredders . . . or anything else up there.

What I'd give for Gabriel to be able to fly as a vampire. He could've done a check to see for sure what we might be encountering. . . .

As another heartbeat crashed through me, I realized that

one silver bullet, one slice of a decapitating blade, was all it'd take for my dreams of a better future to die.

Something landed next to me, and I leaned away from it, my skin blasting with change-heat.

When another smack on the ground followed, I realized that the objects were coming from above us, as if someone were peering over the wall and making debris from the brick shift and fall.

I didn't even have a chance to look up, because that was when it came.

An explosion of sorts that altered the atmosphere—a crack that made me close my eyes for a second. I just knew that, round us, batteries were frying, transformers were shutting down, and generators were whining off.

Power, dying.

The light that had filtered upward, just behind the walls—the illumination from the asylum's windows—disappeared, too, leaving us stranded in the dark.

My body pulled at itself, beginning the usual melting and thrusting, hair pricking my skin as my form lengthened, taller, stronger, while my sight expanded with emerging blue, allowing me to see better.

I panted as I looked up again to see a shape flitting away from the top of the wall.

Shredder?

Thoughts jumbled, I quivered, restraining myself from changing all the way. We'd all decided to fight off a full were-turn at first so we could keep our human wits about us, and I pushed back my animal instincts. Our attack depended on smarts for us to detect any and all cures. We might need to talk to other preters as well as the employees, too, and if we let our monsters fully take over, bloodlust might win out, and we'd mindlessly feed instead of doing our best to investigate.

I heard Gabriel hissing beside me, then say, "Go!"

Taking Chaplin by the scruff of the neck and putting him on my back, where he latched onto me, I backed up to gain momentum, then jumped, grabbing onto the jutting bricks of the wall.

Then we climbed and climbed.

It almost felt as if I were removed from my own body,

half-watching myself go to work from a near distance. That meant my monster was coming, and I struggled all the more to stave it off as the others followed us up the wall, in half were-form, too, while Gabriel scrabbled up just ahead of me, faster, lighter. A quicksilver vampire.

He disappeared over the top of the wall, and I bit back a wild howl, dying to get loose.

As we breached the top, Chaplin sprang off me, sailing through the air until he landed on the walkway. I followed, pouncing, then crouching, peering round at the muddled blue-tinged expanse of empty walkway in my half-were vision. It would've been so much clearer if I'd let myself change all the way. My lungs might've even allowed me to breathe better, too.

The others finally made it up, half-monsters, half-humans with their eyes glowing, wide and alert. They still had the features of people, but with the hint of animals: the oldster with his flesh hardened to semishell consistency, his tail beginning to emerge, his hands half-pincered while other appendages emerged from his sides; Hana, who bounded off the wall in a stiff-legged jump to all four of her feet, leaping about, her skin covered by dark, gray-brown hair with white patches, her large mule deer ears moving constantly to catch sounds; Pucci and his huge, lethally tipped antlers and tannish brown hide.

Like Gabriel and Chaplin, we sniffed. Besides the lowlord bonfire smoke seething off the hub, there was a sharper burning smell—the aroma of cooked hardware. I thought the air even felt a bit warmer, with all the frying and destruction.

Then we were off, canvassing the walkway. My partly heightened hearing picked up the yells coming from the darkness to the right, where the asylum squatted.

Men bellowing about the lights and generators and . . .

Monsters?

The information Jo had gotten us had mentioned force field–protected cages. . . .

Again, my monster prodded me to succumb to it all the way, but I got to all fours and loped along the walkway instead, knowing the stolen blueprints by heart, knowing the most likely place for a cure would be in the labs at the center of the asylum, beyond the cell blocks.

We were all moving right along when Gabriel blurred ahead

of me, then stopped, sticking out his arm and winding it round my waist to yank me back. Then he blurred over to the oldster, Pucci and Hana and Chaplin, stopping them, too, and I got to my four feet, ready to attack whatever he'd sensed.

Didn't take long for me to see our newest problem.

Four scentless . . . things . . . stood about twenty yards down the walkway. Even during this split second of witnessing them, I knew they weren't Shredders—at least, not like Stamp.

"Fuck," Pucci muttered out of his elklike mouth with its already-sharpened teeth. He could've articulated more in his half-form, but not in the face of this situation.

"Angels?" Hana said, as if profoundly fearful of these sentinels.

My hair bristled as I faced the shapes, who really were like angels dressed in white, with hair so light it glowed in my near-preter vision. Two of the beings boasted long curls; two had short, cherubic hair. All of them had big clear eyes, reminding me of some Japanese dolls my father had kept in his collection—little darling toys with pointed chins and delicate noses.

But these darlings had what looked to be dark wings at their backs. It was only after a second that I realized they were wearing chest punchers, which would clamp onto a preter—especially a vampire—and split open its chest, then extract its heart before destroying the organ.

In my half-were sight, I could've sworn the sentinels also had a symbol burned into their foreheads. It looked like the peace sign.

I didn't have time to confirm this, because, without warning, something rushed at me and the group, banging into us.

I tumbled over the ground, more surprised than hurt as I hit the wall alongside Chaplin.

What had hit us? I hadn't seen anything coming. . . .

My dog barked low to me. *Mind powers. These things are more than Shredders.* . . .

Like the rest of the group, I sprang back to my feet, ready to go at them, but I didn't see the sentinels anywhere now.

Where'd they gone?

Onto one of the towers nearby?

Into thin air . . . ?

Chaplin bumped into me. *You're the strongest were. You've still got to go in, even if the rest of us don't make it.*

"He's right." Gabriel came to the front of me. "Whatever these things are, they're using psychokinesis."

"But are they Shredders?" Pucci garbled out of his half-elk mouth just before grinding his teeth, agitated. I could tell he was eager to go full animal, too.

The half-scorpion oldster ducked as Pucci swung round his antlers while scanning for the sentinels.

Hana said, "Shredders or not, one of us has to make it inside."

There wasn't any time to plan, no time to debate. As my body thudded, I pressed back my urges, needing my mind far more than a good, raw meal. . . .

I looked at Gabriel, who'd gone entirely vampire, with exposed fangs, wide red eyes, the works. For a moment, he opened up his gaze and I fell in, hearing his thoughts.

Go for the asylum with Chaplin, he mind-said. *That leaves four of us to hold off these four guards. If we don't catch up to you, do what you have to and we'll meet you at the rendezvous point.*

I let him read me. *But you wouldn't have to be invited into a public place like an asylum, right? You can come, too—*

He knew that I didn't want to leave him behind, so he took desperate measures.

He showed me thoughts of Abby, knowing that it'd be the cruelest sight imaginable. Knowing that when I'd killed her, I'd done it because I'd had to defend my status and existence against a werewolf who'd challenged me.

Blond, beautiful Abby . . . just as *he'd* seen her.

Jealousy throttled me, the memory of her blood covering me and making my skin bubble.

Making me remember why I needed a cure.

And it got even worse as I saw the sentinels suddenly reappear on the walkway behind Gabriel, just where they'd been standing only minutes before. It was as if they'd come out of nowhere . . . or maybe they'd just hidden themselves against the pale expanse of the walkway.

Gabriel saw the look on my half-human face and, as if he wanted to avoid the devastation in me—or as if he wanted to forget Abby—he whipped round, then zoomed toward the sentinels.

It tore apart the pain of the connection between us, and I gasped.

Everyone but me changed into their full were-forms—teeth lengthening, flashing; bodies exploding into wider, more lethal states—then charged ahead to back up Gabriel, rushing the sentinels. Suddenly my friends flew backward, hitting that psychokinetic wall. But the next second, they were right back up again, engaging the angel-beings, getting closer and closer to them with every preter-fueled rush forward.

Then Gabriel changed strategy, beginning to speed round the angel-beings, as if trying to confuse them. The distraction allowed Pucci to barge forward first, slashing out with his antlers just before kicking, trying to stomp one of his foes to death. Hana faked out her own sentinel and pummeled at it with her front hooves. The oldster attempted to crush his prey with his pincers and sting it with his tail.

The change jabbed within me, but I didn't let myself lose my own control—I had to think.

No.

I had to *go.*

I picked up Chaplin, then darted ahead.

Faster . . .

Faster—

Just as I got to the group, I sprang into the air, over their heads, landing on the other side, hoping there weren't any more sentinels to block me.

Nothing.

I zipped ahead to where the asylum door gate stood, wondering if it would be locked, even without the power on. . . .

Chaplin stiffened in my arms, expecting impact as I accelerated. Ten feet away, I jumped and spun so my back would take the brunt of the contact, and—

Bam!

A fireworks display burst through my head and limbs, and I wasn't sure if it was because my body was falling to pieces or because I'd made it through and was only momentarily stunned.

When I felt myself rolling over the ground, I realized that I was still intact.

Panting, I crouched, shaking my head out, what fur I had at this half-stage ruffling. The gates yawned behind me, blasted open from the force of my body, and, next to them, men aimed guns, screaming in Text.

"WTF is tht?"

"Git it!"

Then they were trying to fire, but they must've been using weapons that'd been knocked out by the power blaster. The darkness had to affect them, too, making them flail with no rhyme or reason.

Chaplin laugh-barked, like he was mocking them.

I didn't need my smart-ass dog to start something, so I swatted him on the butt and jetted off, toward a set of doors where a line of white-coated men blocked the entrance.

I don't know what they processed when they heard me coming. There was a wan light coming from their ungloved arms—their fritzed computer screens—but that was all they had to go by except for the subdued glow of my eyes.

A couple of employees weenied out, flattening themselves to the ground. A few of them targeted taserwhips at me, but those didn't work, either.

Chaplin and I hurdled them, but I was faster than my dog, and I flew at the doors, willing to take the hard knock of hitting the barriers first.

But I didn't even break them because their so-called secure locks had been victims of the power blaster, too.

After skidding on the ground, Chaplin and I were back up, pounding ahead like kamikazes.

20

Gabriel

Gabriel knew that Mariah had made it inside the asylum only because he didn't feel her anymore.

The brick walls and distance blocked their link, and the new emptiness felt like a hole that'd been scooped out of him. But the emptiness only made his vampire that much meaner. It left room for hunger.

As one of the angels, a boy with a peace sign burned into his forehead, readied himself to spring, appetite munched on Gabriel. Out of the corner of his red vision, he saw three of the other sentinels engaging Hana, Pucci, and the oldster; the kids had gotten out some blades and the steel was sparking against the were-mammals' hooves and the oldster's emerging exoskeleton.

Gabriel leveled a glare at his own challenger. He doubted these kids were anything more than human, just like the first version of Shredders that the government had obviously discarded for this next generation. But *these* fighters were psychically enhanced. Still, Gabriel hadn't felt any of them reach into his thoughts. These Shredders were only mind movers, not readers, and they weren't from any heaven, either.

You're no angel, he thought as he stared at the boy, who wisely avoided Gabriel's gaze, glaring instead at the space between his eyes.

Angels. Gabriel had once believed in them, but seeing this boy here . . . It made him think that sentinels were only a cheap imitation if there was a real thing.

As expected, the boy blasted out at Gabriel with his mind. Prepared as Gabriel had been, it still made him stumble back a couple of steps before he regrouped, then launched himself at the angel, fangs and claws ready to rip.

But the sentinel had already reached back for his chest puncher, whipping it forward and targeting.

Mariah, Gabriel thought during that split second between now and when the angel would pull the trigger. Mariah was in that asylum, alone with Chaplin, needing Gabriel to keep these sentinels occupied.

Unless there were more in the asylum . . .

Gabriel kicked the chest puncher so hard that it flipped out of the sentinel's hands, hanging in the air for what seemed like an endless second—one in which the angel boy focused his wide gaze on the weapon.

Before the boy could mentally manipulate the puncher back into his hands, Gabriel used his lightning speed to snatch it and aim at the boy's chest.

All Gabriel saw before he pulled the trigger was the peace symbol on the boy's forehead.

There was a kicking metallic sound, then the puncher flying out, clamping to the boy's chest, pulling him open, digging into him and extracting his heart in a splash of blood and cartilage, then a burst of flame as the puncher decimated his heart.

Gabriel tossed the chest puncher away and bared his fangs at all the others, who'd halted their fighting during the sudden conflagration. His were-friends were even gaping at him, just like the sentinels, looking as if he were their worst fear.

Red streaked the angels' white clothing. Blood. And even through the burning stenches, it wafted to Gabriel like smoke from a drug. He wanted some, needed to taste it.

The sentinels must've seen the raging appetite claim him, because, all together, they used their minds to blast out at him.

Gabriel was hurled backward, landing on his ass.

He laughed. He wasn't sure why. He just knew that no one else was laughing with him.

Then he smelled the blood, and he stood, slowly, his hunger screaming.

Blood. All he wanted was the water from these sentinels, who would carve him up just as surely as Stamp had intended to. And now that Gabriel really thought about it, there was *nothing* wrong with spilling blood. All his codes, his rules about overcoming his vampire . . .

They were nothing when the world really came at you.

He saw it all so clearly now. And he could also see that the remaining angels were reaching behind them to pull out their chest punchers. It was fascinating how they moved as one, as if they all knew they were about to die and instinctively agreed that they had to do something about it.

The oldster, who was all monster except for the facial details that remained and marked him as a man trapped under a hard face, struck out with his tail, stinging a girl angel, lifting her off the ground as she yelled and dropped her chest puncher while jerking because of the poison that'd been plunged into her. At the same time, Hana turned around, then flipped onto her front hooves to kick back with her rear legs at the second angel girl. Pucci slashed at his boy with those huge, pointed antlers.

Hana's girl flew backward with the thrust of the were–mule deer's kick, and Gabriel smelled the blood before the body got to him. Hissing, he jumped up, catching the angel girl in his mouth and falling to the ground where he pinned her. He ripped out her throat and gulped down her blood.

Blood.

Such good blood—different blood, with a tinge of something sweet and familiar—and he was drinking it for such good reason.

Finally a good enough reason . . .

As he gorged, he heard the were-creatures behind him, taking care of the final sentinel. Hana kicked again, sending the boy toward Gabriel.

More . . . blood . . .

Without lifting his head from the girl, he reached out, catching the angel and slamming him down right next to the girl he still fed from.

With just one twist, Gabriel broke the boy's neck.

He kept drinking, the girl's blood nearly gagging him because he was taking so much in. It made him just as drunk as he used to get as a human, when he'd nullified the pain of losing his family to the mosquito epidemic with booze. But this was different. Unlike the alcohol, this made him stronger, not weaker.

Mariah was right, he thought as he gulped and gulped. She'd had the right idea all along about being a monster.

He could hear the others panting around him as he kept drinking, sucking, loving every gush. And when he finally couldn't take in any more, he looked up, finding the were-creatures with their heads cocked.

Animals every one of them.

Hana bent to the boy with the broken neck, sniffing at him. It was the full were-creature inside her, not the mule deer, that wanted blood. Pucci got down beside her, sniffing, too.

Even the oldster dipped a pincer in the blood.

As the were-creatures tested the red, then dove into their prey, Gabriel felt something tremble inside him—a recognition.

He let his food roll off his lap.

But just as he was wondering what'd just happened, he heard the barking of dogs.

By the time he got to his feet, his gaze was the thickest of reds, and he could barely see through it to a pack of beastly, big, yellow-eyed canines as they sprinted along the walkway.

Logic screamed at Gabriel. *Get them before they get to Mariah.*

As if in a waking dream, he ran at the dogs, leaving the others behind. The beasts caught air as they jumped at him, teeth bared, and Gabriel punched through their chests, one by one, throwing each bad guy away as he went to the next.

When he was done, he stood there, listening for any more.

But there was nothing, unless you counted the continued panting of the Badlanders.

Gabriel turned to them, only to find them still cocking their heads, their hooves and pincers shining with liquid. Unlike him, they were in control, as if they hadn't expected to react any other way tonight. They'd even disposed of the bodies by throwing them over the wall.

He didn't feel like the savior who'd helped them back in the nowheres. He was them.

One by one, the Badlanders stood and, as if they'd only taken part in what was natural, sped off down the wall path, securing it against any other threats while leaving Gabriel behind to catch up.

21

Mariah

Once I was inside the depths of the asylum, a barrage of sensation had attacked my half-turned were-facilities.

The darkness dotted by the pale, blank, nearly useless glows from arm screens; whimpers and panicked words from confused men and women all round me as they grasped at the walls, trying to find their way; the burned hardware stench lying just below fright-induced sweat that covered delicious skin.

Juices rushed my mouth, and I panted.

Food. Blood. Hungry, always hungry.

Chaplin nipped me on the leg. *Cure,* he said. *This may be your only chance for one.*

I started repeating it all in my mind. *Cure. Go get it. . . .*

I mentally accessed our blueprints of the asylum. I'd run through them a million times in my mind, and Chaplin had them even more down pat. He led me past the whimpering workers sitting against the walls, some of them trying to speak into comm units and arm computers; past the deadened cameras that weren't functional enough to record us; past unlocked doors and offices and straight into the first cell block.

The lab was supposed to be just beyond.

I could see everything as blurs, and I strained, wanting a better view. But my patience paid off when I saw the first monster in its cell, where emergency bars—some coated with silver, some barbed—had obviously crashed down to take the place of the former laser fields.

A preter with tentacles was spurting some waterlike stuff out, as if to test those barriers, and the liquid splatted into the corridor. The creature hadn't been fast enough to escape before the bars had crashed down, but there was a door with a lock in each barricade. The creature raised its tentacles, as if about ready to stick one of its wavy fingers in to pick that lock.

I glanced across the way at another stunned monster, and this one had gotten outside the bars before they'd fallen, although it was refusing to leave. The only way I could describe it was as one of those stone fertility statues you'd see in a book about ancient cultures. A tall, rotund creature with pendulous breasts and a featureless face, just standing in the corridor as if it didn't know which way to go now that it'd been sprung. Another monster was just behind it, but Chaplin barked, consuming my attention, and I translated the best I could through teeth that were lengthening a bit more every minute.

"You're free," I said to the stone thing. "Run!"

But it just kept hesitating, and, once again, I saw why humans had never needed to deal with massive monster attacks.

Maybe the stone creature couldn't talk without a mouth—at least not in any way I could understand—so I went to the monster behind it, a half-man/half-serpent. A chimera?

He uncoiled himself from behind the stone thing. I think he'd been trying to push his buddy forward, and he'd just given up on trying to move it.

"Could you come with me to the lab to find cures for werecreatures?" I asked, way too politely. I had no idea where the civility had even come from.

The chimera seemed to have some dignity, with his beard and steady glowing gaze. "Cures? Surely you jest. Here, they study us, not help us. If there's a cure, I failed to recognize it."

Then he reared back on his coiled tail. I got the hell out of the way as he shot down the corridor, landing next to Chaplin, who dodged, too, his hair standing on end.

The man-serpent roared, then pounced to other monsters who had begun to mill about. "Let's go!"

There was a whispering sound nearby, and I saw the reason for it. A woman—I knew she was a doctor or high-level person because she was talking to herself in Old American—cowered against the wall, dressed in a full-bodied suit with a mask hanging down from her head. She must've seen my glowing eyes, because she raised her taserwhip.

I smacked it away from her. "Cure. You're going to take me to that lab of yours and show me where I can find cures for werewolves, vampires, and dymorrdia." I didn't want to waste time riffling through every bottle, test tube, or computer file that Jo hadn't had access to.

"No cures," she said, voice shaking. "Not for any of you."

Chaplin made a "hmm" sound. *I think she's telling the truth.*

The dog was no slouch in judging people, so I took him at his word.

I cuffed the woman across the face. I'd meant to do it gently, just to get her out of her funk, but I left a deep scratch, and she cried out. The scent of blood made my head spin, but I hung on.

No dummy, she obviously knew that I'd kill her if she didn't level with me. Good thing bad guys were usually cowards when called out.

She pointed down the corridor. "No cures, but . . . last cell . . . Subject 562 . . . we questioned it a lot . . . experiments. Other asylums said it has important blood . . . most powerful . . . could help—?"

And she passed out from the fear of me. I suppose I would've, too, back in the day.

Chaplin was already running to where the employee had indicated, and I wasn't far behind. My pulse took everything over—my near-blue sight, my chest, my mind—but I didn't change. Not now.

When Chaplin got to the barred cell, he scuttled backward, as if he didn't like what he saw. That should've given me a clue, because when I got there, even I almost backtracked.

It wasn't because of Subject 562's hideousness. Not at all. Its pale arms were marred from fresh scratches, but what was more disturbing was its . . . stillness. Only Gabriel had exhibited this type of utter, eerie tranquillity during his worst vampire moments, and this preter could give off that kind of balefulness even with its back turned.

It was facing a corner, as if it didn't realize what was happening outside the cell. But, somehow, I knew that it had a bead on every little thing that was occurring.

Most powerful, the employee had said.

Was 562 an old were-creature or vampire? Would it know history and, perhaps, a location or formula for a cure outside this asylum? Was that why the employee had directed me to it?

I looked at the silver coating the bars, then at Subject 562. "We're not here to hurt you—we're getting you out."

It didn't move except for a slight tilt of the head, as if it recognized my warped voice.

But it couldn't have.

Chaplin got right behind me and pushed.

As adrenaline cut through me, I hoped my human side would hold long enough for me to articulate what needed to be said. "A group of us—we need some help and that's why we're here. We're looking for cures."

Slowly, the creature turned its head, almost as if it didn't have neck muscles. Its long silver hair hung over its face, but I could see two slits of red through the strands, just like Gabriel's own eyes when he was worked up.

Vampire?

But there was a hint of softness in that gaze, even though it burned through the hair. Again, I almost thought it knew me.

"Please. Would you come with us to the lab, show us where we should look? Or maybe you could give us information. Either way, we don't have much time—"

Subject 562 moved so quickly that I didn't get out the rest of my sentence.

As if it had no bones, it just sort of dart-slumped its way to the opposite corner of the cell.

I heard barking from somewhere in the asylum, and I turned to Chaplin.

"Intel Dogs?"

No, he said. *From the sound of them, these are government-issue beast dogs. They're just as strong but not as smart. They don't have the capacity to rebel as the Intels started to.*

So the asylum workers were fighting back, leveling their

own playing field with weapons that hadn't been affected by the power blaster.

Time had run out.

Subject 562 was looking up at the ceiling now, and Chaplin seemed to understand the gesture.

He said, *Who knows when the government will know something has happened here? They'll send a Dactyl if we don't get out soon.*

Dactyl drone planes had been in use before the world had changed. The government could've built up their stocks again since China had started manufacturing them in bulk. The craft had bombs, lasers, and blades that could pinpoint a target on the ground from miles away. It was even quiet enough to assassinate an unknowing entity from ten feet yonder. Hell, it could get here from outside the range of our power blaster real fast, and because of that, it'd be fully functional.

"Will you come?" I asked Subject 562, not wanting to kidnap the monster, even if I could get past that silver on those bars. But if I had to, I would. It seemed like the only option I had.

The barking got louder, and Chaplin began to pace. He was smarter than the beast dogs, but we'd be outnumbered. And what if there were more of those sentinels, too?

I heard howls and preterlike screams from the bowels of the asylum. Monsters versus sentinels and beast dogs? But there were human yells, too. Death keens.

Subject 562 hadn't answered my question. It just kept staring at me with those slit eyes as my body began to lose control, unable to hold off any longer, my bones and muscles shifting, making me even taller, my wolf hair longer.

God-all, here I went. . . .

As I writhed with pain, still fighting for as long as I could, 562 suddenly just sped forward, blasting through the door in the bars. The entire bank clanked to the floor, and without paying much attention to the whimpering the creature was making—because of the silver?—I grabbed it under one arm and Chaplin under the other, finally bursting into my full form.

Mindless now, I faintly remember zooming out of the cell, out of the asylum, over the wall and down the hill, far away out of the hub to the planned meeting place where my friends would hopefully be, too.

Miles and miles away.

By the time we arrived at the old mine shaft that Taraline had recommended—a spot that was no more than a hole in the side of a rock-strewn hill—my bloodlust had eased and I'd gone back to half-were thinking mode. Maybe the asylum hadn't housed a cure, but 562 might be a mother lode of information instead, and I needed to question it.

After entering through a tunnel littered with jagged rocks, clawed pieces of old track, and a rusty pipeline, we came to a cold, larger area where we'd already planted solar-powered lanterns, which had been encased in Faraday cages that were supposed to have protected them if the power blast got this far. Taraline's clothing hung round, too, side by side with tawnyvale herb, just in case they really did throw off any scent trackers.

I set 562 on the ground. My half-were sight worked well enough for me to extract a lantern and fire it up to life. It gave light to the specks of aquamarine and smoky quartz crystals embedded in the walls, although 562's red eyes glowed even brighter, like those monsters in the closet that we used to worry about when we were children, not knowing we should've been even *more* afraid.

Chaplin watched our guest while I willed myself back to full-human form, put on my spare set of clothing against the chilliness, then set to rubbing my aching arms and legs. My joints and muscles were killing me from all the back-and-forth and holding back.

I went to 562 and offered it the last drops from my canteen. The creature didn't move, so I drank what I could.

Chaplin hadn't taken his gaze off the creature, and his hair was still standing on end. He barked at 562, just to show it who was boss, and the creature's eyes got real red.

Then it opened the biggest mouth I'd seen in my life, lined by more fangs than any monster had *ever* possessed.

My tired, yet alert body started to burst into change again, but when 562 sprang at Chaplin, the only thing I could do was howl.

22

Gabriel

Gabriel and the others were on their way back when he heard Mariah's scream-howl from a couple miles away.

Her terror made him speed up, his sight going even redder as he left the others behind while zooming to the rendezvous place under the cover of every boulder and tree he could find.

Why would she be screaming this far away from the asylum?

If she was dying, he'd never be able to apologize for forcing thoughts of Abby on her during the attack. He'd never be able to say a lot of things. . . .

The miles passed in a flicker, and he came upon the mine shaft, where there were grunts, sounds of a struggle—

He barged inside. Mariah, in half-wolf form, fighting, pulling back on the neck of a thing that he couldn't even begin to describe except for the medical gown it was wearing, the long silver hair that covered its face, plus . . .

He barely had time to register the canine vibes that he intuited whenever he was around a dog or a werewolf as the creature reared up its head at his entrance.

The mouth—the teeth . . .

He realized that Chaplin was under the thing, flashing out

with his paws and biting at it, keeping the creature at a distance with nothing but Intel Dog strength and determination.

The monster flashed its teeth at Chaplin, and Gabriel dove in, crashing against the creature and slamming it against the rock wall.

The wall shook, releasing a tiny shower of stone and dirt in front of the many saberlike teeth that gleamed right in front of Gabriel's face. The creature hissed, its teeth jutting out even more, like knife blades coming out during a street fight.

But then, just for a second, it stopped, tilting its head, as if it knew exactly who Gabriel was.

He turned on the sway in his voice. "Calm . . . calm down . . . don't attack . . . *just sit still*."

The creature slowly closed its mouth, mostly out of curiosity, it seemed, and, through its long, thin silver hair, Gabriel could see its red eyes.

But as Gabriel continued swaying the creature, he realized that those eyes held intelligence. Questions. And something else he wasn't sure of except for the strange sense of familiarity.

Without quite knowing why, Gabriel backed off. Then he heard Mariah's hollow half-wolf panting just behind him. He didn't have to look to know that she'd stopped herself from changing all the way.

She was getting pretty good at that.

Chaplin was ready to attack the creature, but the thing had already sat down, crossed its legs yoga-style, neatly smoothing its medical gown over its knees. It had scratches on its pale arms and, for some reason, that spooked Gabriel.

"I don't know what happened," Mariah said, her voice warped. "It went crazy."

Chaplin kept glaring at it while opening his mind to Gabriel. *I think 562 only wanted me to know that it's not afraid. I have a feeling it would have killed us outright if it'd wanted to.*

Couldn't the creature talk for itself? As it made like a Buddha and just sat there, Gabriel had to wonder.

Now Mariah's voice seemed way more human. "Your sway, Gabriel. It got to 562 like a charm. We brought him or her with us from the asylum, but that's a long story."

Gabriel wasn't so sure if it'd been his sway or if this 562

thing had just decided to show that it wouldn't take any shit, then backed off, point made, just as Chaplin had said. Any way about it, Gabriel wasn't the one with the upper hand here, so he kept tabs on the lotus-positioned monster.

"Why do you call it 562?" he asked, almost as if it weren't even there.

Chaplin answered. *That's what the employee at the asylum called it. Subject 562.*

Mariah whimpered as she began the full change back to human form. He didn't want to think about her, but her scent . . . her proximity . . .

Hunger.

Yet she wasn't his next meal. She was much . . . more than that. Shit, at the asylum, after Gabriel had faced the beast dogs and the bloodlust had been strong in him, he'd almost forgotten about why he was there. For her. For their connection. It'd only been after the Badlanders had scoured the outside walls for more angel-Shredders and failed to find any that they'd crept toward the asylum doors. There, he'd overheard from some panicked employees that a few of their staff had left the asylum and made a run out of the hub, toward an emergency comm station miles away. It'd brought Gabriel back to rights.

The GBVille humans would be trying to call on reinforcements, and even as the sound of beast dogs echoed in the asylum while the Badlanders had prepared to go inside, Gabriel hadn't sensed Mariah anywhere.

He'd known that she'd already left.

Here and now, they were still watching 562 with a keen eye when he realized that Hana, Pucci, and the oldster had arrived, lingering far back as they, too, checked out their guest. From their beast breathing, Gabriel could tell they hadn't switched back to human form yet. Why would they, with 562 sitting there so weirdlike?

The thing had come out of its trance long enough to notice the other were-creatures. Gabriel heard it whimper in greeting, then pant, before it went back to staring at the ground.

It was almost as if . . .

No, it couldn't be. But Gabriel couldn't stop thinking that this 562 was somehow on comfortable terms with the other Badlanders, too.

He kept his hands curved at his sides, though he wasn't wearing firearms. "Why did you bring it back here, Mariah?"

"Because . . ." Her voice was human again, and he could hear . . . *feel* . . . the post-change agony in it. "Because the only person and monster I talked to in the asylum said there wasn't a cure on the premises. But an employee told me 562 is powerful, so I went to it. I thought I'd find out more information from 562, because . . ."

"Because what?"

She came forward, into his line of sight, clutching her torn clothing around her. "I couldn't leave that place without anything to show for it."

Chaplin nodded while never taking his sight off 562, who, in Gabriel's mind, resembled a monument to imminent danger. He could hear its vital signs, which were so slow that they barely even existed.

What kind of creature was it? It had eyes like a vampire, teeth like a werewolf, the body and skin of a human, and the sounds of something he'd never heard before, though they harkened back to the familiar wild cadence of a were-creature.

Now that matters were less dicey, he could hear the others shifting back to their human forms, then shuffling around for their clothing, groaning every so often at their aches.

The oldster, who was revitalized by the experience rather than tired by it, said, "I'll assume that those beast dogs persuaded you and Chaplin to get out of the asylum, Mariah. We beat down a few of their butts near the wall, too."

Hana wasn't quite as sprightly. "I would not be surprised if the surviving ones came for us within a few days by tracking our scents."

Chaplin barked and growled, and Mariah translated.

"If they do, Chaplin's going to hear and smell them long before they get here. But we've used tawnyvale in here, so we just might fool their noses."

The oldster sighed, and Gabriel thought that it might be because, like all of them, he hated the idea of having to run away from yet another shelter.

The others had donned their clothes by now, and the oldster was wearing a pair of Hana's extra robes; they'd destroyed all his other clothing back at the GBVille cave.

All of them stayed in back of the vigilant Chaplin as the old man said, "Just so long as more angels don't come with those beast dogs, I think we can take the heat."

The sentinels. Idly, Gabriel glanced at 562, seeing that its hair-filtered eyes were focused on him.

Its gaze caught his and, for an inexplicable moment, something like an image combined with thought flashed over Gabriel's consciousness: the sentinels, white and graceful as they attacked with those peace signs branded into their foreheads.

Then he heard words, though they hardly sounded like words at all. More like . . . hauntings.

Witches. The specterlike sounds whispered in his head. *That is what the other monsters called the new Shredders who kept us inside the asylum.*

Gabriel took himself out of his daze just in time to see that 562 was staring at the ground as if it'd never been doing anything else.

Something had gone down with this creature, and he wasn't sure what it'd been about.

"Okay," he said, matter-of-factly. "I just had an experience."

"What?" Pucci asked.

"562. It was sort of . . . talking to me. I heard . . . saw . . ." Gabriel shrugged. "I'm not sure, but our guest may have the ability to communicate mind-to-mind."

"Like a vampire?" Mariah asked. "Were-creatures don't have psychic abilities. Or maybe 562's a demon or . . . Well, let's just say that I saw creatures I never thought existed outside of fiction."

"Whatever it is," Gabriel said, "it was trying to tell me something about those sentinels. 'New Shredders,' it said. 'Witches.' And their job was to keep the preters inside."

Hana's voice lowered. "Witches?"

Had she really been expecting angels? Maybe. The government was so full of hubris that, like the Christian God, Gabriel wouldn't have put it past them to create a version of their own pseudocelestial beings.

Pucci wandered off, laughing to himself. "Because life really needed to get more complicated than it was."

"Whatever they're called," Mariah said, "there were probably more Witches inside the asylum than what we encountered outside. I think they might've been trying to keep the monsters from fleeing. I wonder how successful they were, especially when those weapons Jo designed were rendered useless by the blast."

Weapons that Jo had unknowingly designed to imprison monsters.

Hana asked, "Are these Witch Shredders monsters? If they are, why would the government be employing monsters to kill monsters? Would that not be a conflict of interest if we are so unworthy of their trust in the first place?"

The oldster held up a finger. "Correction. The purpose of a Shredder *used to be* to kill monsters."

"But we're supposedly not a problem now," Gabriel said.

So the government had lied—they knew that certain, select monsters were still around because they had them inside asylums. For what purpose, though?

A swatch of thought came to him before he let it float past.

His maker. Supposedly, she'd been taken by a Shredder, not killed. That was why Gabriel was still a vampire, because she was as alive as could be somewhere. . . . In an asylum?

Mariah's tone was smooth, as if she didn't want to scare 562 with any volume. "Gabriel, when you fought those sentinels, did they exhibit any bloodlust?"

"Nothing aside from an ordinary Shredder." He tried not to recall his own frenzied hunger while fighting. He still couldn't believe he'd acted so out of character. Or too much in it.

"Then if the sentinels didn't have bloodlust," she continued, "they wouldn't be your garden-variety monsters or water robbers."

Gabriel nodded, seeing where she was going with this. "They were only humans with enhanced mind skills. One mark of a monster is that it's harder to kill, but the Witches weren't. And they wouldn't be banned like rogue psychics, either, because the Witches weren't doing any intrusive mind-reading as far as I could tell. With mere psychokinesis, they wouldn't be able to dig into any government minds."

He looked at 562. It was slyly checking out the other Badlanders, as if hoping they'd glance over at it again. So far, there hadn't been any takers, but much to Gabriel's vampire chagrin, it caught his gaze another time.

In its mental hold, Gabriel received an image/thought of one of those Witch Shredders lounging in a chair inside what looked to be a sterile government lab.

Turn on . . . turn off, 562's mind relayed to him.

Gabriel took a moment. Was it saying that the Witches were products of the state, and their mental powers could be activated and deactivated? Freakin' warriors who were being programmed?

Stories about how the CIA had experimented with psychic powers had been around for years, even Before. Maybe the government's projects had come to fruition now that they had finances to play around with again.

562 gave him one more thing to gnaw on. *Original Shredders . . . not good enough.*

Shee-it.

Gabriel told the others what he'd just seen and heard from 562, and everyone's gazes slid over to the creature.

Mariah had been right. It *did* know some things of value.

Too brave by far, she moved a little closer to 562, as if either inspecting it or baiting it.

"I wouldn't do that," Gabriel said.

Chaplin barked in agreement, and when Mariah gave her dog a warning look, he took a step back, as if . . .

Chastised? Surprised?

"I won't hurt 562." Mariah wasn't talking to Gabriel or Chaplin as much as she was to the creature. "I only want to express how much help we still need. I want 562 to see it in my gaze."

But the monster didn't look at her. Its red eyes didn't even blink. Gabriel noticed that they never blinked.

Pucci was rolling his shoulders and kneading the back of his neck, as if his antlers had felt extra heavy on his head this time out. "So what do we do with it?"

"First off," Mariah said, "we stop calling 562 an *it.*"

The big man snorted. "I can't tell if this 562 is a he or she. Why don't you pull up its gown to find out, Mariah?"

"Always full of good ideas, Pucci." Mariah tucked a strand of her short red hair behind her ear, then addressed 562, her voice soft, just as if she were talking to a wayward child. "Do you have a real name?"

562 stared at the ground.

Pucci chuckled, then found a spot where he could slump down against the rock wall.

Mariah tried again. "As I said, I'm sorry for taking you out of that asylum. Did you want to stay?"

This time, 562 glanced up, looking straight at Gabriel again. There was no use avoiding its eyes since he wanted to see into the creature's head, anyway.

562's gaze seemed to root right into him, and at the same time, Gabriel heard an emphatic *Wanted to leave* echo through him.

Like before, the sound wasn't really a voice. It was just . . . there.

"Mariah," Gabriel said, "why don't you talk to 562 some more?"

She went right ahead. "Why were you in the asylum?"

The mental connection came again from 562, like vague ghosts flying around the room of Gabriel's mind: He saw dwellings built into mountains, heard the wind moaning through the hills, one of which had an ash tree. He saw and felt the heat from the fires surrounding that tree, saw the people with dirt-smeared faces wearing nothing more than rags and bowing on the dirt.

And they were bowing before 562.

The people rose to their feet, revealing one old woman with a dagger. She walked like someone who'd been sick, and her other arm hung at her side, withered and limp. A desperate gleam filled her eyes as she slashed into her palm, offering her blood to 562, who leaned forward eagerly to suck at the female's wound. 562 was hungry. Blood hungry. And when it was done, a pair of fangs thrust out of 562's mouth while the old woman offered her neck. . . .

562 . . . just a vampire, but unlike any they'd ever seen before?

As if excited about Gabriel's receptiveness, 562 assaulted him with another image/thought: a man with vampire fangs, drinking from 562's extended wrist until letting go, slumping to the ground, looking up with the most peaceful expression on his relaxed face . . .

562 gave Gabriel another: It was bending over a dead woman in a fetid room. A stillborn baby was being taken away to be buried, and the woman's family was pleading with 562 until it finally bit the corpse, something it had never tried before. It took a bit of blood from the body, which made 562 sick, but it carried on for the sake of experimentation and pity for the dead woman. It extended its hand, scratching enough blood out so that drops fell into the corpse's mouth.

Then, a blink from the dead woman. A cry as she sprang up in bed . . .

And another image/thought: 562 alone in the woods, curious about what else it could do. Finding the carcass of what looked to be a rabbit, then biting it, too, feeling ill again as it tasted what was left of the animal's corpse blood. Then, just as with the dead woman, 562 fed the rabbit with its blood. This corpse also came alive, its body shooting out every which way into arms, legs, sickly yellow fur, black eyes with thorn-long lashes, and slabby teeth as it pounced on 562, sniffing wildly for more blood and snorfling it in through its nose. . . .

562 was getting braver, and the next image/thought spiraled into Gabriel, obliterating everything that'd come before.

This one featured the same people he'd seen originally—the vampires—except on a different night.

The same old woman, healthy now, her arm clearly mended through her blood exchange with 562. With gloved hands, she yanked 562's hands behind its back, binding it to that ash tree, whose bark weakened 562. Through its silver hair, it could see clouds rolling over the sky, tumbling away from a full moon.

562's body violently shook, then started to split apart—

With every ounce of strength Gabriel had, he forced his eyes closed, pulling himself out of the image/thoughts because he didn't want to experience what he believed might happen next.

Did it change with a full moon, like were-creatures? But what about those other things it'd created, the strange blood-sniffing animal, the woman risen from the dead. Was 562 all of those, too? Most important, did it have the capacity to bring peace, as Gabriel had seen it do with that male vampire?

It came to Gabriel that 562 hadn't even changed into its full form when he'd seen it attacking Chaplin earlier. Unlike in these image/thoughts, it'd probably learned how to bite back when it felt cornered nowadays.

"Can't you speak to us?" Gabriel asked.

The silver-haired creature continued staring through its hair, eyes oceans of red.

The color reminded Gabriel of bloodlust. Of what he'd committed at that asylum tonight.

Pucci interrupted. "Just let the thing rest. *I'm* gonna be tuckered out for the next few nights with all this changing we did. You all will, too."

"Pipe down," everyone told him.

Gabriel gestured toward 562. "Mariah, you look into its eyes now."

"*Her* eyes," Mariah said softly.

Gabriel couldn't say for certain what 562 might be in any shape or form, but he wasn't about to make an issue out of it.

He guided Mariah in front of 562. Chaplin woofed under his breath, but didn't make a move.

"Show her what you showed me?" Gabriel asked 562.

When he let go of Mariah, she stiffened. But he'd bet it was because she was receiving the image/thoughts, not because he'd stopped touching her.

When 562 ultimately averted its gaze from Mariah, it left her green eyes wide.

"That injured woman with the arm . . ." Mariah said. "She was healed through an exchange. And that vampire man—it looked like he was on cloud nine after taking 562's blood . . ."

"Are you thinking 562's a cure-all?"

Her eyes went glassy. "That employee at the asylum pointed out 562 when I asked for cures for were-creatures, vampires, or dymorrdia."

Hana, the oldster, and Pucci seemed to hold their breaths.

Gabriel hated to break their hearts, but . . . "We didn't see what happened to that male vampire after it took her blood. And just because 562 healed a woman's arm, that doesn't mean anything to us preters. Don't make what it showed us into what you need to see, Mariah."

The oldster said, "But what if Mariah's on to something?"

"I'm saying you all shouldn't get your hopes up," Gabriel said. "We don't know what 562's all about. He or she might be sending false images . . ."

Mariah had furrowed her brow. Her connection to Gabriel was just as sore as the rest of her body probably was.

He was real sorry about that, but he didn't want her jumping into a no-win situation. Mariah would do anything for that cure, even mess herself up further, and that worried him.

"Did you see the rest of the image/thoughts?" he asked her. "The part with the blood exchange? The raising of the dead? Then the full moon?"

"There was that, too . . ." Mariah began before Pucci interrupted.

"Vampire? Werewolf? What's this now?"

Gabriel described what 562 had shown them, and the Badlanders got real thoughtful. None of them offered a theory about what 562 might be . . . or what it'd turn into come the next full moon.

Chaplin woofed again, getting their attention, and Gabriel found 562 watching him, as if the creature had been wishing that he'd return his attention to her. Or it.

Or . . . hang, he didn't know.

At any rate, as he looked at 562, he latched onto a wispy thought, and he emerged with what felt like the most solid answer the creature had offered yet.

"We're to keep calling it 562," Gabriel said. "It doesn't have any other name."

The oldster had wandered closer. "No name, huh?"

He smiled at 562, as if reaching out in camaraderie. For some reason, Gabriel thought the creature smiled big and wide, welcoming the oldster's attention, though he really couldn't see what it might be doing through all that hair.

But then he felt any hint of a smile disappear as the creature caught Gabriel's gaze and extended more thoughts to him.

"562 was caught," he heard himself saying from that hazy place. It was as if it was using him to talk.

"Caught by what?" Mariah asked.

"Original Shredders." Just as his own maker had been?

As Gabriel was about to ask 562 why the government

wanted to pack particular monsters away in asylums, the creature flashed him another image/thought.

Your search for a monster cure . . . There is no concocted potion for you and the others to drink, no shots to take for you to return to humanity. . . .

He hesitated to repeat this. It'd slay Mariah and the others. Gabriel wasn't even sure he wanted to hear himself speak it.

"Gabriel?" Mariah asked.

He couldn't keep the information back, so he relayed it to them.

It was as if the air had been let out of the mine shaft, leaving the atmosphere deadened. He felt the same anesthetic disbelief in Mariah, too.

She was shaking her head.

Then 562's eyes fixed on something behind him.

He should have registered Taraline's scent long before now, even with her liberal use of tawnyvale, but he'd been too preoccupied.

She started talking, as if thinking an explanation for her fast journey—which should've taken days, thanks to her human slowness—was primary. Obviously, she hadn't seen 562 behind them all yet.

"I caught a ride with an escaping were-puma as I made my way out of the hub," she said, short of breath. "He saw me stranded and brought me out of the city. A gallant. Who would have guessed? I had him drop me a half mile back, and he didn't even ask me what I was doing around the asylum tonight. No questions at all. I only told him I had a home out here, but he was too excited to get back to the hub to listen to any more explanations."

Pucci said, "Not all monsters are gallants, Taraline. You could've been killed."

But Hana was more concerned about the bigger news. "Most of the escaped monsters stayed behind?"

Taraline didn't answer, because she'd caught sight of 562.

And 562 couldn't take its eyes off her. It was even making a sound with its tongue, though not quite talking.

"Tik-tik, tik-tik . . ."

Gabriel turned to see Taraline in the shadows, just under a beam from a hanging lantern. She was carrying her own light, and it threw a sheen over her veil, lending nefarious angles to the curves and slopes of her hidden face, making it seem as if there were nothing but a skull beneath the material.

"It seems you found a cure," she said in that deep voice.

Had they? At least for Taraline?

But it looked as if that old woman with the injured arm in the image/thought had become a vampire after drinking 562's blood. . . .

Gabriel went very still. All along, he might've been able to offer Taraline a fix for dymorrdia since vampirism healed, though maybe not enough for the damage done to Taraline. But it wasn't in Gabriel to offer salvation for the price of a soul in exchange. He wasn't any kind of cure.

When he glanced back at 562, its eyes were on him again, locking him in, wishing to communicate.

"*Tik-tik . . .*" It kept making that sound. Then it sent an unadulterated thought to Gabriel, and he found himself talking.

"There's nothing that will turn you into the human you were before, Taraline."

Maybe he'd been thinking that, too—that even if he, the vampire, were to try to heal her with his blood, she'd probably never be what she once was. Dymorrdia was too damaging.

He switched his gaze back to Taraline just as she jerked, as if hit, the light from her lantern squiggling over the walls. He felt another burst of the same jagged disappointment in Mariah, too. In himself.

An awkward moment passed. Then another.

"Well," the oldster murmured, clearly trying to save them all from depression. "I suppose this means no champagne tonight."

His comment fell like a ten-ton rock.

As Taraline moved to a side tunnel, where she obviously intended to be alone, 562's gaze followed, as if it were fascinated. Then it uttered a tiny cry, trying to regain Taraline's attention.

She paused, the lantern light casting rays over the walls as 562 parted its hair, revealing its face.

Gabriel could feel Mariah's shock through their link. Then it mellowed to a sense of wonder.

562 had the face of a half-human, but with downy silver

gleams of hair and a nose that resembled a small snout. Black lips. Unblinking red eyes that Gabriel had never seen on any of the were-creatures he knew.

Delicate, Gabriel thought. 562 looked as harmless as a pet from yesteryear except for those eyes.

As 562 kept its hair spread, it was as if it were inviting Taraline to show her face, too.

But the mysterious woman only paused, the lantern hanging in her hand.

Then, without further response, she retreated into the side tunnel.

562 blinked only once as it looked after Taraline, then finally allowed its curtain of hair to fall back over its features, those red eyes not giving away any other reaction. After a few seconds, the creature seemed to shut down, no matter how hard Gabriel tried to win its focus again.

That weight continued pressing down the air as Mariah led Gabriel away while Chaplin kept guarding 562.

"Should we give up for the night?" she asked. "Let 562 sleep?"

"Probably. But what about after that?"

Mariah got real hushed. Gabriel tried to read their link, but she'd made it go numb.

"Mariah?" he asked.

"I say we find out anything we can from her, no matter how long it takes. We also need to find out more before we talk to Taraline about the possibilities."

So she'd caught on, too.

He sought input from the others. Hana and Pucci were holding each other as they lay on the floor, silent, which Gabriel took to mean that they agreed with Mariah. Neither of them had their eyes closed, though they were struggling to keep them open. Gabriel was pretty sure he'd be the only one knocked out once dawn broke, since he couldn't fight off vampire rest.

As for Mariah, she looked beaten, so Gabriel put his hand on her arm. His flesh seemed to flame through her shirt and into her skin, but he didn't remove himself this time, even if he could feel them both pulsating.

The oldster was no dummy, and he pushed Gabriel's hand away.

Right. He was being stupid, forgetting how he'd glutted himself on those Witch Shredders back at the asylum. He shouldn't be touching anyone, most of all Mariah.

Separating himself from her further, Gabriel was thankful that at least the oldster had his head about him.

"Listen," the old man said. "According to 562, there isn't a cure for us, so we need to talk about taking care of business here before we move on."

"How do you mean?" Gabriel asked.

"Did either of you take a look round GBVille? Did you see what I saw? And, if you did, can you honestly say that you can live the rest of your days with that on your mind?"

The oldster was talking about those kids who'd sold themselves for water.

Gabriel had known that the other man had been ill at the sight, but just look at how things had turned out back in the Badlands, after he'd told the community to fight Stamp. Letting 562 go its own way, then lying low, wouldn't come amiss.

It'd sure help Gabriel to get his own bearings back.

"Oldster," he said, "sometimes you have to pick your battles. There's sure to be trouble in the hub right now. Everyone's going to be watching everyone, and it's the last place we should be."

"Eh," the oldster said, waving a hand at Gabriel as if wishing him away. "All your talk about standing up and fighting. Who knew a vampire could rustle up that much hot air?"

"Oldster—"

"You know, Gabriel, you're a real cold vamp, through and through."

The accusation should've hurt more, but it didn't. Gabriel knew he was right about staying in hiding, just this one time. He'd learned.

As the old man plopped to the ground, turning his back on them all, Hana and Pucci looked to Gabriel, as if his opinion about the subject still mattered.

Then they looked to Mariah, and he realized that there might be a place for her in this community after all. She'd always been the lone wolf, but they needed a leader, and maybe Gabriel wouldn't always be it for them.

She'd shut off her emotions, fully closing down their link,

but he could sense confusion in her gaze, as if she didn't like what she'd seen in the hub just as much as the oldster.

Without comment, she went to Chaplin, digging her hand into her dog's brown fur as they both sat in front of 562 to guard their guest.

Gabriel sought his own position, away from the group, far enough so that Mariah's heartbeat faded inside him.

When he drifted into the darkness of rest, her vital signs grew even fainter, but he still held on as long as he could.

23

Stamp

When the power had gone out, Stamp's leg and personal computer had done the same.

Fortunately, as the gears in his leg ceased to work while he and Mags were scouring the western fringe of GBVille for that blip he'd seen on his scent tracker, she'd been there to act as his crutch.

While darkness had swallowed the hub, she'd tucked him into a space between two boulders near Little Romania, then told him to stay put while she hit the road to the hub and procured materials for two makeshift crutches—steel rods that she'd padded on top with small pillows.

Stamp hadn't asked about the details of her scavenging because his leg felt as if it were burning off—same with his left arm, which had held his computer. Thank-all the doctors had put plating over most of the gears in his leg, because it seemed to protect at least some of his mechanical abilities, allowing him to at least walk like a gimp.

Yet who cared about poles and pillows and even a power strike when he was on the scrubs' trail again?

He and Mags had followed his scent tracker just before the

device had also fizzled out. But he hadn't needed a tracker to show him the dirt with boot prints matching those he'd seen back in the Bloodlands.

The scrubs had definitely been here, and since he and Mags had no decent light source, save for a weak glow from their arm screens and the tracker, Stamp had been forced to seek the means for fire so he could continue searching, messed-up leg or not.

While sloughing off her traveling bag, Mags glanced at him, her dark slanted eyes cool in the faint, deadened glow of her arm screen. "If I didn't know any better, I'd guess someone pulled an old e-bomb on GBVille."

Stamp halted in his drag-legged search for two rocks to strike together. The very thought of terrorists sent a patriotic jolt through him, and he wished he'd been a Shredder during the days when those domestic freaks had blown off the West Coast. They'd been traitors, and he would've gone after them like . . .

Well, like a wolf after blood.

The comparison didn't sit well with him and, spent, pissed off, and ready to kill whoever had set off that e-bomb, he sorted through some rocks and found two that would suit his purposes.

"My leg's still workable," he said. "When they find out who set off any kind of e-bomb, I'd like to set off after them, too."

"You don't want to skip down to Waltonburg to get yourself repaired? It's the closest hub, and you could get your leg taken care of, as well as these computers of ours."

"We can do without."

Repaired. Stamp hated the notion of taking a pit stop when he needed to forge ahead.

"John," she said, "it was off-putting enough in the New Badlands when we didn't have reception for the Nets on our computers. I'd like to have mine back."

"Mags," he said, falling into the same chiding tone, "since our van and any other transportation around here would no doubt be disabled by a power-sucking bomb, I think a trip to Waltonburg might turn out to be a hell of a long walk. Besides, what if other hubs were also attacked?"

If so, he just might put the scrubs on hold to answer the call of humanity's duty. The military hadn't been much for waging offensives in a long time—he'd been too young to ever fight as anything more than a Shredder. But if internal terrorists were resurfacing, in spite of sure and immediate death punishment . . .

Stamp tried to bend over so he could discard a rock and take up another, but his leg smarted, reminding him of what he'd already sacrificed for humanity. And what'd his payment been? Nothing but the government setting him aside, retiring him before his time. Turning its back on him.

Mags was quiet for a moment, thinking. Then she said, "I'd like to try to get down to Waltonburg. The police up in the hub were using manual bullhorns to spread word to anyone still paying attention that the power went out because of a grid malfunction, but that doesn't explain why all the vehicles I came across aren't working."

"With the lights out and the zoom bikes and FlyShoes nonfunctional, how are people filling their time?" In spite of his pique, Stamp was genuinely curious. "Did they all join the running ones?"

"Some of them. You know how distractoids can barely stand to wait a nanosecond for a Nets page to download, so they were on to the next activity pretty quickly."

Stamp would bet his good leg that the government was lying about a "power grid malfunction." But he could see why they were acting as if nothing were terribly amiss. A hub full of whacked-out citizens would be a nightmare.

"But then," Mags continued, "I saw a bunch of bodies lying around, and I figured out what was happening to the rest of the people."

Suicides?

Stamp tried to make sense of that as Mags said, "I heard some cops talking. They had out more primitive tools, like riot batons and spears. They'd been prepared for mob uprisings because of how the video screens and jolly box corners had shut down, but I heard one guy talking about the announcements they'd already made to take the pills."

That's right. Since Stamp had worked for the government, he knew that the pills, which every hubite carried, were secretly called *stunners*. The populace had been told that the pills should be taken if a biological attack ever occurred—that they would ward off any impending damage. It wasn't true, but most people who were a part of society would do anything the government said, and the pills acted as crowd control. It whittled down the numbers that the authorities would need to deal with, and the people who didn't take the stunners or who weren't enthralled with running could be rounded up and monitored through other means, like riot measures.

"Apparently, the pills knocked out everyone who was hanging around outside their homes, and probably inside them, too, if they heard the announcements," Mags added. "I didn't want to be rounded up, so I kept to the edges of the city when I came back. The squares are littered with sleeping people, but they'll be waking up soon enough, thinking that they've been in a healing phase or something."

"That's what they'll be told. And I'm sure they'll be instructed to take even more while General Benefactors scrambles to clean up this debacle. Afterward, the hubites will be happy about the kindness the authorities showed in saving their hides."

He took his rocks and started to flint them off each other, creating sparks.

Mags grabbed one of his shirts that he'd kept in their now-defunct van and wrapped it around the nose of a corner gun. The sparks from his rocks eventually caught on the material.

Mags carried the torch, spreading orange light around as she waited for Stamp to stand with the aid of his crutches, then head toward the entrance of the cave, where the scrubs' boot steps led.

To the naked eye, there wasn't anything inside but for the rock and dirt, yet to Stamp and Mags, there were signs of upset ground, indicating that a man with big feet had paced around in one corner. Dog prints. More boot steps leading farther back to a place where indentations in the dirt showed where the scrubs had bedded down. And there was a charred ring of fire with a few minuscule clothing scraps among the ashes.

Yet there weren't any clues telling Stamp where the group had gone.

Or why.

As the torch burned out, he and Mags exited the cave. The sky was struggling out of its darkness, still a few hours from dawn. Above, GBVille remained quiet with the aid of those stunner pills.

"Gone," he said, leaning against a flat rock to rest his burning leg. He also needed a break from those damned crutches. Padded or not, they dug into his armpits. "God*damn* scrubs."

He'd been hoping to corner them in an isolated spot, just like this, where no one would capture his activities on their arm cameras. He'd also been sorry that the chase was over before he'd gotten here to find the scrubs absent.

Mags flicked his gun so that the rest of his embered shirt crisped to the ground, then climbed on top of that flat rock, sitting, drawing her knees up, and resting her arms on them. She was still wearing those featureless light clothes that they'd put on previously, and he kind of missed that tight, one-piece suit she'd had on before they'd arrived in GBVille.

For a distracted moment, Stamp thought of how that suit reminded him of old pictures of Catwoman in Nets comic books. He'd liked Catwoman.

There was heat in the depths of his belly, but when Mags talked, it brought Stamp back to utter coolness. Shredders didn't get distracted like the populace. Shredders kept their heads.

"The scrubs probably got scared when the power went out and they were smart enough to leave, just in case all hell broke loose," she said. "God-all knows they wouldn't need zoom bikes to escape trouble if they thought it was on their heels. I wouldn't be surprised if they've speeded far away by now. That's what I would have done if I were a scrub."

There was a note of something unidentifiable in her voice. Admiration?

Nah. Mags was all the way on his side. She wouldn't have any feelings for the scrubs beyond disdain. People like Mags and him didn't have many feelings.

But as soon as he thought it, she went and made him think again.

"What're you really going to do about your leg, John?"

It made him shift, the way she used his first name softly like that.

"I'll get it fixed," he said. "But later. First I'm going to follow any trail that the scrubs left."

She slid him an exasperated glance, as if she couldn't believe what she was hearing. He didn't like how this conversation—and a few others they'd had—was going. He didn't like anything he couldn't fully grasp.

"What's your glitch now?" he asked.

Like she'd been doing so much lately, she sighed. Sighs were never a good thing with Mags.

Then she came out with it. "You want to hunt down the scrubs while the trail is fresh, is that it?"

"Sounds practical to me."

"You realize, of course, that you're on crutches. And that we'd need to walk all the way to wherever the scrubs have gone, even if they have the ability to speed there much faster than we can stroll. And if we did find them, you wouldn't be very fleet of foot and they'd probably kill you within two seconds."

"You'd rather give up and go to Waltonburg, then start hunting down the scrubs all over again, after their trail might fade? Mags, they can't be *that* far away. I'll find them, then snipe at them, one at a time from a safe place, with some well-aimed silver knives or darts, duty done."

"If we go to Waltonburg, and if it hasn't been bombed, we could get some transportation there. Plus, there's good repair help. It'd be more efficient if you value your damned life."

"I'm not an invalid who needs to be rebuilt again." But when he took a step forward while making his point, he almost lost his balance.

Stamp pushed his crutches away, and they thudded to the ground. Mags's shoulders tensed, but otherwise, she didn't react.

"Who're you to fly in the face of my orders?" he asked, his voice hoarse. He'd never heard himself like this.

"I was only suggesting, John."

"And when did we get to be on a first-name basis?"

Unlike his tone, hers didn't sound weak. "Oh, I don't know—I think it was around the time I saved your ass from the scrubs back when they ambushed you in the New Badlands."

Fuck this. She didn't own any part of him just because she'd performed a quick-minded rescue for them both.

He began to drag himself away, but she stopped him.

"Is it so wrong to give a damn about you?"

It was as if something caved inside him, and he nearly halted in his tracks.

But he couldn't look back at her. If he did, he'd face something he couldn't deal with, something he'd been trained to avoid as a Shredder.

As a survivor.

Stamp gathered himself and kept on going, locking his sight on the scrubs' boot steps, which would surely lead him somewhere.

Mags dogged him, and he was sure she'd grabbed his crutches. He wouldn't admit it, he wouldn't even thank her, but he'd need them later.

Sure enough, he did, right around the time he heard the staccato barking of dogs on the cusp of the hub, less than a mile from where he was following the prints toward the asylum while skirting the edge of GBVille.

Stamp recognized the signs of beast dogs on the prowl, and he wondered if they were even farther ahead on the trail of the scrubs than he was, sniffing them out, tracking.

Or if they were hunting something else altogether.

It might be a good idea to see what they were up to, *if* he could catch up.

Bolstered, he looked behind him to his partner, who was already holding out his crutches to him, her expression a study in *You misheard me—I actually* don't *give a shit about you.*

He couldn't help grinning, even at Mags.

24

Mariah

Three Nights Later

Once again, I was sitting in front of 562 in the main area of the mine shaft, willing her to look at me so I could listen to any more tales she had to tell.

Being so consumed with her, I'd battled sleep, although I'd find myself nodding off frequently, my body needing to regenerate after our activities. But no matter how many times I availed myself to 562, asking her to look into my eyes to tell us what she knew about all the years she'd lived and just what she was when a full moon appeared, she didn't respond.

At least she was moving round today, but all she was doing besides staring at the floor was scratching at her skin—that pale expanse of flesh that didn't have a down of hair on it, like her face. It was as if she were trying to get at something far below, bringing it out.

"Please stop that," I said, but I didn't reach out to grab her hand. There'd be huge teeth and hell to pay, no doubt, even though I suspected that 562 had a soft spot for all of us except Chaplin.

Was it because everyone was a were-creature or vampire,

and 562 had a bit of both in her? That would explain why she seemed so familiar with me upon our first meeting.

But what about Taraline? Why was 562 so enraptured with her?

I suspected it wasn't because 562 was related to Taraline in some way; it might've had more to do with the veil. The covering oneself beneath some hair or material or whatever it might be that made a thing or person feel safe.

562 responded to my request to stop scratching by folding her hands together in her lap, then going back to her still resting. But those scratches had left blood on her arm, and I couldn't help longing for the red.

I trembled a little inside, as I always did at the sight of blood, especially since that asylum employee had spoken so highly and enigmatically of 562.

This creature held the key to everything, the employee had said when I'd asked her about cures for weres, vampires, and dymorrdians. . . . *Most powerful . . . could help.*

I glanced round the mine shaft, but nothing except for the lanterns and winks of minerals from the walls returned my interest.

Then I looked at 562 straight on. A fellow were-creature's blood was poison to me and my type, and if 562 was one of mine in some way, I shouldn't even be thinking what I was thinking.

But I went ahead and thought it, anyway.

One taste, just like that vampire in 562's image/thoughts had taken. The peace that had come over him seemed worth the risk, if 562's blood healed already converted creatures in that way.

Breathing in, I prepared to fight my inner monster if it should get too excited at any hint of blood in my mouth—even poisonous blood. As I hesitated, I also noticed that 562's scratches weren't closing up.

Didn't she have healing powers like vampires? Or was she more like us were-creatures, who mended only when we turned into our monsters? Or maybe she was like those other things she'd shown me and Gabriel in those image/thoughts—the corpse of the mother she'd brought back to life, the mutant rabbit.

Could it be that 562 just willed herself *not* to heal for some reason, choosing instead to wear the wounds as a punishment? I could understand that.

Slowly, so as not to scare 562, I reached toward her scratch. Just a little, little drop.

I talked softly. "I wonder how long you've been round, 562." I was halfway to her arm.

She didn't stir, so I kept on. "I sure do wish you'd trust me and Gabriel with even more of your visions, so we could see just what you went through during your life."

Almost there . . .

As I was about to touch one of her scratches, 562's eyes widened, going redder than ever.

What happened next flashed right by, almost as if it weren't happening at all.

562 opening her mouth—A pair of needle teeth flicking out from the middle of her gums— 562 grabbing my hand and pricking my palm with a tiny bite and a hint of a suck—My veins seizing up as she touched the tiny wound, healing it—

In the next second, I found myself with my hand still reaching out and 562 sitting calmly, staring, as if she'd never even moved. Her eyes were averted.

Checking out my hand, I didn't find any injury whatsoever.

Had 562 just sent me one of her image/thoughts?

I didn't know what she might be trying to communicate, but her blood was right there, and I wanted it. I *needed* to feel the same utter, maybe even permanent, peace that the monster vampire in 562's image/thought had experienced.

So I went ahead and touched the fresh scratch on her skin while I still had the guts.

Just a *tiny* bit of that blood. Surely it'd be enough to supply us with answers.

There was a twitch under her curtain of hair, right near her mouth. Had she known that I wouldn't be able to resist my curiosity?

A glint of red colored my fingertip, and I pulled back my hand, just as slowly as I'd extended it. My pulse jumped and, when I finally closed the distance between my mouth and finger, I tasted the blood, shutting my eyes, ready for a miracle.

I swallowed.

There was a pop of coppery taste, a numbing sensation on my tongue, yet it wasn't as if I'd drunk a magic potion and I was suddenly a princess instead of a beast. I didn't even wallow in the blood, because I wasn't in were-form.

Then I got sick, just as if I'd nipped a spot of blood from a fellow were-creature. Cramps, the works, and I held my stomach.

But I never threw that blood back up.

Afterward, I crawled away from 562, toward a canteen of turtlegrape alcohol that Taraline had brought with her. It washed away the aftertaste, flooding my belly and easing me for a moment. And, although my appetite wasn't piqued, I have to say that the feel of blood on my fingertip had brought up an urge to change and run outside to hunt and drink.

I spent some time fighting that off and, when I finally sat back down in front of 562, laying a piece of cloth over her fresh wounds so the blood would be blocked, I couldn't help but feel like an ass. I'd done something stupid, and it could've turned out pretty bad. When would I learn?

Not that 562 noticed my embarrassment because, really, the only time 562 seemed to snap out of her malaise was when Taraline passed through the area.

I think Taraline was warier of 562 than anyone else was. Odd, because she'd taken my and Gabriel's monster statuses in stride, but that could've been because she was so desperate to get where we were going, toward a cure.

Just like the one sitting right in front of me. We hadn't told Taraline our theory about 562 and dymorrdia yet. Why break her heart before we had more to go on?

When 562 raised her head a little later and started doing that *"tik-tik, tik-tik"* sound while her silver hair curtained off everything but that red gaze, I knew Taraline had to be near. Everyone else was outside, on lookout, probably chatting about what our plans were. I couldn't stand the talking in circles anymore, though. We never decided on anything, and I wasn't certain that we did have another place to go. It was useless to seek another asylum, since 562 had basically told us to forget about finding any cures in other areas. And wherever we ran, Stamp was going to catch up.

This no-man's-land of choice left me drifting, without purpose, and the closer the full moon got, the more restless I became . . . and the more I lost what I'd gained recently.

I couldn't go back to being the old, troublesome Mariah. When I'd had a purpose, I'd been so much better.

So what was my purpose now?

I heard a rustle of clothing, and I glanced behind to find Taraline, her gloved hands clasped in front of her long skirt and the hem of her veil.

Something scuttled through me, and I wasn't sure it was in response to Taraline.

Was it 562's blood in me?

Taraline said, "I thought I would come inside. Sometimes talk can tucker out a person." She shrugged, and it was in such an elegant way that, for a second, I forgot Taraline was anything but a fine lady.

She came nearer to me and 562, and our creature guest made a happy little sound, kind of like she did whenever our vampire or one of us were-creatures was close. It reminded me of how Chaplin would act when he saw me after he woke up, too.

"If I didn't know any better," I said, "I'd say that 562 missed you."

My voice didn't sound different, but my body seemed to be getting all restless inside. . . .

Taraline spoke again. "And I'd say you've been spending quite a bit of your time sitting in front of her. Why, Mariah?"

How to explain the inexplicable? "There's something that keeps niggling at me." I faced 562 again, only to find her gaze trained on Taraline. Naturally.

"And I thought *I* was stubborn about a great many things."

"Stubbornness is an attribute. That's what my father always said. He thought that a strong will was the only thing that would keep us alive." I *really* thought I felt my cells perking up now, as if they were being introduced to 562's blood.

Could something be happening inside me?

My words came a little faster with my excitement. "After I got bitten, I wasn't sure I even wanted to live. But I couldn't imagine dying, either. There's something about us, even when we're made slightly inhuman by what the world brings, that keeps us going."

Taraline wandered even closer. She actually took a knee and opened her veil eye covers to show a watery blue gaze. As you can imagine, that pleased 562 no end, and our guest sat up straighter. If she'd had a tail, she would've been hitting the ground with it, *thud-thud-thud*.

Then I heard Taraline laugh. When I gave her a curious look, she dropped her eye covers and said, "I just did it. I peeked into her."

"Into 562?" Oh, crap. All we needed was for 562 to tell Taraline about a blood exchange as a possible dymorrdia fix. She wasn't ready for that.

"Looking was inevitable," Taraline said. "Everyone else has tried it, so I figured, why not I?"

"And?"

Taraline shook her head, as if she didn't believe she'd done it, herself. "She asked me a question. I think she wants to know how I got like this."

Phew, for now. "I think she knows what dymorrdia is. She hinted as much when she said you'd never find a cure that'd make you like you used to be."

"No, that's not what she meant when I looked at her just now. . . ." Taraline laughed again. "I think she wants to know about my voice. Why I sound like I'm halfway to being an alpha male."

Oh. This was uncomfortable.

Even so, I had to admit I wouldn't mind an explanation, too.

562 was still raptly tuned in to her. I had the feeling that if 562 could adopt Taraline, she surely would've. Maybe she'd even like to do just that, via a willing blood exchange.

"I almost expected 562 to just go ahead and read my mind," Taraline said. "But since she didn't, I'll be polite enough to carry on the conversation."

She opened those eye covers as she faced 562 again, and I felt a little left out because she had closed those covers to me.

Meanwhile, Taraline continued talking. "I went to a doctor who thought part of a treatment for dymorrdia might include some ultrasteroids. That's all there is to the change in my voice, really."

562 was equally on fire to share, and she parted her hair, just like on that first night, revealing her tiny snout and shining red eyes. She looked like the cutest evil little puppy dog ever.

Taraline reared back for a moment, as if 562 had pushed an image/thought on her.

"Did she tell you something?" I asked.

"She showed me a . . . I don't know what it was, but it was like she was being born. She slipped out of darkness and into the world, and there were screams when everyone saw her."

"She was aware of that, even as a baby?"

"I'm not certain she was what we think of as a normal baby, Mariah. . . ."

562 tilted her head, and my heart went out to her, mostly because the world hadn't wanted her, and here she was, living on in spite of them.

"She wants to know how I got here, with you all," Taraline said.

"Simple enough story, right? After you contracted dymorrdia, you went to live in the necropolis nearest GBVille." It felt as if my cells were opening up now, swallowing 562's blood.

Or maybe my mind was just playing tricks on me.

"And then the psychic told you to find me," Taraline said. Then she got quiet, as if she were gathering herself.

562 tilted her head even more, so interested in Taraline.

When she talked again, her voice was thick, emotional. "The psychic must've picked up on how much I needed something . . . *someone*. And then you came along."

I didn't know what to say. I'd missed having people close to me, I think. Except for Chaplin, I'd put myself far away from my Badlands neighbors for good reason. Then again, maybe I was close to Gabriel in a way I was still trying to figure out, but at least it seemed Taraline was grateful that I'd come into *her* life.

I heard a whimper, and at first, I thought I'd made the sound. But when I heard it again, I realized it'd come from 562. Maybe she wanted to be a part of whatever was between me and Taraline. Or maybe she only wanted to tell us what *she* needed, just as Taraline had yearned for a rescue back in the necropolis. Just as I had needed one, too, back in the New Badlands. It was merely that 562 couldn't say it so easily.

But then I saw Taraline looking into 562's gaze, and I suspected that she was finding out what our guest wanted.

"Oh," was all Taraline said, as if she were slightly horrified. Then, while she pressed the covers back over her eyes, she said another "Oh," but this one seemed heartbroken.

Had 562 just made an offer to heal her through blood?

"Taraline?" I asked.

But she only raised her hand, as if to put me off, then stood, leaving while 562 put her hair back over her face and stared at the ground again.

As I watched Taraline go, she passed the robed oldster, who'd been hanging back, listening.

After a moment, he summoned me with a crook of his finger, and I realized that he wanted to do some talking.

How long had he been there?

For a second I thought he might've been standing round long enough to have witnessed me tasting 562's blood, but I hadn't seen him when Taraline had entered.

Hell, wondering about it wouldn't get me answers, so I went to him, feeling a strange sensation through my limbs, almost as if there really were a change going on. . . .

25

The Oldster

The oldster hadn't been hanging round inside the mine shaft too long. For one thing, it was colder in there, and his bones seemed to warm themselves better outside. For another, 562 made him uncomfortable; the creature always seemed to be trying to engage him in some way, maybe even *appealing* to him. Besides, he'd taken to obsessively keeping vigil in the direction of GBVille, wanting to be prepared in case Stamp or anyone from the hub showed. Unlike the last time his community had been attacked, back in the New Badlands, the oldster wanted to be on his game.

But there was also another element to his watching. The oldster was dying to return to the hub, and he wasn't sure yet just how he was going to finagle that.

He'd started measuring his neighbors very closely, wondering if any of them were also still thinking about the indentured servants and all the other wrongs that the hub held. And, night by night, he'd recognized something in Mariah. She was just as fit to fly out of her skin as he was.

Did she feel just as aimless, waiting round here like a sitting duck? Unlike Gabriel, the oldster wasn't entirely persuaded

that "lying low" was the best use of their time. Also, unlike a
live-long vampire, he didn't have many hours left in the count-
down of his own years.

When Mariah excused herself from 562, she had her hands
tucked into the back pockets of her mended pants. For a part-
time big bad wolf, she sure looked sheepish, as if she'd been
caught doing something she shouldn't have been doing.

The oldster hadn't been watching her long enough to see
what that might be, though.

"Hey," she said to him. "What's on your mind?"

The area was clear except for 562, so the oldster didn't
entirely beat round the bush. Might as well see if he'd been
right about his assessment of Mariah.

"I've been thinking about the hub, and I decided that I'm
not going to sit round here while there's so much still left to
tend to up there."

For some reason, she seemed relieved. "Are you talking
about those water servants again?"

"They're a part of it."

She rested her hands on her hips, and it made her come off
like the Mariah he'd always hoped she'd be.

No one had ever really been the leader of their Badlands
community, but when he'd accepted Mariah into it, he'd seen
a strength hidden under all the fear and prickliness. From previ-
ous experience with were-creatures, he'd known that inviting
her inside would be okay since their kind didn't crave the blood
of each other, even if Mariah was a predatory wolf and Pucci
and Hana were an elk and a deer—they'd all be toxic for her.
They'd needed a protector who was territorial enough to defend
her community from outsiders, someone they could depend on
if it ever came down to it. But then Annie—or Abby, as they'd
found out her real name was—had come along, another werewolf, and he'd foolishly allowed *her* in, too, after he'd started
to believe that Mariah wasn't a leader after all.

Abby had challenged Mariah not because of a lust for her
blood, but because she'd wanted the alpha role, and they'd
fought it out, Mariah coming out the winner. Yet then Mariah
had withdrawn, becoming more of a lone wolf than ever, even
in the midst of a community.

A pariah. A sad woman they tolerated.

But, deep down, the oldster supposed he had never really given up faith in her, and now he needed to know if it'd been justified.

Her gaze searched his. "Do you know what you're proposing, oldster?"

Sure, he thought. *I can't stand to know that, not too far away, there're some people who could use my help, and sticking it to the ones who're taking advantage of their weakness sounds downright delicious to me.*

He tempered his explanation, still testing her out. "If we're going to dig in here for a while, it might behoove us to find out what we're up against. Do the authorities know who's responsible for the power blast yet? Are they on our case? We also might want to discover if GBVille has even recovered from the power failure. If they haven't, then that means we still have an advantage over them. Just look outside—there've been no signs of increased surveillance. It's as if no one beyond GBVille knows what happened there."

"You think nobody made it out to any comm stations to inform the authorities of an attack?"

"I might be thinking that." The oldster shrugged innocently. "There were a lot of preters we set loose. A lot of different abilities that humans tried to erase because they thought monsters would overcome society one day. I wouldn't underestimate the vengefulness of a captive monster."

He had her. She wasn't posing any counterarguments now.

Pressing his advantage, he said, "Let's just go over to GBVille—you and me. We'll tell the others that we're off to hunt locally. We've been hunting in shifts, anyway, so it wouldn't look out of the ordinary."

Her skepticism hadn't totally left. "And if something happens to us in the hub and we don't come back?"

"Damn, girl, if it makes you feel better, I'll scratch out a note with the sharp end of a rock on a bigger one and leave it behind for them to find."

She pursed her lips. Yup, he was winning her over, and it hadn't taken all that much. Then again, that was why he'd approached Mariah and not any of his other neighbors.

"Gabriel would kill me for going behind his back," she said.

The oldster thought she was talking about something more

than just deceiving Gabriel for a trip to the hub. She'd hated
herself for lying to the vampire back in the Badlands, when
they hadn't revealed their were-states to him.

"We're doing this for the common good," the oldster said.
"And, don't mind my saying so, but the last I looked, you were
your own person. Unless you up and married Gabriel without
my knowing."

He hadn't meant to belittle her, but her expression fell, anyway. Certainly, everyone knew that there *was* something going
on with Gabriel and Mariah, and the oldster almost apologized
for questioning it.

She'd stiffened, as if maybe there were more strain between
her and the vampire than the oldster knew about.

"When it comes to Gabriel," she said softly, "I suppose I
should be on my own."

She looked so sorrowful that the oldster wanted to reassure
her, yet, before he could, she was already glancing back at 562,
who was mutely resting in that peaceful yogi pose, shutting the
rest of them out.

Then Mariah bit her bottom lip, almost as if tasting something on it. But that had to be the oldster's fancy. She was
probably only making a final decision about his proposal.

"Can you wash off any trace of Taraline's smell with that
dry shampoo of ours?" she finally asked.

"I'll scrub as hard as I can."

"We could also rub as much tawnyvale as possible over
ourselves. It should throw off those beast dogs if they're
tracking. . . ."

The oldster stopped himself from doing a little shuffling
victory dance.

"But," she added, "we need to be back here way before
dawn. No shenanigans up in GBVille. This trip is just so we
can take a little look-see at what's going on. Understand?"

"No shenanigans." He had his fingers crossed behind his
back.

Mariah gave him a stern look, but he just grinned.

"How about you get Chaplin," he said, "since there's little
likelihood of anyone caring that he's an Intel Dog now? We'll
bring him along."

For some reason, Mariah was already shaking her head,

and that startled the oldster. Chaplin and Mariah were like grain-peas in a pod.

Mariah said, "Chaplin's tuckered out. We should leave him to rest."

Ah, okay. The oldster got it. "You think the dog's gonna lay into you for leaving this mine shaft. No need to explain."

And he wasn't about to argue, even if Mariah did have a confused sort of expression on her face, as if she maybe weren't leaving her dog behind for the reason he'd cited after all.

She walked off to prepare herself, but somewhere underneath it all, the oldster saw a spark of excitement in her pace, as if, like him, she was dying to get out of this mine shaft. Dying to do some good as she made up for doing so much bad.

Fifteen minutes later, he'd written the best note he could manage on a flat rock in his own private nook of the mine shaft—a note that confided their trip to GBVille, should he and Mariah fail to return before dawn. Then he told everyone they were going hunting. After that, the oldster and Mariah sped off into the darkness, which was lit only by an emerging sliver of moon over the rocky, gray-spun landscape.

It didn't take long to get to the hub, even while taking cover, as usual, on the way there. Once they arrived, changing back into their human forms and dressing in the clothing they'd carried in Mariah's backpack, it seemed like a ghost town.

And that was no exaggeration. GBVille appeared to consist of those buildings that leaned over the streets like watchers, accompanied by blanked show screens and a straggling army of abandoned zoom bikes. The acrid stench of fried hardware made the oldster's nose scrunch, and he had to labor even more than usual to fill his lungs with air.

It was only when they passed the concrete expanse of an open General Benefactors dome that they were able to see a slew of bodies, all just lying there, side by side on the ground.

"Did the power blaster kill people?" he whispered to Mariah. Higher volume might break the silence, which felt like a glass partition between him and the rest of the surreal hub.

"It wasn't supposed to," she said, heading toward the bodies. She bent to a woman who wore a broken smoker unit, which consisted of two tubes running from her mouth to a smoke box connected to one arm while another tube connected to a filter-ing air recycle bag on the other. Nicotine addicts wore them to keep secondhand smoke away from others.

After Mariah felt the woman's neck for a pulse, she said, "She's alive."

The oldster did the same to a man wearing a General Bene-factors ad jumpsuit. "This one's beating, too," he said.

Nearby, he saw a hefty woman dressed in a gray overcoat and a water necklace—a luxury if there ever was one. And she had hold of three leashes, even in her sleep.

Those leashes connected to two young men and a woman.

The oldster itched to release the indentured water servants. It'd be so easy right now . . .

But then voices sounded from behind them, ricocheting off the dome and back down to the ground.

He and Maria scrambled away from the bodies and, just before they got to the shadows, they heard another voice com-ing from the darkness.

Deep. A man's?

"Those are the police," the anonymous person said, as if he'd already hidden himself from the authorities.

The only human the oldster knew who liked the shadows was Taraline, but this wasn't her—

Two gloved hands reached out of the darkness to pull the oldster and Mariah in, but he wasn't stupid enough to yell. Neither was Mariah, and they both shut up as the cops, dressed in white suits with riot helmets, strolled into the dome area. The oldster could imagine Zel a few years ago, garbed in the same gear, upholding the peace, and his chest stung with yearn-ing to see her, just one more time.

These cops used batons to nudge at several passed-out citi-zens, then left, obviously on regular patrol.

Their shadow-bound rescuer or captor or what-have-you held tight to the oldster's arm for a minute longer. A smell reminiscent of Taraline's traveled to the oldster's nose.

When the person let go of him, the oldster said, "You're not Taraline."

"No, I'm not, but she made certain we were familiar with you and your friends." This shadow man had a measured news-announcer way of speaking, just as anchormen used to sound before being phased out by computer-generated broadcasters.

The oldster wished he could see whoever was talking, or if this person was also veiled, like Taraline. If he was a victim of dymorrdia, too.

When Mariah spoke, she didn't sound afraid. "Taraline did say that there were many others round the hub who moved through the shadows like she does."

"Yes, and she wanted to make sure you were always trailed while you were in the hubs." The man paused. "We know what you did."

The oldster could hear Mariah's intake of breath, but before she could start to change into were-form out of defensive instinct, the oldster asked, "Who are you?"

"Friends. We're only friends, and what you did in that asylum won us to you for life."

The oldster thought he heard Mariah exhale. Thank-all, because having a wolf-girl on the loose again would mess up all the oldster's best intentions here in the hub.

"We know you asked about a cure for dymorrdia in the asylum," the man said, "and we appreciate that. Even before you came, we'd all been thinking of ways to go into that building ourselves to see what secrets it holds."

"Taraline had a lot to do with the plan," Mariah said.

"She left for the necropolis before she would've needed to go into hiding here, like us, so she never had need to plan before now."

The oldster asked, "And when she came back here, she found people of her own kind that easily?"

"We're everywhere, oldster," the man said.

Everywhere. "Then have you been present enough to see a kid with a scent tracker and a female partner wandering round as if they're searching for someone?"

"Johnson Stamp," the shadow man said. "Taraline told us about your ills with him. And, yes, I believe we've seen him. Besides Mr. Stamp, his associate, and the running ones, we haven't observed awake hubites outside any homes lately. Not after the police announced that it was time to take the biological attack pills."

"Ah," the oldster said, finally understanding those bodies laid out on the ground. He recalled the pills being introduced just before he'd left society. He'd heard that even the lowlords and their followers had been allotted their share.

The shadow man said, "Now that we're here to watch, we see that the government didn't bother to relate the truth—that the pills are meant to stun during an emergency like this one."

"Why didn't you take one?" Mariah asked the shadow man.

The man laughed. "How much more harm would a biological attack have done to me?"

He uttered it with the agony of a person who'd given up before this moment had come along.

After a pause, Mariah said, "So you're sure you saw Stamp?"

"A young white-skinned male and a female with dark skin who's a few years older than he is."

"Those are the ones," the oldster said. So much for ditching Kid Trouble.

The shadow man added, "The last we saw of them, they were tracking some beast dogs who were on a trail."

"Our trail?" the oldster asked.

"It could've been yours or any one of the hundreds of monsters who escaped."

"Hundreds, huh?" the oldster said.

"It's been a thing of beauty. The monsters have been hiding on the outer limits of the hub, then taking down anyone who's tried to make it out. They're doing it with stealth so they won't be seen by satellites. And, thanks to the cover of these buildings in the hub, it's a good bet we're not being watched from above here."

"And no one has contacted the government," Mariah said.

"No humans, to our knowledge. But some very old vampires made it quickly to the nearest emergency comm station. However, before they left, they 'met' with some General Benefactor authorities to perfect their voices."

"They imitated the authorities on the comm," Mariah said.

Hellfire, that was some kind of ability that vampires had. Did Gabriel even know he possessed this talent, too? He'd mentioned some kind of pamphlet he'd gotten from his maker, and that was all the education he'd received.

It scared the oldster sometimes—what Gabriel might be able to do if he realized it.

"The vampires told anyone on the outside," the shadow man said, "that a mosquito was spotted within GBVille and destroyed, and they needed to close off the hub as a precaution, in case there were more around."

The oldster grinned. The vampires had played on fears of a resurgent mosquito epidemic. Pretty damned smart.

The shadow man went on. "They explained the power malfunction by saying that a panicked grid employee was so intent on getting to a safer place, far from that fictional mosquito, that he carelessly programmed the babysitter software they use when they'll be away from their stations for a while, and the hub has been trying to get the juice back up ever since. They even said that a few monsters almost escaped before the sentinels contained them again, and that would explain any activity a satellite might have caught up there. Human-looking monsters, like you, have been barricading GBVille, keeping transits from coming in by pretending to be epidemic authorities in disease suits. The government wanted to send some reinforcements and medicines, but the vampires told them we were already well prepared."

Mariah laughed incredulously. "And they think this story's going to hold up?"

"No one wants to come round a hub that might house mosquitoes. In the meantime, other monsters are literally running the asylum. The more bloodthirsty of them killed any and all authorities in there, as well as employees, but more levelheaded breeds have calmed matters by now."

The oldster had fantasized about the monsters turning the tables—he'd even speculated as much to Mariah. But this?

This was amazing.

"What about the cops?" he asked.

"There's a new chief in town." The shadow man sounded amused. "That particular vampire's been swaying the force's high-ranking officers and using them to instruct the lower employees to go about regular business for now."

So the monsters had emerged. This meant that even the worrywart Gabriel wouldn't have to worry about using his powers in front of humans anymore.

Our own Shangri-La, thought the oldster. *At least temporarily.*

"The monsters are in charge of more than the asylum, then?" Mariah asked.

"That's right," the shadow man said.

The oldster could almost feel Mariah looking in his direction, even in the dark.

This was what Gabriel had been talking about when he'd told them to fight back in the Badlands, before everything had backfired. Monsters were standing up, and the Badlanders had been the ones to start the process.

But how long *could* it last?

If the oldster had anything to say about it, this would be only the start of something.

The shadow man said, "The cops will keep instructing the citizens to take their pills until they know better, so as matters stand right now, we have the run of the hub."

The oldster laughed. "Monsterville."

"It definitely appears that way," Mariah said. She simultaneously sounded afraid, pleased, excited.

The oldster's thoughts were flying round. When the Badlanders had used that power blaster, they hadn't done it for a higher reason than finding a cure for themselves. But look what'd happened.

God-all, the time to organize was now, while confusion still dominated. Was it possible that other monsters hiding outside this hub would hear about what was transpiring? And would *they* do anything or would this just be a sad, short chapter in the history of their entire demise?

Nearby, outside in the dimness, the clatter of running ones shook the ground—people who'd been too distracted to take the pills, although they hardly needed them to be controlled by the higher-ups. Humans, doing the same as they'd been doing before, hardly changing course because of a little old power outage or a mosquito.

When the clamor had passed, the shadow man said, "I want you to believe that at least one of us will always be around if you should return to the hub."

His meaning was clear. The shadows were on the monsters' side. They were like guardian angels, but . . . different.

"And who are you?" the oldster asked.

"Leon," he said. "They used to call me Leon when it mattered."

Mariah's voice came soft and low. "It does matter. Thank you."

When Leon answered, his tone held all the respect that a soldier has for a leader. "We will do *anything* to help you."

Then, with a sudden blankness of space, he was gone.

But the oldster felt fuller than ever. The shadows were looking after them. Ever since Stamp had come to the New Badlands, the oldster had been longing for allies, just like Gabriel. Just like he thought Mariah could be, too.

And he was finding them, slowly but surely.

Life wasn't the same as before, and it'd never be the same again, but it was the creatures that refused to fight and move on that died off. The oldster was damned if he'd be a casualty.

Mariah's voice floated out of the darkness, but it was more fully formed than anything he'd ever heard from her, except for the night she'd been bound and determined to save Gabriel from Stamp during their Badlands showdown.

"So do we have what we came for?"

And there was so much more meaning to it than that. He hoped that he was hearing the first words from a new woman, someone who'd finally decided that an opportunity was here, and it was time to grab it.

"Yeah," the oldster said, almost overcome by the magnitude of what lay before him. He'd lived a long time, and he'd been starting to think it'd been for near nothing. "I got what I came for."

He reached out for Mariah, grabbing onto her shirtsleeve. "But there's just one more thing."

She didn't protest as they moved into the dome area, circumventing the bodies until they came to the woman with the water necklace and indentured servants. This time the monsters didn't creep round, as if they'd be caught.

With a nod to the oldster, Mariah took out a machete from her backpack, then lifted one of the servants' leashes and sawed right through it. Her skin had a glow about it that the oldster had never seen before, and he couldn't help staring.

Where had she gotten that glow? Was it because of tonight?

The leash hadn't been designed to hold—it was meant to be a symbol of wealth and domination—and as Mariah cut into the second one, the oldster stripped off his clothing, packed it into Mariah's bag, then prepared to pick up the first freed young man so he could speed him to an improved place.

"Done," Mariah said after making quick work of the third leash. "You ready, oldster?"

He thought of what Leon the shadow man had said about his name—how it'd been what everyone had called him when it mattered.

It mattered now.

"Just so you know," he said, "my name's Michael." Because that had been his name before he'd turned old and so-called useless.

Her eyes shone as she nodded, then discarded her own clothing before she underwent her change into a full werewolf, her body shooting tall, the hair sprouting, her mouth gaping with the fluid pain running through her. Then, opening her glowing eyes, the hulking she-wolf scooped up the two remaining indentured kids and flashed her elongated teeth, as if daring a cop or a waking hubite to recognize what she was.

Before the oldster changed into his scorpion form, he yanked the water necklace from the former master's neck. On the other side of the hub when he and Mariah set these freed people down, he'd leave the water jewels with them.

As the were-scorpion anguish took over his body with the change and the last of humanity left his consciousness, Michael knew that they *would* be returning to the hub.

And it would be in a blaze of righteous glory.

26

Gabriel

Gabriel found the note long before the oldster and Mariah came back.

He'd thought that the two had been gone a pretty long time on this hunting trip, so before looking for them outside, he'd decided to check the mine shaft, just in case they'd returned without his knowing it. Mariah hadn't been in her nook, and the only thing Gabriel had found in the oldster's place was a barebones message scratched out on a dark, flat rock near his belongings.

So Gabriel had waited, seething a little more with every passing minute.

When the duo finally sped into the oldster's nook, they immediately changed back into their human forms, fell to the ground because of their overextended muscles, then started laughing as if they'd performed some cleansing, wonderful joke on the world outside.

From Gabriel's spot by the entrance, he cleared his throat.

Laughs cut short, the naked humanlike duo trained their gazes on him.

Ignoring their state of undress the best he could, Gabriel gestured toward the rock.

" 'GBVille,' " he said, having memorized the contents because he'd read the note so many times. " 'Getting info. Back by dawn. If not, you must leave *quick*.' "

Mariah slid the oldster a glance that indicated the note could've been a whole lot more instructive, but there was something about her that snagged the greater part of Gabriel's attention.

A flush. Even a sort of glow. And it was over every inch of her skin.

She and the oldster pulled clothing out of her backpack, then dressed. With a brief glance at the older man, Gabriel noticed that his skin wasn't like Mariah's. She clearly hadn't gotten that glow from running free or anything they'd eaten.

"We can explain everything, Gabriel," the old guy finally said, not sounding worried about the possible danger he and Mariah could've introduced to the group by going up to the hub.

Concern for the Badlanders' safety made Gabriel feel like its puppet, and he almost attributed that anger to his link with Mariah. It wouldn't have been out of the realm of possibility for her to be upset with Gabriel for confronting her and the oldster.

But he didn't detect any hint of pique about her.

Instead, her glow kept his focus, her normally pale skin almost seeming to pulsate with a rosy flush. Her green eyes were alive with something he'd never seen before, too.

Confidence?

Gabriel definitely felt *that* in her now, and it was inching into him, too, via their link. But there was more to it than even that. She generally seemed more comfortable in her skin than ever. Or it could've even been something besides that—a change he just couldn't describe.

Whatever it was, Gabriel wanted it, too. And it was only now, after sitting here wondering if she would make it back alive from the hub, that he realized how impossible it might be to live without her influence on him, which was funny, since it'd been the other way around not too long ago. He'd offered her the peace to calm her down. Now, *she* offered *him* a connection that pounded with more than the hunger he normally felt for other prey. This thumping was more like a genuine heart inside him—the only one he thought he might ever have again.

Unable to resist, he allowed himself to meld with her, and it was the most profound moment he'd recalled in years—her beat, beat, beat of life within him. He could even say he was inches away from a certain truth in the black area that had once held his soul.

How was it that she goaded him to such bloodlust and, at other times, she allowed *this* to happen? How was she the bad and good in him at the same time?

Then Mariah said, "We went to the hub to see if anyone knew we attacked the asylum. We thought it'd be smart to find out if we needed to be worried about anyone besides Stamp. But our trip turned out so much better than expected."

She looked into Gabriel's own gaze, sending him thoughts and images, faster than she'd ever done before during one of their mind connections.

Almost as efficiently as 562 had done, he thought.

He received the messages like vague wisps: the escaped monsters in control of the hub. The citizens who'd taken pills that knocked them out. A shadow man named Leon who'd pledged loyalty. Setting indentured people free by unleashing them and moving them across the hub . . .

When Gabriel came out of the connection, he saw that Mariah's skin was even rosier, her smile wider. It was as if she expected him to understand something that he just wasn't getting.

Had he finally reached his limitations as a vampire? Was he unable to go beyond what she *could* give to him?

He listened to her vital signs, but instead of the restless cadence of her buried were-heat, he heard very, very, very slow thumps, like the trudge of unstoppable footsteps.

She almost matched the dirgelike pace of 562's body. . . .

The oldster seemed to comprehend that there was something between Gabriel and Mariah that he had no part of, and he finished adjusting Hana's robes around him, then headed for the main tunnel.

Mariah buttoned her mended white shirt, and Gabriel couldn't say that he noticed when the oldster was actually out of the area, because all he felt and saw was her and the terrible suspicions that were building in him.

"What did you do?" he asked, and he wasn't talking about the trip to the hub.

Under the light of a solar lantern, her gaze darted to the left, in the direction of where 562 would be resting in the main area.

Gabriel's knees weakened, but he caught himself before he lost strength. Mariah couldn't have. She wouldn't have. . . .

"Did you try its blood?" he asked. "Please tell me you didn't."

At his cut tone, her gaze darkened, and he could see down to what he thought to be her soul. She knew she'd disappointed him yet again, and it gripped his supposed heart right along with hers.

"Mariah?" It was a question that didn't have the will to form all the way into what it truly was. A plea. If a vampire had any soul remaining whatsoever, Gabriel's was here, in her name.

"It was only a little drop," she said. "I had to. If I didn't . . ."

He finished the aching thought for her. If she didn't try, she'd never know if 562's image/thought of that vampire man drinking its blood and achieving such peace was true.

Jesus, he thought, and the curse ate at him, along with the knowledge that she was just as destructive as ever.

"But Gabriel," she said in a tiny, hopeful voice. "I feel better than ever. 562 is curing me, no matter what we thought she *wouldn't* do."

She didn't even realize she'd attempted something terrible. But that was Mariah—wanting to do good, but always screwing it up somehow. That was her tragedy, and his, too, because he was a part of her.

"At least it didn't bite you for an exchange," he said. "It sounds like that's how 562 transforms things, not just heals them."

Her expression fell.

"Right, Mariah?"

"I'm . . . not sure."

As she told him about what she'd thought to be an image/thought from 562, in which the creature bit Mariah on her palm—just a small bite, she said—he sat on the ground.

"The both of us," he said after her words had faded off. "We're going to finish badly."

"No we won't."

"You've got your obsession to get better. And I've got my bloodlust . . ."

At his confession, her posture echoed the crumbling of his voice.

"I know you've gotten hungrier." Now she didn't sound or feel so happy. "*I* made you worse—"

"No." He couldn't let her take that kind of blame. "My creator made me this way, not you. Maybe all vampires fight this battle during their first years, clinging to what they've lost in their humanity and slowly giving in to the inevitable."

But he had her and their connection. That had been *his* best hope for getting better.

He remembered what she'd told him all those nights ago, while they'd trekked across the Badlands. *You're one of our own, too, whether or not you like to see yourself that way.*

"I don't know what to do to stop either one of us anymore," he said, his tone dead.

She moved, as if she meant to come to him—or maybe he felt the motion *in* her, their link pulling them together once more. But when she held herself back, it was for the best.

"Gabriel, it'll all turn out, you'll see. You want to stop your bloodlust, and that's why I took 562's blood—not just for me, but for you, too. We saw how that vampire man felt after he drank from 562 in the image/thought. It was like instant comfort for him."

"And you don't care about being bitten?"

She had her fists bunched. So frustrated. He could imagine her leaving him alone now, just because she thought it was best for him, but Gabriel would only chase her down, unable to bear the absence of their link.

Or . . . the absence of her.

He tried to reconcile himself with that bald truth, but then a prickle of awareness scuttled down his spine, and he looked in back of him to find 562 in the entrance to the nook. Under that silver hair, its red eyes stared straight ahead, fixed on the wall near Mariah.

It was the first time the creature had left its Buddha spot in the main room, and Gabriel couldn't help thinking there was a reason. That maybe it'd been drawn by their conversation.

But why would 562 be so invested in their problems? Why would it care?

Motioning to Gabriel and Mariah, it urged them to sit together.

It had something to say.

Though the proximity of Mariah nearly broke Gabriel, he waited until 562 caught both their gazes at once, communicating what it couldn't speak out loud in a smash-jab of image/thoughts that encompassed both of them. . . .

It started out with the villagers gathered, the same rag-garbed people from the other night's image/thoughts, but Gabriel understood that this moment was occurring before the night that the one brave, injured, sick old woman had exchanged blood with 562.

None of them were vampires . . . yet.

They'd brought a young girl to 562. She was their first experiment, and they bound her, then cut her flesh as she cried out. They forced her forward, to where 562 could scent her blood.

Tempting, lovely blood.

As 562 panted, they pressed the girl's wound to 562's lips. It drank. Drank. And just when it was on the edge of bursting, the people guided 562's mouth to the girl's neck.

It bit, sucked, the blood thick and heady, the girl's soul leaving her. Lack of a soul made a human more into an animal, like 562, and 562 fed on that spirit before it even left its own body.

Then they cut 562's skin, leading the girl's mouth to that wound, and she took blood in return, suckling as hungrily as a new child.

All too soon, they ripped the girl away, her mouth ringed with red. As 562's eyes filled with tears—it had never experienced the beauty of an exchange before—the girl's fangs flicked outward, her eyes reddening as she begged for more blood.

And the vampire child of 562 got it by spinning around and attacking one of the humans before the rest could restrain her with wooden crosses smaller than the ones that had made 562 freeze in the past. . . .

562 brought on another image/thought that echoed one of the first ones the creature had given to Gabriel and Mariah: the

dead rabbit, after 562 had exchanged with it . . . how its ears had sprouted, how its fur had turned a nasty yellow, how its eyes had grown such strangely long lashes and its mouth had suffered those front slab teeth. 562 watched as it darted about a forest, attacking a deer, sniffing up its blood, cackling, then zooming over to a squirrel, which the creature tore apart as 562 blankly observed this child it had experimentally resurrected. . . .

Another shift in time, back again to another of 562's first shared memories: the dead woman with the dead baby—the lady who'd also been brought back to life with 562's exchange, just like the rabbit. 562 was in the same room as the resurrected woman, watching her as she sat on her bed, crying for her deceased child. As nightfall swallowed the room, the revived woman went still, but there was an eerie *"tik-tik"* sound coming from her mouth now. Then, as if it were the most normal occurrence in the world, she simply reached up and removed her head, her body still sitting while her head floated up in the air, entrails straggling out of its neck. All the while, she kept making that sound—*"tik-tik, tik-tik."* She stopped at the bed of her pregnant sister and, using her teeth, tore into the woman's swollen belly, gulping in the blood, working her way to the baby within—

A flash of horrific time, of pain, red and liquid, and then Gabriel's and Mariah's minds revolved to another image/thought: 562 stripped of clothing while it slumped against a wall, a giant wooden cross suspended from the ceiling over it, freezing it.

With no clothing, it was obvious that 562—she . . . he . . . it—had no sexual parts.

There was a different group of people in front of it now, in a different place, where the walls were made of crude grass and mud. A stringy-haired man in black robes stood by 562, who wanted to sob but couldn't—spirit broken, will broken, caught by these humans who didn't seem to understand. . . .

The door opened, and a man pulled a creature into the room. It was bound with chains, its muzzle wrapped, allowing it to make only muffled, frightened growls.

A black dog . . .

Behind 562, a woman screamed. She had been chained there, stripped of clothing like 562.

The men cut the dog and brought it bloodied to 562, who couldn't stop two slim fangs from popping out of its gums. Then the men forced 562's fangs into the canine, making 562 drink and drink. Unlike it had done with the humans, 562 didn't take the dog's soul—not during this rape of both of them. A willing soul tasted so good, but this could not.

When they were done, they took the dog away. They bled 562 with blades, its life water seeping into cups and vials. They opened the pitiful animal's mouth, forced it to imbibe blood from a cup, then jumped away from it as the canine flailed, howling in spite of its muzzle, squirming over the ground until it stopped altogether, its eyes staring into space.

Yet it wasn't dead. Gradually, bones prodded from underneath its skin, stretching it and sending the black-arts man into an indecipherable chant that burned 562's ears. The dog grew, creating a sound like a scream as its teeth lengthened, its eyes glowing while it fought its silver chains.

With a howl, it jumped up, standing on two feet, its limbs looking so very human under the black hair.

It saw the woman behind 562, and she screamed even louder as the huge creature bounded over to her. . . .

The moment whisked to darkness until objects began to float past in Gabriel's and Mariah's consciousness: a parade of different animals—wolves, cats, bears undergoing the same rituals with 562 and the black-arts man . . . forced breeding . . . birth upon birth of the were-creatures humans had created from 562's blood out of curiosity and arrogance. . . .

Then, blackness again, and just as Gabriel and Mariah believed it was over, one last image/thought rose up: 562 hiding on a rooftop in modern times. It had escaped the black-arts crowd years ago, and it didn't need much blood anymore. It was old, and its tastes had changed to finer blood than humans'. A feeding every few months during full moons was sufficient, although tonight it fed under a waning moon.

Earlier, 562 had been attacked, but now, after it had fought off its enemy, good blood should not go to waste.

Something lay at its feet in the image/thought.

A Cyclops . . . ?

Just as Gabriel's and Mariah's minds tried to take meaning from that, 562's consciousness overshadowed theirs.

My children, it thought as it peered over the roof to the streets below. Its children were somewhere out there. It only wished to be with them, to help them grow and prosper.

That was why it had come out of hiding many years ago. Being alone was unthinkable for a creature that hadn't found a way for itself to die. It had roamed, refraining from making more children, instead searching for descendants it already had. In old Europe, it had come upon evidence of another origin of vampires—a raging prince who'd been annihilated Before, and his composition had seemingly been much different from 562's. It had also discovered another origin and remnants of its vanquished line in Mexico.

Otherwise, it sought its own surviving vampires, plus the gremlins and tik-tiks it alone had given existence to. It had never discovered any were-creatures because they hid themselves among humans so well, but from the others, 562 heard tales of murder. And, with every one, 562 realized a little more each night that all its progeny seemed to be slipping down the food chain, extinction looming, just as it had for the lines that hadn't been birthed by 562.

Its children's blood was weaker than its own, because with every passing generation, the power thinned. It didn't like that its progeny were dying off, even faster than the other monsters out there. . . .

In the image/thought, 562 heard a stealthy sound, and just as it prepared to spring off the roof, five Shredders roped it with cross-dangled lashes, hauling it in.

Then . . . more flashes of image/thoughts for Gabriel and Mariah: years of holding cells; force fields holding it back during the full moon; transfers from asylum to asylum; 562's blood taken out of its body through syringes, the doctors probing, investigating its composition, never learning the lessons from what their ancestors had done to 562 so long ago . . .

Then, in a flurry that ended in a bang, 562 let Gabriel and Mariah go, leaving Gabriel alone in blackness, devoid of any image/thoughts. He scrambled to piece everything together.

562 was a she *and* a he, the mother and father of every type of blood creature he knew on this earth, and all its progeny were bonded by one commonality.

562's bloodlust.

As Gabriel's vision solidified, the mother/father's slit red eyes came into sight. Then 562 found a voice in Gabriel's mind, and Mariah's, too, because he could also feel the hum in her.

The sound was unearthly. A vibration that reminded him of a spirit in a cursed place. A call from the grave.

My children, 562 thought, mentally embracing them.

It was enough to give even a vampire shivers.

Mariah shuddered with him, the sensation jittering through their link as 562 held out its scratched arms to them. No wonder 562 had looked at him and the other Badlanders as if it knew them.

Its children.

What parent wouldn't want their progeny to live on and flourish? it asked. *I hate to see you floundering.*

Gabriel and Mariah's connection rotated, and they shared the knowledge about why 562 had been scratching itself.

It'd tempted Mariah with those scratches—tempted its failing, desperate child, into exchanging blood with it. It had merely wanted to strengthen her.

Were all of the other Badlanders meant to follow?

"You told us there wasn't a cure," Gabriel said, because that was all he could think to say right then.

I told you that there is no concocted potion for you and the others to drink, no shots to take, came that awful voice. *I never said there was no cure. I am only not the sort of cure you were searching for.* 562 focused on Mariah. *Tell him how you have felt since taking from me.*

"I don't know how I feel," Mariah whispered. "I'm better, though—even more improved than I've been lately. It's just not in the way I expected."

Gabriel thought it would be logical to be angry, but he wasn't. His words almost made up for that.

"Why would you appeal to us, make us trust you, and then turn on us like this?"

Please do not look at me as a threat. I have experienced what they do to us. You have seen it, too. It started with them discovering that I could heal them through an exchange. It continued when they found that my blood changed them altogether after they drank it. But then my vampires realized they would have to exercise secrecy to survive, and they left me

*behind while they hid. Other humans came to take their place—
greedy, perverse, in their need to push boundaries. They tested
my blood on live animals, seizing more than I was willing to
share. But, at the very least, out of their efforts, my weres were
born.* 562's red gaze seemed to gentle. *Then I hid myself away,
wanting no more of these humans, but I was lonely. I sneaked
out twice, wondering if there was a type of child who would be
so grateful to me for caring for them that they would live with
me. So I raised the dead, once with a human, once with an
animal. I would give them life again, and for that, surely they
would adore me. Both attempts produced baser monsters than
I would have liked, so I refrained from ever doing more, though
they took care of reproducing themselves.*

Its inner voice had been steeped in something Gabriel
would've called parental love and protection. 562 had explained
a lot—the resurrected dead woman and crazed rabbit—but
there was something else. . . .

The Cyclops in the last image/thought. A bleeding, dead
monster at 562's feet.

Just as Gabriel was about to ask about that, 562 thought,
*Being taken by the Shredders was the best thing that could
have happened. I had my children in the asylums, and I was
content to be near them, even while the humans kept us apart
with their invisible shield doors. I realized that the time has
come for us, children. The world is ready to change.*

Change how?

Mariah asked, "Were you calling to your progeny by
scratching yourself and letting out blood? Was I the first to
exchange with you?"

562 seemed to smile under its fall of hair.

"What if you'd tempted a *human* to drink from you?"
Gabriel asked.

562 didn't blink. *Humans do not crave blood as you do,
Gabriel. They are curious about it, yes, but it is not a calling.
Yet, if they do drink from me? There is only healing. It takes
an exchange with me to become a vampire.*

Mariah's next question rushed out of her. "And what if
someone who's already a were-creature exchanges with you?"

562 leveled its red gaze on Mariah.

"What happens?" she added, but she didn't sound as afraid

as she should have. "Will it give me more power to go after the bad guys?"

Gabriel closed his eyes. The bad guys. The murderers who'd gotten to most of Mariah's family.

When he opened his eyes, 562 relayed more.

My bite—my saliva—transports power into another being, but my blood mixed with theirs brings out different attributes in an exchanger, based on what is already present in them.

"And Mariah?" Gabriel asked, demanding more.

562's hair moved near its mouth again. Definitely smiling. *She will survive them all.*

Gabriel had expected a jarring reaction from Mariah—a sense of terror . . . but that wasn't what he got. A floating energy lifted their connection, as if she thought that 562 had given her . . . a gift?

Hunger tossed and turned inside Gabriel as he considered this. What would an exchange mean for him?

But he was an undead vampire. Would he become like that tik-tik woman 562 had raised from the dead, with her floating head and appetite for unborn children?

What would he become even without a full moon?

At his opened mind, Mariah's link nestled into him, as if burying itself, trying to find a place within Gabriel. The blood-lust and the raging hunger within him responded, pushing up more possibilities.

What if being undead was different from all-the-way dead, and 562's blood just made him a better vampire? He'd seen the peace just a drink had given to the male vampire in one of its first image/thoughts. Surely the full treatment would be . . .

Divine.

562 tilted its head. *Gabriel, the invitation is there for all my children. You, the oldster, Hana and Pucci, and . . .*

He should've wondered who else was on the list, but he was already imagining a perfect world, populated by even stronger monsters.

Yet something struggled in him, as if it were trying to get out of its bindings. He identified it as the last of his humanity, and it was wondering what he thought about a world in which there were things worse than the monsters he already knew.

The things a full moon might bring out . . .

As he glanced at Mariah, he saw that she was completely enthralled with 562.

He couldn't help feeling as if she'd left him behind.

When he looked back at 562, the creature eased into his mind again. *When I was caught, I saw that human weapons were more advanced. They studied me and, several times during their experiments, I wished I would die. Yet I often wonder what might have happened if they had found a way to do it. . . . Would my vampire children turn human, as they do when their direct maker expires?*

It took Gabriel a moment to come to terms with what 562 was saying. According to that pamphlet his maker had given him, her death alone would've meant the return of his humanity.

But what if 562, the well of the remaining blood monsters, died?

This notion balanced against the bloodlust simmering in him, and it was only made stronger every time he thought about 562's bite and blood.

His veins buzzed.

I have also wondered, 562 thought, *if I should die, would my were-children go back to what* they *originally were?*

Mariah took a deep breath. "Animals. Is that what I'd become?" Then she seemed to recall the part where the dog in the image/thought had bred with the captive woman. "Or would we be twisted humans combined with animals?"

562 stared at her, unresponsive, totally unhelpful. After all, it hadn't died yet, so how would it know the consequences?

Even as Gabriel felt Mariah's despair in their link, he wondered what 562's termination might do to a vampire. Turn it back into a human, its original form?

562's death could be a cure for him, but not for Mariah.

Their origin mentally spoke again, as if it'd sensed Mariah's turmoil. *You drank my blood. It* will *make you stronger. Wait and see.*

"What will I be after the full moon, though?"

Certainly not human. 562 sounded as if it didn't wish to encourage that in Mariah anymore. *And the change during the full moon should last only as long as the lunar pull is upon you, though I cannot be certain. During my time out of hiding and captivity, I never did find any were-creatures to strengthen through an exchange, and, besides, you did not take much of my blood during your own exchange.*

Mariah's panic expanded.

562 tried to comfort its child. *You've always been willing to be a monster for the rest of your life if a cure didn't present itself, isn't that true, Mariah?*

She stole a glance at Gabriel. It wasn't that she'd wanted to be human as much as she'd wanted to protect her own the best she could, either by having her powers taken away altogether or never subjecting her community to the consequences of her killer instincts. She hadn't wanted 562's blood to filter through her—she'd wanted the full force of it.

The mother/father reached out a hand, as if to touch Mariah's ever-increasing glow.

But it let its hand fall back down to its lap. *At least I see that your two kinds can coexist. At the root of you, you are animal versus human, and you bring out the defensiveness in each other, even while being drawn to a sameness between the two of you.*

Yes, he and Mariah encouraged what they'd figured to be the worst in each other. But Abby, another werewolf, had never driven him to these depths when he'd been around her. Then again, he'd never bitten her and tasted her blood, had never gotten as close, and most important, they'd never connected or imprinted.

Mariah was both a poison to him and a salvation, and it was the blood that'd brought them together and apart.

Gabriel could feel that Mariah was gradually accepting 562 as a parent, and the emotion carried to him. In a logical way, 562 was more like an anti-cure than a cure. They'd all have to make a decision: to take it or not?

To perhaps live better, or to die at the hands of humans?

As if predicting the direction of Gabriel's musings, 562 thought to him, *I think you should see what changes occur in me first during the full moon. I would not want you to regret strengthening your blood through mine for all the years a vampire would live.*

Though 562 hadn't known him for long, it knew him well. Even so, the bloodlust in him slammed.

Take what it offers, his lust seemed to say. *Live better.*

"Would I be like that resurrected woman?" he asked. "Would my head float and . . . ?"

It almost sounded amused by his question. *No, you're a vampire, not entirely a traditional corpse.*

Then 562 perked up, going back to the innocuous creature it'd seemed to be before it'd revealed itself to Gabriel and Mariah. It started to go, *"Tik-tik, tik-tik . . ."*

Taraline, Gabriel thought. She had to be nearby.

And he didn't like the ideas he was getting by associating that *tik-tik* sound with what he'd seen in 562's relayed stories.

He caught 562's gaze, and a fleeting image zapped into him: 562 hugging Taraline, as if it felt sorry for her. As if a half-dead creature with dymorrdia could be 562's child just as easily as that dead woman it'd obviously sympathized with long ago.

Taraline's situation wasn't the same as that of a woman whose baby had died just before she'd expired, too. But 562 had a parental streak, especially, it seemed, for any female who'd lost a part of herself.

Now he knew whom 562 had left off its list when it said the offer of its blood was open to all of them. Taraline.

Had 562 been playing a puppy-dog game with her, putting Taraline off guard, bringing her closer and closer, luring her in? He'd seen that old woman mended in 562's image/thoughts, but the healing had come after an exchange.

Was 562 tempting Taraline into trusting it? Gabriel's durned heroic urges blasted away his bloodlust, and he stood before Taraline could even get in the room.

He went up the tunnel to her, even while feeling tugged back to Mariah at the same time, their blood, their link. He tried to forget it as he saw Taraline, a breeze fluttering her veil and skirt as she stopped in her tracks at the sight of Gabriel. She held her solar lantern in front of her.

"I didn't find 562 in her normal place," she said.

"No need to check on it. In fact, you should probably just keep your distance."

He ushered her down the tunnel, though he didn't know what good that would do. But Taraline's steps were slow.

"Did 562 ask you to take its blood?" he asked bluntly.

She straightened, as if this were the last subject she'd

expected him to broach. Or as if she couldn't believe he gave a rat's ass.

"I think she took a fancy to you," he said.

She raised her chin. "Yes, Gabriel, she showed me what she could do for me."

Shit.

"*Would* a bite heal me?" She said it with such rawness that he almost didn't notice that she'd said *bite* instead of just *a drink of blood.*

"562 wants to bite you?" he asked.

"She said she'd heal me, but only with an exchange. I took that to mean she wants my blood, too."

This was no time to mince words with Taraline. "I'm not sure what her mere blood would do to someone with dymorrdia. But I'll bet 562 is thinking that an exchange would hold even more power than a drink. It'd make you into a monster. A vampire."

The word seemed to hover there, as dark as her veil.

Then she asked softly, "When you became one, did you have scars that disappeared?"

"I had dyslexia." He supposed that was a scar of sorts. "My cognitive process improved. But I'm not sure it's the same as what you're suggesting."

"I'm only thinking my appearance might be . . ." She sighed. "That this burden"—she pointed to her veil—"might be lifted."

"Is it worth the trade of your soul?"

Taraline's veil fluttered, the lantern light making her look like a statue in a cemetery, but she didn't answer.

Maybe she didn't have one to give.

27

Gabriel

The next night, after sleeping throughout the day, Gabriel came awake, feeling a body stretched out next to him.

A furry body that wasn't as big as most adult humans'.

When he realized that Chaplin was cuddled up to him, he rested his hand on the dog. It reminded him of the early days in the New Badlands, when the canine had welcomed him into his and Mariah's home and had stuck to him like brown on old tree bark.

Hey, boy, Gabriel thought to the dog.

He could hear Chaplin's mind stirring since he was already awake, but there was a disturbed heaviness that sneaked into Gabriel's chest, too.

He didn't even ask what was wrong with the dog. Just before dawn, word had gotten around about how Mariah had exchanged with 562.

Chaplin just sighed, and Gabriel rubbed his side.

She's beyond me now, the dog thought. He sighed again, longer, wearier. *I remember when I first came into the Lyanders' home. She was a little girl with such big eyes—eyes that were so curious as they watched the world. Her dad told me to protect her, but I would have, anyway, even if he hadn't asked me.*

Clearly, even an Intel Dog didn't know what to do with Mariah now. And, although things had seemed bleak before, this seemed to bury Gabriel.

Chaplin didn't move, except for his shallow breathing. *I used to try to get her to confront what was within her—the animal—just as everyone else in the community had faced what was within them. And she did become comfortable with herself. But I didn't realize that seeing her embrace it so fully would be like this.*

She's an alpha, Gabriel thought. *It just took her a long time to accept it.*

I didn't know she would cross so many lines, Gabriel.

He recalled how Mariah had been ushered into the were-world—through what pretty much amounted to a rape.

Chaplin sensed his musings and winced, fully understanding. When he laid his head on Gabriel's arm, the dog looked like old pictures of any other canine, with big, watery eyes that didn't quite understand their masters, although they loved them unconditionally just the same.

In that moment, Gabriel knew that Chaplin would keep his distance from Mariah because it hurt too much to see what was happening to her.

Should *all* of them be doing the same thing?

They stayed like that for a while, until a voice called out of the silence Gabriel had sought when he'd left Taraline alone.

It was the oldster. "Gabriel?"

"Yes."

He was standing in the nook's entrance, outlined by Gabriel's vampire vision.

"You need to come outside. Everyone should."

And the old man was off to fetch the others before Gabriel could ask why.

When he went outside into the dusk with Chaplin, they found Pucci and Hana standing opposite three monsters, the likes of which he'd never seen.

One was a creature that resembled a very tall, chubby of faceless stone—it'd been wearing a hood and ca second was a thing with the top half of a bearded r bottom of a big, thick snake—he'd also been covered until now, as he shed his cloak. The third was a normal-enough-looking guy with reddish-gold hair; a small, neatly trimmed mustache; and a wardrobe befitting a gentleman who'd rustled up the best of the gray garb from the asylum.

Chaplin began pacing around Gabriel while the gentleman greeted Gabriel with a nod, just as if he saw vampires all the time. A few seconds later, after Taraline came out, too, the man smiled and bowed, like he knew her.

"I apologize for showing up unannounced, but I brought a couple of friends out here so we could formally meet."

Taraline, who'd collected herself from what had to have been a stunning conversation with Gabriel last night, acknowledged the man, then said to everyone, "This is the were-puma who sped me out of GBVille. Hiram, yes?"

"Yes," he said. "My friends Neelan and Keesie"—he indicated the man-serpent and then the stone blob—"accompanied me. Not to be rude, ma'am, but since I'm a were, I took the opportunity to scent out the area around the asylum. The trail led out here, and I remembered it was near where I dropped off Taraline."

So their tawnyvale masking hadn't thrown off any werecreatures.

Gabriel sensed Mariah coming outside, too. That glow on her skin seemed to have suffused their link, as well, making it burn with the distance of a sun. Destructive if you got too close, glorious with just enough space between.

Chaplin halted to the side of Gabriel, as if using his body to block him from Mariah.

She didn't notice, though, because she was focused on the stone blob and snake man. Then, as if she knew them, she came forward. "You escaped in one piece."

They bowed their heads, almost as if she were of a higher rank.

Neelan peered up and said, "You're quite lovely out of your were-body."

"Oh. Thanks." Mariah shifted, embarrassed.

Gabriel could feel the emotion tumbling through their link. It was like he was getting pulled into it, a tunnel that would char him alive.

A result of 562's stronger blood?

Something within him wrestled back the helplessness, unwilling to be consumed. Maybe Gabriel could be as strong as she was, if he would take what 562 had to offer, too.

Their three visitors kept their end-all-be-all gazes on Mariah while Hana leaned toward her, as if she were subtly taking up her back. Meanwhile, Pucci wandered away from Mariah, toward Gabriel.

"We heard that a couple of you returned to the hub last night," Neelan the man-serpent said. "Why?"

He was speaking to Mariah, not the oldster.

"We wanted to see what was happening in the aftermath of the asylum trip," she said. "A shadow person told us how some éscaped mònsters have been barricading the hub. You've pretty much taken over."

"For the time being," Neelan said, moving side to side as he balanced on his scaled tail.

The Badlanders glanced at éach other, as if every one of them knew that things were about to change. It was in the air.

Neelan said, "The government was holding every kind of monster you can imagine, except for demons. Authorities wouldn't have anything to do with them because they work off possession of human bodies. Their abilities come from a mental place that turns physical, unlike us. And, yes, we've all been rather busy."

"How about those sentinels?" Gabriel asked. "Did you get rid of them?"

Hiram the were-puma chuckled. "Those bastards retreated out of the asylum early on, and we haven't heard hide nor hair of them since. We think they're somewhere in the hub, hiding like we monsters used to."

Neelan was a little less flippant. "Our monsters didn't catch them leaving GBVille. That's why we're assuming they're still there. But our faster creatures did intercept the humans who were running toward the emergency comm station."

The oldster stood between Mariah and Gabriel. "Why were those sentinels keeping you inside that asylum? What was the government doing to you?"

Pucci added, "Were they trying to create some kind of monster army out of your genetic material?"

When Hana glanced at him, he said, "That's what I'd do if I were them."

"No, sir," Hiram said. "I heard of no plans for an army. It's only that humans are curious about how some of us are able to live so long, adapt so well, and heal so quickly. They're looking for ways to become like us without all the less appealing traits, such as being awful to look upon if you're a Civil monster like Neelan or Keesie, or craving raw meat and drinking blood if you're a Red like me."

"Red?" Gabriel asked.

Hiram grinned. "A nickname for blood drinkers. We're two different camps, us preters, but we started getting along like gangbusters in this asylum once we apologized for giving all monsters that water-robbing reputation. Most Civils don't love to be thought of that way."

Neelan merely kept his gaze on Mariah, and it was almost as if he were reluctant about admiring her. Maybe it was because she was a Red. Then again, she'd charged into that asylum like a savior, and even the Civils would think she was pretty decent for that.

The Badlanders had gone quiet, getting used to the notion that humans might want to be like monsters, but without the ugliness and bloodlust. But of course that'd be the case. Humans had been searching for eternal or extended life all along, even way back when they'd first discovered 562.

Neelan said, "We kept hearing about genetic tampering for the elite in particular. The first to receive any services would be corporate bigwigs and government officials."

"Yes," Hiram said. "Buy your way up the food chain, be the first to inoculate yourself from all disease. Why not? The government's been catering to the elite for years and no one seemed to be willing to challenge the status quo."

Neelan kept swaying on his tail. "The geniuses in the labs were injecting monster blood into test subjects, but they could never find a way to change them into monsters fully."

That was because an exchange would've been needed, Gabriel thought. But he wondered what could happen to humans if they had regular injections. Might they get stronger, healthier . . . ?

Then an awful notion crowded Gabriel's head. Had the government found out what made 562 tick?

No. 562 would never have allowed the authorities inside its brain.

The chubby stone creature clapped its hands together, and a tiny hole opened up in its otherwise blank face.

"Busy, busy, we been busy in the hub."

Then, seemingly from the folds of Keesie's hard skin, something popped out and landed on the ground.

Gabriel couldn't believe it as he stared at the gremlin that was cackling at Keesie's big feet. The thing's ears had grown way longer than the normal bunny size, and it was just as barf-yellow and ugly as it'd been in 562's image/thoughts.

A stream of flame escaped from Neelan's mouth and barely caught the pest in the ass. It scuttled off toward some rocks.

Chimeras, Gabriel thought. Fire-breathing monsters of myth, but they were all too real.

Neelan rolled his eyes at Keesie. "Next time, check your flab for gremlins."

Then he slithered toward Mariah, as if drawn to her. "The main reason we came out here is to tell you we caught a pack of beast dogs outside the hub. We think they were on your trail, but monsters took them out. It's not as safe out of the hub as you might believe."

"Are you telling us to run?" Mariah asked.

"No," Neelan said, winding his tail into a comfortable position. "We meant to ask you if you'd, perhaps, consider coming with us to GBVille, where it's much more secure."

"That's the truth," Hiram added, shooting Taraline a wink. "And besides that, I think it'd be spiffy if the heroes didn't miss out on the rest of the rebellion."

28

Mariah

In what used to be an asylum office, I watched a group of vampires crouch, then let out a primal yell just before jumping up toward the ceiling and crashing into it, sending down a shower of debris.

Unscathed, they landed, laughed, and sprang upward again while creating a shatterproof skylight that would allow in a peek of the moon and could shut out the sun with a sliding door. Stucco and debris kept raining down as I stepped back even farther to avoid the dust. The vampires—ex-prisoners of the asylum—sped about cleaning up the mess, almost before a lot of it even hit the floor. Above us, the nearly full moon posed in the mottled sky. It'd be a big night tomorrow, when it bloomed all the way.

With a full moon, I was finally going to see what I was made of.

I'd experimentally changed into were-form only once since the exchange with 562 about a week ago, and I hadn't found myself to be too much different, although something seemed to be growing inside me, almost like it was waiting to make an appearance. But I was stronger, for certain. Quicker. I hadn't known what else I'd expected.

Vampire, gremlin, or tik-tik tendencies? The ability to leap a tall building in a single bound?

I had no idea because 562 had gone into a quiet state after revealing her story to me and Gabriel, so it wasn't as if she were mentoring me or anything. It could've been that she was saving herself up for the full moon. If so, I wasn't sure I liked the idea of that.

Why would she have to prepare herself?

At any rate, the monster community had decided that all of us were-creatures, especially me and 562, should go into chained and guarded lockdown tomorrow night. Those who'd been held captive here had said that the old force fields would've been enough to restrain 562 and us weres before the power had gone out, but that wasn't an option now with the far less secure bars. And it wouldn't do to have wild things running uncontrolled outside the hub, attracting attention from anyone waiting for that fictional mosquito scare to lift. It also wouldn't do to have me and 562 springing any unwanted surprises on the community.

I said good-bye to the vampires, and they gave me a jaunty salute while manipulating the unbreakable glass they'd discovered in a depot on the other side of the hub. They were workhorses, and part of me felt bad about their great efforts because, these past nights, after we Badlanders had relocated from the mine shaft, we'd mostly been resting from what we'd put our bodies through, changing to and from our were-forms with such frequency. We'd been changing so much that we'd needed some downtime while the other monsters guarded us from the threat of Stamp and those sentinels, none of whom had shown themselves.

At the same time, the monsters built natural light into the asylum, and they were working on ways to better transport the water stores from the General Benefactors corporate buildings so that those who needed it could have good access. We didn't have any tech at all since the power blaster had fried everything, but, seriously, we were doing just dandy without any.

But another part of me did very much enjoy the gratefulness the other monsters were extending. Aside from the Badlanders, I didn't know what most preters were really like, and they were making a good impression, although Pucci kept reminding us that there were crappy preters who wouldn't be so helpful, too, just as there were good humans with the bad.

I took one of my group's solar lanterns in hand—one of the few that had been saved in our mine shaft from the power blaster—and let the light guide me down the hallway, which already had a couple of unbreakable, sliding-door skylights installed. The idea was that vampires slept during the day, so they wouldn't be about while the skylights were open, but the doors were there as a barricade just in case an intruder had a way to break the unbreakable.

Monsters were on top of things, all right. Thanks to their ingenuity, the government hadn't invaded GBVille yet. The oldest vampires were still out there, imitating voices of civic officials over manual bullhorns to any distractoids who might be listening. We'd also sent out our most humanlike monsters as messengers so that word would spread about the imaginary mosquito that was keeping travelers out of the city.

The mosquito story wouldn't last too much longer as an excuse, though, so the monsters were already planning for that, too. When they did start allowing humans to enter GBVille, a few at a time, they intended to capture them.

All of this would need to be done under the protective shields of the hub buildings, though. We didn't know where satellites might be aimed, if there were any.

If we were careful enough, a full monster takeover just might work, because some of the escaped monsters had made it to other underground sanctuaries outside GBVille where preters were hiding. More of us were trickling into the hub by night; none of us had known there were so many monsters out there—especially the Civil ones, who didn't have the Reds' human appearance. My dad's monster book had never really talked about these kinds of preters, who didn't drink blood. I'd always thought monsters were just what humans called water robbers, but they were sure coming out now, emboldened by the change, just as the mutant animals in the Badlands had done after the world had altered. As a matter of fact, we had so many new recruits now that I couldn't keep track of who was coming or going.

We really were becoming Monsterville.

As I walked down a darker part of the hallway, the lantern

light bounced off the surroundings, creating wall-bound, grotesque shapes from the other passing monsters—humanlike were-creatures, more chimeras with lion and tiger bodies mixed with human features as well as reptilian. I even saw what looked to be a mummy, but without bandages; his skin was real shriveled. I would bet that, somewhere in those shadows, we even had people like Leon and Taraline amongst us.

I hadn't seen her for a few nights, not since the monsters had come to the mine shaft and invited us up here. Gabriel had told me that 562 had asked Taraline to do an exchange. It must've been when Taraline had gone into 562's head that one time, and that was what had made her so unsettled.

I think, now, our shadow friend was turning the option over in her head. What was better, being a vampire or a dymorrdia victim? Losing your soul was a major choice—it was something I hadn't literally needed to deal with as a were-creature—and Taraline had so much of a soul that even I had a flitter of doubt about what she should do.

Sometimes, I even believed that she stalked me in the shadows, waiting to ask me for advice but too reticent to come out. At least, I hoped I'd be worthy of that.

I was so deep in thought that, as I strolled, I came upon two monsters—probably were-creatures, based on their humanlike forms—who were garbed in hats that rode low over their eyes, their bodies swathed by scarves and huge coats. One was helping the other down the hallway, as if there'd been an injury during construction and one of them wanted enough privacy to change into were-form and heal. Accidents happened, even to weres.

I said hi to them, noting that the shorter were-creature had a bump on his back and walked funny. Probably a hunchback shapeshifter gargoyle or something. Who knew?

The two monsters didn't even look at me, just kept their heads down as they disappeared through a side door.

Okay. Not that I was a diva, but usually the preters treated me differently. It was because of the whole busting-into-the-asylum thing. They kept calling us Badlanders "heroes" and singling me out in particular because I'd been the first monster inside. The Saving Grace, some had nicknamed me.

But I didn't need to be worshipped.

As I kept walking, I thought I saw Chaplin up ahead.

"Hey, there, boy!" I said. Throughout all the chaos, he hadn't been round much lately, and I missed him like the dickens.

Yet just like that, he was gone.

Had he darted into one of the rooms?

Why?

I rushed down the hall, toward a room where I thought he might've disappeared to, but he wasn't there.

I lowered the lantern, and the light it cast on the walls sank, just like something else inside me.

I could've sworn that Chaplin had been there, and he'd seen me. And, deep inside, I knew what was going on.

Chaplin had always told me that he'd never leave me behind, but ever since I'd taken 562's blood, that was what I'd done to him. Did he think I liked 562 better now or something?

Did he think he'd been replaced?

The more I thought about it, the more I couldn't stop comparing me and my dog to people like Pucci and Hana; no matter how much of a jerk he was to her, she stayed. Had Chaplin gone the other route? Was he showing me that, no matter how much he loved me, he needed better treatment than I was giving him?

Or was he . . .

Scared?

Dismissing that notion, I left the empty room, coming upon another office that was under construction. The oldster—we all had such a hard time remembering that his name was Michael—was helping Hana and Pucci turn it into a bedroom. The monsters had agreed that we heroes deserved to have our own newly designed spaces, and it was kind of embarrassing. But turning them down would've been rude, I think.

"How's it coming?" I asked the oldster. I needed conversation or something to get my mind off my dog.

They all started at my voice, and they got those looks on their faces—the ones that said they were watching me closely to see what effect 562's pure blood had wrought—blood that hadn't been filtered through the generations. When I'd told them about the exchange, they'd thought I was foolish, but I reckoned that they considered me their test case. Another possible cure. They were also thinking about how 562 might affect bitten were-creatures as opposed to born ones. My friends were all true-born creatures, so their situations might not even be the same as mine.

The oldster had even asked me what would happen if a true-born just drank 562's blood without an exchange, since he'd never technically been bitten. Like I knew. It was the full moon that would reveal more about where we were going and where we'd come from.

My pulse began to skip at that, but none of my fellow Badlanders seemed to notice. They just pretended not to be checking me out so thoroughly.

The oldster—*Michael*—brushed off his hands on his trousers. He'd found new clothing in one of the hub wardrobe closets, but it was gray, a color that hardly suited him.

"The room's coming along." He fairly beamed, what with nesting into a new home.

Even Pucci seemed contented. At least he didn't toss any smart-ass comments my way as he worked on hammering nails into a bedpost by the light of a lantern.

Hana was measuring out sheer mahogany material that she'd probably hang round the room, giving it some style. "I will be ready to meet with you in an hour, Mariah. How does that sound?"

A nurse to the end, she'd been monitoring my temperature and keeping tabs on my body because of 562's influence.

"I'll drop by then," I said.

Pucci finally deigned to address me. "Gabriel's been looking for you."

My stomach did a flip-flop. I hadn't seen much of Gabriel since he'd found out about me and 562. He'd pulled away, and I'd missed him so badly, like a part of me had stopped working. Lately, he'd been filling his time by fraternizing with older vampires, probably asking for tips on how to contain his blood-lust, knowing him. Or maybe he was beyond that by now. Maybe he was soliciting ideas on how to get blood with more ease. . . .

Anyway, he hung round with the vampires going in and out of the hub and masquerading as humans to keep outsiders from discovering what was really going on in GBVille. I hoped he was learning a lot from them.

But I also felt as if I were losing Gabriel as he got further and further away from the guy I'd known. The arrow-straight, honorable man inside the vampire. I'd wanted him to be comfortable with what he was, but now that the process had finally started happening, I was second-guessing myself.

Should he take 562's offer? It'd probably mean an increase in his bloodlust, and even though I'd encouraged him to embrace his vampire, I felt possessive of what had made him different from other monsters in the first place—the belief that he didn't have to conform. The capacity to weigh decency against overkill.

His full acceptance was a death of sorts, and I didn't want Gabriel to die, although he was already dead in a lot of ways. Something inside me wanted to save him, just as he'd always saved me. I wanted to keep him . . .

I grappled for a word, but then again, I'd always known it.

Pure. I wanted to keep Gabriel, the best thing to happen to me, just as he was. Maybe, when I'd told him that we couldn't be anything but monsters, it was because I thought this separated him from the vampire who'd loved Abby.

Yeah, that was *exactly* what I'd been doing.

I gestured a thanks to Pucci for him telling me about Gabriel, then at Hana and the oldster, before I opened myself up to Gabriel's presence, trying to find him amongst all these other monsters.

My connection to him was functioning on high lately, and when I sensed him near the asylum doors, I didn't move for a full minute, overwhelmed by how good it felt just to be near him.

Through the moonlight shining inside, I could see he was with a couple of other monsters, probably vampires, judging by their pale skin and lithe movements. Two women who wore painted, flirty glances, even though they were actually garbed in the gray fashion of a GBVille citizen. No matter, they reminded me of how saloon girls might've acted in the 1800s with cowboys who had some pay to spend. For all I knew, the females could've been ex–sporting girls from a watering hole of old, what with them being long-living vampires and all.

They sure acted like floozies, getting too close to Gabriel for my comfort. But it also struck me that most of the monsters had been putting off a bored, restless vibe. A communal sexual stirring. Maybe even one that touched us far deeper inside than that.

We all tried to make up for a soul sometimes, I think, even those of us who still had one.

Feeling plain against the vampire women, I merely held to the sight of him leaning against the wall with one hand on a hip, his expression showing neither interest nor boredom.

A poker vampire face that had been so much more expressive and humanlike in the Badlands.

He must've felt me near, because his gaze wandered to me, and the expression that came to him shot me straight through.

It was the way men used to look at women in films before carnerotica had taken over, like he was surprised and rattled, yet so very happy to see me. Like his breath had been taken away.

But Gabriel didn't have to breathe.

Even so, the inside of my chest got light and fluttery, and our link imitated the silliness as he kept looking.

Looking.

At me.

Then he broke off the glance, leaving me hanging, and I busied my hands, tugging down my untucked shirt, as if I'd meant to stand in the middle of the asylum doing just that. How smooth I was.

He excused himself from the ladies, and they watched him walk away. In all honesty, I'd have loved to gut them, but I restrained myself. Yay for Mariah.

"I heard you were looking for me," I said. *My* breath had sure deserted me.

"Just wanted to see how you're doing."

Aw. But he didn't say it tenderly or softly. He sounded like I was his charge, his responsibility.

And hadn't the oldster . . . Michael . . . pointed out to me the other night that I was on my own?

We began strolling, passing those vamp women, whom I expertly ignored, then moving outside to the walkway, which we felt free to use because, even if there was satellite coverage, asylum employees would've strolled, too. It was as if we tacitly agreed that we had to keep moving or else there'd come a moment that would be too quiet, too strained.

The breath still didn't come easily into me, even though I was getting used to the thinner air in GBVille. I thought I felt a skitter over my skin, as if someone else were near, but when I turned round, all I saw were shadows from the moonlight.

"If you're checking up on me," I said, dismissing the niggle, "I should report that I haven't grown teeth like 562 yet. I haven't scratched myself silly with my nails. I'm still pretty . . . normal."

Or what-have-you.

"What've *you* been doing?" I asked lamely. "Hanging out with all those vampires must've shown you a thing or two."

"Yeah, today there was . . ."

He seemed to think he was being too enthusiastic and, really, I have to say that his rushed words did give the impression that he was a little excited.

He toned it down. "A couple old ones taught me about mind freezing."

"What's that?"

"I guess I can really hurt someone's brain if they goad me enough. You look in their eyes and shoot away. It takes a lot of energy out of a vampire, though, so I was advised to use it sparingly. Vampires didn't survive all these years by leaving trails of brain-deads behind. I think my maker didn't put it in her pamphlet because I might hunt her down and use it on her someday. Or maybe she was young, and she just didn't know about it. From what I'm hearing out of the older vampires, that seems more and more likely." He paused. "It works on preters, too, the mind freezing."

I didn't know how to take his comment.

Then he added, "And there're other things I'm learning."

"Like what?"

He shrugged it off, as if he didn't want to tell me. More proof was in the pudding when he quickly altered the topic.

"I've been looking around for Taraline. Monsters have been going through old hard-copy files in the lab because the computers are fried. They've been trying to match data to the blood and liquid specimens in vials."

I went with the change of subject, wondering if he'd ever

open up to me again. But what he said was important: There'd been a debate amongst the monsters as to what we'd do when we identified 562's stored blood. We'd have to experiment to see what her mere blood would do to all levels of preters, but if it offered improvement for us, we could transport it to other Reds out of the hub without having to move 562 or approach our origin to extract more from her. Some vampires argued that we could strengthen up our numbers that way, even in other hubs. But if humans ever got hold of the blood, could they get stronger, even beyond only healing themselves? Just imagine Stamp as a superhuman. We *had* to contain 562's blood, but how would we quickly fulfill the needs of monsters in other hubs who wanted to launch more efficient rebellions?

I stopped by a spot where the wall overlooked a part of the hub where monsters were dismantling some jolly box corners.

"Did anyone find news about dymorrdia?" I asked. "Is that why you're asking about Taraline?"

"Just incidental news." He rested his arms on the wall, squinting straight ahead. The wind played with his short brown hair, and he seemed so stoic, with his tough-guy face, his placid gray eyes that seemed to have depths I couldn't reach. "They found an old report on dymorrdia that's been kept from the public."

Wow. I hoped this would hold good tidings, and that Taraline wouldn't have to make a decision about exchanging with 562. Don't get me wrong—she'd make a conscientious vampire—but I could just see her being as conflicted as Gabriel.

"According to the report," he continued, "they didn't discover the cause of the disease, or why it affected good-looking people as opposed to others."

"Some used to say that the powers that be were striking back at humans for their vanity."

Could be that dymorrdia was nature's way of extending justice. And, believe me, I understood justice, but this seemed extreme. Nature had to be a real bitch for a reckoning like dymorrdia. But I wasn't nature, so I didn't know how it might form its opinions.

"Dymorrdia was a flesh-eating, bone-shifting malady that

originated from a patient zero in old Europe," Gabriel said. "That's all we've found."

Really, that was it?

Anger stretched in me. It didn't seem fair that there were mysteries of life without answers. With all the years we'd been on this earth, you'd think we would've learned just about everything, but we were more in the dark than ever.

I leaned on the wall, next to Gabriel, and he closed his eyes. He had to be hearing me, scenting me, and I wanted him to take all of me in. No matter how bad I was for him, I couldn't help needing him.

Below us, a group of running ones sprinted past, way off the usual paths they took through the hub. The crowds had grown, night by night, as regular humans awakened, discombobulated, and humanlike monsters directed them to start running with the others. The preters would just flash a General Benefactors badge and tell them, "Everything is good. We're fixing it all, even as we speak. We're laboring our best for you. Meanwhile, carry on with your activities."

And, just as they'd been doing for years, the distractoids believed them.

The few shut-ins who didn't run had been brought to the asylum when they had come outside to see what was happening, and then put in newly barred cells. I wasn't sure I was keen on this solution. These were the people who looked as if they weren't on many neuroenhancers, and a lot of them had refused another dose of stunner pills or hadn't taken them the first time round. And, after getting used to us, a lot of them turned out not to be very afraid, either.

I sighed, and I swear it wasn't meant to get Gabriel's attention. But it goaded his appetite, making it rear up in our link. The force of it made my heart rate zoom and my veins quiver. He was very hungry.

"When's the last time you ate?" I asked.

"I've had blood from animal hunting."

It clearly wasn't enough. I had the feeling that he'd graduated to human blood lately, and nothing else was going to do. And I'd stoked that in him.

"Maybe I should just let you be," I said, getting up from the wall.

"Don't go."

It was the closest I'd ever heard this proud man come to begging, and I didn't know what to do. I couldn't soothe him with a touch. Too high a risk. And I couldn't leave.

"You were the good one between the two of us after we left the Badlands," he said, his gaze containing a hint of red. "You were the one who started to give me some sort of peace through our link, just like I used to give you."

"And tomorrow night when the first phase of the moon hits?" I asked. "If I go really bad with this new, more powerful blood in me, how good will I be for you then?"

"It can't be any worse. My body takes me over now. I used to be able to control myself, but . . ."

He trailed off.

"Gabriel, you've fought for as long as you can," I said, seeing him leaving me. I wanted him to fight longer, harder. I wanted to punch myself for ever suggesting he could keep pace with me and my bad side. I even wanted to stop believing that, tomorrow night, I might miraculously turn out to be wonderful, suddenly better than any human or monster, and he'd come with me.

He lowered his head, the burgeoning moon's light hiding half of his face, making his red eyes blaze.

"I've been thinking a lot lately. The logical side of me says that if I'm going to be a vampire—and that's the way I seem to be going—I should embrace it all the way."

I started to get a bad feeling about this. "What do you mean?"

"Sometimes, I want to take 562's offer, and I want to do it just as much as you did, no matter the consequences."

And that was when *I* deserted him. Not literally, but if he took 562's blood, he probably wouldn't be the Gabriel we all knew and . . .

Well, loved.

My heart seemed to crack open as his eyes got all the redder, seeming to take up the color of the blood that felt as if it were spilling out of me.

"You already hate what you are," I said.

He put a hand to his chest, as if his heart were doing the same as mine, but I knew it was only an echo. "Don't you know that, where you go, I've got to go?"

A whimper, from me. Another desire to touch him, even though I knew it'd result in an ugly explosion for both of us.

Our link seemed to wrap round itself, twisting into complex patterns that I'd never be able to unwind. A rope, a leash . . . whatever it was, it bound us, and not always in a way that made for the positive.

I'd dragged him into a direr situation than I'd intended.

"Gabriel," I said, trying to put him off, "please wait until after tomorrow. See what 562 is like when the moon calls, just in case it matters. See me, too."

The real me.

But his fangs were already extending past his lips, his gaze a piercing red.

The idea of 562's blood was too tempting for him.

He wanted to go to our origin. He'd probably been wanting to do it all night, but being round me had goaded him to the limit.

"Wait, *please*," I said. I'd fight him on this.

He took a step back, flashing his fangs, and I realized that if I blocked him from this nearest door, he might just use the other.

Just as I thought Gabriel was going to make a break for it, he looked at a point behind me. I followed his line of sight, thinking too late that he was trying to fake me out.

But instead of finding nothing there, I saw shadows, then a couple of monsters on the walkway, almost as if they'd sneaked up on us like . . .

Shredders?

My skin started waving, my bones melting as I recognized those two individuals I'd bumped into inside the asylum. One helping the other balance as they wore their scarves over most of their faces, their hats shading their eyes, their bulky coats covering their bodies.

The shorter one let go of the other, then shed his coat in fast motion. But with that coat off, I realized he was actually a she—not that it mattered because, lickety-split, she reached back to bring out the chest puncher she'd been wearing low on her back.

At the same time, the taller figure opened his coat, revealing two crutches propping him up on one side as he brought up a throwing knife.

"Gabriel," was all he said.

I recognized the voice, and my body exploded all at once into my werewolf form as the first attacker fired the chest puncher at Gabriel and Johnson Stamp threw his silver-bladed knife right at my heart.

29

Stamp

Stamp held his breath, watching the projectile from Mags's chest puncher zoom toward Gabriel while his own silver knife spun toward the redheaded woman's heart.

Two for one—a vampire, plus what he recognized as the she-wolf who had come to Gabriel's rescue back at the Badlands showdown.

Just before the knife got to the wolf, Gabriel jumped out of the way of the chest puncher and blasted against his were-friend—

Stamp's knife swished over their heads, along with Mags's projectile.

Shit!

By the time Mags yanked back on the chest puncher cable, hauling back the projectile for another go, the vampire and the freakishly huge, red-haired, blaze-green-eyed werewolf had rolled to the side of the walkway, disappearing behind a jut of wall. Only the solar lantern that the redhead had been carrying lay on its side, amber light spilling over the pale ground.

Mags quickly cranked the chest puncher, locking the projectile into place again, but Stamp raised his crutchless hand, telling her to keep still. Then he extracted a silver throwing star from his Shredder suit belt.

When he attempted a step forward, the plate-protected gears in his bum leg whined and burned, working overtime, and Stamp bit back a grunt. He and Mags had been hoping sneak attacks would get them Gabriel, then more monsters, one right after the other. They'd pick them off like bad fruit from a dying tree.

He'd been lucky Gabriel was so distracted during their approach, until his luck had seemingly run out.

Stamp listened for any signs of his enemy. Had Gabriel sped his female pal away already? Or had he and the woman taken a secret tunnel back to the asylum to get some of their friends to help them?

If so, Stamp could wait here all night long, finding a place to hide, a spot that would cover him and Mags while they did some monster picking, offing the water robbers one by one as the preters ventured out here.

This time, Stamp wasn't going to run, not as he'd done in the Bloodlands.

Mags, who was back in her one-piece suit, obviously heard the weakened gears in his leg, and she steadied Stamp with her hand. Under the shade of her low hat, he could barely see the dark of her slanted eyes or the curls from her black hair peeking out at her nape. He'd given up his chest puncher to her only because it required both hands. It looked foreign in her grasp, but perfectly natural at the same time. He was almost jealous, seeing the two of them together.

Stamp shrugged off her grip, and, hardly fazed, she gestured toward the tops of the walls, where small towers loomed close by, striking out against the moonlight.

Was she thinking that Gabriel and his friend were taking cover in one of the towers?

Mags signaled over the wall, relaying that they should just go. But Stamp knew that if the monsters became any more organized, he'd never get to Gabriel and the scrubs. The time was now.

He shook his head, fingering his throwing star. Primitive weapons. They were the only things working after the outage, and he would've preferred some help from bullets or ultraviolet bombs. But silver was silver, and it'd weaken a vampire as well as a were-creature. And if the silver pierced a were's heart? One more monster down.

Mags paused, and then her jaw went firm. Stamp knew this spelled out trouble even before she strapped the chest puncher onto her back and pointed toward a tower.

He could tell what she had in mind.

She took a run toward the wall, then scrambled up, finally straddling the top of the wall. She reached down to him.

Stamp couldn't run, but he could use his crutches to bolster him while jumping, and he caught Mags's hand, climbing the wall with her help. She was a wiry one, deceptively strong. Once he was up, they balanced on the top, crawling toward the tower, slipping inside its stark lookout emptiness. It'd give them a clear view all around if Gabriel and the wolf showed themselves again. But Stamp would put good water on the fact that Gabriel wouldn't leave any adversary alive. Not if the vampire was smart.

Stamp and Mags waited, just as they'd waited outside the asylum all that time while the moon had phased toward its full form. All those nights ago, when they'd decided to follow those beast dogs, their plans had come to nothing, because the slobbering canines had been attacked by a pack of were-cats just outside the hub. Stamp and Mags had seen it from afar before beating a hasty retreat back to the relative security of GBVille.

It hadn't taken a genius to figure out that the monsters had gotten out of the asylum.

So Stamp and Mags had hidden nearby, near rocks, scentless and undetectable as they'd seen a bunch of vampires and were-creatures going in and out of the asylum. And from the looks of the hub at large, Stamp guessed that the monsters were controlling things all over the place, wrangling the running ones and somehow keeping the authorities in other hubs clueless.

He and Mags didn't dare make a break from GBVille themselves. It'd be a death wish. Besides, if Gabriel and the scrubs were still around, Stamp wanted to be here.

So they'd waited.

Then, several nights ago—pay dirt. They'd seen the Bloodlanders entering the asylum. After coming up with a plan, he and Mags had slunk around the hub, gathering heavy coats and hats. Disguises. With the obvious new influx of monsters from outside GBVille, they would pretend to be one of *them*, just until Stamp slayed his enemies.

They'd infiltrated the asylum, mapping out the best, most out-of-the-way places for hits. Finessing their plan bit by bit . . . until tonight, when the perfect opportunity had introduced itself.

And when Stamp had seen the redhead meeting Gabriel outside, there wasn't a thing Mags could do to talk better sense into him.

A smacking sound wrested his focus to a lookout tower across the walkway. But Stamp had played every game while hunting for preters, and he knew a distraction when he heard one. He didn't take the bait.

But Mags did.

She stood with a fistful of knives in hand, ready to fire, and Stamp was just about to whisper for her to get down when the massive werewolf popped up and over their tower's wall, baring its long teeth, its green eyes pissed as all get out.

He had just enough time to recognize a woman's distinctive features on its face, as if the creature had reverted back to half-form.

Stamp's normally cool blood fired through him as he yelled, "Mags!"

But she'd already let loose with the silver knives, and as the blades whished toward the werewolf, the creature flipped back from the tower, disappearing.

Extracting the last knives from her belt, Mags was over the wall before Stamp could stop her.

A momentary flicker of panic made him want to go after her, but Stamp's developed hunting instinct sensed Gabriel nearby.

He whipped around with his throwing star, aiming at the vampire, who was just appearing over the other side of the tower wall, fangs threatening.

But Gabriel, with his nasty heightened vision, saw the blade coming toward his throat, and even as he jumped into the tower, then arced to a landing, he ducked, and the star glanced off the brick, sparking and flying away.

"Stamp," Gabriel said, the name guttural, filled with hunger.

Stamp didn't remember Gabriel like this. The vampire had been more wily than bloodthirsty when Stamp had faced him last. Gabriel had tried to get him to think he was human, and it'd been a clever ruse, a fresh change from the usual mindless preter defense strategy.

Yet newer vampires were usually like that, slow to surrender the last of their humanity. And this made newer vampires weaker. . . .

Even as Stamp avoided Gabriel's direct gaze, he saw how red the vampire's eyes were. How far Gabriel had gone down the road to what he truly was.

Stamp stilled his vitals and readied his hand to grasp a silver-loaded, crank-action dart gun strapped to his thigh.

It sounded like Gabriel laughed. A serrated laugh.

"You bring a little gun to a personal Armageddon?" Gabriel said in that damned vampire voice. It was on the edge of sway, but Stamp had been trained in how to block that out.

Yet a tap of doubt introduced itself to Stamp, especially when Gabriel gave a pointed glance to Stamp's leg. He'd seen how it impeded movement, probably heard the damaged gears, too.

Gabriel was a predator standing over wounded prey, and he didn't care about any throwing stars or silver darts.

Stamp drew his gun, anyway, and just as Gabriel swatted it out of the tower, a howl cut the air.

Gabriel glanced over to where Mags and the werewolf were obviously having their own faceoff below.

Mags . . .

What did that howl mean? Was the monster standing over her, gutting her?

Mags came flying backward over the tower, as if the werewolf had punched her away. But Mags already had out a cable gun that she was firing, even as she dropped over the other side of the wall.

The werewolf went flying after her.

In the fractured second when Stamp had lost concentration, Gabriel had already crouched, ready to spring—

But he didn't do it toward Stamp, instead diving out of the tower in the direction Mags and the werewolf had gone over the outer wall.

Stamp rush-limped to see them, leaning over the wall, where he saw Mags down among the rocks, wielding two dart guns and firing silver at the dodging werewolf while Gabriel crawled down the bricks toward them.

They were going to kill Mags.

Using the best weapon at hand, Stamp yelled a holy curse at the vampire. "God*damn* you, Gabriel!"

Curses had almost worked the last time Stamp had met the vampire, but now, Gabriel only froze for an instant, shaking his head as if ruffling off a nuisance.

He was deep into his bloodlust, all right, and out of pure desperation, Stamp doffed his coat, took out a knife, then ripped off one of his gauntlets. He pushed up his sleeve, cut his arm just over his useless computer, then reached over the tower wall.

At the same time, Mags yelled at the werewolf.

"Government! We know how the government's going to infiltrate the hub!"

Even Stamp came to a halt.

The wolf cocked her head at what Stamp knew to be a huge lie from Mags. But, good God-all, the half-changed wolf understood what she was saying because the redhead hadn't gone all the way into were-form, and her mind would still be fairly intact.

Would she care about Mags's plea?

Didn't matter, because Mags's appeal hadn't stopped Gabriel yet. He was still crawling down to them, stalking, as if feeding off Mags's fear.

And Stamp knew how another's fear could inspire.

"Hey!" he cried, his voice echoing back at him. "Blood! Gabriel, you and the wolf want *my* blood, not hers!"

His head felt like a toy top, spinning, everything around him a mess of confusion. What the hell was he doing?

The vampire, halfway down the wall now, glanced over his shoulder with those red eyes as Stamp allowed his blood to drip down. A bead of red landed on Gabriel's forehead, marking him, and he reared back, as if reveling in the scent.

Below, the werewolf with the humanlike face was staring at Mags, as if trying to decide whether to chase the blood she scented or hearing out this woman who had information about the government. Mags was sprawled on the ground, not daring to move.

"Blood!" Stamp yelled.

Mags gazed up him, her dark eyes wide under the moonlight. *Don't do this!* she seemed to be thinking.

Gabriel hissed at Stamp, hunching his back.

Come on, Stamp thought. *Get up here.* He had to remove them from Mags. He was the Shredder, not her.

Gabriel reversed direction, crawling back up to Stamp.

He drew a machete from its holster, hiding it behind his back as he saw the werewolf jumping up the bricks, too.

But then Gabriel hissed and—

Damn.

The vampire cocked his leg and kicked down at the wolf, slamming her to the ground, as if he didn't want to compete for the blood.

Although a second couldn't last forever, this one sure seemed to, as the werewolf looked at the vampire with that eerily human face.

Devastated. Destroyed.

Gabriel didn't seem bothered by it as he kept climbing up. But the wolf sprang from the ground again, grabbing at his ankle.

"Gabriel!" she yelled, a half-howl. "If they know something about the government . . ."

But it was also as if she hated to see him this way. How could that be, though, when these things were only monsters?

Stamp pushed away from the wall, still hiding his machete. If he ran, he wouldn't get but a few feet. Best to make a stand so Mags could do the running.

Gabriel's bloodied forehead appeared over the wall first, slowly, as if the vampire meant to stalk Stamp and take deep pleasure in it. Then came his crazed eyes. His fangy mouth, which smiled.

Then he kicked down again, and the pained howl of a were-wolf split the night.

There was a thud, as if Gabriel had kicked hard enough for the were-creature to hit the ground this time.

Stamp gripped the machete and pressed his cut arm to his

hip, hiding the blood. Hopefully Mags had run far enough to set herself up in ambush mode, with better weapons drawn if the wolf decided to chase her.

Gabriel focused those awful eyes on Stamp again. Here went nothing.

"We found a working comm outside the hub," he lied, hoping Gabriel was lucid enough to understand. "We heard the government on it. They're planning to do some real nastiness with you monsters."

Gabriel must've heard the wolf climbing again, because he levered himself up, sitting on the wall's ledge, looking down, hissing, warning her.

Then the strangest thing happened: The vampire paused, as if his humanity had kicked in again.

Amateur, Stamp thought.

But, just as quickly, Gabriel fixed his gaze on Stamp and, with a blast of speed, the vampire pushed off the wall, coming down to a graceful landing a few feet away. He touched his forehead, where Stamp's blood reddened his skin, then sniffed his fingers. Shivered.

His whole body was shivering, as if he were . . .

Still fighting himself.

"If you don't want to know what you're in for with the government," Stamp said, appealing to Gabriel's weakness—his remaining sense—"then go ahead and kill me and Mags. It'll be your last mistake."

Gabriel tilted his head, his hand quaking as he lowered it from his nose. Then, as if unable to resist, he pressed his bloodied fingers to his mouth.

He groaned.

Stamp had always wondered what a Shredder's last thought might be before getting whacked. And if this was it, he'd go out wondering if Mags had made it, but that was only because she was the only one left around here who was equipped to fight the monsters. . . .

Stamp waited only a second more, the time it took to breathe a prayer, and then he brought out the machete.

But his leg made him slow and without decent balance, and as he lurched forward, swinging, Gabriel simply ducked, then knocked the machete away. The vampire grasped Stamp's bandolier, jerking him closer, his fangs flashing as he reared back his head for a killing bite.

Stamp barely saw that, behind Gabriel, the recovered werewolf had jumped over the wall, reaching out to Gabriel. When she got him in a headlock, pulling him away from Stamp, it was as if she really did want to stop him from destroying a person who had information about a government attack, even if it was a Shredder. Her leg was bleeding, as if Gabriel's last kick had split open her thigh and she'd been were-healing the worst of it before being able to come up here.

Seeing an opportunity, Stamp raised his machete again. Two heads in one.

But then, out of nowhere, *he* was yanked backward, his machete pulled from his grasp, his body weighed down by a tawny were-puma sitting on him and hissing, its short, half-human face and clawed hands showing it hadn't gone into full were-form, either, although its long tail spoke of an eager animal underneath it all.

Before Stamp's brain could find an explanation, he discovered that he was inside a circle of monsters, almost all of whom were in their half were-forms.

One of them was fully human, though—the old man from the Bloodlands—and he was watching as the other monsters went for Gabriel and the she-wolf, leaping forward to restrain the snarling pair before they really got into it.

"Back off!" the oldster was shouting at the pair. Then he looked down at Stamp, and there was no doubt he recognized him. Hated him.

Gabriel was fighting the other monsters, snapping at them, but their numbers were too great. The werewolf had already backed away, pointing to her leg, which hadn't healed all the way yet. It might take longer to mend up here in the thin air of GBVille. So might Stamp's hand.

The others gave her room to rest and mend while they turned their attention to the vampire.

But Mags—where was Mags?

The oldster continued chiding Gabriel and the half-wolf. "A patrol spotted you, and they put out an alarm. One of them changed to full form so, even from a distance, he could hear what Stamp here was saying about the government. Think, Gabriel—wouldn't questioning him produce some information we could use? If not, *then* we could kill his ass." He talked to the other monsters. "Separate Gabriel and Mariah and take them somewhere to cool off."

Mariah. That was the wolf's name.

And right now Stamp had a reprieve. A few more minutes of life. But when the monsters started interrogating him, what would he do then to survive?

In spite of his predicament, he didn't lose composure. He'd think of a way to escape. What mattered was that Mags had gotten to safety.

The old guy bent to wipe Stamp's wound with some disgusting medicine and wrap a cloth around his arm.

"Dumb shit," he said, his voice trembling, no doubt because of the blood. The were-puma held out a zip bag and the old man disposed of the medicine cloth in it. "Were you *trying* to get killed?"

Stamp only grinned, and he could tell it unnerved the guy.

The ancient man still had a lot of pluck and strength to him, though, and he proved it when he tugged Stamp to his feet, then pushed him toward some stairs in the tower. The monsters trailed as Stamp dragged his bad leg behind him. He'd left his crutches behind, damn it.

"What's with your leg?" the old man asked.

"Nothing." No one had checked him for weapons yet, but they were sure to get a surprise when they did. He even had devices on him that would go unnoticed in anywhere but a high-security facility.

The oldster pushed Stamp down the stairs, and he stumbled, but didn't fall.

They took him to a cell block, where crude steel acted as bars. It looked as if the monsters had shoved the rods into the concrete through brute strength, taking the place of whatever had been there before. To Stamp's keen interest, there were more than just vamps and were-creatures around, too. He'd never run into any of those in his experience.

He'd never even been in an asylum.

In the cages, humans clung to the bars, eyes wide, skin dirty. They watched Stamp pass.

The old guy shoved Stamp into a cage and, as monsters surrounded him on the outside, a humanlike monster patted Stamp down. He was wearing gloves, no doubt to avoid any silver, and he removed all the obvious blades and throwing stars. And just when Stamp thought of the weapons buried *inside* the suit, the old guy made Stamp strip.

Oh, well.

They tossed some gray clothing at him, and he put it on, already peering around his cell for items he could use as weapons. It was pretty sparse in here.

Stamp went to the back of the cell to sit, locking gazes with the old man, who remained outside gloating.

He found out why minutes later, when they dragged Mags to the cell opposite his.

Stamp rushed to the bars, bad leg and all.

As they patted her down, she didn't look at him, as if too mortified at being caught. And when they divested Mags of her clothing, that was when *he* looked away.

"Did you think she'd get very far?" the old guy asked. "You're just damned lucky Mariah didn't change all the way and stopped herself and Gabriel from getting your blood for the sake of the information you say you have."

He'd uttered that last part with plenty of doubt. Stamp just let him wallow in it.

The old man looked the cell up and down. "Did you know that this is where they used to store monsters?"

Stamp had made an educated guess.

Then the old man delivered the zinger. "Maybe you did know, maybe you didn't. But I'll bet you had no idea that the government was using new models of your precious Shredders to keep the monsters inside."

New Shredders. Stamp wanted to spit.

"That's right," the old man continued, seemingly content at Stamp's silent reaction. "New *and* improved, just like mutants everywhere these days. It looks like your counterparts deposited some of their prey in asylums, where the new Shredders—they call them Witches—guarded them."

There must've been another tell on Stamp's face or body, because the oldster's voice got soft.

"Well, I'll be—you're rather unhappy about this, ain't ya?"

After another thoughtful second, the old guy left, leaving other monsters to guard Stamp and Mags.

He could feel the weight of her gaze, but he wouldn't meet it. He was remembering how he'd shed his blood at the heat of the moment for her. He'd have to tell her it was because she'd been his last hope of gaining vengeance on Gabriel.

"They didn't kill me, John," she said. "They could've, because they had you in custody, but they didn't."

He glanced across the corridor to her. She was wearing that gray uniform now, and her face was bruised from the fight with the redhead. He'd expected to find her sporting a matching grimace, too, but instead, she just seemed sad. And grateful that she hadn't been killed. And . . .

There was a soft gleam in her eyes that told him that, in spite of whatever excuse he might put forward for cutting his skin, she was thinking it was because he'd sacrificed himself for the good of her, not any cause.

Stamp couldn't face that, so he went to the rear of his cell, his back to everything outside.

He made himself think about how much he'd wanted to kill the scrubs before, but it didn't remotely compare to how much he wanted their heads now.

And, suddenly, he felt better.

Much better.

30

Gabriel

Gabriel awakened from his day rest, bolting upright.

He saw red . . . just red—

Then the colors of reality descended on him, lifting the blackness of his sleep, and his gaze took in the sterile cell around him, the silver bars.

Had he been here since last night?

Last night . . .

And it all returned in a backward rush: his fellow monsters tossing him into this cage to "cool off." Stamp, holding out his bloodied hand in invitation.

Blood.

Blood.

And . . .

No.

Next came a memory he tried to reject, but it forced itself into him, anyway.

Kicking at a werewolf while the smell of Stamp's blood tied him up inside and strangled his senses.

The werewolf . . . it'd been Mariah . . .

Remorse pried at Gabriel's chest, and he wasn't sure how.

He wasn't supposed to feel, only need, and he'd needed blood to the point where he'd turned on her. He would've even fought her for Stamp's blood.

Gabriel held his palms to his temples, squeezing, as if he could rearrange all the pieces that had fallen into place with a little pressure. But it did no good. Mariah hadn't wanted Stamp's blood; she'd been trying to stop Gabriel from killing Stamp and throwing away the prospect of getting that government information the Shredder said he possessed.

Right? It all repeated in Gabriel's mind—the torturous image of him sending a brutal kick to Mariah in her half-wolf form, her falling to the ground, where she'd cried out, holding her leg. He heard her saying his name over and over again. . . .

Shame. Gabriel was *sure* he could feel it in him. He'd lost every other connection to humanity but this, and he wondered when even the shame would leave.

But he had an idea now, after meeting older vampires and hearing what they had to say. *After we exchange, our brains don't adapt to vampirism as quickly as the rest of our bodies. . . . It's our psyches that cling to humanity—it's our memories, our conditioning—but that doesn't mean we're still human. . . .*

And he hadn't been able to tell Mariah any of that.

He crawled to the bars, avoiding the silver. He could smell were-creatures all around him in the other cells, could feel the heat from their skin and hear the escalating rhythms of their bodies.

The first night of the full moon—that was why the were-creatures were being held captive, too. Every monster affected by the lunar cycle was already in lockdown now, including 562.

And Mariah.

Gabriel's blood churned at the very thought of her, and his veins felt as if they were roaring with appetite. But that was also because, somewhere in the cell block, Stamp was around, though Gabriel couldn't smell the Shredder or the blood the monsters had probably cleaned off him. It was the mixture of need and proximity of an enemy that addled Gabriel most of all.

"Hey!" he called out to someone, anyone.

He caught the attention of a guard down the way, a large, long-limbed female whose naked body was covered with auburn hair. A Civil Sasquatch with arms that swung at her

sides as she came over. Wicked knives were strapped to both
her thighs.

Gabriel trembled from his hunger, a drunk without a drink
or a junkie without a fix. All he wanted was blood from
Stamp . . . and 562. But there was still a part of him—his mind?
or something much deeper?—that needed to know how Mariah
was doing under the threat of the full moon.

The guard peered at Gabriel with big dark eyes in a hairy
face, her lips thick and pursed, as if judging him to be calmer
than he actually was. She took out earplugs, showing that she'd
been prepared for his swaying powers if he was still in an ill
mood.

He'd fooled her, because he was already picturing teeth—
bigger teeth than he possessed. More efficient killing teeth,
like 562's, that would make it easier to dig into a body for
blood . . .

Gabriel stayed still, hiding his growing bloodlust. His vision
hadn't gone red . . . yet.

"What is it, Gabriel?" the guard asked in a surly, snuffling
voice that sounded just a step above Chaplin's in articulation.

She knew Gabriel, but not vice versa. His reputation had
preceded him.

"Night's falling." He could barely get the words out. "The
moon. Mariah . . ."

The guard's words sounded slurred, but Gabriel knew that
was only how he was hearing things in this quiet fever.

"She visited you earlier, but you were out cold, like every
other vampire is during the day." Some of her words were
high-pitched, then low, snorts and breaths.

But Gabriel's mind was on Mariah. She'd been here?

"Did her leg heal?"

"She's fine now, and she went into lockdown just before you
woke up. She's in a secured room with 562."

He almost yelled *"Why?"* but kept himself serene, even as
he wondered if anyone realized Mariah should be in her own
room.

Gabriel managed to sound reasonable. "When can I go
to her?"

He wanted so badly to think that he was going to help
Mariah in some way, but he kept seeing himself kicking her

instead. Kept seeing the betrayed look in her glowing green eyes as his boot connected with her shoulder and she fell to the ground . . .

The guard snorfed out a response. "She asked to stay alone with 562 under the guard of a lot of vampires and Civils. After your Badlands were-friends hung around to see Stamp and his partner questioned by a vampire, they went under restraint, too."

"And Stamp?"

The Sasquatch shook her head, her long facial hair flowing. "Neither of them gave up information about a government attack." Grunt, snorf. "He's good at mental blocking, and I think he might've taught his friend Mags how to do it, too. We have to keep them around until we're sure we've gotten all we can from them."

"I have to be with Mariah." No matter what 562's blood had done to her.

The more Gabriel thought he could help her, the more he could forget about kicking Mariah, when he'd forfeited every last piece of good in him.

The guard weighed his comment while, down the corridor, the werewolves began to howl softly, the were-cats hiss, as the pull of the full moon summoned their true monsters.

31

Mariah

As I sat in front of a near-comatose 562 in a white, padded room deep in the bowels of the asylum, I could feel the full moon expanding within me, pressing out to its rounded sphere like a ball blowing up with air and light.

It was coming.

I exhaled, and the chains and crosses that bound me to the wall rattled. Like the other were-creatures, I'd requested the restraints, but with me, the monsters had really done a good job of containing. Same with 562 because, during a full moon, no were-creature that I knew of could stop from changing once we started up. We couldn't even hold ourselves to a half-change . . . unless 562 had given me something via our blood that lifted me to a higher, more intelligent form that allowed me a control that I'd never heard of before in a moon-changing were.

I could only hope.

Just outside, Chaplin stood upright at the long, unbreakable window, his paws against it. Even with the weird estrangement we'd been going through, he'd come here, and his big brown eyes were full of worry. He looked as fearful as my heart felt.

Next to him, four vampire guards cocked their heads, extremely interested in what was about to transpire in me, their blood cousin, as well as in 562, their origin.

Civil monsters were guarding all of my friends, plus the other were-creatures, but 562 and I had more security than anyone else, including those crosses that tamed 562. Across from me, my origin seemed to be as smooth as marble, with that all-encompassing silver hair and those unblinking red eyes staring at the wall as if there were something spellbinding in the molecules of its padding.

Another second nattered by . . . then another . . .

With every shuddery heartbeat, I regretted what I'd done with 562. Why'd I taken that blood before the full moon when I could've waited to see what my origin really was?

Why did I always get myself in these messes?

I must've been wearing a jittery expression, because Chaplin barked in encouragement outside, although I couldn't hear him behind that glass.

A force was rising higher in me, raying out in every way, and I sat up straighter at the odd sensation. It was more breath-taking than the usual were-change. It felt like you do when you jump down from a high rock and your stomach turns, except it was happening throughout my entire body.

I strained at my chains, the crosses now making the skin beneath them hurt a little, like needle pricks. I wanted to ask her/him what was happening. "562 . . . ?"

But my origin gave me nothing as she/he continued to stare.

The blankness of alienation surrounded me. My restrained friends weren't nearby. My own origin didn't even seem to know I existed right now. And Gabriel . . .

I lowered my head as I felt his boot clobber my shoulder, pain screaming through me, centering in my heart. I'd been in half were-form, so I'd been able to process the shock. The awfulness of being put aside for his new intimate—the bloodlust.

As a growing were-force began to chop at my sides, almost as if a moon goddess were inside me being born, I started to panic.

I should've waited . . .

Should've never done this at all . . .

Just as I was about to moan in fear, 562 snapped her/his gaze to me. Red, shining . . .

Awake.

Her/his gaze sucked me in, and there was nothing I could do to stop the image/thoughts from assaulting me with what I knew was my future.

A future in which I was a wan imitation of the original 562 since my blood wasn't as pure. Vaguely, I saw myself sitting outside . . . or maybe it was inside . . . staring, hungering as I waited.

A deer loped by, but I had no appetite for it.

A human strolled past, so easy to catch, but that wasn't good enough, either.

Then . . . a chimera, just like Neelan, half-man, half-snake, slithering toward me and . . .

God-all, I was hungry. Oh, the want of the blood in this monster who wasn't a relation of mine. Civil blood—

Then, from 562, I understood that to drink this blood was to thrive. The very definition of peace to 562 was seeing her/his children dominating everyone, even the other monsters. . . .

The change inside me brutally pulsed outward, and I gagged as my origin's gaze kept burning into mine.

Survival of the fittest, even among monsters. I want my children to outlive them all.

Everything made sense: that one image/thought of 562 and the Cyclops, which had been bloodied and gutted at 562's feet just before the Shredders had captured her/him. The progression . . . from animal to human blood, then to this. We blood monsters had inherited a pattern from 562, but we only seemed to get to the point of wanting humans, not other monsters.

And Civils were our allies against the bad guys. They were going to help me visit justice on humans like the ones who'd hurt my family. . . .

My blood thrashed in me as my body rebelled. Monster blood? I couldn't. Wouldn't.

Ever.

562's gaze broke from me as she/he succumbed to the moon's turning before I did, maybe because I was so afraid of what I'd seen in my origin that I was gripping to the last of myself tightly, as I'd done when the bad guys had attacked my home in Dallas with that werewolf in tow—when I wouldn't let go of my bedpost until they got me, dragging me off the mattress, screaming and scraping my nails along the floor.

I *wouldn't* give in. Nothing could make me.

Oh, God-all . . .

The force of change pummeled me inside as 562 gave in to her/his full-moon fate.

First, her/his red eyes rotated, going to vertical slits instead of horizontal under all the silver hair.

Then, everything else at once—

Longer teeth in a seething cavern of a mouth as she/he opened it wide and flexed her/his arms, sending the restraint chains and even the crosses into bits of clanging pieces that hit the padded walls . . . then *another* set of arms blasting out of her/his sides as 562 got taller . . . silver hair sprouting all over the body while a serpentlike tongue waggled out of her/his mouth . . .

I didn't see the rest, because the change consumed me, too, my vision spinning from a blue tinge to violet, then a bloody red. Without the benefit of easing me into it with the melting bones and simmering blood of my normal were-state, my body blasted into its new form in a vicious hurry, sending my own bindings into oblivion.

But, all the while, my mind remained intact, and it was as if I were in a glass coffin, my body buried in this clear container. It left me staring in jumbled numbness up at the ceiling while Civils—no Reds amongst them—rushed in.

They had crucifixes out, and I randomly thought that in this much more powerful full-moon state, holy items weren't going to matter. Then they screamed, and there was a ripping sound just before their blood splashed over the white of the room, over my face, and I heard 562 screech in the same otherworldly, controlled tone that she/he had used while talking directly to me and Gabriel.

The blood's smell, its wetness, owned me and, in spite of myself, I licked round my mouth with a tongue that seemed to stretch three feet.

Through the opened doorway, I heard Chaplin barking.

Mariah!

As I rolled my head toward him, I saw him standing in the

window with a horrified expression. Then he lost his balance
and disappeared.

My dog. I'd seen him retreat from me only once, when I'd
been an out-of-control werewolf in the Badlands. But this was
worse.

So much worse.

Outside, monsters wailed in their death throes. 562 had
gotten out, and she/he was drinking Civil blood—my new
friends. The army we were putting together to beat the bad
guys.

The memory of those bad guys who'd come into my family's
home, murdering my mother and brother, was the only thing
keeping me sane right now. Without the help of Civils, I'd never
find my attackers. I'd never see humans just like them come to
justice.

I was hungrier for their reckoning than anything, even
though this new form might make me stronger than ever.

But would that be only during a full moon phase?

I sprang up, finding that I had two sets of arms now, like
562, but I didn't feel as tall. I didn't feel as hungry.

Not for Civil blood, at least.

I sped away, following the trail of gore 562 had left in her/
his wake.

32

Gabriel

When Gabriel first heard the monsters screaming, he thought Stamp was loose.

But then all the captive humans began yelling for help, and they wouldn't be doing that with a Shredder, who was bound to protect humanity.

Just as the moon-changing were-creatures began barking and yowling, a banshee-like screech shook the walls, and Gabriel recognized the tone.

The terrible cry of 562.

But Mariah—where was *she* if 562 had gotten out of its heavily protected containment?

In Gabriel's haste to get out of his cell, he grabbed the bars, and the silver hissed against his hands, burning. He let go as his skin began vamp-healing.

"Get me out of here," he said to the Sasquatch guard, looking into its eyes and finally injecting sway into his voice, hoping it would work.

The hairy female picked the lock of the cell.

Just as Gabriel launched himself into the corridor, a wall at one end blasted open. Keesie the huge stone-creature punched the rest of the way through and stumbled out, leading a flood of Civils, all with eyes wide while they screamed and ran toward Gabriel. He saw a Red tik-tik woman who hadn't detached her head yet sprinting past Keesie while a Civil chimera turned around and breathed fire behind his horse's quarters before continuing at a fierce gallop.

In the midst of it all, through the dusty rubble, a thing appeared in that hole in the wall.

All Gabriel could see in the beginning was its gaping mouth, a collection of saberlike teeth. It seemed to take its time, screeching, before locking onto a Civil with a dart-shaped skull who was running.

Then everything happened in what seemed to be a splash of time.

562's tongue zoomed out, splitting in two. One part went one way, the other the opposite, both sections flexing, then coming together like two swords, decapitating the dart-head. Even while the skull was still air-bound, 562's tongue scooped up the headless body, shoving the corpse into its mouth, where it sucked on the neck like it was enjoying an old-fashioned lollipop.

Many of the faster monsters were upon Gabriel now, but their frantic motions didn't detract from the scent of blood down the corridor.

Gabriel's veins started to tremble, his vision going scarlet, especially when the dust cleared all the way, revealing all of 562.

A red diamond-eyed monster with the same fall of silver locks on its head but, now, shorter strands of hair were also sprinkled over its stretched body, and the silver . . . it somehow looked like ash rubbed over skin.

Then there were the arms . . . four freakin' arms, waving out of the sides of its body.

A name floated out of Gabriel's growing bloodlust and into his consciousness.

Kali?

He'd once seen the Hindu blood goddess—or what others called the goddess of time and change—in an old, old movie.

Kali with the ashes of Shiva on her—woman and man, almost like 562 but without the same number of arms. But this wasn't any goddess or god munching on a Civil monster twenty yards down the corridor. 562 was merely a creature Gabriel didn't understand, and his mind was merely grasping at a more familiar explanation for it.

After gnawing on the last of the dart-head's body, 562 tossed away the corpse, and its tongue melded into one entity. A group of gremlins skittered by, blatting out screams, and 562's tongue followed them, then quickly shrank back.

Gabriel didn't have time to think about why, as 562's tongue hovered, like it was picking out its next victim from the fleeing monsters. Then it zapped out its tongue so far forward that it caught Keesie, who was still lumbering away.

Taking Keesie by the neck, 562 raised the bulbous, stonelike creature high, then slammed her to the floor. Rocks burst from her as she opened her tiny mouth in that otherwise featureless face and cried out.

Then 562 slammed Keesie down again, as if trying to find a way to break her open.

The Sasquatch guard seemed frozen next to Gabriel as everyone else bumped into them on their way out.

"It's eating monsters," she mumble-grunted.

Even in his growing fog of bloodlust, Gabriel noted that Keesie wasn't just a monster, she was a Civil. Same with the very dead dart-head.

But the gremlins? 562 could've had them easily, and it'd shied away.

Gremlins were Reds.

Shit, 562 wasn't eating any of its children, just the Civils. It thrived on their blood.

And the smell of that blood was taking over rational thought now, making Gabriel feel like a machine with someone else at the control panel.

As the Sasquatch started running away, the only reason Gabriel didn't rip into her was that 562 got to her first.

With a massive leap from down the corridor, it abandoned Keesie, leaving her broken on the ground with shards of stone surrounding a pocked body that wasn't bleeding—

562 screeched through the air, snatched the Sasquatch with its tongue even before it landed, and yanked the Civil straight to its mouth, where the teeth were waiting.

The were-creatures were howling and hissing, making the asylum sound like a madhouse. But even above that, Gabriel could hear sarcastic cheers erupting from one of the cells down the corridor.

Stamp?

Was he feeling safe behind those bars as he watched one monster eat others?

Gabriel's blood hunger spiked as he remembered the cut on the Shredder's arm. And while he watched 562 dismembering the Sasquatch, spitting out the hair while reveling in the blood, he wondered if he would ever have to worry about Stamp—or anyone else—again if he were like a 562.

By now, the were-creatures howled and yowled in their cells, but the other monsters had secured them so well that they couldn't break out of their bindings. Their cries only inflamed Gabriel's cravings, and just as he was about to go to 562, joining it in splashing around the Sasquatch's blood, he felt it.

The sensation of a cushioned cord pulling at him.

Heavy, sawed breathing sounded from behind Gabriel, and it curdled his blood.

562 didn't stop snacking as Gabriel turned around.

He witnessed vertical-diamond green eyes, and in spite of the different shape of them, it was the same gaze he'd looked into that night in the Badlands when, as a full werewolf, Mariah and the others had come to his rescue. Though he hadn't known what she truly was at that point, he'd recognized her then, and he recognized her now.

But this time, Mariah was even more of a monster. She was a visual echo of 562, smaller, though not by much. Her hair—the hair that had always caught his fancy with its sheen and sharp edges—was still red, not silver, and it dusted her entire body, even her four arms. Her mouth and pointed teeth were slightly smaller, too, and her body had more of a womanly shape—waist, long legs, breasts—than the androgynous 562's.

Yet there was an even bigger difference. Mariah wasn't attacking the dwindling number of Civils jostling past her.

Why? Didn't she have the same appetite as 562?

As her gaze landed on him, he saw and felt the truth in her—the numbness of finding out the worst about a parent. The disgust and refusal of what she was supposed to be.

She looked into his eyes and sent a thought to him. *Without an army of monsters, we can't get the bad guys.* Then, deep in her mind, he heard the screams of her brother and mother as the bad guys murdered them.

Revenge. That was what had always defined Mariah, and killing Civils wouldn't provide that for her. Funny how her idea of justice still overrode everything else in that new full-moon body of hers.

But was that only because she was holding on to the last of her humanity, just as he'd been doing after becoming a vampire?

Linked to her like this, feeling her pain, her own longings, Gabriel momentarily forgot about 562's blood, the yearning for a liquid that might be his own remedy, making him faster, better.

She sent another quick thought to him. *562's death might reduce me to something so primitive and weak I'll never survive in this world, Gabriel. Help me contain her/him before the Civils regroup and go after 562?*

He didn't want their origin to be terminated, either—if it could even be killed. Not when he was so close to wherever it was he was meant to go.

But . . . somewhere in his mind, Gabriel knew that its death might make *him* human.

Wasn't that what he wanted more?

Wasn't it?

As his and Mariah's link wound through him, a vine that would tie him up and never let go with its buzzing wisps of energy, he kept looking into her, seeing a trace of memory she hadn't meant for him to discover—the kick of his boot, the fall she'd taken because he'd wanted Stamp's blood more than he'd wanted her at that one, red-crazed moment.

The last of his humanity rushed back, nearly strangling him. *I'm sorry,* he thought. *I'll do anything to help you.*

A screech brought Gabriel out of Mariah, and they both looked at 562, who'd spied a Civil chameleon woman pasted near the ceiling back near where Keesie was still lying. The chameleon was blending into the concrete, where she'd hoped to go unnoticed.

At the discovery, the creature scrambled downward, toward

a cell—Stamp's—and tried to suck itself to skinniness, easing between the bars. 562 huffed out a wheezy-banshee breath, then bounded back to Stamp's cell, tearing off those bars just after the chameleon squeezed past them.

With a thrust of speed, Mariah shot past Gabriel. He took off, too, as if the connection were pulling at him. He stopped in front of the bar-gaped cell just in time to see the chameleon using Stamp as a shield from 562, whose tongue kept flickering out, trying to snag the Civil monster.

Stamp was dodging that tongue, but his dark eyes were glued to 562, as if trying to figure it out. As if thinking of a way to kill it—

Mariah and Gabriel didn't even have enough time to get 562's attention before it wearied of this game and darted out an arm, clawing Stamp out of the way, slashing one of his legs clean off.

In what seemed like a carnerotica slow-motion clip, Stamp's leg flew one way while he flew another, blood spraying like a dissipating bridge between them.

As the kid crashed into the wall, he screamed, holding what was now a stump. On the other side of the cell, the leg spilled gore, steel plates, and gears, some of which spun like dying toys.

Across the corridor, Stamp's partner screamed, too.

But all Gabriel recognized was the blood.

Everything became a red-tinged blur of action for him: 562's tongue snagging the fleeing chameleon and popping her into its mouth. Stamp crying out and holding his bleeding stump. Mariah's connection flaring in Gabriel as he stumbled toward Stamp.

But Mariah couldn't hold Gabriel this time as he readied himself to jump at the Shredder. It was like he'd never promised to help her when she needed it the most.

One of her four arms hit him with as much vigor as he'd kicked at her last night, but she was stronger than any vampire, and she knocked him to the opposite corner of the cell, where the stab of rejection weighed on their link, pinning him for a moment.

Her message had been clear—if he wasn't going to help, he needed to get out of there, before he became part of the problem. She couldn't have him around this time to bring her down. . . .

As that returning shame mixed with his bloodlust, he could only watch as Mariah engaged 562, jumping at it, creating a whir of hair, claws, and teeth. After what seemed an eternity of screeching, 562 finally swatted its child away, and Mariah busted into a wall, creating a four-armed imprint.

But Gabriel didn't look at the damage for long. His attention was too consumed by a line of blood marking the ground, as if a fatally injured person had crawled away.

Stamp.

Instead of wondering how the Shredder had managed this feat, Gabriel crawled to the blood. He couldn't stop himself, and he pressed his mouth to the ground, to the red.

He moaned at the taste of his enemy.

Then 562 let out another screech, and it was so ear-piercing that Gabriel put his hands over his ears and cringed. When he glanced back at 562, he saw that Mariah was facing off with their origin, hardly giving up the fight.

But it seemed that 562 was done with sparring altogether.

As it looked at Gabriel, its red diamond eyes even seemed . . . exhausted. It didn't seem to understand why its children weren't cooperating.

His hands lowered from his ears as 562 sent him an image/thought: a baby in a mother's arms because children were all 562 had ever wanted. Then, a picture of Gabriel drinking its blood, just like it was mother's milk . . .

But the tempting offer broke off as Mariah jumped at 562, swiping out with her claws with such speed that all Gabriel could see was red, teeth, waggling tongue, and arms.

As Mariah landed on her parent, driving it to the ground, 562 let out a series of whines, holding off the attack by pushing at Mariah's four arms with its own and avoiding her teeth. It was trying to connect with Mariah's eyes, beseeching her, but Mariah was on a mission, snapping at 562 while the bigger, older monster dodged, ultimately rolling Mariah over, then opening its own mouth and letting out a rattling roar.

It was angry at Mariah. *Too* angry?

"562!" Gabriel shouted. He didn't know if he'd said it to redeem himself with Mariah or to get his origin to come to him so it could make good on that offer of its blood.

But 562 was beyond sweet talk now, and as Mariah jabbed

up with her tongue, as if she intended to choke 562 into submission with it, 562 lashed out with its own tongue, splitting it in two, wrapping it around Mariah's long appendage and holding it, as if ready to yank it out.

No—

The threat to Mariah overcame all else in Gabriel, and he reacted the only way a lesser monster could in the face of its stronger parent.

Mind freeze, just as the older vampires had been teaching him.

He conjured up power in his mind, and it swirled.

A cold blast of ice. That was what the other vampires had told him. He had to at least try.

"562," he whispered, and it peeked over at him, its tongue still capturing Mariah's.

With every ounce of energy possible, he forced out what felt like a mental icicle, fast, hard—

Swish-crash!

He reared back, feeling as if he'd run into a black wall and chipped away at a small part of it, leaving mental debris to crumble over him.

562's vertical red eyes flickered under its hair, as if it were surprised.

His and Mariah's link joined up again as 562 seemed to realize what it was doing to Mariah, its child. Its tongue loosened from hers and fell away.

A panting Mariah peered at him from under the cage of 562's arms. *What did you do?*

Something I shouldn't have. 562 was more of a parent than even his maker. He hadn't meant to hurt it.

As Mariah held still under 562, waiting to see what it . . . and maybe even Gabriel . . . would do next, he heard a sweeping sound in the cell. When he peered out of the corner of his eye, he found movement.

Shadows.

Within a second, the forms of several shadow people coalesced in his gaze. What were they doing?

The answer shaped itself gradually. They were wiping the floor of Stamp's blood, leaving behind a medicinal smell that made Gabriel's nose sting.

Then he heard Taraline's voice from the corridor. "562," she said in that low, assuaging tone.

Gabriel couldn't believe it. The shadow people had come when most of the monsters had run. They knew that no preter was stopping 562 on its rampage, but maybe a different sort of defense could do it.

Mariah just stared with that half-human Kali face, the diamond-green eyes, the jutting teeth. He could feel that she wanted to scream at Taraline in warning, but for some reason, she wasn't doing it.

When the shadow woman came into the cell, Gabriel saw why.

She'd taken off her veil, and the sight of her tightened a vampire's throat.

Dymorrdia had stripped the skin off Taraline's head, nearly down to the skull, save for a few jaundiced patches. Her forehead and cheekbones were high, but her cheeks contained bones that had broken and shifted, small and piled upon each other like crisscrossing splinters. Her nose looked like an inward snout, but her eyes and mouth . . .

Those eyes were a watery, heartfelt blue while her mouth was perfect, pink-lipped and full. It was the eyes and mouth that told Gabriel just how beautiful Taraline had once been.

562 whimpered, and it was strange to see that sort of sound coming from a mouth with killer teeth and a face with a bloodred gaze.

Mariah still bided her silent time underneath 562 while it was transfixed on Taraline.

"Chaplin wanted to come to you, Mariah, but we told him we needed him to round up the vampires and other Reds down below," Taraline said, obviously trying to reassure everyone while she also calmed 562 with her smooth tone.

Even in her monster body, Mariah's love and longing for her dog wavered outward, smacking against Gabriel.

"They were excited by all the blood," Taraline added, "so my friends and I are cleaning it away. And one of us was in here to remove Mr. Stamp and his partner after his unfortunate accident. We still need to see if they have information about a government attack."

Gabriel's fangs were long, his gaze reddened, even though

the blood had been scrubbed away. "You need to get out of here, Taraline."

562 puppy-dog panted, as if trying to get the shadow woman to come closer.

"No, 562 could use some soothing," Taraline said. "So, actually, you two are the ones who should leave."

Gabriel had met brave people who'd risked themselves for a higher cause before, like Zel Hopkins, and now Taraline joined their ranks as she walked to 562, just as if she weren't a bit afraid of the consequences.

He knew exactly what she was doing. She'd taken it upon herself to placate the creature by giving it another child. Or maybe Taraline had just chosen to take part in an exchange, and now was as good a time as any to do it if it assuaged 562.

562 held up all of her arms, welcoming Taraline, and it was almost beautiful to behold, a fan of silver-glinted limbs wavering with the grace of preter movement.

As the creature leaned toward Taraline, Mariah slipped out from underneath it, rolling away and arching her back as she balanced on all sixes.

Taraline offered the sacrifice of her neck while 562 tenderly laid its four hands on the shadow woman's arms. It bared all its teeth, giving Mariah the opportunity to slide over to Gabriel faster than even his vampire eyes could track.

He didn't know what was going on until Mariah touched his skin, imprinting, linking to him with such ferocity that he felt tunneled out, as if she were using all of him to fuel her.

His mind spun, because it didn't even feel like his own anymore. Mariah . . . becoming him . . . becoming his body, and now his brain . . .

She'd seen him stun 562 with his mind freeze, and she was making him do it again—but on her terms.

He was barely aware of 562 cupping Taraline's face, then bending to her neck as two long fangs flicked out from the center of its upper gums like lethal, slender needles, because Mariah joined with him full force, their link spinning, picking up speed, binding and blazing—

562 drank from Taraline as the shadow woman gripped two of her predator's free wrists. Her knees buckled, and she gasped in pain, sinking to the ground. 562 tenderly let her go,

extending one of its long nails to slash into its own skin for a blood exchange.

Mariah didn't wait a moment longer. She roared, as if calling out 562.

Gabriel moved in front of her out of pure instinct and the heroism that had once defined him. . . .

562 looked up at Mariah, and Gabriel felt the link with her plunging through him, out his mind and through his eyes, into their origin.

In an explosion of consciousness, Gabriel went to another place: a red-tinged film on the screen of 562's mind, flashes of people and monsters bending in worship, flickers of love, happiness, dancing. Ecstatic new vampire children who shared in their parent's bliss.

And, then, 562 was strapped to that ash tree, and it wasn't the burning of the bark against its skin that hurt so much as the betrayal of creatures that wanted even more from it than it had already given. . . .

Gabriel knew that this was his and Mariah's future as well as 562's past. Betrayal happened to all monsters at some point.

As if finally fighting back, 562 turned its mind to a screen of blood, juicy and thick, and Gabriel's appetite reared up again.

With a swatting flash, his consciousness was blasted aside, as if Mariah had swiped at his mind, depriving him of the temptation. Their link heated up even more, and he knew he had no choice but to take strength from her.

Then Mariah turned his mind outward, slamming into 562 as he'd done with his first mind freeze, and the creature reared away.

Mariah directed Gabriel's mind at 562 again, coming at it one more time, another, *another*, until the screen of 562's consciousness began to crack—

Gabriel couldn't move, and his head physically began to ache, sharp and dull at the same time, but Mariah wasn't allowing any weakness in either of them, and his consciousness punched forward again—

In a shattering spray of mental glass, 562's mind went to pieces, and Gabriel saw the sublime sparkle of rotating fragments, each reflecting a single memory for 562, before he was pulled back by Mariah and the link. . . .

With a violent pop, he found himself back in his own mind, alone. His skull seemed to be on fire, but, worse, he smelled Taraline's blood, and it was close.

Too close to him.

He recovered from the mental onslaught, seeing 562 sitting so still in its Kali form, staring ahead with those shattered diamond eyes. It was still alive; he could hear its almost non-existent pulse.

It was still a parent to all its children, even in the containment Mariah had invented for it.

Gabriel's slow gaze traveled to Taraline, who was in a pile next to 562. The origin hadn't been able to infuse Taraline with its own blood, so she was rasping, as if struggling for breath as she pressed one of her gloved hands to her neck. Blood seeped through her fingers.

Taraline would die if she didn't get an infusion, but as Gabriel hissed, his fangs erect, his sight red with need, he couldn't have cared less.

He zoomed toward Taraline, but just as he got there, Mariah screeched in front of him, arms spread, her claws extended, those huge teeth ready to defend her friend.

Feinting to the side, as if he could beat her, Gabriel jumped at Taraline, but Mariah was ready, crashing into him, jamming him to the ground with her four hands.

Stop it, Gabriel! she thought as she pinned him, her gaze firing into his.

He hissed at her again, but he saw something else in her eyes, too.

A time from the Badlands, back when he'd been the one holding Mariah to the ground after she'd gone wild.

Now, he was the one under her.

But even with those humongous teeth and green eyes, she had enough grace to infuse him with the link that had first saved her, only to save him now.

Peace, and it seemed to be sewing him up pass by pass, containing him.

Don't, Gabriel, she thought to him from deep inside that grotesque body. *562 didn't die, so we're still here. We're still stronger than ever, better than any cure we could've ever hoped for. We still have a chance.*

To do what? he wondered as she continued stitching him, their link like thread that hushed through his body. *To beat the bad guys?*

Or did she think they still had an opportunity to conquer what they were becoming in this ever-changing world?

He tried hard to accept Mariah's aid, the stitches, the peace, but Taraline's blood kept luring him.

After Mariah was done, she backed off, as if feeling through their link that he was done attacking, and he was safe . . . for now.

The sounds of Civils came from the corridor, accompanied by the hint of shadow people, all brandishing crosses as they moved into the cell.

The religious items didn't seem to work on Mariah in her new form, but she was lucid enough to back away in surrender. There was no doubt that the holy objects worked on Gabriel, though, and he shuddered, turning away his gaze while hearing the shadow people telling the Civils to take it easy on Mariah, because they'd seen her defend them against 562.

When he next opened his eyes, he saw her bending over Taraline, the shadows and Civils circling the pair as others bound 562 with those probably useless crosses and silver chains.

It was the Mariah-enhanced mind freeze that had gotten 562, and he feared nothing else was ever going to work.

Mariah raised one of her four arms and, with a claw, opened her skin so blood dripped down onto Taraline's lips.

Who knew what would happen next. Wouldn't Taraline need 562's blood, not Mariah's, to become a vampire and be fully healed from dymorrdia, since 562 was the one who'd bitten her?

Or was there a chance Taraline would get some of 562's blood from Mariah?

It was only when Gabriel started shaking from the scent that the Civils flashed their crosses at him again, and he closed his eyes, naturally going toward the darkness instead.

33

Mariah

After the full moon phase ran its course, we hid 562.

We took our mind-broken origin to the boulder cave near Little Romania, far from where the humans still waited for that fictional mosquito threat to disappear. Here, where our group had first hidden, Pucci had built a nook way far back from the entrance. He'd merely moved some rocks away from a wall, and Gabriel had put 562 in a new resting place, arranging our origin in her/his favorite sitting position, legs crossed, gaze an eternal stare.

Yet now 562 and her/his shattered gaze stared at nothing. Or maybe at everything, for all we knew. With the dying of the full moon, 562's body had automatically reverted back to regular form, smaller, just as humanlike as she/he had been when I'd first seen her/him, with fewer teeth and arms and that long fall of hair to hide her/his face. Obviously, 562's body still worked, although the mind couldn't control it.

Only the lunar cycle could. That was what I figured, at least, and come the next full moon phase, there'd be old, strong vampires here to make sure 562 hadn't recovered from the damage Gabriel and I had visited on her/his brain.

We'd brought some unbreakable glass from the asylum with us, too. In the end, we planned to roll the rocks in front of the shield for camouflage. But I didn't like to think that we were putting 562 into a glass coffin, because the very thought made me think of the way I'd felt in my new body during a full moon. Instead, I justified 562's nook as more of a vault, where a treasure could be protected. She/he was our relic.

But 562 was also our secret.

Gabriel had seen to that last night, while the last of the full moon hovered and I was locked up under the tightest security possible while I was threatened with silver swords and told that I'd be chopped up if I misbehaved. All that time, Gabriel had been enlisting his friends, a bunch of old vampires—the ones who'd promised to look after 562 at the next full moon. They lied to the entire community about 562 having recovered from her/his mental affliction and run off, out of the hub. As far as we knew, no one but me and Gabriel, plus the dead Civils, had figured out that our origin had an appetite for the other monsters. If the shadow people knew, they hadn't said anything, so we assumed they'd been busy with the blood cleaning below, where the vampires had caused such havoc until controlled.

It was only when the full moon had waned and we Badlanders had left our lunacy behind that we'd discovered the vampires' subterfuge.

And we hadn't disagreed.

Maybe we were utterly selfish, but if the Civil community knew we were keeping 562 alive, they'd want to try and kill her/him, if they could, and all us were-creatures might end up turning into powerless regular animals . . . or something worse. The tik-tik women and gremlins would probably become what they originally were—corpses. Most important, the older vampires valued 562's existence—and how powerful she/he made them—just as much as the rest of us Reds, and they didn't want to destroy their origin, either.

Yes, we were ruthless for keeping 562 here, but we'd be stupid to possibly resign ourselves to a position of weakness in the world. I didn't mind lying in this instance.

The more I thought about how 562 had gone about introducing us to her/his blood, the more I admired my origin. 562 had known that I would do anything to be a better monster. But she/he had chosen an ambassador for her/his ambitions while not realizing that I'd never give in to an appetite for Civils. Giving in would be like one type of human—say a distractoid—eating a shut-in; two of the same kind, yet different. Cannibalism.

In spite of everything, we'd wanted to honor 562, and with that came the acknowledgment of our other dead. So, in our hidden relic cave, we gathered. Hana went forward first, setting down Sammy's comm device next to 562's clear, upright coffin. The oldster lay down a stone on which he'd written Zel's name, since we'd kept nothing else of her.

Although Gabriel had nothing material of his own to offer, I felt him thinking of Abby and his own mosquito-victimized human family. I felt the heaviness of a promise being made inside him.

Was he musing that he'd make them proud by still trying to be better than his nature was leading him to be? Or was he mulling over experimenting with 562's vial-stored blood whenever someone finally identified it? Perhaps he wouldn't need to be bitten by 562 to be more powerful after all.

I could understand his temptation, since I was the strongest and most peaceful I'd ever been. I'd also proven that I could control my new self, and Gabriel only wanted the same thing.

In celebration of that, I made my own offering to 562, standing before the glass coffin, silently vowing that I'd protect her/his children. They would all take the place of my own family, whom I'd lost to bad guys like the ones who'd first victimized 562 for her/his blood.

I'd find justice for us, because that was the only thing that held the world together.

Pucci had his hands clasped in front of him. Reverence from a man I hadn't thought capable of it before now.

"Where do you think 562 is?" he asked. "I mean, where's its consciousness, do you think?"

"Who knows?" I said. There were no explanations. 562 hadn't even known what had created her/him. For all we realized, 562's birther could've been some kind of entity that'd thought to exercise destruction on humanity.

I didn't expect to find any kind of answer, just consequences. Taraline finally approached 562's coffin. Thanks to my blood, she'd survived, but that was the extent of it so far. I heard that her surface hadn't shown signs of healing in these first couple of nights, so she was back to wearing her veil again. It could be that 562 had been right, and an exchange was the only thing potent enough to fully mend a human dymorrdia victim. Besides, I wasn't the one who'd bitten her before feeding her my blood, so I was pretty sure she wouldn't become a monster, just by drinking from me.

Unless I was wrong.

I wanted to tear her veil off, just to be sure, but we all knew Taraline was a deliberate sort. Maybe my powerful blood *was* already working away on her, and she didn't want anyone to see her face and body until she'd fully healed. To me, she seemed just like a lady preparing herself in her boudoir and not coming out until she was dressed to the nines.

She bent to 562, leaving her/him a necklace of water that a monster had confiscated from a sleeping human.

As if overwhelmed by every sacrifice Taraline had made, whether she'd wanted that exchange from 562 or not, Gabriel walked away, taking a part of me with him. I'd been caged away from him since we'd last been together, and tonight was the first I'd seen him since the confrontation with 562.

Chaplin, who'd gone right back to avoiding me—maybe even worse now than before—nuzzled up to Taraline on one side as Hana hugged her from the other. As Pucci closed up 562's grave, then sat down to guard it, I began to follow Gabriel.

But I waited a moment, hoping Chaplin would come with me.

I glanced back at him, but he just slid a look to me, then turned away.

I didn't know what to do, how to show him that I wasn't as monstrous on the inside as I'd seemed on the outside when I'd turned into this new form.

But I'd think of a way to win my Chaplin back. He had to see that I hadn't changed so much.

My chest squeezing itself into oblivion, I walked all the way out after Gabriel, allowing him some distance while he exited the cave. Thanks to our link, he would know I was nearby, and he would slow down when he was ready for me.

But he kept going toward the hub. Miffed, I continued

trailing him, even as he entered the asylum. Avoiding the other monsters who were walking round, he mounted some stairs, and I was about to, also, when I heard the oldster right behind me.

"Mariah."

I could tell he wanted to chat. Before we'd come to the cave tonight, I'd overheard him talking with some monsters about more solid plans to spread rebellion to other hubs—including the worst of them in old D.C.—and how they'd found some preters who had flying capabilities that could eventually post themselves round GBVille to bat down Dactyl planes and surveillance robots, if they should come. They also spoke of other monsters who could post themselves outside the hub and emanate radiation enough to block satellite activity.

It was as if the oldster wanted to tell me every little detail, like it was important that I sign off on them. I could tell by the way the other Red monsters—even the Civils—greeted me when I entered the asylum that they felt the same way. The gremlins followed me with their gazes when I walked by, too.

Very weird. Me, commander in chief, just because I'd barged into the asylum first on the power blast night and, now, because I was . . .

Whatever I was.

I sighed, watching Gabriel disappearing up those stairs. The oldster—Michael—caught up to me. So did Hiram the gallant were-puma.

He talked before the oldster did. "We've got an interesting visitor." Hiram jerked his head toward the direction of the cell block. "A human, and she's claiming that she worked with a vampire to bring down the hub."

I hoped he wasn't talking about Jo, our contact via Taraline who'd designed our power blaster. How could she remember working with us when Gabriel had swayed her . . . ?

The oldster went with me and Hiram to the cell block, where they'd stored this visitor because she was a human. Unfortunately, I passed Stamp and his partner, Mags, first.

He was sitting, propped against the bars, the stump of his leg capped off by a manual medical doodad they called a coagulator. After some shadow people had dragged Stamp out of harm's way and into a lab that night, a mummy man who'd once been a doctor had saved his life with that device. Stamp and Mags were alive only because some vampires believed they were just real good at blocking and they actually did carry information of value to us. I didn't think so, but I was sure the vamps considered them entertainment besides.

Anyway, you'd think a Shredder would've gained some humility from his inferior position, but he still had a dark fire in his eyes. I recognized vengefulness.

"You know they *will* be coming from the outside, right, Mariah?" he said, trying to scare me with his bottomless gaze. "Mags and I might've been the first to get to you, but we won't be the last."

I would've laughed at him, except he was pitiful, sitting there with a nub for one leg. I even felt a little sorry for him and this Mags girl because they'd gotten desperate enough to launch a half-baked attack on us; I'd been desperate like that at one point, too.

Logically, though, we monsters *were* still concerned about those sentinels who were out there somewhere. And then we had to worry about the unstable state of our charade, which could fall down all round us any day now.

Mags was standing at her cell bars, but when I glanced at her, she was looking at me funny with those dark almond eyes of hers. Almost as if she had a million questions she wanted to ask me.

I refused to glance at Stamp again and, instead, moved on quickly, to where Hiram was waiting in front of a cell at the end of the corridor. Keesie, who'd recovered from 562's attack but bore the gouges of missing rock in her body, was standing guard, too.

Ironically, they were in front of 562's original cell. But, inside, Jo faced us straight on, unlike 562 had when I'd first come to her/him.

Jo's long mahogany hair was slicked back, and she was still wearing that disease mask, plus the generic clothing. I acted as if I didn't know her, and that she hadn't been the force behind our asylum takedown. But, without preamble, she said, "A word in private?"

Hiram, Keesie, and a reluctant oldster left us. The latter hung round not too far away down the corridor.

"There are a lot of people like me out there," Jo said when we were alone, "and we don't plan to offer up resistance, ma'am."

Ma'am?

It occurred to me that if Gabriel's sway hadn't worked on her, she'd probably recall my name. It was just that the monsters had thought to bring Jo to *me*.

The more I looked, the more I saw that there wasn't even a speck of recognition in her eyes. She really didn't know who I was.

"You sound as if you're flying a white flag," I said, still gauging her, anyway. "Why would you surrender to me?"

This was a good time for her to subtly say if she did know me.

"There are those of us who've stayed in our homes, too wary to come out, especially now," she said instead. "We've been as tired of the world as you seem to be, and I don't know how much longer we can stand to hang back."

"Are you saying you want to . . . join us?" I asked.

Jo nodded, her gaze intense. She looked at me as if I were someone who'd already made a difference, and it didn't matter to her that monsters had been the ones to start bringing it about.

My skin tingled. It hadn't stopped doing that since the full moon's leaving, when I'd turned back to my normal form. Thing was, I didn't hurt as much as I used to after a regular were-change.

I motioned over the oldster, asking him to bring a seasoned vampire who could go into Jo's mind to ascertain her level of loyalty. I didn't trust humans who weren't under sway.

As I walked through the cell block, I thought, *Well, I'll be. Human backups . . . and they're coming to me.*

The monsters I passed seemed to see the strength that a little faith in me brought out. As they watched me, a smile threatened my mouth, but I fought it down. I went to my room, with its comfy bed and skylight, which showed the waning moon. I leaned back against the door, finally giving in to that smile, even though it felt a little wrong, as if something nasty and way too powerful had infused me, and it was only waiting until a perfect time to really come out.

Maybe another full moon.

But I could control myself. I'd faced down my biggest challenge yet, and I could do it again.

I heard a sound to my left, and Gabriel eased into sight. He'd slunk out of the darkness, just like one of the shadow people. Or maybe more like the pariah I used to be.

I hadn't known he was even present, but I think he saw that smile I'd been wearing.

At his stricken expression, I sobered.

He shook his head, as if my moment of indulgence were his fault, just like so many of my bad behaviors.

"I can't tell you how often I've thought about leaving since the other night," he said, "but every time I try, I can't."

He couldn't bear to watch me change, just as much as I couldn't stand it with him. Still, neither of us made a move to go anywhere, although I could feel that an urge for him to run was pulling at him.

We both realized it and, in spite of the danger, he took my face in the palms of his hands, leaning his forehead against mine, closing his eyes. Our link encompassed us, pressing against our skins, and then . . .

I sucked in a breath as Gabriel flinched.

The link had done . . . something. Attached to him, sucked some of him in. He'd felt it, too.

It was almost as if I were the stronger one. As if I was taking him over.

There was no way I could know what my new form was going to do to Gabriel, as well as everyone else round me, and I should've run, but Gabriel still had his hands under my jaw, and the next thing I knew, he was kissing me, hard and desperately.

I couldn't move as the kiss melted into a slow draw of lips and pressure, causing our link to settle further into him as my mind swam with Gabriel, my body wanting to own everything about him.

But wasn't that what should happen between two beings who were meant to be together? Surely there was no bad about us. We'd put 562 to peaceful sleep, where she/he couldn't harm the Civil monsters while she/he kept us functioning. We could provide an example for our new community as different types of monsters who could get along.

There had to be a million things we could do together.

As he rested his mouth against mine, still holding me, he felt the same momentary optimism—our link told me so.

We were two monsters who might actually be able to save the world if we tried hard enough.

One hub at a time.

Turn the page for a special preview of
Christine Cody's next novel of the Bloodlands

IN BLOOD WE TRUST

Available October 2011 from Ace Books!

Mariah

I woke up that night, my arms and legs tangled in the sheets of the bed that I'd been assigned to in our liberated asylum.

Even during the fog of post-sleep, I felt him right away, on my bare skin. Or maybe I should say *through* my skin—on top, under, in.

Gabriel.

As he lay behind me, still in the throes of vampire rest, he didn't make a sound. That was because none of the vampires I'd met so far needed to breathe to survive. Animation kept them "alive" or "undead" or whatever they chose to call it. But those of us in the monster community who lived under the title of *were-creature* were pretty much the opposite of a vampire, what with our strong ties to the humanity that ruled us whenever we weren't in creature form.

But just listen to me, claiming myself as a were. Hell, ever since I'd messed up and taken part in a brief exchange with the mysterious monster we'd rescued in this asylum a couple of weeks ago—a cipher named Subject 562 who turned out to be the mother and father of our blood monster line—I couldn't really call myself a normal were-creature anymore.

I, the stupid and impulsive Mariah Lyander, was now a curiosity for my community. I was even more of a pariah than ever, although the others—the Red blood-drinking monsters and the Civil non–blood drinkers—seemed to respect me for kicking 562's ass in the end with Gabriel's help.

We had psychically joined together and broken 562's sanity, using Gabriel's newfound ability to freeze minds. That full-moon night, when I'd first changed into a form that I could access only once a month, seemed so damned long ago.

I didn't like to think of what everyone had described to me: long teeth, a split tongue, flowing hair, four arms, and cravings that went beyond even a normal monster's.

Yeah, I'd really done it by allowing 562 to exchange with me. Hell, I wasn't even your garden-variety werewolf anymore when the moon *wasn't* full. I'd been testing myself over these last couple of weeks and, thanks to my origin, I could call up my new nonlunar form at any time, like when I got pissed off. Or when I got too excited.

This one featured big teeth in a huge mouth. Claws. Fast and mean.

No, in any case, I wasn't quite a werewolf anymore at all.

Now, as I lay here next to Gabriel in bed, I didn't move a muscle. I hardly breathed, wondering when he would sense that dusk had fully fallen. I pressed my face into my pillow while his mere presence sent my blood rushing, heating, as if it were waiting for him to put his fingers on my back, where the blood would gather at his touch. His imprint.

Our strange link.

My instincts told me that I should probably slide off the mattress before he did wake up. But when was the last time I'd listened to my conscience? It sure hadn't been present when I'd been off-guard enough for 562 to bite me in a rapid, willing exchange that I had barely even registered.

My heartbeat twisted as I heard Gabriel stir.

Awake.

I felt his fingertips skim over my spine, and I shivered as the blood rushed there, mocking the shape of his touch.

"I can hear your pulse," he said.

He'd told me once that my body's rhythms sounded like

musical chaos to him, that it was like no other's. He couldn't resist the volatility in me; it was what drew Gabriel, but there were times I wondered if that could ever be enough in the long run for us. Or if it was *too* much, and it'd already led us to places we never should've gone together.

As I pressed my face into my pillow, he slipped his fingers over my back, to my waist, going even farther, inserting his hand between the mattress and my belly. My stomach muscles jerked. My blood did, too, as it tumbled from one part of my body forward, rolling over itself to get to him.

An ache pierced me low, stabbing and swollen. It was almost as if my blood were doing two things at once: trying to get out of me and go to him, as if it couldn't stand to be inside me anymore. Yet it seemed like it was also attempting to bring *him* into *me*.

When Gabriel traveled his hand a little lower, my blood jammed to a sharp point between my legs, and I groaned, burying my face in my pillow even more.

His thoughts mingled with mine through our link, which had always grown stronger when we did sex.

Give in to me, Mariah, just this once . . . give me everything. . . .

No blood, I thought back. *Don't even ask for a taste.*

His vampire sway should've been enough to get me to surrender, but I was resolute these days. 562's blood had made me stronger than anyone or anything I'd ever known. Even so, I was already damp for him.

I resisted Gabriel, not wanting to lose control of my body, becoming that new nonlunar creature.

Even though the full moon and my more dangerous shape was twelve nights away, I knew that if my passions got the better of me tonight, I'd still regret it.

Got to stop now . . . I thought to Gabriel.

You won't change form, Mariah. I'll make sure you don't.

He was patient, waiting for my answer. But he wouldn't be that way for much longer if he kept rubbing me like this.

I told myself to pull away, but somehow, I wasn't doing it. I kept thinking that whenever we got together, we always managed to tear ourselves from each other before it got lethal, and we'd be able to do it this time, too. Gabriel would just go for his animal blood–filled flask at the side of the bed, drinking down the sustenance while he slid into me, giving me pleasure in that way while I held back my monster. It was a risky game that we'd won so far.

One night, though . . .

As I started to tremble, my mind kept grabbing at logic, even though it seemed as if emotion and need were eating it right up.

Gabriel had changed so much during the last months, just as much as I had, his bloodlust growing and growing as a maturing vampire. What we had wouldn't end up in a good place.

I'd first met him in the New Badlands, out in the nowheres, when he'd been able to masquerade as a human well enough. He'd contained his thirst, holding on to his humanity as best as he could back then. He'd even been a hero to our secretive were-community, going up against the Shredder who'd wanted to slay every last one of us.

But even as he'd been so noble and honorable, he'd met me, and I'd brought out the worst in him.

Maybe that wasn't altogether true, though. Since coming upon other vampires here in the urban hubs, Gabriel had been schooled proper. He'd learned that vampires eventually let go of their humanity anyway, and his escalating need for blood and the lack of caring about it was only natural.

Yet something inside Gabriel was still fighting his instincts—I could feel the push and pull inside him even now through our link as he pulled me backward, closer to him, where I could feel the buzz of his bare skin. His remaining humanity was the only reason he still drank from that flask instead of sinking his fangs into me. Besides, he knew that if he tasted the blood of 562, he might get even nastier than any regular old vampire.

Obviously done with all the waiting, he coaxed his fingers between my thighs. I held my breath. Then, even though I should've stopped him, he delved between my folds.

Up, into me.

I sucked in that breath while my blood flooded and tingled,

hurting in such a nice, scary way. He churned his fingers in and out, and my hips moved to meet every stroke.

I clung to my logic while I still could, but the heat was taking me over, a pounding that would lead to a burst, an explosion into my new form. . . .

From the back of me, his stiffness probed between my thighs, and I knew that this was the time to leave that bed, but I didn't. I parted my legs, because I was his already.

My blood was his blood.

Thudding in every place that his skin touched mine, I started the change I so wanted to hold back.

First, there was a blue-tinged wanting. . . .

Then something that had been building for the past couple of weeks—a bigger hunger that just got redder and redder by the second.

A craving unlike any I used to feel, and it split me down the middle in a streak of cruelty, a need to hurt . . . especially those who'd hurt me.

But somehow I shut out that hunger, angling my head into Gabriel's arm, where my cheek met his skin.

Smooth. Cool. No scent.

Vampire.

I bit into him, not rough enough to break his harder-than-human skin. Just enough to warn him that we were getting to a point of no return.

He growled, and if I turned round, I'd see that his eyes had gone from their usual silver to a blazing red, that his fangs had popped, changing him from a seemingly human drifter to a seething devil.

He pushed his fingers into me harder, and I groaned, trying to hold back the meanness that was about to come out in me in a series of boiling, stretching, agonizing pulls.

His fangs scratched my shoulder.

"No," I said out loud now, my voice low, garbled.

God-all, he wanted a bite. I wanted it, too, but I wouldn't be limited to sinking my teeth into one of his veins. My bite would rip, tear, decimate.

And I had the feeling it wasn't regular blood I wanted, either. That split of cruelty prying me apart needed a certain sort of blood tonight—hot, violent, brutally earned—and I pushed back at the craving as Gabriel took his fingers out of me, using his hand to spread my legs even wider.

He probed at me from the back again, and I winced. At the sound, he teased a little more, slipping against me, sliding until I couldn't take it anymore.

"Gabriel." My voice on the edge, a warning. My vision gone to a pulsing violet.

Laughing low in his throat, he thrust into me, and I clutched at the sheets, yanking them off the corners of the bed, rocking my hips back against him, wanting him to go deeper so I would forget everything else.

But that was the human side of me, fighting this other . . . thing.

He rammed in again, and I moved with him—one drive, two, more, again . . .

My blood buffeted me from the inside out, forging toward him, beating against my skin like fists even as I drew *his* own blood to my skin.

He bent to my neck, fangs scraping my flesh.

"No!" I grappled for his blood flask, not really knowing where it was, only knowing it had to be close.

But then he drew himself back, in striking position.

I tried to move before he could bite, yet he was faster than I was in my mostly human form, and his fangs needled my neck before I dodged out of the way.

In a crash of white, our mind connection went blank, like a lightning strike that had wiped out all power. But I didn't need to read his thoughts to sense the anguish in him.

He had reared back from me, as if something had jerked him away, and when I got to my knees, one of my hands pressing against my slight neck wound, I saw that he was tearing apart the bedclothes on his way to where he'd stored his flask near the edge of the mattress.

My body rhythms were shredding me, my breath like icicles puncturing my lungs as heat wrestled with the coolness of my will to stay strong.

Stay human.

He spit out my blood, gulped from his flask, spitting that

out, too, then drinking more. His back was to me, and I hunched down, shamed. A power within me was pressing outward, as if my monster didn't want to stay in. My gaze was still violet, beating and fuzzy.

No, I thought again, but this time it was to myself. *Just stop. . . .*

He finished draining the flask, then slowly looked over his shoulder at me, his gaze a little less crimson, but not all the way back to its humanlike appearance. His short hair was tousled, his face a wounded scape boasting a nose that had been broken and hadn't healed correctly back when he'd been human. All in all, he was a bruised, haunted revelation of all the remorse he could muster.

But there was a terrible slant to his mouth that negated that.

"The way you taste . . ." he said.

He ran a bewildered gaze over me, and for a moment, I thought that maybe I had started to turn without having realized it. But with one scan of my body, I saw that I was still as human as I could be, considering the circumstances.

As I calmed my pulse—*don't think of the blood, think of breathing, just breathing*—I watched as Gabriel tossed the flask away.

"I can still feel your blood on my tongue," he said. "It . . . numbs me."

I still didn't get it. Not until I thought about the word *numb*.

"Like a poison?" I asked. My muscles ached a little, and not only because I'd tempted my body to change. It was because I wanted him back inside me.

"Like a poison," Gabriel repeated.

I didn't think I'd heard him right, and I retreated to the wall, near my pillow. Before I'd turned into this new creature, he'd taken my were-blood. It had bolstered him, and I'd even thought . . .

Well, I'd thought that maybe I might be the only being in this world who could make him feel that way. But that was before I knew better.

Before I'd exchanged with 562 and become real poison.

My mind spun as he wiped the back of his hand over his mouth.

God-all, *poison.* Were-creatures worked that way with one

another. We didn't yearn for each other's blood, because it pained us to taste and digest it. That was a good thing, too; it kept the more powerful creatures, like the wolf I'd been, from attacking the weaker ones, such as the were-elk, were–mule deer, and were-scorpion who'd been a part of my Badlands community.

Had 562's blood changed the composition of mine to the point where Gabriel couldn't stomach it now?

I wasn't sure how I'd even been able to digest 562's blood in the first place, but maybe it had something to do with the way 562, my origin, had quickly and deceitfully taken my blood before I'd taken it from her/him.

Gabriel stayed on the other side of the bed, having turned away from me again. I wanted to reach out, run my palm over the lean muscles of his back.

"I don't get it," I said. "The night of 562's rampage, she/he kept mentally appealing to you with the notion of feeding you with blood. Why would 562 have done that if it would've poisoned you?"

"Maybe its blood just tastes bad enough so that none of us would try to drink from it. 562 offered it out of love. That's what it kept thinking to me, anyway."

I'd always thought of 562 as more were-creature than vampire, with its snout and fur, its copse of long teeth, and its response to a full moon. Maybe that was why it had chosen me to be the drinker—because for the rest of the Reds, mother's milk wasn't healthy.

Besides, now that I thought about it, I *had* gotten sick on 562's blood, just as if it were a poison. But I'd swallowed it. I'd taken it right in, unlike Gabriel.

"Why did you take it from me?" I asked. "You knew that my blood could be dangerous in other ways."

His shoulders slumped, and the sight of such a strong man weighed down did the same to me.

"Whenever I'm with you," he said, "I tell myself I won't give in. But I did this time."

"Maybe we should . . ." What? I was out of ideas, and I couldn't stand the thought of never feeling Gabriel again.

"Tonight," he said, "it was a prick on your neck from my fangs. Next time . . ."

Next time he might get even more violent, and I could see . . . *feel* . . . that the part of him still clinging to humanity might survive only if he was miles away from me.

My blood gave one last desperate stretch in my core, then began to cool. My vision went from violet to blue as it turned back to normal.

When he stood, I looked away from him, hardly able to afford for my body to heat up again. I couldn't stand to see how beautiful Gabriel was, pale and streamlined, his belly flat, his legs long. And his skin . . .

I liked the coolness and hardness of it. I'd grown so used to it.

He gathered his dust-worn clothes—the beaten white shirt, the jeans, the boots that had always reminded me of a lost cowboy from the movies of yore. He put the articles on, one by one, seeming so far away already.

"I need to go to the cells," he said, as if we'd only been in the middle of some discussion and were just now taking it right back up again. "I've got to talk to Stamp."

"Now?"

"Me and the other vampires have to keep at it. We've got to chip away at him until he brings down his mind blocks to let us know if there're other security threats outside the hub, just biding their time to come in and attack. And Stamp *will* break. The old ones tell me that all humans do, at some point."

Johnson Stamp, the Shredder who'd tried to kill us more than once. He'd even chased our group out here to the hubs, although he'd gotten his due in the end.

When I didn't say anything else to Gabriel—what could I possibly utter?—he turned round, all dressed now.

I held a sheet in front of my body. I don't know why when he'd seen it all more than once.

When he came over to me, it seemed as if he were going to bend down, kiss me softly. But all he did was touch my neck, healing my faint wound just before he headed back to the door, walking right out of it.

I should've told myself that it wouldn't be the last time he would need to leave me hanging, either. Not if we wanted to keep ourselves—and probably every one round us—safe. I was so easily riled, and I had caused enough trouble in the Badlands to know better than to cross lines now.

Reassuring myself with that mantra, I set about getting ready for the night, aimless, restless, and even now under the thumb of a hunger that Gabriel had brought out in me but hadn't assuaged.